THE RAILWAY

Hamid Ismailov

The Railway

TRANSLATED
FROM THE RUSSIAN
AND WITH A PREFACE
BY

Robert Chandler

Harvill Secker
LONDON

Published by Harvill Secker 2006

First published as *Zheleznaya doroga* in Russian in 1997 by Voskresen'ye

2 4 6 8 10 9 7 5 3

Copyright © Hamid Ismailov 1997
English translation copyright © Robert Chandler 2006

First published in Great Britain in 2006 by
HARVILL SECKER
Random House, 20 Vauxhall Bridge Road
London SW1V 2SA

Random House Australia (Pty) Limited
20 Alfred Street, Milsons Point, Sydney,
New South Wales 2061, Australia

Random House New Zealand Limited
18 Poland Road, Glenfield,
Auckland 10, New Zealand

Random House South Africa (Pty) Limited
Isle of Houghton, Corner Boundary Road & Carse O'Gowrie,
Houghton, 2198, South Africa

The Random House Group Limited Reg. No. 954009
www.randomhouse.co.uk

A CIP catalogue record for this book is available from the British Library

ISBN 9781843431610 (from January 2007)
ISBN 184341610

Map on pages xxviii–xxix by Reginald Piggott

Typeset in Adobe Caslon
by SX Composing DTP, Rayleigh, Essex
Printed and bound in Great Britain by
William Clowes Ltd, Beccles, Suffolk

Preface

I first met Hamid Ismailov after a lecture at the Pushkin Club in west London. A colleague was talking to me about his experience of reading Andrey Platonov, a writer I have spent many years translating. As I listened, I realised that two other people, a man and a young woman, were listening no less intently. We introduced ourselves. The woman was Rosa Kudabaeva, a BBC journalist with whom I was later to travel to Uzbekistan. The man was Hamid Ismailov, who also worked for the BBC – as well as being a poet and novelist who wrote in both Uzbek and Russian. Hamid said that Andrey Platonov was one of his favourite writers; he had wanted to translate him into Uzbek but had found this impossible. He also said that many years before, after first reading *Soul*, Platonov's novel set in Central Asia, he had felt so depressed that he fell ill. This had not been because the novel was itself depressing but because Platonov seemed to have said all there was to say about Central Asia. Nothing was left – Hamid had felt at the time – for him to say himself.

A few weeks after this first meeting, Hamid and his wife Razia came to supper with me and my wife Elizabeth. It was a June evening, we ate and drank in our small walled garden, and it was as if they had brought something of Uzbekistan with them. Hamid told stories about his grandparents and great-grandparents, while Razia raised her eyebrows in mock-scepticism. I myself was captivated – both by the exotic quality of the stories and by their strange familiarity. Hamid and I evidently had much in common. His maternal grandfather, who was shot long before Hamid was born, had been a mullah; my maternal grandfather, who died of cancer a year before I was born, had been a canon at Salisbury Cathedral. Both of our families had owned land. Hamid's family had lost theirs because of the 1917

Revolution; we too had lost our estates, though as a result of high death duties rather than of violent revolution. And both Hamid and I were living lives very different from those of our parents and grandparents. We both wrote and translated; we both loved Platonov.

In 1997, a year or two after these first meetings, Hamid gave me a copy of the first Russian edition of *The Railway* – a charmingly produced volume with a picture of a little train at the bottom of each page: a locomotive, one coach and one goods wagon, the page number printed in white in the middle of the goods wagon. He said that he had also tried to publish *The Railway* in Tashkent, in the main Russian-language literary journal, but that the Uzbek authorities had fired the editor and blocked publication of the issue containing the second half of the book. Hamid's generally sceptical attitude towards authority had, it seemed, alarmed a government that takes itself very seriously indeed. The Uzbek translation of *The Railway*, completed in 1997, remains unpublished to this day.

I soon realised that – for all his anxiety after first reading *Soul* – Hamid had found his own voice and his own subject matter. I translated three chapters of *The Railway* and began looking for a publisher. I am grateful now that this proved difficult, and that I had the chance to learn more about Central Asia before returning to the novel. Most important of all, it was around this time that I was commissioned to translate *Soul* – and Hamid and Razia were among many people I turned to when I had questions. Hamid helped me with regard to the work's religious and philosophical aspects; Razia, a musicologist, helped me to understand Platonov's treatment of song and music – an important theme of both *Soul* and *The Railway*. And then, shortly before *Soul* was published, Hamid – who was by then Head of the BBC Central Asia Service – phoned to suggest I visit Uzbekistan; he wanted me to travel, together with Rosa Kudabaeva, to the area where *Soul* is set and to make a series of programmes to be broadcast in Russian by the Central Asia Service.

What has stayed with me from my two weeks in Uzbekistan is a sense of the age and sophistication of Central Asian culture. I sensed these qualities vividly in the Shah-e-Zindah in Samarkand, a steep narrow street which – unlike the city's over-restored grander monuments – embodies both the continuity of tradition and the continuity between art and nature. All twenty-two of the modest buildings, built in the fourteenth and fifteenth centuries, are mausoleums for the city's rulers. Walking round behind them, I found blades of grass growing from cracks in the walls; the street is sunken, so poppies and yarrow flowers in the fields beyond were at eye level. Perhaps half of the mosaic and majolica tilework has disappeared from the façades and even from the inside walls, but what remains is astonishingly fine. Beyond the shrines, which are still regularly visited by groups of Sufi pilgrims, stretches a whole series of cemeteries: Muslim, Jewish, Korean Christian and Soviet. The Koreans, I learned, had mostly entered the Soviet Union during the Second World War, to escape the Japanese; Stalin had sent them to Uzbekistan. As for the Sufi pilgrims, they seemed tolerant and welcoming, glad if I joined in the gestures they made as they prayed but accepting me anyway.

I sensed this age and sophistication no less vividly in the Friday Mosque in the silk-road city of Khiva. This was built in the eighteenth century, but many of the carved black-elm columns supporting the flat roof were taken from a tenth-century mosque nearby; one column, worn by time and silky to the touch, looked as if it had evolved from tree to work of art and back again to tree. I was oddly pleased to learn that the columns' silkiness came from their being treated for five years with chicken dung before being worked. There was clearly no substitute for natural processes and the work of time; impatient Soviet restorers, unwilling to wait five years, had replaced missing columns with new columns that felt painfully rough.

In the old centre of Bukhara I talked to a blacksmith by the name of Sharif Kamalov; like most educated adults in Central Asia, he spoke Russian and we were able to understand one another easily. Despite the decline in tourism since 11 September 2001, his business was clearly successful. He had a line in scissors made to look like birds; when closed, they resembled the profile of a cock, or a stork, or a pelican. He began by speaking enthusiastically about the freedom he had enjoyed since Uzbekistan became independent. He could make what he wanted, and he had travelled to blacksmiths' congresses in England, France, Germany and Pakistan. When I asked about his life under the Soviet regime, his tone changed. All he had done, he said sadly, was to turn out three different kinds of agricultural implement; he felt particularly sad about his father, whose whole life had been lived under the Soviet regime.

After a while, I ventured a few words in Farsi – a language I had been studying for only a few years. Although Stalin chose to incorporate them into Uzbekistan, Samarkand and Bukhara are really Persian cities; the first language of most of the inhabitants is Tadjik, essentially the same language as Farsi. Kamalov was delighted by my stumbling attempt to speak his mother tongue – and still more delighted when I said I was learning it in order to read the poetry of Hafez. He began to recite one of Hafez's most beautiful ghazals; I happened to have been studying this very ghazal only two weeks before, and so I was able to join in with him. We were both moved by this unexpected discovery of another, seemingly deeper, shared language. And I was astonished at how quickly we had moved back in time. Beneath the enterprising businessman was a dissatisfied Soviet worker, and beneath that – a man familiar with a tradition of mystical-erotic poetry going back seven or eight centuries.

*

The Railway is as multi-layered as the cemetery of Shah-e-Zindah or the cultural inheritance of Sharif Kamalov. There are several different narrators, and it is an open and tolerant novel that has room for crude sexual jokes and sophisticated multi-lingual puns, for allusions to Soviet political slogans, Sufi philosophers and to Claude Lévi-Strauss; it is this linguistic breadth, this variety of perspective, that enables Hamid to give a truthful account of the history and politics of twentieth-century Central Asia without slipping into mere polemic. Such complexity, however, is not easy to translate; I could not have unravelled the sometimes baroque syntax and deftly interwoven stories without Hamid's help. There were many points that I found bewildering, many references to details of everyday life – or matters of philosophical or political controversy – with which I was unfamiliar. In one chapter, for example, somebody comes 'under salty fire' from a nightwatchman; I had all kinds of ideas about what this might mean, but it never entered my head that the nightwatchman was simply firing pellets of salt. It was, Hamid explained, common practice for guards and night-watchmen at collective farms or small factories to be issued with an air rifle and salt bullets – to wound but not kill.

More often, however, the answers to my questions were more complex than I had expected. Near the beginning of the circumcision chapter, for example, Hamid writes that the boy didn't want to leave the house and lose his *imenitost'*, his 'name-day specialness'. I asked Hamid whether it really was the boy's name day – or perhaps birthday – or whether the phrase was being used more loosely, to mean the sense of importance one feels at any time that one is the centre of attention. Hamid's answer was that the term 'name-day' was, in effect, a code word. Circumcision, though widely practised, was the object of official disapproval; the boy would have heard his parents inviting friends and neighbours not to his circumcision party but to his 'name-day party' . . . There were scenes I did not understand because I did not know enough about Muslim life, scenes I did not understand because I did not know enough about Soviet life, and scenes – like the above – where I was confused by the complexity of the interface between the two.

Towards the end of my work on the novel I began to feel as if I were restoring a precious carpet. Patterns I had sensed only vaguely, as if looking at the underside of a carpet, began to stand out clearly; seemingly unimportant details in one chapter, I realised, reappeared as central themes of other chapters. Colours grew brighter as I sensed their inter-relationship. Occasionally I even felt able to suggest to Hamid that a particular thread should be moved from one part of the carpet to another.

The world of *The Railway* – like that of Andrey Platonov's work – contains a large number of orphans. Hamid has said to me many times that there is nothing in *The Railway* that is not based on reality, and there is certainly nothing exaggerated about this emphasis on the theme of orphanhood; throughout the twentieth century a huge number of children in all the Soviet republics were brought up in orphanages. Many lost their fathers during the First World War and the Civil War. Others were orphaned during Stalin's purges; still others in the course of the Second World War. During the first decades after the Revolution there was a sense, encouraged by Soviet children's literature, that orphanhood was the ideal state; an orphan's father was Stalin, his or her grandfather was Lenin, and there was no rival father whose influence might corrupt.[1]

The world of *The Railway* and the world of Andrey Platonov are also both home to a surprising number of cripples. *The*

---

[1] There is a Soviet joke: a teacher asks children in his class what they want to be when they grow up. First child: 'Russia is my mother; Lenin is my father; I want to be an engineer.' Second child: 'Russia is my mother; Lenin is my father; I want to be a nurse.' Third child: 'Russia is my mother; Lenin is my father; I want to be an army officer.' Fourth child: 'Russia is my

Railway even contains a chapter about a false messiah who encourages his followers to mutilate themselves, proclaiming that only the limbless can enter paradise. I asked Hamid what had inspired this. After saying that he had indeed witnessed a short-lived cult of this nature, Hamid talked about the Soviet faith in what was known as dialectical materialism or *diamat*; he thought that, in truly dialectical fashion, this faith masked its opposite: a profound contempt for the material, for the earth and for the human body. Not all of the many amputees – he went on – had been injured in the Second World War; many were the victims of industrial accidents, often caused by alcohol abuse and a disregard for safety precautions.

The Railway and *Soul* – though not Platonov's other stories and novels – have at least one other shared feature; they are among the surprisingly few Soviet novels that engage with one of the favourite concepts of Soviet propaganda: 'the brotherhood of nations'. Platonov describes the *Dzhan*, the heroes of *Soul*, as 'a small nomadic nation, drawn from different peoples and wandering about in poverty. The nation included Turkmen, Karakalpaks, a few Uzbeks, Kazakhs, Persians, Kurds, Baluchis, and people who had forgotten who they were.' As for Gilas, the small town where most of *The Railway* is set, its inhabitants include Armenians, Chechens, Germans, Jews, Koreans, Kurds, Persians, Russians, Tatars, Ukrainians, a variety of smaller nationalities from Siberia, the Arctic and the Caucasus – and, of course, representatives of all the main nationalities of Central Asia. Gilas is a Noah's Ark of humanity – and a microcosm of the Soviet Union. Once again, there is nothing fictitious about this emphasis; for several decades after the Second World War,

mother; Lenin is my father; I want to be an orphan.' Orphanages remain important in much of the former Soviet Union even today; often parents take their children there because they feel unable to support them. During my trip to Uzbekistan in 2003, the director of an orphanage told me that the number of children in her care had doubled during the preceding five years.

Tashkent was a thriving and cosmopolitan city. Some of its inhabitants had freely chosen to make their home in Central Asia; others had been exiled or deported there.

The path that has brought most of these people to Gilas is, of course, the 'iron road' (the standard Russian term for a railway) that provides the novel with its title. Hamid's iron road, however, is not only an actual railway but also a symbol that brings together the novel's Soviet and Sufi themes. To a group of pilgrims returning from Mecca not long before the 1917 Revolution, this twentieth-century equivalent of the silk route is 'a never-ending ladder whose wooden rungs and iron rails lay stretched across the earth from horizon to horizon'. To Obid-Kori, the mullah who is imprisoned in the 1930s and then taken off in a goods wagon to be shot, the two rails and the sleepers that bind them together are like a seemingly infinite extension of the iron grating of his prison window. To a young woman born in exile, the railway is an inexorable force that 'warps the earth and its people, twisting lives out of shape'. To Gogolushko the ex-Party functionary and failed mystic the railway is a spiritual path that has gone rigid and that has led him nowhere; it is covered in shit from the toilets of passing trains.

A particularly striking chapter evokes the nomadic Turkic tribespeople who were press-ganged, during the last decades of the Tsarist regime, into building the first railway to Central Asia. At the cost of their lives they struggle to assert the vertical dimension of spiritual belief, repeatedly tearing up small sections of track and transforming them into the ladders the souls of their dead need in order to climb up to heaven. The novel's most truly redemptive moment, however, occurs in one of the chapters about the character known simply as 'the boy'. Angry and depressed after running away from home, the boy wants 'to get his own back' on a train that has startled him as he stands dreamily beside the line; in the event, however, he surprises himself by throwing a kiss and calling 'I love you' to an unknown girl standing by the door of one of the carriages. The boy is still free; he is the only character whose identity has not been fixed by a name; and it is his gradual initiation into the adult world that constitutes the heart of the novel. His unexpected 'I love you' is central to this process of initiation; his simple and spontaneous words transform a Soviet iron road – the unyielding way of linear thinking and material progress – into a Sufi path of Love.

If the boy can also be thought of as a passenger on this train, then the self-contained anecdotes that constitute many of the chapters can be imagined as scenes glimpsed by the boy – and the reader – in the course of a long journey. As Hamid wrote in a letter to me, 'each individual story is like a station flashing by. Some of the stories disappear without trace, others wander from chapter to chapter; sometimes the reader can get down from the train, look at people's faces, hear words, take something away in his memory.' And if the individual chapters are scenes glimpsed by the boy, stories heard by the boy, it is possible that it may be the boy himself who has written them down.

The general tone of *The Railway* is exuberant, even if this exuberance sometimes seems to mask a pain so deep that the narrator cannot allow himself to dwell on it for long. There is an exuberant humour in most of the individual stories, and there is an exuberance in the way that the stories multiply; one story, or even just the beginning of a story, quickly generates another. Many sentences seem so full of energy that they are reluctant to settle down and come to a full stop. The wordplay is dense; its unruliness exemplifies an important theme of the novel, that words – whether they are the words of magic charms or of Communist slogans – are endowed with an autonomous power. We read how Granny Hadjiya writes an Arabic charm on a scrap of paper, wraps a bit of cloth round it and hangs it from a tree in a cemetery; her magic charm then terrifies a group of schoolboys. We read of people who collect stories, people who collect manuscripts, a man who collects slogans, a man who collects words . . .

I soon understood that an adequate translation of *The Railway* must recreate this exuberance – even, if necessary, at the expense of literal meaning. There is often an element of paradox in the work of a translator; I have never before had to work so hard to understand the literal meaning of the original text – and I have never before allowed myself to depart from the literal meaning so often and so freely. Not every pun in the original is translatable, and I have omitted jokes that needed too much explanation; I have compensated, I hope, by gratefully accepting any appropriate pun that English offered. Sometimes these puns seemed to arise without any effort on my part; it would have been hard, for example, for an English translator to avoid a pun (a pun not present in the original) in the passage where the sight of Nasim's huge 'male member' makes Khaira 'remember' facts about her life that she had forgotten for decades. And it would have required a restraint out of keeping with the spirit of the novel to have refrained from adding the words 'trans-oxianic' to a sentence about a couple from the USA who are about to travel to a part of Central Asia once known in English as Trans-Oxiana:[2] 'And so the young couple set off on their trans-oceanic – and even trans-oxianic – ravels.' The words between the dashes are my addition, approved by Hamid.

Sometimes, however, even when wordplay seemed to arise of its own accord, it took many revisions before a passage felt right. The last sentence of the following passage did not come easily: 'Trying to forget Froska behind a veil of words, ex-Master-Railwayman Belkov succeeded in forgetting everything except her act of betrayal; losing his whole life to oblivion, he struggled to recapture it in a web of words. But his webs and veils were in vain; his verbal virtuosity was to no avail.' 'Veil', 'avail' and 'in

[2] i.e. the land beyond the Oxus – the Latin name for the great river now known as the Amu-Darya.

vain' are all literal and obvious translations, but it took me a long time to find a way of taking advantage of the sound pattern they create; at first its insistence seemed not to buttress the meaning but to distract from it.

There were many other comic moments that came to life only after patient but determined coaxing; humour, of course, tends to be what gets lost most easily in translation. We speak of jokes being 'barbed' or 'pointed', and jokes do indeed have something in common with darts or arrows. If a joke is to survive the journey into another language, if it is to hit the mark even when its cultural context can no longer be taken for granted, its point may need to be adjusted or somehow re-sharpened. A sentence about Bolta-Lightning the town electrician sounded irritatingly plodding even after several revisions. It was only after Liz suggested replacing the literal 'explained to' by the wittier 'explained over the heads of' that the English version began to seem as funny as the original: 'Bolta-Lightning climbed the column in the middle of the square, hung the banner on the loudspeaker and explained over the heads of the entire backward bazaar both the progressive meaning of the slogan and the precise time the proletariat was to unite.'

Just as puns sometimes seemed to appear of their own accord, so did instances of alliteration; once we had hit on the phrase 'gloom-dogged Gogolushko', we soon found that this unfortunate Party functionary (a caricature of Nikolay Gogol) was 'struggling doggedly' on one page and 'gazing glumly at every bit of garbage' on another. And on one occasion I went home from a meeting with Hamid and noticed that the letters 'f' and 'l' occurred surprisingly often in the notes I had made while he explained a particular passage. The alliteration seemed in keeping with the tone required, and so I expanded a shorter original into the sentence 'Something inside him really did seem to break off and fall – fulfilled or perhaps full of failure – to the ground'; almost every word here is Hamid's, but not all of them are in his original text.

There were occasions when I incorporated oral explanations in the text of the translation. Once, merely as an aside to me, Hamid said 'enough money to buy two Volga cars' while we were discussing some other aspect of a sentence about two fantastically rich Chechens. I at once asked if I could include these words. The English version of the sentence now reads, 'and they had once bought ten thousand roubles' worth of goatskin coats and astrakhan hats in a day – enough money to buy two Volga cars or for Granny to live on for the rest of her life and still leave something behind.'

Curses and swearwords present a particular problem for translators into contemporary English. Our lexicon of abusive language is oddly limited, and the more florid curses still common in Russian tend to sound laughable if translated at all literally. Reluctantly, I have simplified much of the foul language. In one chapter I have tried to compensate for this impoverishment by adding my own brief evocation of the essence of Russian *mat* or foul language: 'those monstrous, magnificent, multilayered and multi-storied variations on pricks and cunts and mother-fucking curs'.

Many people hold oddly absolute views about translation. Some see translators as unsung heroes; others see them as inveterate traitors. Some believe that translators should concern themselves only with literal meaning; others believe that nothing matters very much except tone and readability. My own view is that translation is an art, and that no art can have absolute and universal rules. Every book, every stanza or paragraph, every phrase may have its unique requirements.

The Railway reminds me in some ways of a jazz improvisation or the paintings of Paul Klee. Hamid keeps to a delicate balance between imposing order on words and staying open to suggestions from them, between telling a clear story and allowing words to dance their own dance. In translating the novel, I have tried to observe a similar balance – both to be attentive to precise shades of meaning and to listen out for unexpected ways in which English might be able to reproduce the music of the original. Fidelity, after all, is never simply a mechanical matter. To stay faithful to people or things you love, there are times when you need to draw on all your resources of creativity and imagination. If I appear to have taken liberties with the original, it has been in the hope of being faithful to it at a deeper level. I have never – I hope – simplified anything of cultural importance. The character known as Mullah-Ulmas-Greeneyes, for example, is not really a mullah; 'Mullah' is a nickname, given to him by people around him because it alliterates with 'Ulmas'. One reader suggested I omit this 'Mullah', arguing that English readers are not used to Muslims using religious terms so light-heartedly and would find the word confusing. This had the effect of bringing home to me how important it was to keep the 'Mullah'. The Muslim world has never been monolithic; Central Asia has nearly always been religiously liberal – with Sufis having the upper hand over dogmatists – and during the Soviet period secularism made considerable inroads. Even believers tended not to take their religion over-seriously.

The same wish not to simplify has also led me to include over 150 endnotes. Soviet Central Asia is an alien world to a modern Anglophone reader, perhaps no less alien than the Spain of Cervantes. We take it for granted that there will be notes in a new edition of *Don Quixote*; it is my view that notes are no less necessary in a translation of *The Railway*. This short novel can be read as an encyclopaedia of Central Asian life. Its pages are doors into many realms; I will be glad if my notes make these doors easier to open.

Robert Chandler
September 2005

Acknowledgements

The Railway is, in a sense, a collective work. Hamid made free use of stories told him by friends, relatives and colleagues; I have heard him describe the book as 'a folkloric novel'. This translation is still more of a collaborative work. First, as well as answering countless questions, Hamid has read through the translation several times and made many suggestions and criticisms. Second, I have twice read the entire translation out loud to my wife Elizabeth, and there are many sentences we must have discussed twenty or more times. She drew my attention to passages that were unclear and helped me formulate questions to put to Hamid; she also contributed many phrases and some elegant puns herself, as well as making a crucial suggestion about the order of chapters. Third, I sent drafts to Hugh Barnes, Olive Classe, Mel Dadswell, Gill Gregory, Mark Miller, Dzhanna Povelitchina, Caroline Sigrist and John Spurling; all made valuable contributions, as did Katerina Grigorak, Eleanor Yates, Danirand Rano Ismailov and – above all – Stuart Williams at Harvill Secker. A translator is more likely than an original writer to have to find words for realms of experience outside his or her imaginative grasp; this is part of the reason why so many translations sound wooden. I send drafts to as many readers as possible, hoping they will draw my attention to passages I have failed to make clear or bring to life.

I should also say that Hamid abridged the original by around 20 per cent before I began work; I later agreed with him on a few further cuts.

I am grateful to the journals *Index on Censorship*, *In Other Words* and the *TLS* for publishing earlier versions of parts of my preface; and I am grateful to *Moving Worlds* for publishing the final chapter and to *Index on Censorship* for publishing earlier versions of the Obid–Kori chapters. I also wish to thank Robina Pelham Burn and Christopher MacLehose for their faith is *The Railway*.

Most of the characters bear Uzbek names, and these are stressed on the final syllable. Where the stress falls in a Russian word, however, is unpredictable. In the following list stresses that do not fall on the final syllable are shown by italics:

Abdulhamid: childhood friend of Mahmud-Hodja. Becomes a poet and is shot.

Abubakir-Snuffsniffer: school caretaker.

Adkham-Kukruz-Popcorn: gypsy who sells popcorn in Gilas.

Aisha-Nogaika: a Nogai Tatar, mother of Saniya.

Akmolin: driver of shunting locomotive.

Alihon-Tura: a cousin of Mahmud-Hodja the Younger and also of Oyimcha.

Ali-Shapak: younger brother of Tolib-Butcher.

Alyaapsindu: old Korean man. His name means 'Greetings!' He is called this because, being very polite, he is constantly repeating the word.

Amon: nephew of Faiz-Ulla, who brings him up after death of his mother. (See Zainab.)

Artyomchik: a friend of the boy.

Ashir-Beanpole: Gilas station announcer.

Asolat: the elder sister of Hadjiya; the wife of Pochamir-Hodja; and the boy's great-aunt.

Asom-Paraff: half-Uzbek, half-Tadjik, sells paraffin in Gilas.

Bahriddin: famous Sufi singer.

Bahri-Granny-Fortunes: gypsy fortune-teller, mother of Lyuli-Ibodullo-Mahsum.

Bakay-Croc: son of Mukum-Happy-Trigger. A double-amputee. Uchmah transfers her powers of prophecy to him and he becomes the leader of a disabled movement. His name is that of one of the heroes of the Kirghiz epic

Manas.

Banat-Pielady: wife of Oktam-Humble-Russky.

Basit-OrgCom: disciple of Gogolushko during his phase of mysticism. Appointed First Secretary of the Gilas Party Committee after the dismissal of both Gogolushko and Buri-Bigwolf.

Belkov: Master-Railwayman and caretaker of Gilas Party Committee Building.

Belyalov: the first 'capitalist' to appear in Gilas, under the Brezhnev regime.

Boikush: half-blind old woman, mother of Tadji-Murad. Her name, the standard name given to folk-tale owls, means 'rich bird'.

Bolta-Lightning: electrician; husband of Vera-Virgo.

Buri-Bigwolf: First Secretary of the Gilas Party Committee.

Chilchil: Garang-Deafmullah's main competitor with regard to the carrying out of circumcisions.

Chinali: the fabulously rich director of the main warehouse; father of Soli-Stores.

Democritis-Chuvalchidi: son of Aristotilis Chuvalchidi, a Greek Communist exile.

Djebral-Semavi (Gabriel of Heaven): fled the 1905 Iranian revolution; father of Huvron-Barber.

Djibladjibon-Bonu-Wagtail: wife of Kun-Okhun.

Dolim-Dealer: trades in cattle; heir to Oppok-Lovely.

Elias: a guard in the Bukhara jail; he employs Pochamir to make boots.

Ezrael: a son of Huvron-Barber and grandson of Djebral-Semavi.

Faiz-Ulla-FAS: one of the two sons of Umarali-Moneybags. The suffix FAS indicates that he is the director of the Factory Apprentice School.

Father Ioann: Russian priest responsible for the Apostolic Church of St Thomas; known to the inhabitants of Gilas as

Old Vanka.

Fatima: one of two Uighur twins made pregnant by Kara-Musayev.

Fatkhulla-Frontline: a veteran of the Second World War, during which he lost one eye.

Froska: wife of Belkov; sells fizzy water in railway station.

*Fyo*kla-Whispertongue: works at small shop attached to the cotton factory; a notorious informer.

Garang-Deafmullah: the only mullah to remain in Gilas. So as not to offend the authorities, he limits himself to carrying out circumcisions.

Gazi-Hodja (Fighter on the Road of Faith): husband of Hadjiya; poisoned in 1930.

Gogo*lush*ko: Second Secretary of the Gilas Party Committee; turns mystic.

Guloyim-Pedlar: a sharp-tongued Uighur woman.

Gulsum-Khalfa: homeless old woman in a story by Hoomer. She brings up an orphaned boy.

Gumdjadain-Bangamtsaray: Mongolian mother of one of Mefody's 'brothers'.

Habib-Ulla: an alcoholic poet.

Hadjiya ('born during the Hadj'): daughter of Mahmud-Hodja the Younger; wife of Gazi-Hodja, and then of Israel-Warder; grandmother and guardian of the boy.

Hoomer: the Homer of Gilas.

Huvron-Barber: son of Djebral-Semavi; father of Ezrael, who marries and murders Shah-Sanem, and of Hussein, who is murdered by two gypsy boys.

Ibodullo-Mahsum: the son of Bahri-Granny-Fortunes.

Ilyusha-Oneandahalf: a Korean friend of Rizo-Zero. When he was a child, half of one of his ears was bitten off by Rizo's donkey.

Ishankul Ilyichevich: surgeon at the Gilas War Commissariat.

Israel-Warder: second husband of Hadjiya.

Izaly-Jew (Izaly Rabinovich): director of the Papanin Tailoring Co-operative, which is later renamed 'Indposhiv' or 'Individual Cut'.

Janna-Nurse: falls in love with Nasim-Shlagbaum.

Kara-Musayev the Younger: Gilas head of police, married to the daughter of Kuchkar-Cheka. He goes mad after being dismissed from the police, after which he is known as Musayev-Slogans.

Kazakbay-Happytrigger: caretaker at the wool-washing shed.

Khaira Gavrilovna Huzangay: a lost Chuvash who lives, for unknown reasons, with Bahri-Granny-Fortunes.

Kobil-Melonhead: friend of the boy.

Kuchkar-Cheka: deaf in one ear; an informer.

Kukash-Snubnose: interrogates Obid-Kori after the latter's arrest.

Kumri: wife of Kara-Musayev the Younger.

Kun-Okhun: a deaf Uighur who works at the station as a freight handler; 'Okhun' is the Uzbek for 'Uighur'.

Kuvandyk: Oppok-Lovely's son, a car mechanic.

Kuzi-Gundog: buys cartridges on the black market.

Lobar-Beauty: a lame and beautiful woman who runs the Culture and Recreation shop in Gilas.

Lyuli-Ibodullo-Mahsum: gypsy rag-and-bone man.

Mahmud-Hodja the Younger: great-grandfather of the boy.

Mahmud-Hodja the Elder: a successful merchant; uncle of Mahmud-Hodja the Younger.

Maike: a Kirghiz who accompanies Mahmud-Hodja on the Hadj, is granted a vision and becomes an incomparable poet in many languages.

Mashrab: youngest son of Obid-Kori.

Mefody-Jurisprudence: the town intellectual, an alcoholic ex-lawyer who has spent many years in the Gulag.

Mirzaraim-Bey: father of Obid-Kori and great-grandfather of the boy; *bey* means leader.

Mukum-Hunchback: son of Umarali; owner of chaikhana.

Mullah-Ulmas-Greeneyes: brother of Kuchkar-Cheka and husband to Oppok-Lovely. The name 'Ulmas' means 'immortal'; 'Mullah' is a nickname, evidently given to him simply because it alliterates with 'Ulmas'.

Murzin-Mordovets: a driver.

Murzina-Mordovka: sister to Murzin-Mordovets and mistress to Timurkhan. Murzin and Murzina are from Mordovia – one of the many constituent republics of the Russian Federation whose inhabitants are predominantly Turkic.

Musayev-Slogans: see Kara-Musayev.

Muzayana: daughter of Said Alihon-Tura. Her grandmother was one of Oyimcha's sisters.

Nabi-Onearm: propagandist.

Nafisa: daughter of Hadjiya and Israel-Warder; step-aunt to the boy.

Nakhshon Shtonner: wife of Hoomer.

Nasim-Shlagbaum: grandson of Tolib-Butcher, famous for his huge penis.

*Nat*ka-Pothecary: daughter of Bolta-Lightning and Vera-Virgo; works as a pharmacist; confidante of Janna-Nurse; eventually she marries Nasim-Shlagbaum.

Nozik-Poshsho: the youngest wife of Mirzaraim-Bey and mother of Obid-Kori.

Obid-Kori: Originally known as Obid-Bey (Obid-Leader). Grandfather of the boy; a mullah, executed in 1938. The suffix *Kori* indicates that he is a 'Preserver' of the Koran, someone who knows it by heart.

Oktam-Humble-Russky: an accidental revolutionary. Marries Banat-Pielady.

Oppok-Lovely: daughter of Oktam-Russky and wife of Mullah-Ulmas-Greeneyes. First Secretary of the Station Komsomol Committee; then Head of the Kok-Terek Bazaar; then Gilas passport officer.

Ortik-Picture-Reels: runs the Gilas cinema.

Osman-Anon: KGB officer.

Oyimcha (Beautiful Moon): wife of Obid-Kori and grandmother of the boy.

Ozoda: niece of Oppok-Lovely; runs the small bazaar by the station in Gilas.

Pinkhas Shalomay, later Pyotr Mikhailovich Sholokh-Mayev, then Pete Shelley May – Mullah Ulmas's companion.

Pochamir-Hodja: a Bukhara Jew, who is imprisoned first in Bukhara and then in Gilas. He marries Asolat.

Rakhmon-Kul: one of Chinali's younger sons.

Rif: Tatar gravedigger in the Russian cemetery.

Rizo-Zero: son of Fatkhulla; an engineer, supposed to have instigated a terrible eclipse.

Robiya-Baker: daughter of Garang-Deafmullah and aunt of Kobil-Melonhead.

Rukiya: mother of Kobil-Melonhead; in charge of Selpo – the shop for the sale of clothes and household items.

Ruzi-Crazi: lives in Mookat. When Oyimcha comes to Gilas to take care of the boy, she comes to stay with them, to their annoyance.

Ryksy: inspector in charge of shops and all forms of State trade; father of Kutr.

Sabir and Sabit: two gypsy boys, who rape and murder Hussein.

Said Alihon-Tura: the son of Oyimcha's sister; born in Mookat, he escapes across the mountains from the Bolsheviks and ends up living in Brooklyn.

Said-Kasum-Kadi: father of Oyimcha. The suffix *Kadi* indicates that he is a judge.

Sami-Rais: Chairman of the 'Fruits of Lenin's Path' collective farm.

Saniya: widowed daughter of Aisha.

Satiboldi-Buildings: in charge of all housing and public buildings in Gilas.

Sevinch (Joy): head of Gilas music school, Soginch's great rival.

Nicknamed 'Moisey' or 'Musa'. After losing his memory, he becomes an artist.

Shanob: youngest daughter of Oppok-Lovely.

Shapik: son of Uchmah, a mad boy who looks like Hoomer.

Sherzod: son of Tordybay-Medals.

Shir-Gazi: Obid-Kori's nephew; First Secretary of the Mookat Village Soviet.

Soginch (Desire): conductor of Gilas brass band, Sevinch's great rival. Nicknamed 'Aaron'.

Sohrab-Sharpie: homosexual son of Temir-Iul; lover of the Greek Democritis Chuvalchidi.

Soli-Stores: the elder of Chinali's two sons and heir to his great riches.

Suleiman-Haberdasher: father of Abdulhamid, the revolutionary poet.

Tadji-Murad: son of half-blind Boikush; Akmolin's assistant at the station.

Temir-Iul-Longline: regional railway boss, son of Umur-Longline, the builder of the local railway line.

Timurkhan: a wall-eyed Tatar. Dies after being run over by a train.

Togolok Moldo-Ullu: father-in-law of Shir-Gazi.

Tolib-Butcher: a womaniser.

Tolik-Nosetalk: an alcoholic.

Tordybay-Medals: First Secretary of the Gilas Soviet.

Uchmah-Prophecies: fortune-teller, daughter of Saniya and granddaughter of Aisha, both of whom were single mothers. In old Turkish 'Uchmah' means 'Paradise'.

Ulkan-Bibi: the eldest wife of Mirzaraim-Bey.

Umarali-Moneybags: old inhabitant of Gilas, who became rich through money-lending.

Usman Yusupov: First Secretary of the Uzbek Party Central Committee.

Vamek ben Hasan: a Moroccan prince, engaged to Muzayana.

Vera-Virgo: a prostitute; the wife of Bolta-Lightning and mother of Natka-Pothecary.

Yormuhammad: basmach leader.

Yusuf-Cobbler: a kind man who for some reason regularly pisses against the wall of Huvron-Barber's booth.

Zainab: daughter of Faiz-Ulla. She is named after the heroine of *Zainab and Amon*, a poem about the love of two collective farm workers by Hamid Olimjan (1909–44), the most famous Soviet Uzbek poet.

Zakiya-Nogaika: daughter of an eminent member of the modernising Jadid movement in the Crimea; she ends up in Gilas, working as a wool-washer.

Zamira-Bonu: wife of Mahmud-Hodja the Younger.

Zangi-Bobo: sells *nasvoy* by entrance to Kok-Terek Bazaar. He has compiled a huge dictionary of all the words he has ever heard in Gilas.

Zebi: the beautiful wife of Fatkhulla-Frontline, mother of Rizo-Zero and Zumurad-Barrenwomb.

Zukhra: one of two Uighur twins made pregnant by Kara-Musayev.

Zukhur: manager of grocery store.

Zumurad-Barrenwomb: Fatkhulla-Frontline's beautiful but childless daughter.

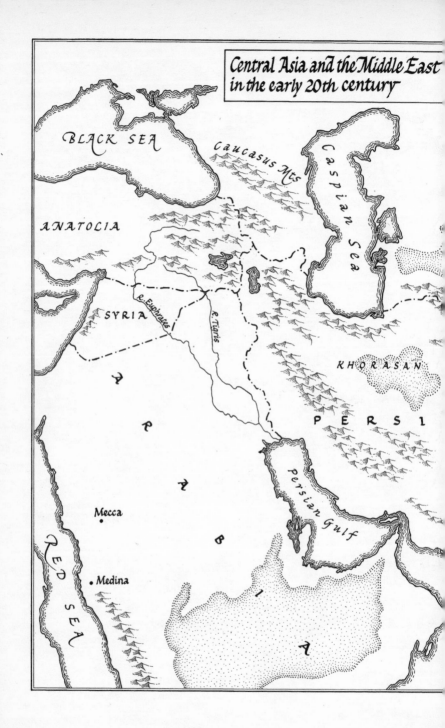

Central Asia and the Middle East in the early 20th century

BLACK SEA

Caucasus Mts

Caspian Sea

ANATOLIA

SYRIA

r. Euphrates

r. Tigris

KHORASAN

PERSI

A
R
A
B
I
A

Mecca

Medina

RED SEA

Persian Gulf

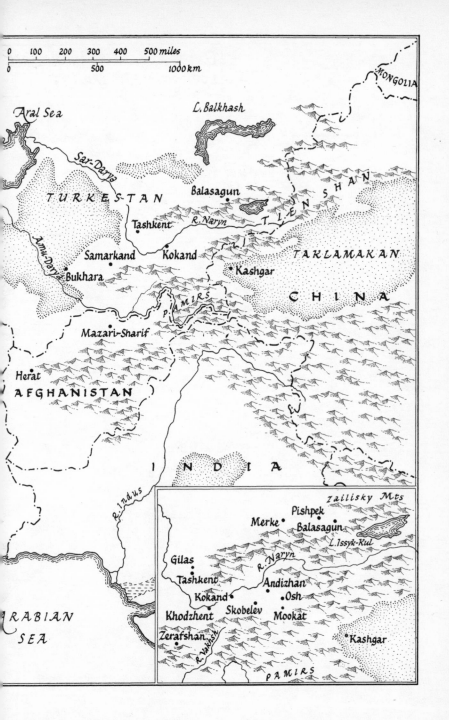

THE BOY'S FAMILY

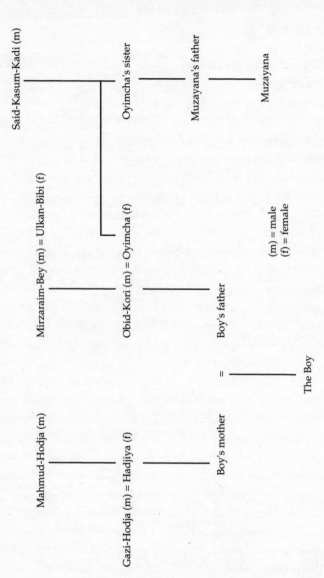

(m) = male
(f) = female

Said-Kasum-Kadi (m)

Oyimcha's sister

Muzayana's father

Muzayana

Mirzaraim-Bey (m) = Ulkan-Bibi (f)

Obid-Kori (m) = Oyimcha (f)

Boy's father

Mahmud-Hodja (m)

Gazi-Hodja (m) = Hadijya (f)

Boy's mother

The Boy

Instead of an Epigraph

O Lord! And you created so perfect a miracle! The elder looked out of the corner of his eye towards where the boy sat bent over the Book, and once again strangely uncontrollable feelings began to run wild in his pure and polished heart. It can happen that, in the middle of intense prayer, the thought of prayer can imperceptibly take the place of prayer and only by prayer itself, only by lifting your voice into a chant and listening to its sound, can this thought be driven out; but the elder (may the Almighty forgive me!) was not granted even this release, although he appeared to have attained not just a momentary illumination – the lot of those who are still struggling – but the light that is even and uninterrupted. I repent a thousand times, O Lord, but the elder was not granted even this release . . . He had long ago left behind our kingdom of dreams and mirages, but now his thought, although he suspected it sprang from delusion, was quivering like a moth between the Creator and his Creation (forgive us sinners, O Lord!) and once again his pale face turned towards the boy reading the Book.

After offering three hundred prayers of repentance, the old man put aside his now warm prayer beads and absolved himself, leaving everything in the hands of Allah. 'A question is the path from the end to the beginning, and doubt, too, is the journey back,' he repeated to himself. In his heart and mind he knew all this – but it made no difference. 'Am I longing, in this extreme of disobedience, for childhood – am I longing again for its unbeaten track?' he thought sorrowfully. 'Has my flesh risen up at its last breath, untamed and untameable?'

The boy had been brought to him seven days before by Mirza Humayun Ardasher; he was on his way to Balkh, where there had been an uprising. 'Amid the sea of vanity and impenitence, you are a pillar of our inviolate faith,' Ardasher had said to the elder. 'The boy has no mother and he knows the taste of bitterness – he will value every minute of peace and obedience under your supervision. Only if he can live here in your sacred dwelling, far from the world's vice and lechery, have I the right to hope. And so may my boy hold firmly to the skirts of your gown and follow you along the straight path of righteousness.'

The elder remembered the warrior's words. Ardasher had found it difficult not to place the boy in front of him on the saddle and take him to Balkh, into dusty and sandy whirlwinds, into a world of battles and wanderings – and the elder had admired the father's act of renunciation. Amid his spirit's settled peace the elder had not resisted a contrary movement of his soul that had been barely perceptible – and now he was ceaselessly repenting before the Supreme One, who had evidently chosen to test him one more never-ending time. But He was free, free to do as He chose.

He stole one more glance at the boy reading the Book – and the boy, as if sensing the gathering weight of the elder's silent gaze, raised his eyes. His eyelashes were like a dark shadow, and this shadow lifted the boy's black clear eyes to meet the eyes of the surprised and embarrassed elder. The elder was no longer used to direct looks from young eyes – his disciples always looked down as they answered him – but the boy's gaze had nothing of the disciple about it, and the elder sensed this clearly in his confused soul. Used as they were now to the even light of the Book, the boy's eyes seemed to linger – as if within them still lingered something of the Book's even and unstoppable light – and the elder's soul, his sinful soul, was tormented in the boy's presence, like a moth that doesn't know what to do with the light.

On the seventh day, when the boy had learned one thirtieth part of the Book, the elder broke with age-old rules and astonished the whole hanaqa[1] by declaring a chella, a forty-day fast. What is more, he declared this fast not for the hanaqa as a whole but for the boy alone, thus exciting long and fruitless self-doubt in the hearts of his disciples and even a certain envy towards a boy judged worthy of initiation after so very short a period of preparation.

Only in the chellakhona did no candle burn that night. The

chellakhona was given over to nature – although it was protected by a labyrinth of underground walls reflected against which the light of night endlessly mirrored its own reflections. There was no place like it, no other place where thought returns to itself and blood imbued with thought polishes the imperfect heart.

After the midnight prayer the boy, whom the Teacher was leading along the path of perfection of the spirit, tried to master the pillars of the formally simple Ikhlas Surah, about the One and Only who neither begetteth nor is begotten, and there is none like unto Him.[2] The first thousand repetitions remained on the boy's tongue, not peeling away from the flesh; then a handful of raisins sent out sweet shoots between the dry, cracked words, and the Teacher told him that they were in the wilderness where the path begins.

Candles burned behind candles; a moth that had got lost in these underground depths, perhaps having been enticed into them by the smell of raisins – a moth that seemed to value its own life, sensing perhaps that there was little other life in this many-layered and resonant emptiness, kept beating against the light reflected off the stone ceiling, and only on the ninth day did it exhaust itself, fall and burn up in the flame. And even this eternal image, which had always imbued the elder with resolve, at first evoked in him only confusion and panic. Sensing hesitation in the measured rustle of the Teacher's lips, the boy suddenly turned round – and the elder's tired eyelids shook off the dust of countless prayers.

The elder at that moment got the better of his desires; he had long known that the Path is only the Path in so far as – whether you have set out on it intentionally or by chance – you accept that you are doomed to allowing yourself to be led by the Path, even to be used by the Path. Submission to the inevitability of this truth had always brought him peace; now, however, no effort of will could eclipse his sense that the Path is not what begins with the first day of the anxiety that is left behind and yet still pierces your spine, nor is it what people consider achievement – not even the fortieth day that glimmers ahead of you and that you anticipate as early as the nineteenth day. No, the elder now understood that the Path was the distance dividing him from the boy – two sideways steps between two kneeling figures, two short steps that must never be taken.

On the twenty-seventh day the boy was seized by a fever. Even Hafez Safautdin Sheikh, as he came silently to them that morning with warm water for their ablutions and to take away the pots with their rare excretions, now devoid of all smell – even Hafez Safautdin Sheikh noticed that the stone shelf in the wall was less cold than usual. The boy was shaking, and at first the elder thought that he had reached the Valley of Terrors that is governed by djinns; the elder was frightened, however, by a strange sense that he himself was not so much leading as being led, and so he hurried in spirit into the midst of these terrors and hallucinations, where djinns dance like tongues of fire, where every dance ends in copulation, where demons like new-born babies slip inside you and use your face as a mask, taking over your body to give free rein to their corrupt natures. With a superhuman effort of will the old man formed out of tongues of fire the single word 'Allah', like a spell, like a talisman, like salvation for both him and the boy, and when the fires died down, quivering their last unruly little tongues, the old man saw that the boy was not whispering a prayer glorifying the name of the Benevolent and Merciful One, but calling to his mother, whose name he did not even know because it was so long since she had died. Sweat was streaming off the boy, mingling below his damp turban with cloudy tears . . . 'What makes a child's tears so cloudy?' the old man wondered in bewilderment; it was, after all, the thirtieth day, and by this time all the functions of our frail bodies usually become pure and insensible, while the body, the body itself, begins to shine with a pale light . . . From where, from what unreachable depths, were these cloudy drops drawn?

Lack of sleep and the demands of the fast had turned the old man's soul into a tangle of strings – yes, he could not shake off this sense that his soul was a tangle of strings that had become knotted together yet were somehow still able to sound; every movement of the boy's inner being echoed long and resonantly in this tangle, but for the first time in many years of enlightenment the elder was bewildered, unable to understand what the sounds meant.

The boy regained full consciousness only after a week.

After the midnight prayer, the old man was laying the boy down on his felt mat and, having covered him with a prayer rug, was wiping his burning face with the end of his own fine turban. Why had he not, at the first sign of weakness, sent the boy back up above? No, even before that, why had he led this young and frail soul underground? Why had he set him on this long path of loneliness and renunciation? What pride had made him lead a child along a path that belongs to Allah alone?

Face to face with these questions, the old man hid for a long time behind a shield of prayers, but not even they could revive his exhausted spirit; the never-ending prayers, which had lost all meaning, were now tearing his soul to shreds . . .

On the fortieth day the boy opened his eyes at dawn. The old man knew it was dawn from the gentle touch of a breeze on his back. There was a flicker of light, reflected through the labyrinth of stone walls. A faint scent of henna from the beard of the hunchbacked Abu-al-Malik, whose turn it must have been to bring them their water and the usual handful of dried raisins and ground nuts, carried into their solitude a memory of the life that goes on outside.

And the boy opened his eyes.

Every summer the chaikhana was moved outside and set up beneath the huge silver poplars that the railway had headed for when, fifty years before, it had first made its way to Gilas. It had been the same during the year the Fascists invaded; the five low wooden platforms were set up beneath the poplars. There were fewer and fewer people, however, to sit on them; the previous tea-drinkers had gone to the Front, and a new Gilas had yet to emerge from the influx of evacuees and the wounded. Really there was only Umarali-Moneybags, whose insatiable greed had led him to be pronounced fit for prison, where he had gained another three stone before the War, but had also made him so fat that he had been pronounced unfit to fight; and Tolib-Butcher, who, as if to spite Umarali, was so thin that he had been entrusted – on the grounds that he could hardly be keeping anything back for himself – with the allocation of the occasional meat rations, although the half-blind Boikush slanderously questioned how on earth Tolib could feed others when he was unable to feed himself; and then there was Kuchkar-Cheka,[3] whom Oppok-Lovely had once struck so hard that he had gone deaf in one ear. As a result he had had to found his career on making the other ear work overtime.

These three would sit down at dawn on three separate plat-forms so that no one could think they were conspiring together; each would put a black pellet of opium under his tongue, close his swollen eyelids and greet either the dawn or his dreams, or else the 7.12 train – Gilas's counterpart to the SovietNewsBureau bulletin.

Now and again the morning rustle of leaves being warmed by the sun would be interrupted by the matured reflections of Umarali-Moneybags. 'They say the Germans aren't far away,'

Umarali might begin, his fleshy head resting on a fist as big as a prize-boxer's glove. 'Yesterday Oktam-Humble-Russky said that one has been seen in Chengeldy.'

After several minutes of the rustling of leaves, Tolib-Butcher, over whose sunny face two newly-awoken flies would now be crawling, might respond, 'If they're coming from Kazakhstan, then there's no way to come but the railway line.'

Silence would hang over them once again. After processing all the information he had taken in through his one ear, Kuchkar-Cheka, his face as wrinkled as a dried prune, would say, 'If they reach Gilas, they'll have to come through the chaikhana – sure as sure can be.'

There was another long and fruitless silence. Then the creak of wooden sleepers or thickset poplars would seem to them like a harbinger of either an approaching train or advancing Germans.

'Parpi-Sneakysnake's no ordinary man. He isn't going to let them through without paying for a dish of *plov*,[4] is he?' said Umarali-Moneybags, and licked his weighty moustache.

The wind blew. The minutes passed.

'*Plov* with meat,' added the skinny Tolib-Butcher.

As startled as if a distant steam-engine whistle were the command 'A-ten-shun!' Kuchkar-Cheka concluded. 'Yes, the rascal will fleece the Germans all right. He'll give them some food, talk them into the ground and fleece them. He'll take all their money and all their gold.' And his eyes burned with indignation like the sun, or like the sun's reflection on the cab-window of a panting steam engine.

The following morning it was Kuchkar who began the conversation. 'Have you heard? Jews are being sent here from Odessa.'

In the opium-filled silence his companions sifted through the news they had heard the previous day, but neither Tolib-Butcher (who had yet to become a fully fledged butcher) nor Umarali-

Moneybags (by then, alas, anything but a Moneybags) was able to find any tiniest scrap of news about Odessa Jews in any corner of his mind or body.

Then Kuchkar-Cheka – and heaven knows where he had got hold of this information – went on cautiously, 'Now if our dear . . . if our First Secretary of the Central Committee, Usman Yusupov, were to build a house for the Jews on the bank of the Ankhor . . .'

The others meditated for a long time on Kuchkar's loyal, even obsequious words; nobody, after all, had provoked him by saying anything untoward. Then Umarali, a dissident before dissidents were thought to exist, had been overwhelmed by the nihilism born of his years in prison. 'Usman won't fucking well build anything. It'll just be the usual fuck-up,' he said at the end of the fifth minute, by which time Tolib-Butcher had forgotten about Usman Yusupov, although he hadn't forgotten the Jews.

'Mister Umarali could build the house,' said Tolib-Butcher, finally remembering what all this was about.

Kuchkar's silence lasted so long that the others began to wonder whether his one whole and zealous ear might also have been damaged.

And then Umarali-Moneybags, yawning so luxuriously that the golden sun shone into his huge slobbering mouth, went on, 'A six-floor house, thirty rooms in each floor.'

'That makes two hundred rooms less twenty!' Tolib exclaimed after another minute.

'And they could be rented out at . . . at . . .'

'That's an awesome sum!' Kuchkar had been bent double like a folded radio aerial, but a steam-engine whistle had woken him up; once again he was ready to receive information.

It was one more day of the War.

Late that night Umarali-Moneybags entered his yard, hung a six-stone chain over his gate and shook awake his wife, who was sleeping under the vine. 'Hey, bitch, have you got anything left to eat?'

'But you've only just got back from the chaikhana!' his wife said with a groan. Umarali then cursed every part of her from head to toe until she relented and said, 'There's some leftover meat and lentils on the shelf in the kitchen.'

Umarali wandered into the kitchen in the darkness, groped on the shelf for the bowl and wolfed down the contents.

In the morning his wife got up and looked around the kitchen; she couldn't find the oilcake she had put to soak for the rams. She cautiously woke her husband. 'What did you eat yesterday, husband? There's no oilcake left.'

And he replied, 'You fucking bitch, I thought I'd eaten something I shouldn't have. I've been shitting all night.'

Another day of the Great Patriotic War[5] was beginning.

Sometimes Umarali, Tolib and Kuchkar were joined by Sami-Rais, the chairman of the 'Fruits of Lenin's Path' collective farm that surrounded Gilas. Because of the War and the consequent shortage of cadres, the collective farm had been so much enlarged that it took Sami-Rais a week to ride to one corner of his fields, and another week to ride to the next corner. During these journeys he slept in all kinds of places, but most often upon his bay mare, who had acquired a useful skill; she always immediately offered Sami-Rais the shoulder towards which his troubled head was falling. She had also developed an ability to sense if her rider's weight was diminishing and deliver him at precisely midday to the Gilas chaikhana, which stood at the intersection of all the collective farm roads. By then Umarali, Tolib and Kuchkar, having finished their discussion of the news from the 7.12 'SovietNewsBureau' train, would be sitting together, about to delight in whatever sustenance All-Knowing and All-Merciful Allah had sent them that day.

During his endless journeying through a collective farm

manned only by women, and during his visits to the chaikhana, where his family sent him letters with requests for rice and flour from the store, Sami-Rais never once suspected, not even with a single hair of his moustache, that Umarali-Moneybags had imposed a tax on the whole of Gilas, threatening its inhabitants with 'labour mobilisation' into a collective space so boundless as to be the equivalent of exile, and that every day at noon either Izaly-Jew – director of the Papanin Tailoring Co-operative – or the half-blind Boikush, or Yusuf-Cobbler, or Chinali, the wealthy director of the huge warehouse, would deliver to the chaikhana whatever the All-Knowing and All-Powerful had chosen that day for Umarali and his fellow-diners.

And when Sami-Rais, unloaded from his horse by Kuchkar-Cheka and Tolib-Butcher, was sitting down, propped against three large mattresses and still rocking in the rhythm of his morning's ride, and when Umarali handed him a letter from his family, Izaly-Jew would look out through the ventilation pane of his tailoring co-operative. By evening the whole of Gilas would have learned from its women that Kuchkar-Cheka's list of saboteurs and enemies of the people had been passed on to Sami-Rais by Umarali-Moneybags.

Sami did not smoke opium but, like all chairmen, he liked to drink vodka. Vodka, of course, served everywhere as a test of political reliability – a final examination that Sami always passed with flying colours and much smacking of lips. During the last such examination, after a decision to amalgamate seven collective farms under a single chairman, he had managed without difficulty, in the presence of a strict Russian referee, to drink his two rivals under the table as if they were mere puppies. Let it be known that true Communist cadres are to be found even among simple folk!

Every bottle of State vodka, however, was being sent to the Front, and Umarali ran into difficulties in his attempts to ensure a regular supply for Sami-Rais. For a while, Umarali was saved by Kolya-Konyak, who used to fill the one remaining vodka bottle with his own sultana brandy. Now, however, like everyone else in a country straining every sinew in the decisive struggle with the Fascist enemy, Kolya had run out of both sugar and sultanas; as a result, he had lost all sense of the meaning of life and was no longer afraid even of the prospect of forced labour in the deserted fields of Sami's collective farm.

But Umarali's fine nose for alcohol, sharpened by years of confinement among Russians, did not let him down. Once, as he was walking past the 16.17 train and thinking about the fate of his Soviet Fatherland, he suddenly sensed something that vividly reminded him of the sour eructations of Sami-Rais. Following his rat's nose, he found the source of this smell not far from the engine's wheels. Surprised in his search by a locomotive driver carrying a revolver, he struggled for some time, summoning all his prison Russian, to explain what it was that he was looking for: 'You Ivan, me Umarali. Me give melon, you give vodka!'

He breathed in the vile smell and demonstrated his appreciation of its beauty. And he pointed to where it was coming from.

Confusing the Uzbek name 'Umarali' with a similar-sounding Russian word that means 'dying' – and unable to make out what on earth was the matter with this apparently dying saboteur – locomotive driver Ivan pointedly began wiping a rag imbued with this same smell over the revolver to which he was entitled by rank. But when Umarali bent down towards the rag – hands clasped behind his back to show he meant no harm – and began gabbling away, the Communist engine driver felt able to adopt an internationalist viewpoint. Deciding that this younger brother to the Russian nation must have run out of brake fluid for the collective-farm tractor (Yes, that must be why he couldn't stop rattling on!), he even went so far as to refuse point-blank the offer of a collective-farm watermelon.

'There!' he said, handing this agrarian worker a bottle of industrial liquid. 'For your socialist tractor!'

'Yes, yes – for socialist *traktir*!' said Umarali, remembering from his years in prison a Russian word that meant 'tavern'.

From that day on, locomotive driver Ivan began to economise on brake fluid for the sake of the triumphant future of the nation's collective farms; once a week he gave what he had saved to his new protégé, and Umarali diligently transferred these half-litres of fraternal aid from his one and only vodka bottle into the innards of Sami-Rais, who was growing steadily greener.

'All this travelling's taking it out of poor old Sami,' Umarali would think sadly, as he watched Kuchkar and Tolib hoist Sami-Rais, now well fuelled, well lubricated and well informed as to his family's requirements, onto the back of his bay mare, who clip-clopped away into the boundless fields of the collective farm, still always offering Sami-Rais the shoulder towards which his great bulk was slewing.

Oktam-Humble-Russky was one of the first revolutionaries, one of the men who had established Soviet power – first in the City, then in Gilas itself. What, though, do we mean by 'established'? In 1916 the sixteen-year-old Oktam – together with the whole of his village, which lay not far from Gilas – was dispatched to form a labour brigade behind the lines in some remote and barren part of Russia; but since Oktam had been born an albino – which was why he was known as Russky – the first frosts almost tore away his skin. Strange scabs spread over his body, as if his platoon had sprayed him with shrapnel, and the battalion doctor, afraid this was some unknown infection, took the first opportunity to send Oktam back to wherever it was he had come from.

But as Oktam, along with some recruiting officers, was about to get on a train, a Tatar came up to him in the station toilet. After satisfying himself that Oktam was a true, circumcised Muslim who squatted down in order to piss, and after waiting for him to finish, he asked him to take a short letter to someone in the railway depot in Tashkent. The accursed Tatar swore by Allah that it was just a message to his relatives but, as the saying goes, 'If your friend is a Tatar, keep an axe close beside you!' The letter turned out to be a Revolutionary Proclamation and the unsuspecting Oktam was dragged off to the fortress as soon as the train reached Tashkent.

Oktam had no complaints – it was better, after all, to be in prison in one's homeland than in a trench beneath a foreign sky . . . And then came the Revolution. The Revolutionary Sailors of Tashkent[6] released Oktam, went through his files and leapt eagerly on the evidence of his revolutionary past. At public meetings in the Buz Bazaar[7] they displayed the scars from his virulent Russian illness as evidence of the darkness of the past and the true nature of the prison of nations that had been the Tsarist Empire.

Oktam did nothing more than lift his shirt and slightly lower his trousers, but at the All-Region Congress of Bolsheviks he was co-opted onto the Central Committee. In short, it was not long before Oktam had become an important figure, and even his nickname – 'Russky' – soon began to sound like a certificate of reliability and political consciousness.

Oktam-Humble-Russky was unable to do anything at all – or rather, all he could do was live in constant fear that someone might be about to expose his incompetence. But his incompetence was of no concern to anyone; on the contrary, it made everyone – builders, weavers, town labourers and farm labourers alike – feel that Oktam was someone they could rely on. No one needed to worry that this splendid Bolshevik might secretly be promoting the interests of some other profession.

Then came industrialisation, followed by collectivisation, followed by cultural revolution. Enemies – and the state seemed to have many of them – were dealt with methodically, one profession at a time. Oktam learned the latest Party slogans at night, syllable by syllable, and slowly came to realise, with his scant mind, that the safest place in a burning house is the yard.

He asked to be transferred to the God-forsaken – and Party-forsaken – town of Gilas. The Party sent him to reinforce the spirit of dialectical materialism in the wool factory; among a group of Tatar women who had been brought there by cattle truck from Orenburg he was to lay down the Party line, a line as clear and undeviating as the railway that cut through Gilas. 'Not Tatars again!' Oktam thought confusedly, but then, remembering the end of his first encounter with Tatars, he said to himself, 'Oh well, all's well that ends well!' and accepted the post of factory director.

*

And so he ended up in Gilas, where, in order to have some influence on this collective of women, he had no choice but to marry their team-leader Banat-Pielady, a woman as full of words as a radio and as noisy as a steam-engine . . . It was not long before they had a daughter, to whom they gave the name of 'Oklutsiya' – or October Revolutsiya.

During the Great Patriotic War, in the absence of trucks to fetch the wool, the factory personnel were evacuated to the Sary-Agach steppe, closer to where the Kazakhs grazed their flocks; and in order that these young Tatar women, who were now washing their wool in a muddy river immediately after the sheep had been shorn, should not all end up marrying Kazakh shepherds and then wandering off with them across the steppe, thus multiplying private property, Oktam was ordered to accompany them. In the steppe he exposed the anti-Communist sabotage of shearers who left tufts of unshorn wool around the members of rams and the teats of ewes. By way of a demonstration, he sheared these sheep several times himself, so terrifying both the Kazakh shepherds and the Tatar wool washers that, when the War came to an end, he was able to return to the wool-factory all of its personnel – although he did in addition bring back the three sons that Alfiya bore to Kypchibek the woodcutter, who himself became the factory watchman and remained in this post many years.

After the War, when matchmakers came to Oktam-Humble-Russky in respect of his daughter Oklutsiya Oktamovna, he was sitting in what he called his office and cursing that thrice-accursed Tatar at that station in Moscow where the track of his life had so suddenly changed direction – and the reason he was cursing this Tatar was that the finance inspector had called the previous day and, having failed once again to obtain payment of the household taxes now due, had begun to make a list of Oktam's possessions: Item: 1 felt blanket; Item: 1 iron bedstead;

Item: 1 stove, bourgeois.[8] At the sound of the word 'bourgeois', which the inspector pronounced out loud and without abbreviation, Oktam had been seized with fury. He had gone into his office and, using the only telephone in Gilas, asked the young lady to connect him to First Secretary Usman Yusupov. After several minutes of crackling, Usman picked up the receiver; without listening to the imposing voice Usman adopted for the benefit of the telephone, Oktam shouted into the mouthpiece, pointing at the same time to the still obstinate inspector: 'Usman, is this what we made a Revolution for?' Without waiting for an answer, he had then thrown the receiver down onto its cradle of two gilded ram's horns.

And as he sat in his office, cursing that thrice-accursed Tatar, his wife Banat came in. Not wasting words for once in her life – she must have expended all her urge for conversation on the matchmakers – she said: 'Speak to Usman, old man. After all, we are Uzbeks – how can we give our daughter away without any dowry? We'd never live it down!'

Oktam thought for a moment and agreed: 'All right, I'll go and call on him. But tell me about this young man. I take it he's at least a Komsomol member?'[9]

3

Mullah-Ulmas-Greeneyes was the brother of Kuchkar-Cheka. After their father was shot in the 1930s, he felt he had no choice – if he was not to be shot too, along with the rest of the family – but to marry the sister of the Bolshevik Oktam-Humble-Russky, who like her brother was an albino. This marriage had left Mullah-Ulmas with a secret but profound hatred for all Russians and above all for that honorary – though hardly honourable – Russian, Oktam-Humble-Russky.

When Oktam-Humble-Russky, through one of his Bolshevik decrees, instituted Russian-language clubs in all the *mahallyas*[10] that adjoined, and therefore lived off, the wool factory (some people stole the wool, others bought and sold it; some used to spin it at home, others used to knit with it; some sold the wool that had been spun, knitted and combed, others bought this wool from them, and so on and so on) – when Oktam-Humble-Russky instituted these clubs in order to abuse the unconscious masses more effectively, Mullah-Ulmas-Greeneyes made use of his family connections (after all, he got cursed quite enough by Oktam-Humble-Russky as it was) to opt out of this cultural activity, an act of sabotage that was later to have significant military consequences.

Soon after the Fascist invasion, Mullah-Ulmas-Greeneyes was sent off to the Front. Apart from the usual curse about a man's mother having been fucked by a cur, he knew no Front-speak at all. Nevertheless, his commander Kozoleyev and his political instructor Polityuk managed to instil in him, for the rest of his life, one entire speech: 'Right dress! A-ten-shun! Listen to battle orders! Numerically-superior-fascist-hordes-are-advancing-along-the-front!   ButthesplendidsoldiersoftheRed-ArmyunderthewiseleadershipofthefatherofpeoplesthegreatSTALIN HUR-R-R-AAA-AAAH!'

No sooner had he learned this phrase by heart than he was taken prisoner near Smolensk. Poor Mullah-Ulmas-Greeneyes defended himself against the questions of the Fascists with this incomprehensible sentence, imagining that he was speaking the language of his questioners and smiling all the time with blissful inanity. Eventually the Germans decided that he must be a Jew – didn't he, after all, have excellent manners? – and after confirming the truth of this hypothesis by examining his indisputably circumcised member, they sent him off in the next goods train bound for the death camps, to await his turn there.

There in Maidanek, among Jews of many nationalities – from Russian to Ethiopian – he became acquainted (as a result of a chance oath while they were stoking the crematorium furnace) with a Bukhara Jew, Pinkhas Shalomay. Shovelling coal as he spoke, Pinkhas explained in Uzbek how things stood and just what it was they were doing.

That night, as he lay on a plank-bed in a camp barrack, Mullah cried with his green eyes and prayed to Allah to save him from a faithless death. 'Since it has been your will that I be taken for a Jew, let me become a Jew. I shall learn languages, I shall travel the world, I shall find out about everything and stick my nose into everything. Let me, O Allah, be a Jew, but in life rather than in death!' he sobbed.

His prayer was heard. The following day Pinkhas found in the toilet a soiled scrap of a German newspaper containing an announcement of the formation of a Turkestan Legion.[11] 'A curse on the arsehole of the Kraut or Yid who wiped himself with this blessed news,' Pinkhas whispered as he held the paper up to the light. That same day Pinkhas wrote a letter to the head-quarters of this Legion; the illiterate Mullah-Ulmas-Greeneyes appended an Arabic-looking scribble and pressed against the page the tip of a thumb smeared with human soot. A week later a uniformed gentleman of either Kazakh or Kirghiz appearance came to the barrack and, towards evening, set off with both the blissful Mullah, who in his delight had rattled off his one and only Russian sentence, and Pinkhas, who had passed himself off as the Tadjik Panzhkhos Salom.

The military career of the Jewish Pinkhas Shalomay was considerably more successful than that of the Muslim Mullah-Ulmas-Greeneyes. The reason for this was simple enough: Pinkhas was able to read and write in both Uzbek and Tadjik and he was equally at home with Arabic, Latin and Cyrillic scripts, the various alphabetical reforms having proved no obstacle to him.[12] Mullah-Ulmas-Greeneyes, however, out of a secret hatred for alien letters – a hatred that once again derived from his link to Oktam-Humble-Russky the Bolshevik, even though the latter in fact knew no letters at all – could sign his name only by dashing off a few circles and lines that he thought of as Arabic. Within a month, Panzhkhos had become an influential Tadjik at the Headquarters of the Turkestan Legion, while Mullah – thanks to his irritatingly frequent repetition of his one Russian sentence – had been sent off to herd swine, creatures abhorrent to Allah.

But a vow, above all a vow made to Allah, is a vow, and Mullah took it upon himself, there among the swine, to master his first foreign language. When the owners of the swine cursed him in their native tongue, he remembered his distant brother-in-law Oktam-Humble-Russky and, out of habit, longed to fuck the sisters of his tormentors, just as he had somehow or other fucked his unbearable wife, the albino Oppok-Lovely – and tears would roll from his green eyes and down his long lashes. In time, however, retribution fell upon his ungrateful masters, whom he had mistakenly believed to be Russians and whose convoluted language, with its 'Ishch vaishchishch nishcht', he had reluctantly studied.

Our American allies arrived; Mullah-Ulmas-Greeneyes realised he had learned the wrong language and, either from joy or by way of a curse, rattled off his Red Army speech. This led to his being sent off to still more distant parts – to France, to graze horses in Fontainebleau. There, in the family of Mademoiselle Countess de Sus, whose great-uncle had brought some great obelisk or other from Egypt and set it up in the Place de la Concorde, Mullah learned to tell one wine from another and to discriminate among cheeses; he also, with the help of this Mademoiselle and her friend, the granddaughter of Napoleon Bonaparte's Josephine, he acquired fluency in the most florid and refined of phrases: 'I shall unlace your corset!' or 'How cruelly a man in love is oppressed by tight pantaloons!'

Once, however, taking a break from love and going to Aven station for a glass or two of Saint-Emilion, he came across a drinking companion of his. This man seemed to have been named after some cognac or other – probably either Napoleon or Camus. He was standing in a corner and pissing upwards, trying to reach a '*Vive la Résistance!*' poster high on the wall and make his urine flow like tears from the eyes of his French Motherland. Some unconscious force then erupted from Mullah in the form of his Red Army speech, as a result of which this Camus stood rooted to the spot, his stream of urine hanging in mid-air.

Camus took him straight off to Paris, to a friend with the improbable name of Sartre. In actual fact this Sartre was not a Sart[13] at all; he had just read too many books and dreamed himself up a new surname. In Gilas no one would have got away with a joke as silly as this: if Mullah had introduced himself as 'Mullah-Ulmas-Greeneyes French', he might have been taken, even by his own compatriots, for a Jew – but no one would have believed he was French. Anyway, this Sartre made Mullah keep repeating his speech until well after sunrise, and the three of them washed it down each time with a glass of Camus. By dawn the Frenchmen were feeling nauseous – one kept falling to the ground and the other had to prop himself up against the wall – while Mullah himself was so overwhelmed by the startling power of his speech that he began to confuse the two men with his two aristocratic ladies and to whisper in their ears, in the now blinding sunlight: 'I shall unlace your corset!' or 'How cruelly a man in love is oppressed by tight pantaloons!'

Sartre turned out to be truly a Sart in at least one respect: he proved treacherous. Towards evening, he sent Mullah to Maurice Thorez's people.[14] Maurice Thorez, on account of certain ideological differences, conveyed Mullah through the Black Forest into Switzerland and then across the Alps to Italy. There Mullah twice ate spaghetti bolognese with comrade Palmiro Togliatti[15] and, after washing down some strange filth from the sea with a revolting Italian wine whose bouquet was the same as that of the local fish, he blurted out his sacred and eternal speech. He was promptly conveyed to Palermo.

Amid bombs, arguments and gang feuds he escaped in an unseaworthy boat to Greece, together with an up-and-coming young rascal called Toto whose mother had been loved by Mullah as she had never been loved by any Italian. Confused by the word 'Sart', she would whisper to him the words she had learned from American soldiers: 'Fack me! Fack me!' Growing more ardent, she would wriggle like an eel in between the words: 'Spain me! Greek me! French me! Turk me!' Only at the wildest moment of orgasm would she cry out in a cat-like voice the incomprehensible nationality of this Mullah, 'Sart me! Sart me!', thus inspiring Mullah-Ulmas-Greeneyes to the highest degree of patriotic ecstasy.

In Greece, on the seashore, people filled Mullah's mouth with stones in order to teach him Greek declamation.[16] In Turkey, where the language was almost the same as his own, the main burden fell on his legs. Momentarily entranced as he danced the dances of the Mevlevi order of whirling Dervishes, Mullah came out with his usual sentence – heathen words abhorrent to God. This led to his being taken through Thrace to Bosnia, and from there to Serbia. In Serbia he took lessons from the leader of the Southern Slavs in the language then known as Serbo-Croat.

Once, however, Mullah-Ulmas-Greeneyes reeled off his sentence over some plum brandy; there was, alas, no wise Pinkhas Shalomay beside him to explain that Yugoslav-Soviet relations had entered a period of tension. Josip Broz Tito did not forgive Mullah. He was conveyed to the Soviet Union via eight intermediary countries – whose languages he innocently mastered one after another – and handed over to Stalin.

As a traitor to the Motherland, Mullah-Ulmas-Greeneyes was sent to the Gulag. Four years of terrible Siberian camps and transit prisons imprinted themselves on the speech organs of the doggedly surviving Mullah in the guise of Khakass, Buryat, Evenk, Nivkhi, Inuit,[17] and one other language whose name was known to no one at all.

During his wanderings Mullah-Ulmas-Greeneyes had seen so many countries and places that when, along with a few million other political prisoners, he was rehabilitated at the time of Khrushchev's Thaw[18] and asked where he had been born, so that he could be returned there by train, he could no longer remember the name 'Gilas'. For two days and three nights after his release he lay on the bed-boards of his barrack and tried, without success, to recall the name of his birthplace. But he did for some reason manage to recall the name Kok-Terek, where his brother Kuchkar-Cheka had sold sheep on Sundays – and where his wife Oppok-Lovely had been in charge of the bazaar!

He was sent to Kok-Terek. But he had the misfortune to be sent not to the Kok-Terek he knew, which lay two kilometres from Gilas, but to a Kok-Terek in Kazakhstan where a teacher at the local evening school with the surname Solzhenitsyn,[19] who had also done time in the camps, ended up giving Mullah mathematics lessons in German. This Solzhenitsyn refused point-blank to speak Russian to Mullah or to instruct him in the expansive Russian language; the reason for this intransigence was that Mullah, while downing some Kazakh moonshine to celebrate his arrival in Kok-Terek, had fired off his entire Red Army speech.

After an unbroken eight-year correspondence encompassing the entire Soviet Union, the Young Pioneers[20] of Gilas finally managed to track down the native of Gilas who had served as their very first front-line soldier – Mullah-Ulmas-Greeneyes. Yes, there were indeed many veterans more deserving of honour than the former swineherd Mullah-Ulmas-Greeneyes, but none of them had been born in Gilas. One-eyed Fatkhulla-Frontline had been born in the half-Uzbek, half-Tadjik village of Chust; while as for First Secretary Tordybay-Medals, the retired colonel whose chest was decorated with medals from all the countries of Central and Eastern Europe whose languages Mullah-Ulmas-Greeneyes had absorbed with such remarkable ease – he had only a blank space in his passport under 'place of birth', having acquired his name, surname and nationality at the age of eleven, in a Soviet orphanage.

The mathematics teacher was almost in tears as he said goodbye to Mullah; after Greater Serbian, Mullah had been going to teach him the basics of Albanian, Uzbek and Yiddish – but Fate decreed otherwise.

Like it or not, Mullah-Ulmas-Greeneyes, armed with his Red-Army sentence (a sentence that had protected him over the years more effectively than any conceivable spell or act of sorcery and that now met the needs of the time more precisely than ever) became the First Veteran of Gilas and the adjoining collective farms. His wife Oppok-Lovely, who had by that time taken Gilas well and truly in hand, spared no effort to make sure that her poor husband was granted all appropriate honours. And then one day, during an All-Republic Congress of Veterans of War and Labour, he wandered into the toilet and bumped, as one might say, penis to penis into whom do you think? None other than Pinkhas Shalomay, who turned out to have transformed himself from Panzhkhos Salom to Pyotr Mikhailovich Sholokh-Mayev, to have completed a doctoral thesis on the crucial role played by Uzbek spies behind the lines of the German-Fascist enemy, and to have produced a film, *The Exploits of Farkhad*,[21] based on this thesis, which was to be shown immediately after the Congress. Sholokh-Mayev was now head of the translation and interpretation department of an important research institute, his chief responsibility being to liaise between two mutually uncomprehending groups: the three or four learned Russians with no knowledge of Uzbek who were employed to edit dissertations and theses about to be submitted to the Higher Dissertations Commission in Moscow, and the thirty-seven Uzbek professors, doctors and post-graduates who somehow produced these dissertations but whose grasp of the complexities of Russian declensions and conjugations was, alas, alarmingly shaky. There in the toilet, to the amazement of more simple-minded veterans, who found themselves unable to go on pissing, these two switched casually between Sudeten, Alsatian and Catalan. But when Mullah-Ulmas-Greeneyes, who was used to old-fashioned buttons, caught his penis in the zip of his new trousers and burst out swearing in the language of a fisherman whom a sharp-toothed walrus had bitten in the same place on the shores of the Laptev Brothers Sea,[22] even Pinkhas Shalomay could understand fuck all.

After this chance meeting Pyotr Mikhailovich Sholokh-Mayev managed to get Mullah-Ulmas-Greeneyes appointed to a part-time post in his research institute with the title of 'Bearer of Dying Languages' and succeeded in organising around him an All-Union Centre for the study and restoration of the languages of Siberia and the Far North.

In the days of the ever more decrepit Brezhnev and his fully developed socialism, when Mullah-Ulmas-Greeneyes the renowned Veteran and Bearer of Languages used to have to recall his immortal speech almost every day, Jews began to migrate to other lands. Pinkhas Shalomay applied to leave too. For some reason he was refused – perhaps because he was irreplaceable, perhaps because of the emergence of certain troubling details about his heroic wartime past. Pinkhas reminded Mullah of their old friendship and asked him to write on his behalf to Solzhenitsyn, that former teacher and pupil of his who had apparently become a very big fish indeed.

'But what language can I write to him in? I don't know Russian. And he hardly learned any Uzbek at all. Anyway I can't write!' said Mullah. Pinkhas then wrote something himself and Mullah, just as in the old days, dashed off his 'Arabic' line and circle signature.

What happened next was exactly as the devious Pinkhas had intended. Whether or not Mullah's letter ever reached Solzhenitsyn is uncertain, but a copy certainly found its way to the security organs. And two weeks later Mullah-Ulmas-Greeneyes was called to the City, purportedly in order to receive yet another military-service medal and a certificate from the Koryak National Party Committee.[23] In the event, however, both he and Pinkhas Shalomay were expelled from the USSR.

And so, in his old age, Mullah-Ulmas-Greeneyes, brother of the late Kuchkar-Cheka and brother-in-law of the late Bolshevik Oktam-Humble-Russky, ended up in Brighton Beach, New York, where, finding no other languages he didn't know, he began studying the Jewish-Odessan dialect[24] of the Greater Russian language, roundly cursing anyone he happened across during his drinking bouts with that all-powerful and indestructible Russian sentence whose meaning he had at last fully grasped.

4

But now I must say a word or two about the red-eyed albino Oppok-Lovely, the wife of Mullah-Ulmas-Greeneyes and sister of Oktam-Humble-Russky the Bolshevik . . . In the early 1920s, after Oktam-Humble-Russky had scaled the mountain of Marxist-Leninist thinking, matchmakers began to make more frequent appearances in their village. Oppok, still only a girl, would peep out through a crack in the door of the women's quarters and study the Komsomol bosses petitioning for her hand – a hand that would bring with it the Party patronage of her brother. One of them looked crooked, another looked bald, another too thin . . . In the end her grandmother said something Oppok-Lovely was to remember for the rest of her life: 'Wise up, you little brat – take your clothes off and have a look at yourself in the mirror!'

The Komsomol bosses, however, soon stopped visiting; some married Tatars, some married Kazakhs and the most zealous careerists of all married Russians. At her brother's insistence, Oppok-Lovely the albino then publicly cast off her yashmak – and even the leaders of the veil-burning movement took fright, confusedly crossing themselves as they realised how easily, but for the grace of God, they might have married her themselves. And no one ever again came to the village to ask for her hand.

And so she would have passed her whole life in Communist solitude and socially important labour, had not the mass executions of the 1930s impelled Mullah-Ulmas-Greeneyes to marry the woman who had by then become First Secretary of the Gilas Komsomol Committee.

During their first night, Mullah-Ulmas-Greeneyes, afraid of face to face contact and constantly adjusting his pillow, lay on the

First Secretary and wondered if divorce and execution might not be preferable, while she herself cried out 'More! More!' with Komsomol indefatigability and went on demanding the contributions due to a Komsomol bride.[25]

She bore three children before the War; and after the War had begun, she gave birth on her own to four more male and female defenders of the Motherland, all of whom were given the patronymic Ulmasovich – a mistake Oppok-Lovely would never have made had she thought that her husband might one day be discovered to have been a traitor. The demands of being a single mother forced Oppok-Lovely to leave the Komsomol Committee and become Head of the Kok-Terek Bazaar. This led Oktam-Humble-Russky, as a true Bolshevik who made no compromises with capitalism, to sever relations with her.

Oppok-Lovely bided her time but eventually responded to Oktam-Humble-Russky in kind, saying farewell to her Bolshevik brother not at the threshold of the edifice of Communism but at the threshold of a run-down old people's home. As for her own life, she quickly grasped the fundamental rule of the bazaar – 'You scratch my back and I'll scratch yours!' – and it was as if her wallet sucked in money. She got her children accepted to study in various institutes and, on the eve of the introduction of universal internal passports,[26] bought herself a position – that of Gilas passport officer – which allowed her to delete their unfortunate patronymics. Being a passport officer was, in any case, a great deal more comfortable and secure than patrolling a bazaar.

The position of passport officer also proved a thousand times more profitable than Oppok-Lovely, who had paid out 400 roubles in old money, could have ever imagined. Glamorous women would pay her to erase their column – or rather columns – of marriages and divorces; new Party members would pay for the deletion of their old criminal records. But she received the largest sum of all from Ali-Shapak, Tolib-Butcher's youngest brother; he was the public weigher at the Kok-Terek Bazaar and it was to him that she bequeathed her position as Head of the Bazaar. She also agreed to change just one figure in his year of birth, with a stroke of her pen making him several years older than his elder brother. As a result, Ali-Shapak was soon receiving his pension, while Tolib-Butcher wailed in fury at the prospect of having to toil five more years on behalf of the State that was treating his brother with such undeserved generosity. By then the introduction of passports had brought untold riches to Oppok-Lovely the wife of Mullah-Ulmas-Greeneyes – that Traitor to the Motherland and First Local War Veteran whom she was already summoning back home with the help of her Young Pioneers.

Meanwhile, Tolib-Butcher lived out his life in shame, reduced in old age, because of his own niggardliness, to the position of younger brother to his own kid brother Ali-Shapak.

5

The women in the yard went on crying for ever and ever.

It seemed to the boy that there would never be an end to the many-voiced wailing that met each new old woman as she darted in through the gate and past one-eyed Fatkhulla-Frontline and the two other men who were standing there, waiting for anyone who wanted to come but above all for Garang-Deafmullah, the father of the man who taught history to the senior classes and who had gone out to look for the boy in the wasteland behind the school; at first the boy had felt frightened – not because he guessed what had happened but simply because a teacher had found him messing about on his own – and he had felt still more frightened by the excessively kind voice with which the teacher called to him, standing there by the canal and not crossing over, and the teacher had gone on standing there after telling the boy, he'd gone on waiting while the boy ran back to fetch the satchel he'd left on the ground, and the boy was still feeling frightened even when he looked back round the corner of the school building, somehow thinking that all this might be a punishment for his not being at lessons – even though lessons had ended long ago – and then the still more awful thought that lessons had indeed ended long ago and that he should have been back home long ago for the funeral made the boy stop on the other side of the road, without going into his home at all – and he just stood there and listened to the endless wailing of the old women who kept darting like little mice past the old men at the gates and who then seemed to want to make the most of this opportunity to wail and gossip. Each woman would wail together with the woman who had first greeted her, then gossip with her for a while, and then, yielding her place to someone else, greet a new arrival and wail and gossip with her; it seemed this would go on for ever . . .

The boy stood behind the cherry trees opposite his home, beneath Huvron-Barber's windows, and looked at the belt that one-eyed

Fatkhulla-Frontline had left for the boy on an empty bench beside the wide-open gates.[27]

Now the lamentations were coming not from the yard, but from the house itself.

The boy heard his uncles being called to say farewell to their father and he wanted to rush in there, even though he was still carrying his satchel, which was now cutting into his shoulders and urging him on by drumming against his back; but a force still stronger than what was really the drum-drum-drumming of his heart was making him press more desperately than ever against the wall of this mute house where the children of Huvron-Barber lived; and he stood there stock still while they carried out the stretcher, which was covered by a plain black gown, and while his belted uncles went out ahead through the wide-open gates, followed by one-eyed Fatkhulla-Frontline, and Oppok-Lovely's son Kuvandyk, and that drunkard Mefody-Jurisprudence, and Nabi-Onearm, and blind old Hoomer, and Kuchkar-Cheka's successor – Osman-Anon, and Tolib-Butcher, and Sergeant-Major Kara-Musayev the Younger, and Kun-Okhun and everyone else, and they all disappeared behind the corner of Huvron's house.

He ran to the other corner and then to the end of the next sidestreet, and he caught up with the procession again by the railway line. The men walked on, taking turns bearing the stretcher, and even Akmolin stopped his diesel shunter, leaned his head out of the window and watched as the procession crossed the tracks and the men waiting on the platform rushed to join it, each taking his turn beneath the stretcher and then yielding his place to someone else so he could return to the platform. Finally, not daring to leave his shunter but wanting to make his presence felt, Akmolin gave a long hoarse hoot that startled the boy and made him stumble against a rail. The boy ran on at a distance from the procession, his satchel thumping against his back as he jumped across the rails; eventually the procession emerged onto the road and went quickly past the school, and the boy looked again at the wasteland behind the row of poplars. He felt as if he would see the history teacher there, standing by the canal, but there was no one –

only the barely audible, heart-rending voice of some well-known singer . . .

The boy lingered for a moment, but the procession was moving fast. Cars coming the other way were stopping and their drivers were getting out, bearing the stretcher for a dozen strides, then returning to their cars and quietly driving – almost floating – away, while the procession hurried on. They had to move fast – soon the sun would be setting.[28] The sun jumped from one gap in the high house walls to another, then between gaps in the mulberry trees, then again from one yard to another; and at last the procession turned into the cemetery.

But for the satchel the boy would have been able to creep into the cemetery on all fours, but with it there on his back he had to go round behind the low half-ruined wall to the deep canal on the other side. From the canal and its willows the crowd was only a stone's throw away.

By then, the procession was already squatting down and Garang-Deafmullah was reciting his monotonous prayer. The incomprehensibility of its words made the prayer seem still more melancholy – as dismal as a breath of wind over dry grass, or as a lone ant trying endlessly to climb a dry, dusty, prickly grass-blade.

Everyone left and went back to their homes. The boy sat on the grave and observed the ant trail that had appeared beside the little mound, almost beneath his feet – the ants were going round his shoes, sniffing them, exchanging greetings at every step with those coming the other way and disappearing from sight behind other graves. The boy was looking towards these graves, leaning over so far that his satchel slipped forward over his head, and then he remembered Fatkhulla again and his sense of shame grew as unbearable as if Fatkhulla had been watching him all the time, just as he himself was watching the ants, and then, swallowing down his snot, he began to remember the words of a prayer his grandmother had taught him and he began to say it out loud and, listening to himself, he sensed all the hurried unnaturalness of the words raining down on the ants and pins and needles were pricking his legs and it was as if these same ants were crawling all over him.

The sun was a red spot rolling down from the tall, distant poplars that stood in a row in front of the first yard beyond the cemetery; when the boy looked that way, the black mounds and the long shadows of the wrought-iron railings appeared to move slightly, as if they were settling down for the night, and then, from just above these mounds and fences, from just above the poplars, came a momentary breath of the freshness with which you wake up refreshed after weeping for a long time in a dream, when you wake up well and truly, as if all of a sudden you are being born adult, ready to understand everything – and the boy set off without fear in the direction old one-eyed Fatkhulla had gone.

The door was still open from all the day's visitors, and Fatkhulla was the first person the boy saw as he went in. The yard had been swept and sprinkled with water, and it was quiet and empty there except for Fatkhulla, who was sitting on the wooden platform, opposite the boy's huge granny, chanting a prayer in his monotonous voice. The boy went towards this voice, which seemed to be coming out of the twilight.

He stood behind Fatkhulla's dark back, out of sight of his granny. Now he had even less idea what to do; Fatkhulla's awkward prayer was the only safe and warm refuge he had, and, for the first time in his life, he could feel every one of its incomprehensible Arabic words deep in his chilled heart, and he held the words there devoutly. And when Fatkhulla said 'Amen!' the boy tremblingly lifted his cupped hands and sensed the dry heat in his palms as he brushed them over his face and cheeks. And at that moment, as if able to look straight through Fatkhulla, Granny said, 'So he's come back, has he?'

Without turning round to look at the boy, Fatkhulla said, 'He's been with us all the time' and the boy felt the same shame he had felt at the cemetery when his satchel flew over his head, and now, standing behind the old man, he felt as if he himself were a kind of satchel, attached to Fatkhulla's broad back. If the old man were to turn round or bend forward . . .

6

Once upon a time there lived Mirzaraim-Bey, ruler of all the mountains and mountain pastures around Mookat and head of the Kirghiz 'Wolf' tribe that was the mother of every Turk. He had four wives, and the two he loved most were the eldest and the youngest. He loved Ulkan-Bibi because she had been like a second mother to him; Aichiryok, the beautiful girl from the mountains who was his blood mother, had died when he was only seven, and a year after her death his father had found him a wife: the half-Uzbek Ulkan-Bibi. After a magnificent feast in the high meadows of Ak-Tengri, Ulkan-Bibi had carried her sleeping eight-year-old husband away in her arms. And so she took the place of his mother, carrying him on her back – which was like a strong slim poplar – until he started to become a man.

And Mirzaraim-Bey loved his youngest wife, Nozik-Poshsho, the Princess from Margilan, because she bore him his first son – Obid-Bey.

His first-born son grew not by the day but by the hour; by the hot-blooded age of sixteen he was, at a gallop, slashing off the heads of visitors as they made their way up the mountainside. All this amused Mirzaraim-Bey and filled him with pride, until one day Obid-Turk, as his companions now called him, decapitated the ambassador of Khudoyar, the Khan of Kokand,[29] and Mirzaraim-Bey was faced with the threat of years of war. After his gift of sixty head of large-horned cattle and 200 sheep and goats was accepted in compensation for the ambassador's hairless, moustache-less and even eyebrow-less head, Mirzaraim-Bey decided it was time to regulate his son's boyish amusements. Like an avalanche, he swept down on the plains of Osh and, in the course of an hour, seized a crowd of Sart mullahs and sages and carried them off to his mountain headquarters. There, in his royal yurt, he held a council to decide what should be done with his son.

The mullahs, as is their way, spoke so eloquently and intricately that the straightforward Mirzaraim-Bey regretted his hasty foray and wished he had left them in Osh. More than that, he found himself longing to unleash his son on them at full gallop; yes, Obid-Turk would slice off their heads as easily as if they were cabbages and Mirzaraim-Bey would be relieved of the obligation to present them with gifts of sheep in reward for their wise counsel.

Then one of these Osh theologians, perhaps sensing the rustle of the wings of Azrael the angel of death over the yurt, and over the six folds of his own turban, exclaimed, 'O revered ruler of mountains as lofty and eternal as your own power . . .'

'Get to the point!' interrupted Mirzaraim-Bey.

'O rectifier of speech, whose own speech is sharp as the point of a sword . . .'

'I said, *Get to the point!*'

'Here, in the mountains that bow down before you, in the Ali-Shakhid valley, is a holy sage who knows the flow of life and how it turns the wheel of human destiny.'

Mirzaraim-Bey commanded a sheep to be given to each of the mullahs and, with his son and his warriors behind him, moved like an avalanche towards the Ali-Shakhid valley.

The sage had been sitting beneath a waterfall for sixty-six years, beside the mark left by the Prophet's horse on the night of his Ascension to Heaven.[30] Countless prayers had made his soul as transparent as the mountain stream beside him, and his face was as smooth as a stone that its waters had polished. After the briefest of glances at Obid, he said, 'My son, the Lord has made you pregnant with knowledge!'

Obid-Turk, this wild and unruly young warrior, was at once

quietened by these quiet words that sounded louder than the thunder of the waterfall.

'What must I do, wise father?' Obid asked, dismounting from his horse.

'Your own father will tell you. You have a great and terrible future. Let your father say who you should be.'

Mirzaraim-Bey thought. He knew only two ways of life: that of the Kirghiz up in the mountains and that of the Sarts down on the plains. If his son chose the life of a Kirghiz, he would carry on galloping down from the mountains and slicing off the heads of strangers. And Mirzaraim-Bey would have neither the cattle nor the sheep to pay compensation.

And were his son to take after his mother, he would turn out like those Sart mullahs; instead of a head, he would end up with nothing but swathes of turban on top of his neck. Mirzaraim-Bey made up his mind: 'May my son be like you!'

The old man called out 'Allah Akbar – Great is Allah!' and disappeared into the thundering waterfall.

From that day, Obid-Turk's soul grew quiet, like a mountain wind that has fallen silent. His mother gave him *Beauty and the Heart*, a work of wisdom by an ancient poet[31], and the now silent and reflective Obid-Bey read this book day and night.

And Mirzaraim-Bey bought his son forty cells in the Kokand madrasah. There, supporting himself by renting out cells to the other students, Obid-Bey learned Arabic, Persian and elementary theology and memorised the entire Koran. Seven years later his father sent him to the noble city of Bukhara; now known by the name Obid-Kori,[32] he studied there for another twenty-three years.

He was in his late forties by the time he returned home, full of wisdom and sorrow, to his native Mookat.

*

Oyimcha, one of the daughters of Said-Kasum-Kadi, the Sart district judge, had by then herself reached the unruly age of sixteen. A descendant of the Prophet, from a family whose men were so heavy that they had only to sit on a horse to twist or even break its spine, she was as slim as a poplar from the valley, as light as the breath of the mountains.

Once, as she and her little sister were washing clothes in the pool of spring water behind the white stone house her father had built after a trip to Skobelev,[33] her little sister jumped up and sang out like a small bird alarmed by some animal, 'Sister, dear sister, you must hide. An accursed man is approaching. We mustn't be seen by him.'

She was ten years old, and so she fulfilled the obligations of a grown-up woman with a great deal more enthusiasm than she moulded the clay flatbreads with which a ten-year-old girl was supposed to amuse herself.

The sister looked up, saw a rider approaching and, not pausing in her work, said in a loud voice, 'Why should we hide? It's only a Kirghiz.'

And so the half-Sart and half-Kirghiz Obid-Kori, who had studied in the best Sart madrasahs with the best Sart mullahs and theologians of his time, quite lost his head – over a sixteen-year-old girl whose existence required no evidence, proof or justification.

The now ageing Mirzaraim-Bey paid dearly for this – still more dearly than he had paid for the loss of the head of the ambassador of Khudoyar, the Khan of Kokand. Month after month he sent rams and goats to two Jewish financiers whose names even the cultivated Obid-Kori was unable to pronounce. Only after two years did Said-Kasum-Kadi yield to the persuasive power of the eighty mountain steers, 200 fat-buttocked rams and hundreds of curly-horned goats that constituted all the remaining wealth of the once powerful Mirzaraim-Bey. Entangled in lawsuits, mired in debt and bewildered by the dawning age of bills of exchange and shares, European phaetons[34] and railway lines, Said-Kasum-Kadi gave his eighteen-year-old Oyimcha in marriage to a Kirghiz of nearly fifty. The unhappy girl was sent high into the mountains that stood over Mookat.

Mirzaraim-Bey solved the problem of his son's marriage, but there was another question that his clear and straightforward mind never resolved: had his son Obid-Bey, or had he not, already entered the great and terrible future foretold by the holy old man beneath the waterfall?

Mirzaraim-Bey died without ever knowing. But Obid-Kori himself, after burying a father who in his last years had lost all his sheep and cattle, strode into this future without fear, though not without pain in his heart. In this future he committed to the earth his four mothers – beginning with his eldest mother, Ulkan-Bibi, and ending with his blood mother, Nozik-Poshsho – and began to live a life of poverty with his young and only wife, Oyimcha.

7

On his return from prison, where he had put on three stone, Umarali-Moneybags laid on a thanksgiving feast. A week beforehand he sent Tolib-Butcher to the City to announce that every tramp, pickpocket, beggar and day-labourer was invited. Tolib-Butcher expended four whole days on this task, wearing out his only pair of boots and all the voice left in his puny body. He then asked Umarali in a hoarse, agitated whisper, 'But why only them? Why not get Oktam-Humble-Russky to invite Usman Yusupov and his Party Committee?' Umarali, in his usual way, cursed every part of Tolib from head to toe and said, 'You're a fool, Tolib. This riffraff will tell the whole world about Umarali's feast. There'll be no one who doesn't know. And as for your Usman Yusupov – fuck him! The only gift I've ever had from him is prison.'

Later, when Tolib-Butcher was standing beside Umarali-Moneybags, Oktam-Humble-Russky and old blind Hoomer, greeting the rabble that had poured into Gilas like a Tatar horde, he kept worrying that Umarali might refer to this conversation about the thrice-accursed Usman in the presence of Kuchkar-Cheka. Perhaps for this reason, when the parade of guests drew to an end and Kuchkar-Cheka popped up from a neighbouring gateway, Tolib-Butcher promptly stood to attention, like a soldier before a general reviewing his troops. Umarali, on the other hand, giving Kuchkar only the tips of his fingers in greeting, cursed him roundly, then coolly added, 'Before greeting you, a man needs to eat either several pounds of honey or a stone of the very best *kazy*.'[35]

'What do you mean?' asked Kuchkar, pricking up his ever-attentive ear.

'The mere sight of you, you son of a bitch, is enough to chill a man's soul.'

Umarali-Moneybags died a slow and difficult death. Many times he seemed about to let go of the reins of life – but each time he would come to with a start, grabbing life by the mane as it slipped away from under his vast carcass . . . just one more step . . . one more breath . . . one more moment . . . Just as the women were getting ready to weep and keen, he would glimpse a railway line at the end of the War, goods wagons bound for the textile factories of Ivanovo,[36] and himself as a young man – directing the stolen cotton on its way to those factories: 'One million bales to Ivanovo, one million bales to Orekhovo-Zuyevo . . . Ay, ay, ay . . .'

8

The post of head of police, which was always held by the sergeant-major – at present, the elder son of Kara-Musayev the Elder, who had gone blind in his old age after impiously kicking some flatbreads[37] that Rokhbar was selling illegally at the station – was passed on from one generation to the next. Let me repeat this more clearly: the post of head of police, now held by Kara-Musayev the Younger – the elder son of Kara-Musayev the Elder – was passed on by inheritance. In a word, the post was hereditary. Got it? If not, I've been wasting my breath, as Kara-Musayev would have put it, blathering away to a brick wall.

Everything would have gone well, the life of Kara-Musayev the Younger would have continued swimmingly right up to his retirement, had it not been for the fact that his wife, the daughter of Kuchkar-Cheka, turned out to be barren. There was no one he did not take her to, no one who did not investigate her. Such an army of doctors, healers of every kind and the merely inquisitive examined the poor woman's reproductive organs that, were the eyes of men endowed with even an ant-sized dose of fertilising power, the unhappy Kumri would quickly have brought forth a whole battalion of potential heirs for the post of head of police – which, as it happens, is just what she eventually did do, except that she bore them all to the wrong husband. Had these children been his, then Kara-Musayev the Younger would have had at least a little more right to the light-blue 'Heroine-Mother' medal that he always wore on State Holidays – a medal confiscated from an unfortunate Kazakh girl at the bazaar whom he had once fined for some misdemeanour; it had been tied, along with coins from all over the world, to the end of one of her pigtails. But neither wearing this medal on his uniform, nor any number of non-fertilising male examinations of his wife's non-conceiving womb were of the least help – and so Kara-Musayev decided to investigate his own role in the matter, to confirm by experimental means his own procreative ability.

Among the female population of Gilas there were just two idiot-girls whose obedience to Kara-Musayev was unquestioning: one who yielded at home when she was drunk and one who yielded when she was intoxicated by the fresh air out in the maize fields where the young lads had all taken to grazing their cows – but the sergeant-major's strategic savvy prompted him to decide that an experiment on either of them would hardly prove conclusive; and, in any case, heaven only knows whom or what these idiots might not give birth to. And so Kara-Musayev the Younger waited until the Sunday Kok-Terek Bazaar and then arrested a young Uighur woman for speculating in Indian tea – an activity she was engaging in for the first time, buying the tea from Samarkand Tadjiks and selling it on to Kazakhs from Sary-Agach. Threatening her with exile to Siberia, he ordered her to come to his office after lunch the following day, when even engine driver Akmolin would be asleep inside his diesel shunter.

The following day, when only the sun was still out on the street, hallucinating in erratic spirals over the white-hot asphalt – into Kara-Musayev's office came not one young woman but two. At first Kara-Musayev thought that he too was hallucinating. It was only when one of the women begged him to pardon her sister, throwing herself at his feet beneath the office desk, that he understood they were identical twins.

A moment later, when he found on his knees a packet of second-grade Indian tea stuffed with three-rouble notes – the usual tariff for speculators – the sergeant's strategic savvy prompted him to an unusual response: he seized the bribe-giver by one hand, called on her sister as a witness and accused her of a far more serious crime. Threatening her with forced labour in the uranium mines, he accused her of attempting to bribe an official in the course of carrying out his official duties.

The Uighur girls wept in repentance, but Kara-Musayev showed no mercy. Having indicted the sisters upon separate articles, he led them to separate cells and subjected them to separate personal interrogations that concluded in one and the same fashion – with both twins choosing dishonour rather than prison. True, he did assure each of them, upon his honour as a police sergeant-major, that her sister, released on bail, would never know the physical price that had been paid for her freedom.

Who would have guessed that these two young women, Fatima and Zukhra, would both fall pregnant? And that the first person to know this would be Kumri, whose demand for an immediate divorce quickly led to Kara-Musayev's demotion from sergeant-major to sergeant and from full member of the Party to candidate member? His bosses, however, did not yet know the reason for this divorce, and fear of this being made public led Sergeant Kara-Musayev the Younger, candidate member of the Communist Party of the Soviet Union, to propose marriage, on separate occasions, to each of the twins. Now, however, it was the turn of the twins to be merciless. In the course of a second meeting in Kara-Musayev's office during the afternoon hour when even Akmolin is asleep in his shunter, they discovered the potential bigamy of the divorced Kara-Musayev – a crime which, unlike divorce, was punishable by the criminal law that it was the job of the dumbstruck sergeant to enforce – and the latter's now uncertain strategic savvy prompted him (it seemed better to divorce one sister and face demotion to the rank of constable and the loss of his Party membership than to be charged with bigamy complicated by divorce and end up being sent to Siberia or to the uranium mines of Kazakhstan) to say to the Uighur twins, 'I shall marry whichever of you is first to give birth!'

And that was the beginning of a socialist competition between the Uighur twins, both of whom – to prevent any compromising rumours circulating in Gilas – Kara-Musayev quickly installed high in the mountains, in separate rooms of the Alcoholism Prevention and Treatment Centre on the resort bank of the Aksay river.

Zukhra was first to give birth and so Kara-Musayev married Fatima, as had been agreed, in order to divorce Fatima straight away and then marry Zukhra – but this was more than the jealous and perhaps also brainless Zukhra could bear, so what did the girl do but wait until the next Kok-Terek Sunday Bazaar and then – carrying in her arms a baby whose Musayevan yells were a clear indication of his right to inherit the post of Gilas head of police – proclaim to everyone present the full details of how disgrace-fully she had been treated?

A court was convened in the chaikhana to pass comradely judgment on Kara-Musayev's conduct and, no one being able to suggest any way of further demoting a non-Party-member rank-and-file policeman, it was decided to remove from his surname the prefix Kara and to dismiss him from the police force – and so Kara-Musayev was pensioned off with the decapitated surname Musayev, whereupon he somehow lost his reason.

What remained of his life he for no known reason devoted to reading every poster and slogan he came across – on walls or roofs, in a bus or at the bazaar – hoping to penetrate its esoteric meaning and impart this to others. 'The Five Year Plan is the Law; Fulfilment of the Plan – Our Debt and Our Duty; Over-fulfilment of the Plan – Our Honour,' he would read in Russian on the squeaking cart of Lyuli-Ibodullo-Mahsum. He would then start to philosophise out loud in Uzbek: 'Plan means law. But what is law? The plan. What then is the plan? Once, I remember, there was a plan for fulfilling the law, er, I mean, a law for fulfilling the plan . . . What did Sami-Rais do in my father's day? He appointed my father to subordinate everyone to the law – and what do you think happened to anyone who didn't fulfil the plan? They were lawfully destroyed by the full force of the law!

'And as for overfulfilment – that's as clear as daylight even to the tail of a dog! What does overfulfilment mean? Our debt and our duty. A debt means that someone has borrowed money. And if you've borrowed money, then you'd damn well better return it, you bastard – in accordance with the law. Otherwise? Otherwise it's against all lawful law! But what do the police think they're doing? Mullah-Ulmas-Greeneyes borrowed twenty roubles from my father, and we haven't had sight nor sound of those roubles for twenty years. There hasn't even been a police search. Gunpowder up his arse – that's what he needs!

'And what's this here at the end? Overfulfilment – Our Honour. This is beyond the understanding of reason. This is well and truly super-complex! Yes, comrade!

'"Study, study, study – Lenin". I couldn't agree more! Let him study the same as we do! Think of all those works I've worked through in my day! That's right. Study, study, study – Lenin!'

9

Among the mulberry thickets that stretched between the Korean *mahallya* and the thin line of the first houses of Papanin Street there were also a few fig trees. No one knew about them except Boikush (whom Tolib-Butcher had once led there) and her neighbour Zebi, the beautiful wife of the one-eyed war veteran Fatkhulla-Frontline – the mind, conscience and honour of the *mahallya*. Once, as Boikush and Zebi slipped off into the trees, pretending they needed to relieve themselves when what they really wanted was to enjoy the paradisiacal fruits beneath which Tolib-Butcher had once told Boikush the story of Adam and Eve, they heard a voice calling their names. It was Vera the Korean. Or maybe Lyuba. Or Nadya.

'Damn her! She's been watching us!' Boikush said furiously. And a moment later, in a clear friendly voice, she called out, 'Hey! Come and join us! We can have a feast of figs!' Then she looked at Zebi and quietly added, 'She was coming anyway . . .'

Here in the attic, beneath the chaikhana's sloping roof, the boy had a secret place of his own. This was where he slept when he didn't go home; it was here that he would lie awake until late and listen to the never-ending stories, the sometimes enchanting, sometimes tedious stories that drifted up the chimney, the stories the old men used to tell then just as they do now.

Their endless talk was like a lullaby – as otherworldly as the sleepy light that hovered over the paraffin lamp on winter evenings when the family sat down together to tease out the seeds from the cotton and Grandmother would measure the slowly growing heap of cotton wool with a length of cloth and quietly hum:

> Gunokhim bora-bora togdin oshdi,
> Kiemat kun mani sharmanda kilma . . .
> *My sins climb higher than the hills –*
> *On judgment day forgive my guilt . . .*

And this half-whispered song would draw the boy towards a sleep that was softer than cotton wool between slow fingers and quieter than the light from the paraffin lamp he had just cleaned. But now, after the funeral, the boy was afraid of going to sleep; yes, it would be wrong to go to sleep, just as it had been wrong for his family to eat after the funeral, or maybe it would be still more sinful and wrong, because there would be no one to blame but himself . . . And so he began brushing off the straw that had stuck to his flannelette school uniform – his jacket or, as his grandad called it, or rather had used to call it, his kitel[38] *– and his grandad had called it a* kitel *because his grandad used to call anything he wore a* kitel, *with the result that once, soon after he first started travelling to Moscow by train, he came back home with what he called a summer* kitel, *and he put it on the following morning*

– a kitel *with thin stripes like a mattress – along with a pair of equally stripy trousers, and no matter how much the women tried to dissuade him, he had insisted on setting off to the City, wearing what Uncle Izaly from the Tailoring Co-operative called pyjamas, and wearing them, moreover, tucked into his eternal red canvas boots . . .*

And this flannelette kitel, *which was no less shameful than Grandad's pyjamas, this shameful* kitel *whose only good point was that you could spill ink on it without it showing, this* kitel *was all the more hateful to the boy for being an award from his school; and the shame he had felt when squint-eyed Annushka had announced at the parade in honour of Lenin's birthday that he was being awarded this uniform in recognition of his excellent schoolwork and exemplary conduct, and when in spite of his having run away from that accursed and shameful parade she had got that idiot Natashka to take this horrible uniform to his home, which had led Granny to go on in front of Natashka about how her own children had never been given anything of the kind – this shame had made him run away from home for the first time.*

It had been just before the May holidays – and the mere thought of not having to go to school had made him feel happy, but all of a sudden the boy's heart had filled with aching toskà:*[39] who would he find to play football with?*

Nevertheless, he had been determined not to return home. Instead, he had decided to go and find Grandad – who had also fallen out with Granny and left home: yes, he would live on the streets – he would live anywhere; but he would not go home. What to do about school he could decide later, but after the shame he had felt during the parade . . . And now, as he sat in his attic and removed the straw that had stuck to the kitel, *he hated this garment doubly: because of the shame he had felt in front of the entire school and – still more – because, even as he remembered the shame of it first being presented to him, he also hated the way he looked in it now – wearing this charity uniform that was too big for him and had got covered in bits of straw.*

Granny had said, 'See – the school's looking after you, they've given you a uniform. It was different for your poor mother – she had to go to school in a dress made from sackcloth. I sewed it for her myself in the co-operative . . . They sent sacks of wadding for soldiers' jackets, and one of the sacks tore . . . My poor little daughter . . .' And she began to cry; or rather her voice began to cry, while she herself went on folding his uniform, smoothing out the flapping sleeves and doing up two of the star-embossed metal buttons.

He had refused to put on this wretched handout and Granny had gone on and on at him. At one point she had even brought Grandad into it, saying to the boy's mother that it was quite impossible to be so pernickety, and so what if Grandad was just as bad, he and the boy weren't even blood relatives . . .

This had been more than the boy could bear, and a kind of whirling inside him – a whirling like the whirling of water being poured fast into a large bottle, a whirling that deafened his ears and caused utterly unexpected tears to splash out from his eyes – snatched him up, whirled him out through the gate and down the little street, past Huvron-Barber's fortress-like walls and all the way to the railway embankment, and then swept him in the direction of the small bazaar by the station and then from sleeper to sleeper of the railway line, up towards the depot. On he walked until he came to a place he did not know at all but where at least there was an end to his tears, an end to the snot he spat out after every ten of those hateful 'per-nick-et-y's, and where even that awful word no longer seemed as hurtful as it had done before, although there was still a dry bitterness on his tongue and this bitterness was made still more bitter by a wind blowing from somewhere a long way away, from beyond the thickets of Russian olive and the ploughed land by the embankment, from somewhere in the wormwood-filled steppe.

And the boy felt a strange freedom, as if he were alone on this empty and slowly darkening earth, without hurtful words, without shame and fear, without any need for friends who go away with their parents and spend holidays in the City, without even the City itself, where he too used to go with Granny – but only to buy lollipops that they sold as soon as they got back to Gilas; as if he could now do whatever he felt *like, as if he could shout out at the top of his voice, 'Mummy, Mummy, I love you!' and be frightened only by his very first shout, which startled a crow into shooting up from behind some clods of ploughed-up earth and cawing crossly as it flew off down the line of telegraph poles; yes, he was able to pick up a stone and throw it at that crow, for no reason at all, simply because he was free to, because he was free to do anything he felt like doing – except that there was nothing to do. The boy was amazed by this emptiness – an emptiness very like the sky's, which was getting lower and lower before his very eyes and which seemed to be bringing together the two sides of the boundless earth just as Granny used to fold together the two sides of her oilskin cloth after the boy had kneaded the dough with his fists – and then she would put the bowl with the dough to one side, so that the boy could cover it with a cloth and a blanket while she folded up her oilskin, tapping it on the underside to make specks of flour sprinkle down from it just as stars would soon sprinkle down on the earth.*

The boy was so entranced by the sky that he felt as startled by a sudden hoot as he had been by the crow, and he jumped down off the embankment even before he realised that it was a train – and that the drivers might just have been having a little fun, laughing at him for standing where they had never seen anyone standing before. He was almost certain of this, and still more certain when a light swept over his head and only when he looked back did he realise that this was the sunset reflected by the glass windows of the locomotive cab, but he still didn't feel like climbing out from behind his mound of earth. Only when another hoot, right beside him, made the earth tremble, only when the locomotive thundered past on its heavy wheels did he climb out from his crow's hideaway, meaning to shake his fist at the loco-motive just as he had thrown a stone at the departing crow, but then he saw it was a passenger train and didn't know what to do. It was too late to go back and hide, nor did he want to, especially since people were looking out of the windows at the sunset over the fields and it was impossible for him to stand opposite them as they rushed past – impossible not because he was disturbing them but because they were disturbing him; it was they who had burst into his life, not he into theirs, but as he thought about what he could do to get his own back he saw that there wasn't really anyone at all looking at the sunset and that they were all busy with affairs of their own: a woman was sorting out her berth, unfolding the sheet just as Granny used to unfold her oilcloth; someone was eating; someone was drinking. And in the restaurant car still more people were eating and drinking.

And when the boy had begun to feel quite cross that there was no one for him to revenge himself on, he caught sight of a girl, standing behind an open door at the end of one of the very last coaches and looking out at the sunset. There was no one else for the boy to get his revenge on – everyone else was safely behind a window – and so the boy desperately began wondering what he should do: throw some clay at her, undo his flies, or even pull his trousers right down ... As the coach drew level with him, he felt utterly bewildered and, clumsily kissing the ends of his fingers, he threw a kiss in the girl's direction; the girl, taken aback, stood there and smiled and didn't even hold a finger to her temple and rotate it but instead leaned out of the coach, holding on to the handrail and looking in his direction. And this bewildered him still more and even made him blush – and when the train's red tail-light disappeared round a distant bend, the boy's shame was still humming in the rails, which were warm from the red sun that had been warming them all day long, and this hum passed through his flaming cheeks and into his heart, which was beating out its quick beat just as the wheels of the train were doing on the rails.

And the boy shouted, 'Girl, I love you,' and this time there wasn't anything he was frightened of, because he knew that in the falling darkness his voice would not carry beyond this ploughed earth, beyond these Russian olives, beyond this emptiness which was by now a personal emptiness that he had himself marked and filled, filled so full that now he wanted to leave it alone, like well-worked dough that has already risen to the top of the bowl; and he began to walk quickly back along the sleepers.

II

His mother used to tell Mahmud-Hodja[40] that he had been born in the Year of the Dog, in early summer, when the apricots were being harvested all over the province of Andizhan.[41] On the very same day that Mahmud-Hodja was born, their neighbour Suleiman-Haberdasher also had a son, Abdulhamid – who was later to become a poet and end up being shot. And so, growing up together, Mahmud-Hodja and Abdulhamid lived through both the Andizhan uprising and the great earthquake; during the uprising they were locked inside Suleiman-Haberdasher's stone warehouse along with bats that flew out in alarm from cracks in the walls, squeaking and flapping their wings. Then they were sent to study in the first Russian school in Andizhan, where the teachers were all Tatars, small-minded people with a small-minded way of talking. They were sent there on the insistence of the uncle of Mahmud-Hodja – Hodja Mahmud-Hodja the Elder – a man who had travelled through many lands and countries, both to Mecca and in the opposite direction, to the land of Gog and Magog, and who, being an exceptional merchant, couldn't help but notice even during the Hadj[42] that prayer rugs were more expensive in Mecca whereas dates were cheaper there by precisely as much as fur in Russia was cheaper than Bukhara silk rugs in Bulgaria, and who had also insisted on importing into Andizhan the incomprehensible and new-fangled word 'Jadid', which he had no doubt picked up at some distant fair and which he insisted was the best and newest word for everything new.[43]

Both in matters of trade and in matters of religion (not that it was always easy to tell these matters apart, given Mahmud-Hodja's way of setting out on the path to Mecca laden with prayer rugs and returning laden with dates) Hodja Mahmud-Hodja the Elder was a great deal more successful than his neighbour Suleiman-Haberdasher, who was so ill-fitted for business that he even started writing poetry; consequently, it was Hodja Mahmud-Hodja the Elder who decided the fate both of his nephew Mahmud-Hodja the Younger and of his neighbour's son Abdulhamid. He made up his mind without hesitation: the children were to study languages, and they were to study according to the newest methods.

Mahmud-Hodja lived halfway between the cities of Andizhan and Osh, so as not to belong to anyone but himself. His eccentric habit of opening new-method schools in this city and that city, under the direction of groups of Tatars he had recruited from Kazan, Orenburg and Bakhchisaray, failed to draw down the wrath of inveterate conservatives for the simple reason that in the whole of Turkestan there was no other Muslim who had so many times completed the Hadj.

And so, every lesser holy day, when the orthodox of Andizhan would go and prostrate themselves before the sacred Mount Suleiman outside the city of Osh – a pilgrimage they referred to somewhat unorthodoxly as a 'quarter Hadj'; when Suleiman-Haberdasher would most truly and deeply appreciate the significance of his name and therefore, on the eve of the holy day, order horses to be harnessed to his phaeton – yes, to a genuine phaeton that had been 'written off', in exchange for twenty bottles of sultana brandy, by the local colonel and district governor in the village called 'Soldier', where a regiment of the Russian army of occupation was stationed; when the little boys had sat down in the early morning of this holy day behind their impressive fathers and the phaeton had set off at an insane speed; when, later in the morning of this holy day, the phaeton had reached the halfway point between Andizhan and Osh, having long since overtaken all the crawling and creaking mule-carts – all of a sudden, about fifty paces from a huge stone house that stood alone by a turn in the road, the panting steeds would be reined in and the phaeton would come to a halt; everyone would dismount and, after allowing the dust to settle, walk slowly up to the house. On the rare occasions when Hodja Mahmud-Hodja the Elder was at home, he would come out to pay his respects, offer everyone a cup of tea – and test the children's knowledge of languages; but more often than not the master of the house would turn out to be away on his religious business and they would have to content themselves with making low bows to his house; only after walking another fifty paces would they climb back into the phaeton and resume their wild rush to Mount Suleiman. In the meantime other people's carts went on squeaking and sending up clouds of dust a mile away from the house, on a special road that Hodja Mahmud-Hodja the Elder had had built for them.

In 1905 the Russian Tsar suffered a revolution and Mahmud-Hodja the Elder got stuck with his goods somewhere on the road between Petersburg and Moscow; a Bukhara Jew who found his way back from those parts said that all-out anarchy had already erupted and that revolutionary railway soldiers had shot the merchant and appropriated his goods. Whatever the truth of all this, the disturbances slowly spread further and the Tatar teachers, who were no longer receiving their pay, all disappeared – some to become revolutionaries, others to become journalists, and yet others to become mullahs. It was then quickly agreed that it would be best for the boys to go and study in the same school as their fathers and grandads before them – the Kokand madrasah. But even the madrasah was no longer what it had been; staffed half by Tatar mullahs who had been thrown out of new-method schools and half by migrant Turks, even madrasahs now sowed seeds of sedition in the souls of the young. It was therefore not long before Abdulhamid ran off to the City, intending to become a famous poet and spread the Revolution further. His father was surprisingly quick to forgive him his poetic ambition, after venting his initial rage in verse – and in time he even forgave him his political ambition, deciding reasonably enough that his son was in any case never going to learn anything more, or anything better, from this medley of half-baked mullahs.

The father of Mahmud-Hodja the Younger died soon afterwards, unable to get over the disappearance of his brother, and the young man, deprived by this accursed revolution of his uncle, his best friend and his father, gave up his studies and became a merchant. After his first trip to Khodzhent, his mother died too; when the year of mourning was over, Mahmud-Hodja the Younger married off his sisters, sold the now empty house, bought a flock of sheep from the Kirghiz of Mookat and, together with a cousin by the name of Alihon-Tura, drove this flock over the mountains into Merke and Pishpek.[44]

It was summer, but high in the mountains they were caught by a snowfall that killed half the flock. There and then they roasted the sheep over a fire, eating as much meat as would fit in their manly stomachs and leaving what remained to a Kirghiz called Maike whose home was somewhere nearby. In the course of the next three days Maike put away an improbable amount of this meat and then, big-bellied and rosy-cheeked, hurried off in search of the mountain onions he needed to accompany it. By the upper reaches of the Naryn river he caught up with Mahmud-Hodja and Alihon-Tura; after eating an entire sack of Asakin onions, he drank the icy mountain stream almost dry – yes, in those days men were men.

Then Maike led Mahmud-Hodja and Alihon-Tura through secret ravines and hollows along the southern slopes of the mountains, where the grass grew furiously and the sheep grew fatter even as they walked. Soon the sheep began to multiply, and by the end of summer, when they came down along the shore of Lake Issyk-Kul towards the holy city of Balasagun,[45] the flock – in spite of Maike's insatiable need for meat – was almost as large as when they had left Andizhan.

After selling half the flock to local Dungans,[46] they bought two houses in the Dungan part of the city. Soon afterwards

Mahmud-Hodja the Younger married the beautiful Zamira-Bonu from Sairam, who had been staying in the city with relatives of Alihon-Tura.

For several years life went well, but then there were more revolutionary events; this time it was Alihon-Tura who got stuck with all his goods, somewhere on the road between Tashkent and Djizak. Sensing the beginning of a new round of misfortunes, Mahmud-Hodja the Younger hurried to perform a propitiatory rite – a pilgrimage to Mecca and Medina. In exchange for Chinese gold he sold one quarter of his flock, which had continued to multiply, to the Dungans; he left another quarter of the flock for the upkeep of his family and then – together with Maike and Alihon-Tura, who had just managed to get back to Balasagun – drove the remaining sheep along the spurs of the Tien Shan Mountains and the Pamirs towards Khorasan. During their passage across the high mountains Maike consumed half of this half-flock but, by the time they came down into the valley of the blessed Euphrates, the flock had miraculously doubled again. Maike drank from the upper reaches of the Euphrates just as he had once drunk from the Naryn, while the sheep waded to the other bank through waters growing shallower by the minute.

On the Arabian Peninsula they were more than once buried in sand, and Maike was able to eat only half of what he had eaten before – there was not a drop of water, and certainly no onions, so he washed down the sheep he ate with the blood of those being sacrificed. In the deserts of Hidjaz they left whole sand dunes over the countless sheep that had died of hunger. When they drew near the sacred mountain of Arafat, Maike abruptly refused to go any further. He stayed behind to help the flock multiply, while Mahmud-Hodja and Alihon-Tura went on to worship.

While Mahmud-Hodja was worshipping, a daughter was born to him in far-off Balasagun; she had been conceived the day he set out on the Hadj and for this reason, without consultation

55

with her father, was given the name Hadjiya. Mahmud-Hodja learned this when he met up again with Maike; while Mahmud-Hodja was praying in Mecca and casting stones at the evil spirit that had flooded the world with sedition and revolution, Maike had been granted a vision. A voice had ordered him to sell the entire flock. But there was nothing to be bought with the gold he acquired other than these same sheep – or their butchered meat – and so Mahmud-Hodja and his fellow-pilgrims found the simple-hearted Maike sitting on a bag of gold; he had eaten nothing for over a week.

Maike had eaten nothing, but his every thought was full of light. Towards morning, when the first of the travellers awoke, Maike began to sing. He sang about all he could see, and all he could see became song: poppies on the slopes of the mountain, curly clouds in the blue ash of the sky, curly sheep – sheep he had himself sold – on the burnt-out ash of the hillsides, sunset over the desert, stars close to the horizon. He sang about human fate at the mercy of Providence and about the journey he and his companions had made over the sands. His songs were strange and wonderful; terrifying evocations of fire and dishevelled mountains suddenly resolved into images of fruitful palms and rivers flowing gently between low foothills.[47]

It cost Maike nothing to compose hundreds of lines about a horseman who galloped past or a little hamster whistling in the Iraqi desert, but what inspired him most were the mountains of Anatolia and Akhal-Teke horses; the poems he composed about these splendid steeds were later incorporated verbatim in *Manas*, the Kirghiz national epic.[48]

Strangest of all was the way the sands of the desert no longer swept over them, nor the snows of the mountains, nor the dust of the steppe. And since Maike was almost constantly playing a kobuz[49] – one made from Mazendaran mulberry by the Turkmen of Khorasan – he almost stopped eating and drinking again. Swollen by the rains that Maike sang down from the skies, dried-up rivers would turn to raging floods as he and Alihon-Tura stepped onto the far bank, and mountains rose up behind them like an unbroken stone wall, hiding the gorges through which they had passed.

In Herat, before the burial vault of the great vizir and poet Mir Alisher Navoi,[50] the uneducated Maike began to recite ghazals in Persian; Djebral-Semavi, the Persian keeper of this burial vault, was so struck by the wild magnificence of Maike's poetry that he invited him and Mahmud-Hodja to be his guests, even though he himself was a Shiite and they were both Sunnis.

During theological discussion it emerged that Djebral had escaped the previous year from revolution in Iran, just as Mahmud-Hodja had escaped from revolution in Russia. Maike then sang to them about the falcon of righteousness and the snake of sedition. Moved to tears, Djebral insisted that they stay another seven days and presented the singer with a small flock of fine-haired Kandahar goats. All those seven days Djebral, Mahmud-Hodja and Alihon-Tura ate, prayed and talked of a promised land where there was no sedition and everyone was like Maike. On the eighth day, as they were taking their leave of one another, the unschooled Maike sang in Arabic a farewell elegy to the extinguished hearth, an elegy that the retentive Persian immediately wrote down, although it was subsequently classified as a pre-Islamic muallaka and ascribed to Imr-Ul-Kais.[51]

As they travelled on, Maike once again began to sing in Kirghiz – that way the flock grazed and multiplied better; and after they had passed Mazari-Sharif, as they drew close to the upper reaches of the Vakhsh and the Margi Mor mountain, they were overtaken by Djebral-Semavi, who had disposed of all his property in order that, like the happy Mahmud-Hodja, he might see the promised land which had brought forth such prodigies as the incomparable Maike.

*

Together they passed Gissar and Zerafshan, Djizak and Khodzhent and then, in the steppe near Tashkent, not far from the Gilas river, they came upon a never-ending ladder with wooden rungs and iron rails that lay stretched across the earth from horizon to horizon. As Maike, struck dumb in the middle of his singing, was looking despondently at his feet, he heard a high-pitched whistle in the distance; this whistle, similar at first to that of a hamster in the Iraqi sands, grew louder and deeper and suddenly acquired a fire-spitting face, which filled Maike with terror. Bleating like uncastrated kids, the goats scattered about the steppe; the horses stumbled amid the sheep; Djebral, Mahmud-Hodja and Alihon-Tura wheezed and trembled and prayed towards Mecca. And then, whistling and thundering, a snake-like wonder hurtled past them, packed both on the inside and on top with infidels shouting and waving their hands. 'The End of the World!' thought both Mahmud-Hodja the Sunni and Djebral the Shiite.

Trembling all the while like a shaman, Maike began to sing in some croaking and fragmentary tongue. This hoarse and strange song continued for two hours. Punctuated by the word 'Gilas', which became a kind of refrain, terrible images followed one upon another – of a river frozen solid out of terror of the final day, of water turning into iron before men's eyes, of silt and rushes changing into wooden cross-beams, of blood that could be washed away only by tears . . . Blind old men appeared in Maike's visions, followed by murdered boys, all crowding about the bank of this now impassable iron river. Now it was Maike's words that breathed fire – and the river became the bridge of Sirat,[52] which was being crossed not by people but by a people-devouring monster. Suddenly Maike's voice shot up, far above the dust, into the heights where the steppe sun was listening entranced. No less suddenly his voice melted into blue smoke. The goats calmed down, the horses stood still, and the men arose from their prayers. Then Maike sang his last song about Gilas – a Gilas that was now a happy and barely attainable dream – and bloody saliva sprayed from his burnt and blackened mouth. And at sunset Maike stopped breathing and fell to the ground.

In the morning of the following day Djebral, Mahmud-Hodja and Alihon-Tura gave Maike the burial of a true believer, washing him in the muddy waters of the Gilas river and sewing him up in the travelling turban of a man who has completed the Hadj. They wept for him and buried him beside an ancient burial mound not far from the Kazakh village of Kaplan-Bek. Djebral settled in the nearest inhabited spot – a small town near where they had first come upon the iron ladder and which turned out, like the river, to be called Gilas – and once again became the keeper of a grave: the unknown grave of the unknown Maike. Mahmud-Hodja and all his family soon moved there too, in order that the grace brought into the world by Maike should increase and blossom. But the iron road, the ladder stretching far across the earth, had already become the path of a new Revolution.

12

Obid-Kori was now living with his one and only Oyimcha, but he did not know peace. He was tormented by the thought that Oyimcha – this highborn descendant of the Prophet – was only his because of the power of money. He was tormented by the thought that every one of her many relatives looked down on him; however pious or well educated he might be, he was still 'only a Kirghiz'. When the first snow fell on the mountains, when the first flakes drifted down onto Mookat, one of Oyimcha's cousins had tucked under Obid-Kori's belt a slip of paper bearing the words:

> Men must prepare, should snowy news
> Fall in their lap, a splendid feast.
> Our Kirghiz brother will not refuse –
> He too will prove a gracious host.

According to Sart custom, this 'snowy news' obliged Obid-Kori to lay on a huge feast and invite every one of his relatives. And – Allah be praised! – Obid-Kori intended to be as gracious a host as any of them. But what the sly Sart really meant was only too clear: 'You may only be a Kirghiz – but you must do as we do!'

Allah alone is omniscient. Had Obid-Kori known that Oyimcha's cousin had slipped a similar note under the belt of every one of his relatives, then he might not have been so upset – but, as the saying goes, any stone can sharpen a knife. And so Obid-Kori went on tormenting himself, constantly searching for evidence that his new relatives despised him.

He resolved to teach only Sart boys – the brothers of girls who had been sent to study with Oyimcha. But the Kirghiz – straightforward men from the mountains who came down every week to the Sunday bazaar – went on bowing to him out of respect for his father Mirzaraim-Bey and did not even notice his attempts to avoid them; as for the smug Sarts, they were too full of themselves and their self-centred valley-dwelling ways to realise how desperately he longed for them to accept him.

Most of the time Obid-Kori sat at home, either deep in his own thoughts or else teaching Sart children Arabic and Persian, poetry and philosophy and the Holy Koran. Apart from the boys passed on to him by his highborn wife, his students were mostly orphans and children of the poor – more and more of them every year. It was wartime and their fathers were being conscripted for trench-digging and other manual labour behind the front line.

And then, towards the end of one winter, the Russian Tsar suffered yet more troubles; this time his troubles were called a Revolution. The news, admittedly, only reached Mookat around the beginning of summer, when a mullah accompanied by three Russian soldiers arrived from Skobelev in order to mobilise the benighted population towards Enlightenment and the creation of political parties. The local Sarts were at best indifferent to these appeals, which offered no prospects of better trading in naan bread, potatoes or dried apricots; the warlike Kirghiz, however, were so entranced by the Russians' promise of firearms that they missed the Sunday bazaar two weeks running, leaving the Sarts' bread to go stale and their apricots to rot while they rode from one high pasture to another to spread the good news.

Obid-Kori himself had stuffed both proclamations – the one from the mullah and the one from the Russians – up his sleeve, and he had forgotten all about them while he taught his lessons. As he was washing before his evening prayers, the papers fell out of the rolled-up sleeve of his gown and he put them to one side so they wouldn't get wet; only as he was getting ready to go to bed and Oyimcha was wrapping their first-born Abdulhamidjan in his swaddling clothes did he remember them. By the light of a feeble, shaded lamp, clad in white underwear that made him look like a gawky stork, he unfolded the proclamations, read them one after the other, then tucked the one written in Persian by the Kokand 'Holy Mullahs'[53] into his handkerchief and threw the other one, which was printed in Russian, into a niche from which it was removed the following day by Oyimcha, who looked on anything written in the Russian script as profane.

One proclamation told Obid-Kori how the mullahs of Turkestan had decided to create an Islamic state free of distinctions of tribe and birth; the other told him, in Russian, about some 'classless society' in which everyone would be equal. Obid-Kori pondered all this for a long time. The two documents seemed to be talking about one and the same thing, so what was the difference between them? However many wise books Obid-Kori read, he found that they were always devoted to the same question: how can everyone be made equally happy just like that? But if the Almighty had chosen to make people different, was it in man's power to change this? And then wasn't this the very same problem that had tormented Obid-Kori – who had left the Kirghiz but never quite managed to join the Sarts – for so many years? Wasn't it this that had caused him so much suffering – torn as he was between valley and mountain, between horse and book?

Whatever the truth of all this, Obid-Kori rode later that summer to Skobelev and Kokand, where he met both reformist mullahs and extremist soldiers, both deputies from the list of progressives and progressives from the list of deputies, and where he even took part in a regional congress. Beside him at this meeting sat the chairman of some Peasant Progressive-Nationalist Party for Labour and Peace, a Russian who appeared not to know the difference between a bull and a cow (speaking to some soldiers, he referred to the latter as 'a bull with a cunt') but who showed a passionate interest in what he referred to as 'the situation in the lower depths'. Heavens above! What on earth did he mean by this? The secret parts of a woman? Did the man have no fear of God?

Then this Russian took from his trouser pocket some ungodly scrap of paper – like the paper non-believers wipe themselves with – and held it out to Obid-Kori. 'I couldn't sleep at night,' he said, 'so I drew up this document. Now I'd like your advice. I can see you're an educated man who knows the world. This is a list I made during the night – I'm sure you will appreciate its importance and understand its necessity. It's the men I've chosen as ministers.'

'Heavens above!' thought Obid-Kori. 'The half-Shah in Tashkent[54] hasn't even packed his bags yet, and here's this man . . .'

'So,' the man began, 'the prime minister will be Al-Misakkidin Sarymsak-Oglu.'

'Excuse me. Just how old is he now?'

'Eighty-seven. And what of it?'

'Well, he's certainly not too young for the job.'

'What do you mean? He's full of mind – every bit of him, from head to toe. And anyway, he can always consult us. Now, the Minister for the Indigenous Population – he's the one on the platform now.'

'God forgive me! You don't mean that Russian, do you?'

'He's no Russian, God bless you! It's just that he studied in Petersburg.'

'He'll need a good interpreter – the locals won't be able to understand a word he says!'

'Really? Do you think so?' Taken aback, the man put a large question mark against the name of the Minister for Indigenous Affairs. 'Now, the Minister for Village Affairs', he continued, 'is your humble servant.'

'Excuse me,' said the man sitting behind them, 'but I don't think you've got a Minister for the Affairs of Doctors and Healers.'

'No, there was someone, I'm quite certain of it,' said this Minister for Village Affairs – peering at his list, then giving up in despair. 'But what makes you ask?'

'Well, I've got an uncle who's a healer. He heals just by looking at people. I wanted to suggest . . .'

'Is he a Party member?'

While their neighbour wondered how best to explain away this shortcoming, the Minister leant over towards Obid-Kori and said, 'Listen – you wouldn't like to be appointed our representative for Osh District, would you? Or you could be Minister for Enlightenment and Madrasahs? Yes, that particular position happens to be still vacant.'

'O Allah! O Allah! What evil spirits you place in our path!' thought Obid-Kori, escaping from this regional congress during a break. 'Give me the strength to ignore these whisperings of Satan and tricks of the Devil! Do not abandon me in their presence!'

Back in Mookat, Obid-Kori fell ill for the first time in his life. But Oyimcha healed him with honey and herbs and he soon returned to his usual measured routine and began to prepare for the advent of another winter.

13

As he approached old age, Master-Railwayman Belkov was appointed caretaker of the local PartCom building.[55] Belkov had his own point of view, a strictly Party point of view, on every event in Gilas. It seemed to him that what he was guarding was more than just the building where the PartCom was located – the eight windows, four walls and tiled roof that had come the way of the Party after the expropriation of Mirzokul-Tailor, the original owner of the cotton factory; yes, it seemed to Belkov that he was guarding the very edifice of Communism.

And when he saw the slogans that Ortik-Picture-Reels had written in his crooked hand in exchange for a bottle of Russian vodka – slogans like 'Let Communism be Constructed by 1980!' or 'Long Live our Splendid Nation, the Splendid Builder of Splendid Communism!' – caretaker Belkov would laugh with his toothless mouth, knowing that the building of Communism had already been built and that he himself, ex-Master-Railwayman Belkov, had been appointed to guard it every third night.

'What matters most in Communism?' he would ask to the bewilderment of Froska, his plump and lovely wife, who sold fizzy water in the station and was pined after by the entire male population of Gilas. And then he would answer his own question with the words: 'Communism is human sympathy and the current of life.'

Now and again Froska would try to argue with him; once, after attending a seminar for sellers of fizzy water, she tried to insist that Communism was 'Soviet Power plus the Gasification of the Entire Country!'[56] But Belkov interrupted her current of thought by scratching himself in an unmentionable place – and Froska did not forgive him.

*

Soon afterwards Froska left Belkov for the station's other seller of fizzy water, Uncle Yashka, a Jew who came by train every day from the City. And so Belkov lost an obedient wife – who had never before inflicted any worse punishment on him than rolling over and turning her irresistible buttocks to the wall – and his life was drained, once and for all, of every last drop of the current of human sympathy.

Master-Railwayman Belkov begged for an extra shift as caretaker in order to share his bitter fate with the Party he loved. But Second Secretary Gogolushko not only reprimanded him for exploiting the Party for personal ends but also injected him with a hefty dose of the elemental anti-Semitism that was gradually becoming the Party's almost-official policy. More precisely, Gogolushko opened Belkov's eyes to the underlying economic causes of the cartelisation and monopolisation of the fizzy-water trade in Gilas.

Belkov had managed to accommodate all life's complexities in his simple sentence about human sympathy and the current of life; after losing his wife, however, he not only ceased to believe in himself and his lapidary formula but also – after his conversation with Gogolushko – became an out-and-out anti-Semite. It has to be said, however, that this out-and-out anti-Semitism was directed exclusively against Yashka, and, since Belkov went on selling the leather of the PartCom armchairs to the Jewish Yusuf-Cobbler, it could perhaps better be named anti-Yashkism. And anyway, one could hardly suspect a veteran of Lazar Moiseevich Kaganovich's[57] railways of holding views that contradicted his whole life as a railwayman.

Belkov's forgetfulness, and his resulting habit of repeating himself, soon acquired improbable dimensions. During his long monologues, while he tried to fit thoughts disarrayed by life into his forgotten formula about the current of life and human sympathy, unsympathetic candidates for Party membership found time not only to repeat the Programme and Statutes of the

Party but also the whole of the impressive curricula vitae that Mefody-Jurisprudence, Gilas's solitary member of the intelligentsia, would recently have composed for them. And during the time he took to answer the question 'Where's the Office of the Party Committee?' – or, more often, 'Where's the toilet?' – candidates from the local population were able to repeat to themselves the midday prayer, the longest of the five daily prayers. It was thus with Allah behind them that they entered the Office and began to live the life of a Communist.

During the last census Master-Railwayman Belkov had declared that he knew only the language of the Soviet people; he did, however, once have a go at learning modern Vietnamese. During one of the evenings that Belkov was on duty, a certain Nguyen Dyn Hok, who had accidentally been left behind by his 'Friendship' train, wandered into the building of Communism; he turned out to be searching for a shop where he could buy a metal teapot. By morning, this middle-aged man – lying on a divan the leather cover of which Belkov had already sold to Yusuf-Carpenter, and somnolently embracing Belkov's generous present of the office metal teapot – had not only acquired quite a decent understanding of the mighty Russian language but was also marvelling at the supple expressiveness of his own still developing language as developed by the master-railwayman: 'Ho-Chi-Minh – Hoo-Rah! Hoo-Rah! Sai-gon – No! Ha-noi – Hoo-Rah! Jon-son – No, No, No! Ho-Chi-Minh, Fam-Vam-Dong, Den-Ben-Fu – Hoo-Rah! Sai-gon, Mee-kong – Hoo-Rah, Hoo-Rah! Yan-kee – No! Yan-kee – No, No, No! Jon-son – No!'

Master-Railwayman Belkov accompanied Nguyen Dyn Hok to the station in time to catch the 7.12 train, and, in reply to Belkov's last Communist invocations of 'Ho-Chi-Minh, Fam-Vam-Dong, Den-Ben-Fu!' Nguyen Dyn Hok called out with no less passion, 'Co-mu-nee-sum-ees-cu-llent-of-rife-and-hoo-man-seem-pat-ee!' Belkov, alas, failed to take in this distillation of his own words that the Vietnamese, now on his way back to his motherland with the Gilas Party Committee teapot, had so quickly committed to memory. Had he understood, he might perhaps have found release from his militant tediousness and been able to rest once again within the sympathetic embrace of his all-embracing formula.

As things were, however, the life of the Master-Railwayman was without any current of human sympathy at all, and his ability to bore others was matched only by his ability to forget. These two abilities were, in fact, not unconnected. Trying to forget Froska behind a veil of words, ex-Master-Railwayman Belkov succeeded in forgetting everything except her act of betrayal; losing his whole life to oblivion, he struggled to recapture it in a web of words. But his webs and veils were in vain; his verbal virtuosity was to no avail. At the beginning of his night watch poor Belkov would forget in which pocket he had put his cigarette case with the inscription: 'To Esteemed Master-Railwayman Belkov from his Comrades and Fellow-Railwaymen who will Remember him for Ever'; looking for his cigarette case, he would forget where he had put his nightwatchman's pullover; during his search for the pullover, he would lose his double-barrelled shotgun; searching for the shotgun, he would drop his round-lensed spectacles; without his spectacles he lost all sense of what on earth he was looking for. He lost so much that he lost all count of his losses. Towards the end of his night's watch the vigilant Gogolushko would hand him his cigarette case; the Party chauffeur would remove the pullover he had been lying on as he repaired the Party Committee car; poor Auntie Lina the Greek Communist would be found carrying his gun around in a bucket along with her mop; and his spectacles would drop out of his trousers as he hitched them up before leaving the building.

But there was one thing Belkov never lost: the certainty that he was guarding the building of Communism.

14

The next morning, the boy set off towards the depot. Some goods wagons had been brought there the previous evening and Belyalov's lorries were already starting to arrive. The boy still felt a little sick from the day before. He had washed under the tap but he was afraid to drink, and anyway it was impossible to stay there long; someone coming from the little bazaar the other side of the ice-cream stall was about to start washing two bunches of radishes. The boy did, however, stand there while this man – whom he had never seen before – washed his radishes, and the boy even waited for him to go away, leaving one radish – as red as a red shipping buoy – bobbing about in the stream of water. There was only this one radish; the boy had thought there were several, but when he reached down into the pit beneath the tap, the redness shining beneath the water turned out to be from eggshells dyed red with onion juice – and the boy remembered hearing from the other children that this Sunday was the beginning of Easter.

The radish he had eaten was burning his hungry stomach and, as he walked along the railway track in the fierce sun, he was hoping that the men would be loading fruit. When he came to the first wagon, however, he realised that there had been no need to hurry: the wagons were not being loaded but being unloaded, and the sacks being piled into Belyalov's lorries were full of onions.

Still, if he got himself taken on, he would at least earn a few roubles to keep himself going through these hungry days. He walked round a lorry that had been backed up to the wagon and saw that four winos had already staked their claim: it was no good hanging around there. The boy asked the driver if they were unloading any more wagons; the driver nodded in the direction of a man in a suit and said, 'He's the head clerk, he'll know.'

The boy felt lost: if only Artyomchik were with him . . . Artyomchik knew all these head clerks. The two of them could do a wagon together.

But without Artyomchik . . . He himself was too small. The head clerk wouldn't even talk to him. At the moment the head clerk was arguing with three strangers. They were sitting beneath the wagon and playing hard to get.

'Come on, get cracking!' said the head clerk. 'Don't worry – we'll get you a fourth comrade soon!'

'Nod likely, boss. We dud wud druck – ad dad's your lod! Now we wod our half-lidre.'

'One and a half roubles per ton. Come on now!'

Recognising Tolik-Nosetalk, the boy went up to him and offered to join them. Someone cleared his throat, someone else told the boy to fuck off, but Tolik, sounding as if he himself were the station director, said, 'I dow de boy. Powerful as a forklivd druck, he is!'

In the end they settled on three and a half roubles for two tons. The boy dragged the sacks out from up above and placed them on the men's shoulders. Staggering and cursing, covered in dust and sweat, the men were soon on their fifth or sixth lorry. Sometimes a lorry driver would climb up into the wagon, go to the opposite corner, untie one of the sacks and blather on about how wonderful last year's onions had been. But not even Tolik-Nosetalk would tell him to fuck off, since he too was desperate for something to eat. As soon as they'd unloaded half the wagon, the men jumped out onto the flat space below. Tolik asked for three roubles from the head clerk and said to the boy, 'Rud over do de codod fagdory ad ged some Vermood[58] and ady dam food you like!'

The boy rushed off, but all he could find in the shop was a stale railway loaf, some tinned flatfish and some sticky 'Cherry' caramels . . . And he got so out of breath on the way back that his head was still spinning even long after he'd sat down again. The rail seemed to be transmitting every clack and bang made by the diesel shunter working on the other track, but the sun was at the very top of the sky and it was impossible to move even a centimetre from the shade of the wagon.

'Drig up!' said Tolik-Nosetalk. 'Or some fukkuvadidspector will be roud.'

The boy wanted to join in – especially when Tolik threw his head back and his Adam's apple bobbed up and down and a red stream dribbled from the corner of his lips and down his dusty chin. 'Your turn!' someone said to him as the bottle went round the circle. The boy refused and regretted it. The bread he had chewed so greedily got stuck at the back of his mouth, and anyway there was a piece of greasy tinned fish blocking his throat just a little further down. He didn't in the least want any of the 'Cherry' caramels, let alone any of the stinking onion – and when they suggested he finish up what was left in the bottle he practically grabbed it from them and gulped it all down in one go.

The wine was sweet and disgusting. But it tickled his throat and the unchewed bread at last began to move down, although his head now felt as if the diesel shunter were at work right beside him and his cheeks were swelling up and their heat had dried his sweat and turned it into a tense hot film and all this made him want to let out a volley of curses. Yes, he wanted to tell that damned lorry driver what he thought of him. Feeling as if he were jumping off the edge of a precipice, he found himself saying, 'Fucking cunt – saying the fucking onions are too fucking small!'

But no one listened to the boy's quiet words – one of the three men was spreading out a copy of the cotton factory news sheet as he lay down in between the rails, where a few stems of shepherd's purse were swaying from side to side, the second was throwing away the empty bottle and tins, and Tolik-Nosetalk was rolling some home-grown tobacco. The boy didn't know what to do next, but he felt he had to do something; he tried to clamber out from beneath the wagon, but the fierce sun drove him back, and, no longer able to support his own weight, he collapsed onto the track and lay there just as he had done ages ago – or was it only last night?

Later they made a start on the other half of the wagon. At first the work went smoothly; once they'd finished, they were going to go to the cotton factory shop to get some more drink. The boy was looking forward to this. But when there was only one more lorry to load, a car drove up and even Tolik-Nosetalk was alarmed. 'Belyalov's here — ged fuckig movig widdose sacks!'

First Belyalov went to the wagon next to them; then, along with the head clerk, he came to their own wagon. The clerk nodded in the direction of the boy and began, 'This boy now . . .' Belyalov immediately scrambled into the wagon, walked straight to the far corner, came back towards them — and suddenly there was no stopping him: 'Who put a minor like him in the wagon? Do you really have no idea, do you really not understand, what the law calls this? Exploitation! Yes, exploitation of children! How can a boy like him lift sacks?' And so on, with a lot of drivel about standards of safety technology, and so on.

He ranted for ten minutes. It was a little unclear whether he was ranting at the head clerk or at the winos, but in the end, of course, the one who got thrown out was the boy; and however much the boy pleaded with Belyalov, reminding him how he'd made crates for him at the depot and saying that it wasn't the first time he'd loaded, or rather unloaded, a wagon, Belyalov just went on yelling that he didn't want to be put behind bars and that if a minor was wandering around without parental supervision, then he'd make it his business to get this minor taken back to his school and that the head clerk should take a note of the boy's surname and draft a letter about him — and then off Belyalov went to his car. And when the treacherous head clerk got out his indelible pencil and a scrap of paper, the boy felt he was going to start howling any minute and that nothing could be worse than crying in front of bastards like these, who would exploit his childish tears to tell him to bugger off if he was going to be such a baby — and so he jumped down onto the ground and went on his way, ignoring the head clerk's question, 'Where do you go to school?'

He walked along the dusty road beside the railway line and his tears seemed to run all the way down his body and end up on the ground, transforming the dust behind him to clay. He wanted to escape from all this humiliation and he couldn't; his feet were sinking into a quagmire; and when he got to the first fence between the road and the depot, he fell down beside it, wept himself into a state of desolate fury *and, his insides now clenched tight as a fist, began to wait for Belyalov's car to come round the bend. He was going to smash Belyalov's windscreen with the stone that was burning in his hand; he'd show Belyalov he could do a bit more than just lift sacks . . . He kept thinking up more and more ways he could punish that stupid fat-face — as well as that cheating shit of a clerk — but none of this did anything to soothe a burning in his chest that was stronger than hunger, a burning that made him unable to think of anything else at all — and then, instead of Belyalov's Volga, which had gone on its way long ago, he saw one of Tolik's gang coming round the bend. The man didn't know the way to the cotton factory shop. 'You come with me, my boy, you can show me the way!' he said; and the boy with the parched face went with him, not really knowing why.*

They turned into the sidestreet — and there was the last of the lorries coming up behind them, piled high with sacks. Looking straight in front of him, the man said, 'Quick, one of those sacks is ours! Stop gawping! Quick — there's no mirror on that side!' The lorry was struggling with its load and, before it could catch up with them, they crossed over. The whole of the empty space between the cotton factory and the wool factory was now filled by a cloud of dust like the tail of a comet, and the boy remembered how he had wanted to throw a stone at Belyalov's car; as if they were a curse, he found himself repeating the words, 'I'll show you, you bastard, how I can lift sacks!'

'You chuck it down, I'll do the rest!' said the man, and when the lorry was five yards ahead of them, the boy ran after it, leaped up and gripped the top of the tailboard with one hand as he got his foot onto the trailer hook and pulled on the top sack with his other hand. The sack plopped down into the dust and the boy plopped down after it, landing on all fours and grazing his palms and legs so that they bled — but that was something he only noticed later, after he had thrown the sack onto one shoulder and carried it over to the blind wall at the back of the wool factory. The man was waiting; he'd already taken off his overalls, and he quickly flung them over the sack. The boy's palms and knees started to hurt, but somehow this was exciting — even more

exciting than managing to carry the sack so easily; when the lorry disappeared round the corner, he spat through his teeth and said to the man, 'Come on – get fucking moving with that sack!'

The man quietly heaved the sack onto his shoulder. After they'd gone round the corner, he slipped through a little gate while the boy sat on the bank of the canal and began to wash the blood and dirt from his hands. The man came out, swore and said, 'First the bitch said she'd grass us up. Then she paid me enough for a couple of bottles. Fuck the bloody bitch! Let's go!'

Then the man went to the cotton factory shop, emerged with three bottles of Vermooth and said with a chuckle, 'Here you are, I've got you your bottle too!' These words at once brought to mind the thick slobbery lips of Tolik-Nosetalk and the disgusting red liquid that had dribbled out of them. Yesterday's nausea had never really passed and once again the boy nearly threw up. 'Give me my money!' he said through his teeth, almost weeping with fury. There were no stones or bits of metal to hand, but the man must have felt anxious about his bottles; he at once started apologising, saying nervously that the boy could take all the money he had in his pockets, and why hadn't the boy told him he wouldn't be drinking with them – they had, after all, worked side by side, shoulder to shoulder – and that there wasn't much in his pockets, only small change, but the boy was welcome to take every kopek he had . . .

Who knows, probably the boy would have taken the change, if only to buy a loaf of bread – but just then the man they called 'Malka', the science teacher, came out of the shop. Seeing him, the boy turned round and walked in the opposite direction, full of an impotent fury and despair made all the more shameful by the way the wino called out after him, 'Hey, boy, where are you fucking off to?'

By then he was almost running to the first little sidestreet he could find – to hide there and forget all this and not see anyone, not see anyone . . . It was late afternoon and the crooked little streets were empty and the boy didn't know what to do with himself. He was hungry and ashamed, and his hunger and his shame felt as if they were one and the same thing; he couldn't have calmed one without getting *rid of the other. He wandered along like a stray dog that has just been beaten, shying away even from the old women who happened to pass by, until he found himself on a street at the end of which, outside the house of the old German woman they called Reitersha, he heard the voices of his schoolmates: 'Christ has risen! Christ has risen!' Then he remembered that today was the beginning of Easter – 'Eater' as his schoolmates called it – and he realised that Borat and Kutr, Kobil and Vityok, Shapik and Abos were doing the rounds of the old Russian women, just as they went round the Uzbek houses during Ramadan, and that today they were begging for dyed eggs and Easter cakes. Afterwards they would sit down on a bench somewhere and fight egg-battles till every last egg was cracked; then they would cram all the food down and give themselves hiccups.*

And he wanted to join them – not because he was hungry but simply because he wanted to join them. Yes, he could stay out late with them – only what, he couldn't help wondering, what would he do when they all went home? And so, instead of joining them, he just followed them for a while, quietly murmuring with them the words 'Christ has risen!' and hearing the old women reply to his mates: 'Risen indeed!' But when they all sat down on a bench and began their egg-battles, he felt so lonely, so unbearably lonely, that he just set off wherever his legs took him. After wandering through fields, and through the outskirts of town, he ended up just before midnight by the Russian cemetery; there, on little tables in front of the crosses, glimmering in the moonlight, stood polished glasses full of vodka, and there was a dimmer, paler glow coming from the multicoloured Easter eggs.

The boy stood by the canal, uncertain whether or not to jump across, and the canal, gliding snakily along, seemed to be smearing bits of moon over its skin – and these spangles of moonlight shone like coins and for some reason reminded him of silver fish that he couldn't quite fish out of his memory.

Then he remembered. It was in the autumn, when they had all been sent off for a few weeks to pick cotton; his class had picked their quota before lunch and decided to go to a nearby cemetery in the afternoon to catch snakes. They cut themselves plenty of forked sticks and went past some burial mounds and along the bank of a river, which was thick with reeds, to a cemetery beside the road. However hard they tried, they couldn't find any snakes there, but they came across a holy tree, decked not with leaves but with bits of cloth of every colour, and somebody suggested they look and see if there was anything wrapped in these cloths. The boy had tried to stop them; he had remembered how Granny had once gone to a tree like this and hung on one of its branches a curse against the evil spirits that had entered her aching legs, and the boy had imagined that what she had wrapped in her red cloth was not a curse written on a piece of paper in some strange and incomprehensible script but the evil spirits themselves – and that the evil spirits would fade in the sun and be blown about by the wind, only to escape when the cloth rotted beneath the winter rains and then find their way back into Granny's swollen legs.

All the same, the boys had untied one of the cloths and some coins had fallen out – green from time, sun and damp. Soon they had quite forgotten about the snakes; they had collected nearly a rouble and all they wanted was to get to the little collective-farm shop before it closed. But just as they left the cemetery they heard a loud shout behind them. They all turned round and caught sight of a black horseman, raising a cloud of dust as he tore towards them. The terrified boys rushed into a field. But they could still hear the horse, and the thudding of its hooves was drawing closer. Chest-high cotton cut into their legs and faces; their boots kept sinking into the mud; someone, probably Mofa, stumbled and fell but he just kept going on all fours, not letting go of his stick or falling behind the others, looking like a relay runner crouched down by the start line; at last, galloping to the edge of the field and leaping across a ten-foot-wide drainage canal, they calmed down a little and looked back. There was no one there. Had the horseman been a spirit? Had evil spirits escaped from the cloths?

Breathless but pale, they settled on the bank of this cold and murky canal, leaving Mofa – who was still bent double – to keep watch. They began teasing one another and making jokes. Then the boy threw his coin into the canal and they all leaped to their feet as it plopped noisily into the water. Once again they laughed nervously – until they caught sight of a colt, walking round in circles in the middle of this clover-filled meadow . . .

Perhaps wanting to make up for the fright they'd had, someone suggested they try riding the colt. The boy felt alarmed by the silence hanging over the meadow and didn't especially want to exchange their present shelter – even if it was only a few mulberry trees – for the middle of an open field; nevertheless, they all walked towards the colt and the boy followed. Mofa was first to scramble up onto the colt's back; Artyomchik and Pchela followed. They rode about in circles for a long time, sometimes slipping off the colt's neck, sometimes jumping up and landing on his bony croup, until there was a sudden yell from behind them and they rushed off in a panic.

Afraid that it was the black horseman, and that he was going to make them answer for what they had done in the cemetery, the boys ran towards the edge of the field, desperate to get away from the horseman's ever closer cry: 'Ushla! Ushla!' Whether the horseman was shouting in Russian that the colt had got away or whether he was shouting in Uzbek, calling 'Catch them! Catch them!', none of them had any idea – but when the boy turned round in hypnotised terror he saw that the colt was galloping towards him; it was angry with him for not having been on its back and the terrible thought that the black horseman was shouting orders to the colt, telling it to catch the boy, made him turn round with a scream and take a great swing with his stick at this snorting monster that wanted to trample him under its hooves.

The colt shied away to one side, but repeated cries of 'Ushla! Ushla!' threw the boy into still more of a panic. Finally reaching the reeds by the bank, he sank into the slime and looked round for the last time. The colt was a little spot at the far end of the field, close to the dusty road, and there was no black horseman at all, nor could he see the other boys.

*

And now, standing by the canal, the boy couldn't make up his mind whether or not to jump across to the other bank and commune with something that was already lying softly on his tongue and quietening the burning pain in his insides. He didn't remember how long he stood there, but the chill slipping into him gradually changed his uncertainty to terror, and more cold darkness was creeping across the canal and a dog was barking in the distance and a frog began croaking somewhere near his feet – but then a night bird settled on one of the tables and, quietly pecking at the buns and the Easter cakes, calmed the boy and gave him new heart. He leapt across the canal and, playing safe by whispering 'Christ has risen!', began to make his way between the graves and crosses to the table where the bird had been sitting until he'd frightened it away with his leap. He called the bird back down from its wrought-iron perch, inviting it to a table where he could see bread and a glass and an onion . . .

15

You will remember that Hadjiya was born while her father, Mahmud-Hodja the Younger, was in Mecca, having set out on the Hadj in order to pray that the sins of the February Revolution be forgiven. But not long after he came back home with Djebral, who was seeking a haven from his own Persian revolution, they were both overtaken by the yet more improbable October Revolution. Improbable because it began like a light cold you think you're going to shake off in no time at all . . . but then . . . in the end . . .

Djebral married the first refugee to come his way from Kokand, which had been sacked by the Bolsheviks and then looted by the Dashnaks;[59] probably he was hoping to appease this latest revolution, to pay his dues to it once and for all before building the famous wall behind which not one inhabitant of Gilas ever penetrated – except for members of his household, who were protected from our faithless world by Djebral's unshakeable vow that no revolution of any kind would ever be allowed to enter his own home.

The death of Maike the bringer of fertility led Mahmud-Hodja to switch from rearing livestock to cultivating the land. After selling his countless flocks to the Kirghiz, from whom they were immediately confiscated by men who called themselves the Revolutionary Sailors of the Zailiisky Mountains,[60] he bought some large vineyards just outside Gilas and moved there with his family, reckoning that even if the grapes were all confiscated and taken to Russia at least he would still be left with the vines.

The Bolsheviks did indeed confiscate everything they could eat, drink, or wear – and everything they could sell in order to obtain things to eat, drink or wear – but these homeless, kinless, thieving soldiers who had been sent for their sins into the deserts of Turkestan were incapable of doing anything except waving their flags and revolvers in the air and pissing wherever the need came upon them; and so Mahmud-Hodja's vineyards were not chopped down or uprooted and Mahmud-Hodja was even able to steal – that is, carefully store away – what remained of the harvest after the night-searches carried out by Bolsheviks desperate for anything they could make into alcohol.

In the labyrinthine depths of his infinite vineyards he built secluded quarters for his wife and his two daughters, Asolat and Hadjiya, who from then on saw nothing of the outside world at all. In winter they sorted raisins and in summer they bathed where the Khasanbay canal forms a small pond; they prevented the unclean water from getting inside them by holding their fingers to every aperture of their long-haired heads.

Once, as they were bathing – seeing nothing, hearing nothing, smelling nothing and saying nothing – they were glimpsed by a distant relative. This relative was no mere boy but a fully grown man; his name was Gazi-Hodja and he was helping out in the vineyards of a fellow hodja in order to avoid serving the heathen Bolsheviks. The buttocks of the plump younger sister, rising now and again from the muddy water like white cupolas, deprived him of his reason and made him forget not only what is expected of a hodja but even the foundations of the Sharia itself. From that day he paid ever more frequent visits to his neighbour, pruning his vines, digging the soil and removing dead leaves – especially in the dense thickets penetrated only by the muddy water of the canal.

Regardless of wars or revolutions, autumn was the time for weddings, and this autumn was no different; matchmakers came to speak to Mahmud-Hodja about his younger daughter. Mahmud-Hodja, as obstinate as any true hodja who has eaten a good lunch, was unshakeable: how could he even think of allowing his younger daughter to marry before her sister?

'You can take the elder,' he said guilelessly to the matchmakers

– but they, like true hodjas who have eaten a good lunch, got up and left. As they made their way out through the vines, they forgot that Mahmud-Hodja was a relative of theirs and muttered crossly, 'Damn you and your daughter!'

Cross words from a hodja can have serious consequences, and it was many years before anyone asked for the hand of Asolat, the elder sister who, in addition to being hidden away behind thickets of vines, was herself as thin and dry as a vine-pole. Hadjiya, meanwhile, grew into so splendid a young woman that even her own father felt shy in her presence – while Gazi-Hodja wept every summer by the source of the muddy Khasanbay, seeing in the reflection of the sun the rounded buttocks of his chosen one and praying for the day when that hateful vine-pole of an elder sister was finally married off. And then one day, wanting to fulfil the will of Allah and not be denied the opportunity to continue to praise Him, he offered up a prayer, went over to the Bolsheviks and became a policeman.

In this Gazi-Hodja demonstrated not only spiritual wisdom but also worldly good sense: hodjas unconverted to Bolshevism were already being threatened with exile, and Gazi-Hodja was hoping to save Mahmud-Hodja's family and so win Hadjiya even if her elder sister should remain unmarried.

On the Day of the Death of the Leader of the World Proletariat, when police were sent to the bazaars and chaikhanas to round people up so that they could express their elemental feelings of grief at the mass meetings that had sprung up spontaneously all over the country, Gazi-Hodja was assigned the task of finding praise-singers to console the orphaned soul of the nation. Why, Oh why, had Allah taken Vladimir Ilyich to Himself without first deciding in whose hands to leave the World Revolution and the Labouring Poor? The whole of Gilas, the whole of the City, the whole of the Soviet nation had been brought to its knees. And during this terrible hour, while comrades in Moscow were laying out the body of the man in honour of whom the local Kazakhs were obliged to call their inopportunely born children 'Elesh' – since they could no more distort their steppe tongue to form the word 'Ilyich' than they could push these children back into the womb to wait for a happier day – a certain Pochamir-Hodja from Bukhara was escorted to the police station. A stranger to these parts, Pochamir had taken it into his head that Allah, not waiting for the end of the world, had begun his Last Judgment, and so, there in the bazaar, amid the jars of grocers from whom he had bought a little opium and lapis lazuli as a remedy against toothache, he had hurried to clear his conscience by telling Allah what he truly thought of the Bolsheviks; since he was abusing the Bolsheviks and their lamented leader in a Bukhara dialect beyond the comprehension of anyone in Gilas, the authorities had thought he must be wailing about some pogrom or other, and, in case the exploitative English should seize on this pogrom for the purposes of anti-Bolshevik propaganda,[61] they had decided to isolate this panic-mongerer of a Bukhara Jew in the lock-up. And there Gazi-Hodja, searching for a singer to bring consolation to the orphaned soul of the nation, had found him.

'I call on the spirit of comrade Lenin as a witness', Pochamir-Hodja swore in his Bukhara dialect, 'that I am here in this magnificent town of yours for the first time and I have no idea what is going on here. I implore you in the name of the Communist International and International Solidarity to leave a poor old fool alone in peace.'

'You become comrade Leninandtrotsky – then we'll leave you in peace!' said a warder, a newly Bolshevik new recruit.

The last time Pochamir had been in jail – at the time of the Bukhara Revolution,[62] which he had also interpreted as the end of the world – it had been for over six months, and towards the end of the first month he had grown so bored that he began repairing his cellmates' boots, using waxed thread from his own belt. Noticing this, one of the guards, a Bukhara Jew by the name of Elias, thought of asking the prisoner to repair his own down-at-heel boots. One thing led to another and it wasn't long before Pochamir had repaired the shoes of every one of Elias's relatives; only then did Elias mention Pochamir to his colleagues and to the director of the prison. Then, however, he had a second idea: the boots Pochamir repaired looked as good as new – what if they supplied him with materials and opened a workshop? This might also prove to be a way for Elias to secure an apprenticeship for his son; Yusuf had often taken leather from old boots to make catapults, but only the other day Elias had noticed him using leather from an old catapult to repair a boot that had somehow never been taken to Pochamir.

And so, drawing on generations of cunning and mother-wit, old Elias agreed with Pochamir that they should set up a prison workshop: Elias would supply Pochamir with black leather from the jackets of Chekists who had fallen into disfavour and been shot, Pochamir would make this leather into boots, and Yusuf would sell these boots in the Toki Sarrofon Bazaar. Elias asked for only one thing when he prayed to his Jewish God – for Pochamir to stay in prison for a long time and be forgotten by the authorities – but then the uncircumcised Kalinin[63] had come to Bukhara. As if there were no other places where an old revolutionary could feel at home, he visited all the chaikhanas and prisons and published an indignant article about Pochamir and his boots in the Bolshevik *Local Pravda*. The investigation lasted for several months, during the course of which Elias went on buying up the leather from the jackets of disgraced Party bosses and Yusuf went on trading the boots Pochamir made while he waited for his fate to be decided. But this was not all that Elias accomplished during those months; he also made his son Yusuf sit down by a paraffin lamp and study the seams and insoles of

Pochamir's boots so that, when Pochamir was set free, the bullet-riddled jackets of executed Bolsheviks and Chekists would not be left to rot away in graves.

This time, however, it was not Kalinin but a rank-and-file policeman who came to visit Pochamir-Hodja in his cell. But the policeman turned out to be a hodja himself, and, after talking for a long time about Vladimir Ilyich and his soul's inevitable flight into the inescapable nets of Allah, he suddenly proposed that Pochamir, instead of weeping for the Leader whose death had brought such misfortunes down on his head, should marry the daughter of another of the local hodjas.

It was after lunch – may that hour when hodjas go mad be for ever accursed – and Pochamir agreed to take on a wife and live near the City in exchange for being granted his freedom. He would have done better to wait for a visit from comrade Kalinin; as it was, married to a scrawny vine-pole of a woman who had not only taken him away from Holy Bukhara and its speech and its newspapers and even his own family but even insisted on changing his plebeian name to the more dignified Pasha-Amir, he came to know despair many times. He had nothing against new names – a new life had, after all, begun and yesterday's chaikhana had been renamed a reading-hut[64] – but it was, like it or not, rather awkward to sell lollipops at the end of their little street on weekdays, and in the Kok-Terek Bazaar on Sundays, if one had a name that meant 'Amir to the Padishah'.

And so Gazi-Hodja was able to marry Hadjiya. After his marriage, he had himself transferred to the Party apparatus, to live a life that was a little poorer but also a little less dangerous – given that by then the 'indigenisation' of the security organs had already begun. Gazi-Hodja never managed to grasp that this alien word was supposed to mean the replacement of Russian apparatchiks by local apparatchiks, but he understood very well that it entailed the exile or execution of every other man in the security organs. He would gladly have gone back to working in his father-in-law's vineyards, but the same exiles and executions were taking place there too, in the name not of 'indigenisation' but of the no less mysterious 'collectivisation of agriculture'; and so he had had no choice but to transfer to the Party apparatus and try to save the lives of his wife's family even at the price of their vineyards.

At first everything went well. Children were born to Gazi-Hodja and Hadjiya; and Mahmud-Hodja, fearing more revolutions, stayed at home for years on end – hidden within labyrinths of vineyards that had somehow escaped destruction. After a few years, however, the First Secretary turned his attention to economic matters; the slogan 'Let Village Life be our Focus!' had, after all, been replaced by 'All Eyes on Economics!' And so, in cahoots with the local public prosecutor and the mullah from the mosque in the Old City, the First Secretary imposed on the population a 'K-M' (Kommunist-Muslim, Kapital-Marx and Koran-Muhammad) tax which allowed him to collect 1,931 head of large-horned cattle, five times that number of sheep and goats and an entire 'Rosa Luxemburg Poultry Farm' of chickens and hens. A third of the carcasses were distributed among their superiors and a third were dispatched to the still starving Volga peasants,[65] but the question of how to divide the remaining third gave rise to factional struggles: the public prosecutor opened criminal proceedings against the mullah, charging him with everything from homosexuality to basmach leanings;[66] the mullah exploited his Friday prayers to impose a fatwah on the godless First Secretary, cursing him as a blasphemer and persecutor of the faith; and the First Secretary attacked simultaneously on both fronts, accusing the mullah of rightist-monarchist leanings at the same time as he charged the public prosecutor with leftist-Trotskyist-deviationary tendencies. The very incomprehensibility of the First Secretary's accusations lent them added power; and when Gazi-Hodja and an honourable Jewish Bolshevik by the name of Umansky tried together to make him see reason, the First Secretary made a second two-pronged attack, arranging for Umansky to be packed off to Birobidzhan[67] at the same time as he invited the trustful Gazi-Hodja round for a friendly chat and a dish of *plov*. The First Secretary added opium to the *plov* and, when Gazi-Hodja was fast asleep, he poured into his ear a poison he had obtained from the mullah during their period of Kommunist-Muslim co-operation.

And so Hadjiya lost her first husband. The First Secretary, the public prosecutor and the mullah came round together to express their condolences; by then the three of them had made peace – basmach fighters from·the mountains had carried off the last third of the cattle and poultry and so there was nothing left for them to fight over. But the First Secretary (who gave a speech about the contemporary political situation), the public prosecutor (who read out the verdict of the official inquest into Gazi-Hodja's death) and the mullah (who sang a prayer for the soul of the deceased) were rivals again before they left the house; each wanted Hadjiya for himself. Happily, however, the year 1937[68] was about to begin and all three members of this warring troika – one of them about to hand Hadjiya an application for Party membership, another about to send her a threatening summons, and the third about to present her with a protective amulet – were arrested and sent off to some remote part of Siberia to fell timber and construct a railway. And that was the end of them.

Then the Germans invaded and Hadjiya's two brothers were sent to the Front, along with her brother-in-law Pochamir-Hodja; at the end of the War only one brother would return. Then Mahmud-Hodja himself was arrested; after starting to cultivate an abandoned vineyard, he was accused of 'laying predatory hands on the property of the people'. Hadjiya had to move into Gilas, where she worked in the Papanin Tailoring Co-operative and married a prison guard, Israel-Warder, so as to be able to get parcels of food and clothing delivered to her father. She had, curiously, first been introduced to Israel by yet another prison guard – a Bukhara Jew by the name of Elias; he was a friend of her brother-in-law Pochamir-Hodja and had recently been transferred to Gilas from a jail in Bukhara. And he was the father of the town's new cobbler: a good-natured young man by the name of Yusuf.

In 1945, soon after Victory Day, it was Israel-Warder's turn to be mourned by Hadjiya. Israel-Warder had given her three children – of whom one, a girl called Nafisa, was still living. And since her father had been released from prison on the day of the Victory amnesty, Hadjiya no longer really needed him anyway.

Israel's death was due to sheer carelessness; his comrade Elias failed to observe safety regulations when firing his ancient Bukhara musket into the sky to celebrate the Soviet Victory. It was then Elias's turn to be put behind bars, and it was not long before his son Yusuf-Cobbler got into the habit of saying, 'During the War my father lived opposite the prison, and since the War came to an end he's been living opposite his own home!'

16

Oyimcha was carrying grapes . . . grapes . . . grapes . . . Bunches of grapes . . . bunches of grapes . . .

Why had life turned out this way and no other way? The bunches of grapes were dripping, and the sun was reflected in the drops of water and in the bunches themselves – which seemed like ripe drops of light . . . light . . . light . . .

Obid-Kori was now the only mullah left in the region. Some mullahs had crossed over the mountains to China; others were teaching in village schools or interpreting for District Party Committees, still others were fighting in defence of the Faith.

Life had turned out this way and no other way, and this, no doubt, was an expression of the wisdom of Allah who was, no doubt, testing and punishing his servants, and Obid-Kori accepted in his heart that this was the life he must live. He had not fled over the mountains with Oyimcha's warlike brothers and uncles, although he had accompanied them, in accordance with his duty as a Muslim, from one Alay Kirghiz mountain settlement to another as far as the Kanchyn pass – from which a narrow one-horse track led to Badakhshan.

The horses had plodded gloomily on, gloomily on, and their cold-clouded eyes had kept looking back, past their scrawny flanks – as if the horses had wanted to leave their eyes behind, had wanted to leave their eyes behind in their own land . . .

Oyimcha had wept ceaselessly and amid her weeping had given birth to a child they called Mashrab . . . Mashrab . . .

Life had turned out this way and no other way, and through the Providence of Allah Obid-Kori had become neither a village activist nor an adviser to a District Party Committee nor an editor of the Kirghiz-and-Uzbek newspaper *Herdsman-and-Ploughman* – although activists tried more than once to drag him, like a cow about to be slaughtered, onto one of their Soviet-and-Socialist platforms. Nor did Obid-Kori join the basmach, even though they once abducted him straight from his bed. He had been sleeping out in the courtyard, Allah be praised, and so when he came back home at dawn, on foot, from Chachma-Say, Oyimcha was still peacefully asleep, surrounded by children who seemed like a bunch of grapes ... grapes ... grapes ...

What had happened was this. Yormuhammad – one of the youngest and boldest of the basmach leaders, who had made a surprise attack on Chachma-Say with his Alay Kirghiz and seized control of these heights that command the entire Mookat valley – had happened upon an old woman repeatedly wailing the words: 'The Lord save us from Yormuhammad! May his blood pour from his throat and may he die young!'

It is not for a warrior to correct an old woman, but there were people in the village able to explain why she was wailing: Yormuhammad's basmach had supposedly knifed her two sons and seized her husband, together with all his cattle. It took Yormuhammad only from the sunset prayer to the mid-evening prayer to find out who had been abusing his name: Makhsum-Kulluk, a Sart elder from a nearby village who had recently sent his youngest daughter to become yet another of Yormuhammad's wives. Yormuhammad accepted such gifts as gestures of support for his struggle and did not so much as glance at these new wives, who now occupied a whole mountain village near Shokhimardon, exciting the envy of the local Soviet poets. No one guarded them; they needed no protection beyond Yormuhammad's reputation for showing no mercy on or off the field of battle.

Yormuhammad's treacherous father-in-law was brought to Chachma-Say towards midnight, at the same time as Obid-Kori. Yormuhammad said not a word about his tie of kinship with Makhsum-Kulluk, nor did he even show the man to Obid-Kori. He merely asked the mullah what punishment the Sharia decreed if two innocent men had been knifed and their father, seized together with all his cattle, had met his end in a mountain ravine. Obid-Kori thought for a moment, then quoted al-Marginoni[69] from memory, adding, admittedly, that blood is never washed away by blood, only by tears.

'Write down what is written in al-Marginoni's *Hidoya*', said Yormuhammad drily. When Obid-Kori had finished, Yormuhammad asked, 'Now, how can I be of service to you?'

Obid-Kori shrugged his shoulders, raised his hands in prayer and said, 'May Allah lead you along no path but the True Path!'

Yormuhammad did not try to detain the mullah but simply ordered a horse to be saddled for him and an escort to be provided. Obid-Kori, however, had no need of horse or escort – this was his native land and everyone knew him – and he set off on foot for his village, which lay dark in the valley . . . dark in the valley . . .

That morning, in the most crowded part of the bazaar, where eight smooth-cheeked boys were selling flatbreads and four grey-bearded men were selling cream cheese, Makhsum-Kulluk's head was discovered on a tray, along with a page bearing a quotation from Burkhanutdin al-Marginoni's *The True Path*. The page was wet and swollen; blood was still oozing from the severed head.

'O Allah, why have you made your justice so harsh – and me, so ignorant, so ignorant?' Obid-Kori whispered during his midday prayer, as he prayed for everyone, both the righteous and the unrighteous, but most of all for those who are confused, who in the confusion of their souls and aspirations attempt to amend the pattern preordained by Allah . . . preordained by Allah . . .

Yes, life turned out this way and no other way. A week after this, to warn and edify the local population, the Bolsheviks exhibited the heads of two of Yormuhammad's basmach with the judgment of the Revolutionary Tribunal pinned to their throats. In reply, in the course of a single night, the entire Bolshevik leadership of Mookat was done away with as they slept – from Agabekov the one-armed Chekist to Kuldash the District Party

Committee butcher who had bartered away his faith for the flesh of large-horned cattle. The response to this was the 'Red Terror': every local male between the ages of twenty and forty was exiled to the far North. Those able to move fast joined Yormuhammad in the mountains; those who moved too slowly were shot; and an entire regiment of Red Army soldiers under the command of Chanyshev-Tatar was stationed in the area to carry out the duties of the male population.

The apricots ripened outside, bright and translucent among leaves . . . leaves . . . leaves . . . The cherries grew darker and darker, and the children were unable to pick them all before nightfall. Oyimcha made jam, and instead of sugar she poured condensed grape juice over the cherries – or thick mulberry syrup. The syrup was viscous – and Oyimcha, sitting beside the hearth, moved the strainer slowly and heavily, slowly and heavily through the cauldron.

Obid-Kori was now the only literate Uzbek left in the village. Some Uzbeks had gone to Kashgar, some had been deported to the far North, others had died in the mountains and nobody, nobody had returned. And soon, when the region was declared part of Kirghizstan, there were no other Uzbeks left in the village at all.

Obid-Kori's nephew Shir-Gazi – who was married to Noroon, daughter of Togolok the sheep-shearer – had been the only literate Kirghiz in the village; for this reason, during indigenisation, he had been appointed Secretary of the Village Soviet. He at once reclassified the entire population of Mookat as Kirghiz, imposed traditional tribal tribute in addition to the various Soviet taxes and even asked his uncle to pronounce a fatwah to ensure prompt payment. Obid-Kori, however, sent Shir-Gazi packing as briskly as if he were the devil himself, and Shir-Gazi got his own back by denying his uncle the right to become a Kirghiz. And so it happened that, although all the rest of Mookat turned Kirghiz in the eyes of the Soviet authorities,

Obid-Kori remained irredeemably Uzbek – the only Uzbek left in the village.[70]

Noroon's family, who supplied the village soviets with wool from Alay sheep, naturally spoiled Shir-Gazi, but he was still further corrupted by his power as First Secretary. He became fat and red, like one huge belly, and, seen from behind, his head looked like a sheared hindquarter of one of his father-in-law's sheep. Shir-Gazi threw his considerable weight around to such effect that his envious father-in-law once said to him quite directly and openly, 'By Leninandstalin, I beg you to let me have your place for a fortnight, so I too can enjoy the pleasures of power!'

At first, Shir-Gazi refused, but Togolok had a word with his daughter, the beautiful Noroon, and after a week Shir-Gazi summoned the Kirghiz of Mookat to a meeting of the Village Soviet and decreed that, during his absence on a tour of inspection of socialist mountain pastures, Togolok Moldo-Ullu should take his place as First Secretary. And so for two weeks Togolok did as he pleased, fleecing the inhabitants of Mookat as if they were his own rams; and in return for allowing his father-in-law this pleasure Shir-Gazi acquired a flock of plump and woolly sheep in the mountain pasture of Kok-Bel – which was where he spent his two agonising weeks of separation from Soviet power.

But the children grew in spite of everything, the children grew just as bunches of grapes go on swelling . . . swelling . . . Oyimcha sewed belts for them during the languid summer days, slowly fluttering her swan-white sleeves . . . sleeves . . . sleeves . . . She embroidered lines of her own poetry on these belts in silk thread and the children learned them by heart as a defence against calumny and the evil eye.

Why, why, why did life turn out this way and no other way? And what other way is there? Is there another way in the world, or is that just a dream people dream? Or a dream dreamed by Allah himself, to console people? Oyimcha appears, carrying a full basket of grapes; she appears and disappears. And nothing is left in the place of her grapes, her bright, airy grapes – only patches of sunlight among vine-leaves . . . vine-leaves . . . vine-leaves . . .

Calumny and the evil eye did not fall on the children – Allah be praised! Calumny and the evil eye fell on Obid-Kori. The children had gone off to the bazaar, taking with them hens' eggs for holiday egg-battles; and the youngest, Mashrab, came back in tears, saying that the son of Soat-Moneybags had smashed everyone else's eggs with an egg-like stone he had found in the Kakyr-Say river. And nobody had been able to prove that this stone was not an egg.

Nothing had been forgotten. Obid-Kori was reminded that he had studied in a hotbed of opium for the people, that he had participated in the Kokand bourgeois-nationalist congress, and that he had gone on believing in his illusory Allah during the epoch of militant materialism. He was also accused of treason towards the Motherland and betrayal of the Kirghiz people. And who, you may ask, charged him with all this under article 58?[71] Kukash-Snubnose, whom Obid-Kori had himself taught to read and write. This green-eyed young Sart – now a Kirghiz NKVD officer – was interrogating Obid-Kori every other day in the main jail.

Oyimcha had been carrying a full basket of grapes, bright bunches of bright grapes, grapes, grapes, when Shir-Gazi had come with four policemen to arrest Obid-Kori.

And the children were at the bazaar, and the yard was empty, and only patches of light, patches of light lay on the ground, which was covered by the shade of vine-leaves . . . vine-leaves . . . vine-leaves . . . Oyimcha wept. Obliged as she was to hide from these profane ones, she cried from deep in the house; her tears fell like grapes, grapes, grapes and her wordless howl carried far beyond the gate . . .

Grapes lay scattered over the yard. Shir-Gazi and the four policemen trampled over them in their boots, pressing, squashing, stamping them down like patches of light, patches of light in a deserted court . . . court . . . courtyard . . .

Yes, life turned out this way and how else could it have turned? Words can turn out other ways, words can be replayed and re-plied, relayed and re-lied, rehearsed and re-versed; words can be the tools of a green-eyed Judgment-Day-Devil like Kukash-Snubnose – but life is one, and life is from Allah. And what do we know of it? It cannot be sensed or weighed between words any more than the rays of the sun can be sensed between leaves . . . leaves . . . leaves . . . And only the leaves' shadow catches the little patches of light, surrounds, frames, defines, confines, arrests.

Life happens in words. One person says or thinks of another: 'they did right' or 'they did wrong'. But what is this 'right' or 'wrong' outside of words? Or if words are turned upside down, turned head over heels? If, instead of leaves casting a shadow imposed by the light, the shadow gives birth to the leaves and light is the leaves' product?

The iron grating in the small prison window Obid-Kori looked through after saying his prayers had precisely this relationship to the sky and its blue, to its sun and its occasional white clouds. The grating was formed by two verticals and six rusty crossbars.

And after each interrogation by the Judgment-Day-Devil, when everything he said was turned back against him, old Obid-Kori, refusing to understand anything at all, sat on the stone bed beneath the grating and, between his repeated prayers, which gave words back their meaning, remembered a family legend told him by Oyimcha . . . Oyimcha . . .

Oyimcha's maternal grandfather, Mullah Tusmuhammad-Okhun, had studied as a young man in the Miri-Arab madrasah in Bukhara – the madrasah where Obid-Kori had studied fifty years after him. One winter, after reading the Koran in his cell, Tusmuhammad realized that it had been snowing. It had been snowing so thickly that he could no longer open the door. Snow fell for three days and three nights. Or maybe longer – Tusmuhammad, barely pausing in his studies, ate his entire store of food, all his thin porridge. And it went on snowing. There was no food left in the cell, and time did not stop. And Tusmuhammad prayed and read the Koran . . . prayed and read the Koran . . . He lost count of the days and nights. And it went on snowing. And during one of these countless days or countless nights he was sitting and listening to the falling snow and thinking about the might of Allah, who had sent people down on this earth just as he sends down snow, snowflake after snowflake, snowflake after snowflake, when he heard a strange noise in a corner of his cell. And he saw a shining hen. Together with seven golden chicks, she walked across the cell and out of the door, the snow dissolving before her as the door silently opened. The sun was shining and the muezzin was calling the faithful to their prayers. And the sky's blue, blue, blue pierced Mullah Tusmuhammad-Okhun's eyes so deeply that Obid-Kori was able to see traces of that celestial blue in them even after Tusmuhammad had gone blind in his old age.

Mullah Tusmuhammad-Okhun's teacher had told him that seven generations of his family would live under the protection of Allah, and Oyimcha, poor Oyimcha had believed this as if it were holy writ.

Oyimcha came every week, staying with relatives who lived opposite the prison and bringing sometimes prayer beads, sometimes flatbreads, once a jug for Obid-Kori's ablutions, once a secret note from their children. Her male relatives bribed the prison guards and passed her gifts on to Obid-Kori; there was even one occasion when Oyimcha threw a veil over her face and got as far as the prison gates herself – but a Russian standing there with a rifle drove her away, making the air thick with his swearing and cursing.

What, in any case, did it matter if calumny and the evil eye had fallen on Obid-Kori? Even little Mashrab was already fully grown, already a fine young man – Allah be praised! Mashrab at least had been like a golden chicken, protected from calumny and the evil eye. But Obid-Kori himself had evidently been unworthy to marry a descendant of the Prophet – may he be praised!

Repeated interrogations, repeated prayers, repeated thoughts were beginning to confuse Obid-Kori. Why had life turned out . . .

One night, when a sudden light fell on the metal grating (those two verticals and six crossbars) and the harsh clanking of cell doors made him rise from his iron bed (the same iron grating, the same two verticals and six horizontals, covered by a mattress Oyimcha had stuffed) Obid-Kori's torments came to an end. The wing of a night bird flashed outside the window and he was led into the prison yard. Seven Black Marias were waiting there, and the guards were leading men out, leading men out.

Obid-Kori took in deep lungfuls of the night mountain air – as relieved to be leaving his cell as Mullah Tusmuhammad-Okhun had been when the snow finally melted.

> *'Val Zukha, val laili iza sadja,*
> *Ma vadda'aka rabbuka va ma kala . . .*

> 'I swear by the bright shining of the day
> And by the night, when her darkness is spread wide,
> Your Lord never left you, nor is he displeased . . .'

Obid-Kori whispered to himself, and tears rolled down the thin beard on his cheeks.

Oyimcha, Oyimcha was sitting in the middle of the summer courtyard, beating cotton wool, spinning it with long switches . . .

switches . . . switches . . . In their broad white linen sleeves her arms were like fluttering wings and the cotton wool clinging to the slow, slow, slow switches flew high into the air, into the air, like celestial clouds . . . clouds . . . clouds . . .

The prisoners were loaded into Black Marias and taken off to the station in Gorchakov. There they were transferred to a goods wagon, with the same small grating as in the prison (two verticals and six crossbars) and taken silently-slowly down the iron road. Through chinks and holes in the floor of the wagon they could see two never-ending metal rails and those same short crossbars, repeated again and again and again, to infinity, and it seemed as if the earth herself had been put behind bars, framed, bound, confined, arrested, or as if they, in their goods wagon with the metal grating, had been separated from the earth for ever.

Why had life . . . The soul of Obid-Kori was flying over the earth, leaving Oyimcha behind, and the children were running after Oyimcha, Oyimcha, Oyimcha, whose long hair streamed behind her like bunches of grapes . . . grapes . . . grapes . . .

17

During the campaign after the death of Stalin to recruit new Party members 'from the machine-bench', it emerged that there were no machine-benches at all in Gilas. Or rather there was one – in the Labour workshop of the October School – but no one knew what to do with it. It was looked after by Abubakir-Snuffsniffer, the school caretaker, whose father had been school caretaker in the days of the Tsars, but this Abubakir was already so very old that the Party sensibly enough decided not to recruit him: why should the likes of him be granted the honour of dying a Communist death?

The local Party did, however, manage to respond to the directive: it was decided that new members should be recruited not only from the machine-bench, but also from the hoe, the mop, the broom and the shoe-cleaning brush – in short, from any proletarian walk of life, male or female, in Gilas. Cinema technician Ortik-Picture-Reels quickly decorated a banner with the words 'Proletarians from every Quarter of Gilas, Unite in the School Yard!' – and Bolta-Lightning climbed the column in the middle of the square, draped the banner over the loudspeaker and explained over the heads of the entire backward bazaar both the progressive meaning of the slogan and the precise time the proletariat was to unite.

The Party's call was answered only by Kun-Okhun the Uighur, who, being partially deaf, tried his best to answer every call that he heard; on this occasion, however, he responded because his wife, Djibladjibon-Bonu-Wagtail was convinced that some special goods or other would be on sale at the school, the same as during elections to the Supreme Soviet.

Taking the money she had hidden away in her trunk, she told her soot-black husband, a station freight handler, to clean himself up; then she dressed him in a pair of pyjamas she had bought for him as a summer suit, carefully tucked the trouser legs into his one pair of box-calf boots, which he had inherited from her cattle-dealer father, and sent him off to become a member of the Party, telling him it wouldn't be long before they made him into a man like Oktam-Humble-Russky.

On his way to join the Party, Kun-Okhun bumped into Timurkhan the wall-eyed Tatar, who was resting beside the railway line after intensive love with Murzina-Mordovka.

'Where are you going?' Timurkhan asked idly.

'No, I can't,' answered the deaf Kun-Okhun, assuming that Timurkhan was, as so often, in need of a drinking comrade.

Then Timurkhan looked at him out of his other eye and said with emphasis, 'Lend me ten roubles!'

'To the Party!' Kun-Okhun replied proudly.

'Fuck off then!' said Timurkhan, now turning both his divergent eyes back to the horizon. Kun-Okhun's hearing, however, had by then sharpened, and these words were more than he could pardon. More than he could pardon as a station freight handler, and more than he could pardon as a candidate member of the Party. A scuffle ensued – the wall-eyed Timurkhan repeatedly landing blows around Kun-Okhun's eyes and the deaf Kun-Okhun repeatedly boxing the small but agile Timurkhan's ears. The noise brought Sergeant-Major Kara-Musayev the Younger hurrying towards them with his gun, blazing away within earshot of plenty of people so that he could account for the cartridges he had already sold to Kuzi-Gundog. Kun-Okhun and Timurkhan, locked together like Siamese twins, quickly ran down the railway embankment and dived beneath the first stationary wagon they came to. Kara-Musayev fired a last shot and, pleased that he could now make his records balance, went back to the station to draw up a statement.

Half-blind and half-deaf, the two men ran down a corridor

between two sets of wagons until they tripped together over the protruding arse of Nabi-Onearm; he had been stealing his daily quota of cotton seeds from beneath the wagons, intending to sell them as cattle-fodder at three roubles a sack. The terrified Nabi shot up into the air, holding his one hand high above his head both as a sign of surrender and as a reminder of mitigating circumstances – but the sight of the two men rolling over the stones made Nabi-Onearm think that Gilas had already been corrupted, even though Stalin was barely in his grave, by that terrible bourgeois affliction, that plague from the past once known as 'play-with-the-beardless' and now called something like paedosexuality or homophilia.

His index finger pointing heavenward, Nabi furiously denounced this shame on the town of Gilas, invoking no less a witness than Allah, whom he had not called upon since he first went to school in 1924, the year of the death of Lenin: 'If you feel no shame in my presence, then at least have shame in the presence of Allah! How can you do this? How – at the time of the death of our immortal Leader, our beloved Comrade Stalin – can you sink so low?'

The two men were sitting on the stones beside the track, with no idea why Nabi was arraigning them, when they heard what sounded like the trump of the Last Judgment – Ta-ra! Ta-ra! – but was really the hooter of Akmolin's diesel shunter. The wagons behind the unappeasable Nabi, who was still spitting in denunciatory fury, began to move forward. And as the last wagon passed by, as the fire in Nabi's eyes began to fade at the sight of the deaf Kun-Okhun and the wall-eyed Timurkhan sitting before him like schoolboys waiting for the bell at the end of lessons, whom should they see but Tadji-Murad, jumping down from the footplate of this wagon with his two flags and his one whistle? With a squeal of brakes, the train then came to a stop at precisely the spot that allowed the bags containing Nabi's pickings to emerge from under the last wagon. Nabi desperately shook his head in denial; and his one hand – that sole reminder of his mitigating circumstances – continued to point towards the heavens.

On another day, to be honest, Tadji-Murad might have turned a blind eye – Nabi-Onearm, after all, took every fifth bag to Tadji-Murad's mother, the half-blind Boikush – but now that socialist property was being plundered by an entire collective, and at a time of such universal grief, Tadji-Murad could hardly remain silent. In the intervals between whistles so ear-splitting that even the deaf Kun-Okhun trembled and flag-waving so frenzied that not even Timurkhan's wall eyes could move fast enough, Tadji-Murad began to accuse them of a crime more terrible still. 'Dear Comrade Stalin's ashes have not grown cold,' he cried out to the horizons, 'and already you have created an international bandit-Trotskyist organisation to appropriate and plunder – yes, to loot and plunder – the wealth and property of our socialist Fatherland!'

Nabi's missing arm had rendered him unfit for military service and so he had never had Russian comrades to teach him their Greater Russian language. Tadji-Murad, however, had only recently returned from military service and so could curse and denounce the others in the most expansive of languages; this somehow made the prospect of long years in Siberia seem all the more real.

'You fucker, we should have gone for a drink like I said!' Timurkhan whispered in the ear of the deaf Kun-Okhun. 'Now Murzinka will get to hear of it.'

This thought caused him such sorrow that a tear fell from each of his autonomous eyes. Timurkhan could remember only too well what had happened after judgment was passed on some damned Shistakovich or other and the whole of Gilas – everyone from Tolib-Butcher, who had never held anything in his hand other than his cleaver and his own member, to the half-blind Boikush, who had also once handled Tolib's member – had signed an official condemnation of the anti-Soviet music of this unknown Shistakovich; yes, Timurkhan could remember only too well how his beloved Murzina-Mordovka, his Carmen-with-Eyes-Round-as-Cherries, had made herself unavailable, keeping her distance from him for years on end because of his reactionary individualism and petty-bourgeois mentality – and all merely because, afraid of being looked down on by Mefody-Jurisprudence, he had said he knew no Russian songs except 'Kalinka' and refused to add his name to this expression of collective indignation.

Year after year, in the gloom of lonely nights and lavatories, Timurkhan had cursed that shit of a Shistakovich. And then, at last, he had returned to Murzina's favour . . .

And now . . . now he might just as well lie down in front of a train!

As if hearing this despairing thought, the other train gave a loud hiss and inched forward, wheels squealing. Timurkhan sprang up, ran the length of one wagon in the direction the train was moving and laid his head on the rail. Nabi was so shocked that his already numb arm dropped to his side; Kun-Okhun froze. The wheels continued to move towards Timurkhan; Timurkhan lay still, one eye looking at the wheels and the other looking at the men doomed to remain guiltily in this world. Unable to bear a scream he could already hear all too clearly, Kun-Okhun leapt to his feet and was beside Timurkhan in eight strides; snatching him from under the approaching wheels, he threw him to one side like a sack of onions. Wheezing in some kind of death-ecstasy, Timurkhan tried to slip back beneath the oncoming wheels. Kun-Okhun got on top of him but, realising that he too was now in the path of these wheels and that this was no way to become a Party member, he quickly drew himself up to his full height – as erect as 'The Commissar' on the wall of Tordybay-Medals's office. And then, Allah alone knows how, Kun-Okhun was suddenly kneeling on the ballast beside the line, his right knee on Timurkhan's throat. And Timurkhan was no longer struggling; his tears were washing the foam from his lips and his whole body was quivering in time to the knocking of the wheels of the last wagons.

'Now your fucking Death will want its revenge. It'll be my turn next!' shouted Kun-Okhun, letting go of the puny Tatar.

Afraid of being caught up in yet more trouble, Tadji-Murad and Nabi-Onearm had by then silently slipped away; Akmolin gave a hoot to indicate that it was time to break off for lunch; and then Timurkhan, having wept his fill, stared with his wall eyes at Kun-Okhun's torn clothing and asked in the most sober of voices, 'What are you doing in pyjamas?'

In his usual random way Kun-Okhun answered, 'Mefody-Jurisprudence will know!'

Rather than tell him to fuck off a second time and so start another chain of disasters, Timurkhan gave a feeble shrug of the shoulders and agreed.

'Let's go and see him,' said Kun-Okhun. Leaning on one another for support, the two of them set off in the direction of the cotton factory and Mefody-Jurisprudence, Gilas's Number One Intellectual. Kun-Okhun had in fact imagined that Timurkhan had said something like, 'What on earth will they do to us now?' Knowing that no one except Mefody could possibly answer such a question, Kun-Okhun had suggested going to see him, and Timurkhan had agreed, knowing that no one even thought of calling on Mefody without first getting hold of a bottle or two. Yes, all Gilas knew that a bottle of 'tongue-loosener' poured into Mefody could be guaranteed to flow out of him again in the form of a free consultation about any branch of law whatsoever: Collective-Farm, Family or even Roman.

And so, while Kun-Okhun and Timurkhan wait in the midday sun as they wait for Fyokla-Whispertongue to return to the cotton factory shop from her lunch break, and while

Fyokla-Whispertongue enjoys herself inside the cab of the diesel shunter with one of Akmolin's apprentices, we have time for a few words about Mefody, who is lying in his room behind the depot, still hung over from the previous day's consultations.

Mefody was, apparently, the last illegitimate son of the great Russian traveller Mikhail Przhevalsky, who had journeyed through all the vast spaces between the Caucasus and the Taklamakan desert.[72] Mefody's mother, a widow from the first generation of the colonisers of Turkestan, had been laundering the gentleman's clothes as he rode towards Mongolia to discover his remarkable horse; as she hitched up her skirt to do the rinsing, the great traveller had taken her from behind. It was not until after the Glorious October Revolution, however, that she confessed all this to her family. Przhevalsky, as everyone knows, had the misfortune to die before the Revolution, and so it was only in the Rumyantsev Library that Mefody – who had been sent to study in Moscow by what had once been the Turkestan Geographic Society – first had the chance to acquaint himself with his father's deeds and achievements. He also found out that there were other researchers into the researches of Przhevalsky – and that the most valuable letters and diaries of all had been reserved by the Kremlin.

Who in the Kremlin was studying the heritage of the moustached traveller Mefody was unable to discover,[73] but he succeeded in tracking down three of the other researchers. In spite of differences of race, nationality and age, they all wore similar moustaches and gave off not the colourless and sickly air of scholarship, like everyone else in the library, but something vital and untameable; like colts, they were alive with the power of the steppe! For three months and three days Mefody studied their movements and their preferred spots for feeding and sleeping – and this detective work inspired him with an interest in jurisprudence which led to his transferring eagerly and without difficulty from the Geography Faculty to the Law Faculty. Why without difficulty? Because in those years the Geography Faculty was more popular than the Law Faculty, since it enabled its graduates to take off in a hurry to out-of-the-way places other than the Gulag – the only destination available to graduates of the Law Faculty. But Mefody had failed to grasp this. He merely plodded on, though now according to the discipline of Jurisprudence, along one and the same line of inquiry.

Through organising a centenary colloquium on the theme 'Methods of Capture in the Steppe and Reproduction in Captivity of the Przhevalsky Horse', he met a fourth researcher – a Mongolian with a thin moustache who played an animated part in the discussions. And Mefody discovered with horror, as he got to know the other researchers, that every one of their mothers, including an anonymous Arab and a Mongolian by the name of Gumdjadain Bangamtsaray, had laundered the Russian gentleman's shirts and trousers as he travelled in pursuit of his horse.

The young Mongolian told Mefody, who by then had also grown his hereditary moustache, that he had met three more fellow-researchers in Leningrad, in the Saltykov-Schedrin library. Mefody went there to carry out further inquiries and ascertained that one of them had no moustache at all; his mother had never been a washerwoman; and he was interested in Przhevalsky only because he was studying the spontaneous dissemination of dialectical materialism around the fringes of the Tsarist Empire. This whiskerless youth, however, told Mefody the precise number of the great traveller's illegitimate sons: eight. Mefody knew only of seven: himself, four in Moscow and two in Leningrad. Who then was the eighth?

To this question Mefody devoted all that remained of his studies, and indeed of his life, until the year 1937.[74]

Fyokla-Whispertongue returned to her shop and found the two men; glancing from side to side, she asked them the time.

Learning that she was half an hour late, she at once began, in her usual whisper, to accuse both the deaf Kun-Okhun and the wall-eyed Timurkhan of being good-for-nothing time-wasters. Only when Kun-Okhun asked for three bottles of vodka in exchange for half the savings from his wife's trunk did she, after glancing once again from side to side, disappear beneath the counter.

They reached Mefody's room just as Mefody, in the delirium of being without a single hair of the dog, was trying to recall, article by article, the Civil-Procedural Code, which he had memorised, immediately after the Corrective-Criminal Code, during his time in the Solovetsky Islands[75] – but for some reason he had faltered twice during the Karaganda Criminal-Procedural Code and had even stumbled in the middle of the Land Code, which he had committed to memory during his time as a free worker in Chita.[76]

After one bottle he managed to recall the Civil-Procedural Code not only by articles but even by sub-sections, including the Commentaries.[77] During the second bottle his two visitors kept distracting him; one was asking something about Party member-ship, the other something about pyjamas. After the third bottle Mefody managed to get a clearer grasp of these two questions and even to see them as two aspects of a single broader question, but just then Timurkhan sent Kun-Okhun 'in the name of the Party' to fetch new supplies of vodka. On the way Kun-Okhun was fired upon by Kazakbay-Happytrigger, the caretaker of the wool factory, who had the same concerns as Kara-Musayev about cartridges he had sold illegally to Kuzi-Gundog, and so Kun-Okhun had to return on his belly, executing a flanking manoeuvre around both the wool and the cotton factories that took up a whole hour.

They drank the first two bottles of the second series in silence; a listener might have thought they were mourning the death of their Leader. Mefody-Jurisprudence not only brought together in his consciousness every Law, Code and Commentary he had learned in the camps but also for some reason rummaged in his beloved briefcase – which he used at night as a pillow, in the day as a table, and the rest of the time as a trunk, a home for all the scant property he had accumulated in the course of his life – and took out some battered book or other which he then began to wave in the air, claiming it was the Law of Laws, Code of Codes and Commentary on all Commentaries and telling Timurkhan (who had by then become not only wall-eyed but also deaf) and Kun-Okhun (who had by then become not only deaf but also wall-eyed) that he had at last unveiled the Truth he had always known and that they should now address him not as Mefody but as Benjamin. While he was shouting this crazed gibberish, the book fell from his hands and Timurkhan was impelled by compassion to crawl up to Mefody and read out loud, 'T-t-t-omm-masss Mmma-nnn . . . [he gave a hiccup of excitement] Io-seeff a-and hee-ees brrrothers!'

'Yes!' shouted Mefody-Benjamin. 'Precisely!' Then he began telling a broken tale of exiles and betrayals and hunger and kingship, a tale so terrible that neither Timurkhan, when he had returned to being simply and straightforwardly wall-eyed, nor Kun-Okhun, when he had returned to being simply and straightforwardly deaf, ever again dared to recall it – either in solitude, or in the presence of others, or even when it was just the two of them drinking away their hangovers.

All Timurkhan remembered from this tale about Yusuf was that his mother had been a washerwoman and that, for some reason, Mefody seemed more exercised by this simple fact than by everything else put together. 'His m-m-mother was a washerwoman, brothers! Don't you understand?' Mefody had kept stammering through his tears – and all Timurkhan had been able to say in response was 'Not a fucking thing!'

And what the simple-hearted Kun-Okhun remembered made no sense at all: the Party, Stalin, a beautiful but adulterous wife and then, for some reason, this Yusuf, who not only used to rule but still does rule and for some reason will always continue to rule. Did he mean Yusuf-Cobbler? But then what did Comrade Stalin have to do with it? And so Kun-Okhun had repeated after Timurkhan, 'Not a fucking thing!'

'You don't believe me? You don't believe me?' How could Mefody ever convince the wall-eyed and the deaf? All of a sudden he cried out, 'Pee on my head then, if you don't believe me! Pee on my head in front of the whole town!'

Soon after the three of them went out onto the street, Kun-Okhun had felt a sudden, burning stab – a stab of pain occasioned not, as he first thought, by a fear that he too was being betrayed, that his beloved Djibladjibon-Bonu was seeing too much of Yusuf-Cobbler, but by the impact of a bullet. After saying goodbye to the savings from his wife's trunk and his dream of a career in the Party, Kun-Okhun had passed within range of those whose duty it was to guard the station and its freight trains.

And then, outside Huvron-Barber's little shop, in the presence of Huvron-Barber and Yusuf-Cobbler, poor Mefody's request was answered: Timurkhan executed civil punishment on this drunkard of an intellectual, this brother of his many unfortunate brothers. Yes, he made Kun-Okhun, who was on fire from both physical and emotional wounds, take off his pair of summer pyjamas, the ends of which were still neatly tucked into his box-calf boots, climb up onto one of Huvron's chairs, and piss out all his hatred for the discord-fomenting intelligentsia onto the thin-haired, broad-browed head of this son of a washerwoman and a traveller.

'I'm Benjamin, I'm Benjie,'[78] Mefody cried pathetically when the careful Yusuf-Cobbler, who normally pissed against the wall of Huvron's small shop where no one could see him, decided to take advantage of this opportunity and expend a whole day's worth of urine beside that of Kun-Okhun. 'And he's Yusuf,'

Mefody wept – and his tears mingled with the two streams of urine as he pointed somewhere up above, perhaps at Yusuf, perhaps somewhere higher still in the heavens.

No one understood anything at the time. Nor did anyone remember anything afterwards. What, after all, was there to remember? A stain from some evaporated urine? At the time of the death of Yosif Stalin!

In any case, whatever it was that happened, there was certainly no new intake of Party members in Gilas after the death of the Father of Nations.

18

As he fell asleep, the boy quite forgot whether he was in the cemetery or in his attic in the chaikhana. Everywhere hung the same darkness, full of silence and sleep, and he dreamed of a life he had long forgotten, of a village lying in a hollow in the mountains. From the pass you could see Mookat as clearly as if it rested in the hollow of your hand: every line of its streets and buildings, and the tall, triangular poplars he used to walk under on his way to the house where he had been born.

It was as if someone invisible were walking beside him and saying: 'Tell me what this is! And this!' And with the ease with which you talk about your first home, about where you were born and where you lived your first years, he chatted away to this invisible figure. Here was the park where he had run about with the other nursery-school children, where they had played 'Swans and Geese' while the teacher played on her squeeze-box and sang about the stars and about the word that bound the boy and little Nadya: love. The poplars here were tall and full of air, and the air was deep blue in summer but in autumn it became a transparent yellow and it whirled around together with the slow smooth leaves, like the water around the little fish in the aquarium.

And here was the barn. They were taken to this barn after lessons, and here they sat in a circle on aprons or sackcloth piled high with newly picked tobacco leaves. The leaves were warm and sticky; the children used needles as big as kebab skewers to thread the leaves onto strings, and their hands would become as sticky and fragrant as the leaves themselves. When the teacher could no longer bear the dirt smeared over their faces, the boys went off and washed and then crept beneath the long, long row of leaves that had been hung up to dry, and there they lay, in this dizzying space of drying tobacco, living earth and warm sun, until the next class came to take their place. After that it would be the turn of the girls.

And here, in the bogs by the Kakyr-Say, where you only had to run a few yards and a cold dirty slime would ooze up between your toes, they used to play football . . .

But this was not what he wanted to talk about. What he wanted to talk about was his granny. No, not granny Hadjiya whom he had run away from, but his other granny – the one to whom he was taking his invisible companion, telling him what an astonishing granny she was. She was very tall indeed, and thin. And, to be honest, rather like a vulture. Granny Oyimcha had not a nose but a beak, and her eyes were equally sharp. But that didn't matter, although there had been a time in his childhood when he had been as frightened of her as of a bird of prey . . .

One winter's day he had been standing in the Gilas bazaar selling his naan breads when Ozoda – Oppok-Lovely's niece – told him that a visitor had arrived. Everyone there had heard about Ruzi-Crazi's crazy letter, and so they had all laughed. And then, before the boy had had time to think, he saw not Ruzi-Crazi but Granny Oyimcha, all in black, tall and frightening, walking through the snow with her arms tucked crosswise into her sleeves. It really was as if a mountain bird had swooped down on their little dump of a town. Quite without meaning to, remembering what his mother had once said about Granny Oyimcha, the boy had shrunk into himself like a mouse, unable to forget an image that was imprinted in him as if in the long-ago frame of that long-ago window with the double panes and the glittery cotton wool in between them that looked like fresh-fallen snow.

As for Ruzi-Crazi, the stupid woman had taken it into her head to come all the way from Mookat – nearly a thousand kilometres – and had turned up at the bazaar with no warning at all. She had laid down her baby and, in front of everyone, had rushed at the boy, calling him a poor little orphan as she covered him with slobbery kisses and wailed about the death of his mother. Why did she need to wail if it was neither forty days nor a year since his mother's death?[79] And she had brought the whole mahallya *running into their yard when, on meeting Granny Hadjiya, she started up a second time, howling about the poor orphan and calling him a piece of her own liver, a piece of her own spleen, a precious drop of her own heart's blood.*

And then she had begun living with them. At the depot that month they were loading pumpkins onto lorries, and the children were coming back almost every day with two or three misshapen pumpkins they had been given by way of wages, and so Granny Hadjiya kept cooking either pumpkin in ravioli or pumpkin in milk, or just plain pumpkin soup. Ruzi-Crazi sat most of the time in the yard, feeding her baby and chewing pumpkin seeds. And so the days had passed – and Granny had ended up cross-questioning her grandson, evidently unable to find out from her own long conversations with Ruzi-Crazi what on earth the woman was up to.

The boy knew she was called Ruzi-Crazi, but he didn't know why. He didn't mind her being there because the only way they could feed an extra mouth was by getting pumpkins straight from the depot, and so Granny allowed him to work there instead of insisting he go to the bazaar to sell naan breads. Ruzi-Crazi did, admittedly, often lull her baby to sleep by saying – probably more for Granny Hadjiya's ears than the baby's – that there was nothing more important in the world than kindness and, since they had come to this house to be kind, the best thing the baby could do was to keep growing. The baby would duly fall asleep, but Granny would toss and turn, groaning as if her rheumatism was playing up.

After a while they almost stopped talking in the evenings; Granny was sleeping badly and so she usually went to bed immediately after their pumpkin supper. In the daytime she too started going to the bazaar, with a bowl of hurriedly roasted pumpkin seeds. On one such day – so the other boys told him afterwards – a lame man with a moustache had come to their house and Ruzi-Crazi had once again let out a howl that had brought the whole mahallya *straight to their door. It turned out that her husband had spent all his month's pension searching for this half-wit daughter of half-wit parents who for some* reason or other was feeling badly treated – and since the accepted way for an Uzbek woman to let the world know how disgracefully she had been treated was to go and stay with her parents, or with some other relatives, the kinless Ruzi had had no choice but to travel a thousand kilometres to Gilas, even though Granny Hadjiya wasn't really related to her at all. And so her lame husband with a moustache had given her a good hammering with his fists and one of his crutches and then led her back to their little mountain village as if she were a stray cow.

And a month later she had sent a letter that the boy had read out loud to all the old women in the mahallya. In it, word for word, was what Ruzi-Crazi used to say at night to her baby; it was as if she had written the letter in the middle of the night, while her baby cried and her lame husband slept. This seemed all the more probable in view of the fact that her words about kindness were interrupted by a crazy postscript addressed to Granny: 'All day and night you stuff yourself with pumpkin and you've turned into a great fat pumpkin yourself!' These words had such a powerful effect that for a moment Granny's bloated and helpless face really did look like a misshapen pumpkin.

It was because of this letter that everyone in the bazaar had laughed when Ozoda told the boy that a visitor had arrived at his home. But when they saw tall, black Granny Oyimcha walking through the white snow, they fell silent. Or was it that the boy went deaf? All he could remember was glimpsing out of the corner of one eye how everyone slipped back behind their tables and began fiddling about with their weights.

19

In the end Garang-Deafmullah was the only mullah left in Gilas.

Though nowhere near as talented, he had been a diligent student of Zokhor Alam from the Alam Shakhid district of the Old City. When the heathens from the security organs had arrested his Teacher, they had classified Garang-Deafmullah as an under-age assistant, oppressed by a representative of the dying classes and clergy. Garang was indeed still unable to 'strike letter against letter', that is, to read out loud a sentence written in Arabic, although he had learned by heart much of what he had heard from his Teacher's lips.

It was this very slow-wittedness that had once led his father to box him on the ear. The future deafmullah, unfortunately, happened to have hidden in that ear some Russian tobacco from the bazaar, and this filth burst his eardrum and so earned him the nickname that would stay with him until his dying day.

When those damned heathens arrested Zokhor Alam, Garang saw the way things were going and decided to stop practising all religious rites except that of circumcision, which he continued to carry out in and around Gilas in order to provide for his family. He was as competent at this as one of today's surgeons; ever since he was a child, after all, he had been pruning vines for Mahmud-Hodja, who was a friend of his father. Yes, Garang-Deafmullah was a true professional; wrapped in singed cotton wool, the circumcised members of the local boys were fully healed within a couple of weeks.

Large numbers of baby boys were born in the years before the War, as if people foresaw the need to provide themselves with plenty of male descendants, and Garang enjoyed a stable income. Drying in the sun among his apricots and tomatoes were whole garlands of rings of skin, waiting to serve as charms during the long childless years when the men were all serving as soldiers. Nevertheless, Garang-Deafmullah did not know peace of mind. The security organs were rumoured to be turning their attention to circumcision, and colleagues in Chakichmon, Allon, Akhun-Guzar and Takhtapul had already been arrested for 'sabotage of members'; Garang-Deafmullah's primal fear of these organs gave him no rest until the day he looked at his own adult yet still uncircumcised son – he hadn't dared abandon the boy to the knife of his rival Chilchil, but the thought of cutting into his own flesh and blood was still more frightening – and happened to recall a precept of his late teacher Zokhor Alam (Allah's blessing upon him!): 'When Allah sends retribution, one must hurry to Him with a sacrifice.'

And so he decided to follow the example of Abraham (May Allah grant peace to him and all his descendants!) and sacrifice his own son.

Yes, Garang-Deafmullah recommended his son to Umarali-Moneybags, who recommended him to Oktam-Humble-Russky, who recommended him to First Secretary Akmal-Ikrom,[80] who recommended him for work in the security organs.

For eighteen months Garang-Deafmullah's son participated as a 'witness' in night searches. For two years he escorted prisoners in Black Marias. And at the end of his fourth year, when even most of the NKVD officers themselves were in prisons or camps, a shortage of reliable cadres led to his sudden elevation to the position of Gilas's senior NKVD investigator.

Garang-Deafmullah quietly went on carrying out circumcisions. He even got his son to have Chilchil – whose members, after being bandaged with a dressing of mouldy maize flour, had started healing in only a week – sentenced to several years' exile in the steppes of Kazakhstan.

But the War began and a secret directive was issued to the security organs with regard to 'sabotage of members during military operations launched by the victorious Red Army against the German-Fascist invader'. And so the son, intensifying his activist zeal in order to escape being sent to the Front, conducted a house interrogation – in the presence of his mother and little sister – of his own father. He gathered evidence from around the house – the split reed into which foreskins were inserted, a cut-throat razor, a strap for sharpening this razor, cotton wool, matches and even five dried rings of skin which he discovered among his mother's dried tomatoes and which he identified as 'cuttings from the penises of males between the ages of seven and ten'. All this ended with the son sentencing the father to house arrest and then retiring to his room to write up his records.

Disgraced in front of his women by this drop of his own sperm that was now standing forth as an open adversary,[81] Garang-Deafmullah took the dried rings of skin, said a prayer over them before burying them in the yard, and crept silently into the office of the Senior Investigator for Gilas and its environs.

Yes, like Abraham, Garang-Deafmullah had resolved to kill his own son.

His son was sleeping, over the third line of his account of the interrogation.

What happened next is uncertain – although it is rumoured that Garang's daughter Robiya-Baker once talked to Banat-Pielady, who passed on her words in secret to Zumurad, Fatkhulla-Frontline's beautiful but barren daughter, who in turn spoke to Uchmah-Prophecies. What Uchmah recounted is that Garang-Deafmullah silently removed a TT revolver from his son's trousers. Bending down over the sleeping investigator, he numbly mumbled a prayer. The investigator heard nothing. Garang-Deafmullah twice kissed the terrible instrument of Providence and held it to his son's temples, first one side and then the other. One of his own tears then happened to fall onto the revolver. Using both hands, Garang-Deafmullah pulled on the stiff trigger; nothing happened. Then Garang-Deafmullah called up all his strength, which somehow made him stand up on tiptoe. The trigger yielded. There was a terrible report and Garang-Deafmullah fell to the ground, as if dead.

What had happened was improbable: as the father bent over his son and pressed on the trigger, the teardrop had made his fingers slip and he had lost his aim. And so Garang-Deafmullah shot off the tip of his own manly pride and joy, together with the nail phalanx of his right big toe. Startled by the sudden report, the son jumped to his feet and, seeing blood pouring over his father's trousers and slippers, had been about to send him to hospital when he realised that this was out of the question: his father had carried out the purest act of sabotage against a fully developed male member. The son then resorted to the sacred method employed by his father for many a year; he took from the table the cotton wool and box of matches he had just gathered as evidence, singed the cotton wool and wrapped it round the bleeding source of his own life.

The father was back on his feet only towards the end of the fourth week; his age, and the loss of his right big toe, slowed the process of healing. He then went deaf in his other ear, so as not to hear the gossip.

Witty anecdotes, embellished versions of stories told by certain women with one-track minds, duly found their way to the ears that are always listening. For 'concealment of the sabotage of members on a significant scale, considering the age and social standing of Garang-Deafmullah', his son was dismissed from the security organs and sent straight to a penal battalion on the front line, from which he returned at the end of the war as a Hero of the Soviet Union. He was immediately accepted by the Pedagogical Institute, which even waived the requirement that he sit the entrance exam, and he soon became history teacher to the senior classes of the Gilas school.

During the mid-1950s, when the illegally repressed were being belatedly rehabilitated, Garang-Deafmullah's now middle-aged but still uncircumcised son sent a petition to a Party Congress, begging to be pardoned before the Court of History in view of his heroism both as a citizen and as a soldier. Six months later the Congress replied that he had been reinstated in the ranks of the NKVD as a retired sub-lieutenant, and at the next school parade he was elected Honorary Chekist, in the place of poor Kuchkar-Cheka, who was drinking himself to death.

Garang-Deafmullah had given up carrying out circumcisions in the face of competition from Chilchil, who had also been rehabilitated, but he had begun practising other religious rites. And when he heard that Muslims were now being allowed to perform the Hadj, he went to the Kok-Terek Bazaar and sold a yearling bullock along with its mother, intending to use the money to travel to Mecca and so redeem a life spent in vain.

A month later, as was the custom, he was summoned to the now more decorously behaved security organs for a prophylactic conversation. Gogolushko, who at the time was still Second Secretary of the Party Committee and whose daughter Garang-Deafmullah had once publicly denounced as a prostitute, had inquired in the politest of tones: 'Tell us now, what if the mullahs of Mecca and Medina were to ask you, Garang-Deafmullah, to stay with them and pray for them too in their holy places? Would you agree to stay with them?' Dear Garang-Deafmullah, his simple soul sensing not a trap but a confident faith in his own orthodoxy, replied without a moment's hesitation, 'Inshallah!' At the end of this conversation, the representatives of the Party and the security organs took it in turns to shake hands with him and asked him to go back home and wait. And so Garang-Deafmullah began to wait.

His documents were now far away, floating about in higher realms. And while he waited, every one of his contemporaries passed away. People prayed to Allah for Garang-Deafmullah to live a long life – otherwise there would be no one left to sing prayers over the dying. But not a word was said about his application. The cemetery had by then grown so full that the dead were being buried on the periphery of the 'Fruits of Lenin's Path' collective farm. As a result of this interminable waiting, Garang-Deafmullah at last made peace with his ageing son. But at a banquet of the teachers' collective the Party organiser let slip something about 'the impossibility of allowing the potential defector Deafmullah-Garang Mir-Gaidar Afat-Ullaev to travel beyond the borders of our Motherland and the urgent need for an intensification of politico-educational work among the collective of the cattle-trading section of the Kok-Terek Bazaar, which has allowed . . .'

That evening the son tried to explain everything to the father in the presence of both his mother and his younger sister. The details of this conversation are unknown – unknown even to Banat-Pielady, Zumurad-Barrenwomb, Guloyim-Pedlar and even to Uchmah herself. But that night, bereft of his dream of Mecca and Medina, Garang-Deafmullah died of a broken heart. The following morning his son took him to the Kok-Terek Cemetery, not far from the Cattle Bazaar.

Thus the organs took their revenge on Garang-Deafmullah.

When the War began, no one was happier than the barefoot and bareheaded Tadji-Murad, the son of the half-blind Boikush. He ran up and down Papanin Street, shouting so loudly that the whole street could hear, 'Hurrah! Hurrah! Hurrah! Now they'll be showing new films! Even better than *The Mannerheim Line*![82]

Gilas Party Committee Second Secretary Gogolushko once heard a voice. In the middle of the night this voice said, 'Shit, Nikolay – we'll clean everything up ourselves!' – and Gogolushko for the first time in his life, with no sense of tightness in his guts and without holding anything back, expelled everything that had accumulated inside him. In the morning Gogolushko was woken by his wife, who had a sharp sense of smell, and he discovered with horror that, only two hours before a meeting of the Party Committee, he was smeared from head to foot with his own excrement. Nevertheless, what he felt in his heart was joy – and he threw back the quilted blanket. His wife fell silent and then burst into lamentations, as if he had passed away, and then, as if he really had passed away, began spraying the bed with eau de Cologne – again and again, a third time, a fourth time, a fifth time. And Gogolushko, lying in the middle of the foul-smelling bed, remained immersed in what lay far beyond the understanding of his poor fool of a wife.

Only one thing troubled Gogolushko: the fact that They had not cleaned up as They promised. Still, only the weak in spirit measure their lives by such trifles – trifles that can be put right by any cleaner or washerwoman like Auntie Lina the Greek Communist – and from that day, or rather from that night, Gogolushko was a man with a calling.

For two years, exploiting his authority as Second Secretary, he went into the local bakery every night; at first, he simply smeared his bureaucratic hands with the dough of honest labour, but then a mixture of idleness and some obscure urge led him to start moulding all kinds of little devils. After a while, the Deputy Secretary of the Party Cell at the Bakery appointed himself Gogolushko's production technician and started baking these devils in the oven. Gradually a whole workshop came into being and Zukhur's grocery store began to sell Gogolushko's hand-crafted little witches and devils. Misshapen and swollen but well-baked, these were at first bought only by Djibladjibon-Bonu-Wagtail, who fed them to her hens, but as soon as people realised that these evil spirits were baked from first-grade flour, a quarter of the cattle-owners of Gilas turned their backs on Nabi-Onearm, who had until then supplied them with stolen cotton and sesame seeds, and began instead to make use of the artistic productions of the Second Secretary. Around the same time, two solo exhibitions of the work of this self-taught primitivist sculptor were opened with considerable pomp and ceremony: at the Gilas Party Propaganda Institute and – thanks to the patronage of an influential friend of Gilas, Academician Pyotr Mikhailovich Sholokh-Mayev – in some other town in the region.

When, however – as an example of an approved Party initiative – the whole devilish enterprise was automated, Gogolushko fell into the grip of *toskà*. Once and for all, he took to the bottle.

This marked the beginning of his second life. He had always drunk deep, but the burden of being chosen made him drink deeper still. No less than thirteen times he was attacked by the heeby-jeebies: his own baked devils came to visit him, dancing round him like giant figures out of Matisse and asking why he had thrust them into that burning hell of a bakery oven. It was then, in despair, that he began to look with contempt at run-of-the-mill drunkards who ate while they drank – and above all at that half-baked, half-drunk, half-witted, half-educated fool by the name of Mefody. Gogolushko's wife deserted him, as did his comrade Master-Railwayman Belkov, his faith in Communism destroyed by Gogolushko's embittered decline. The Party, however, did not desert him.

First Party Secretary Buri-Bigwolf was not, as it happened, in the least put out by Gogolushko's drinking bouts. On the contrary, he made the most of the freedom they allowed him; Buri's friends and relatives, and even the friends and relatives of his friends and relatives, soon began to reap the benefits of Party membership. Gloom-dogged Gogolushko was dragged along once a week to Committee Meetings, during which he would silently raise a hand or hiccup his agreement. Buri-Bigwolf supplied him with a weekly special delivery of food, and Marleon – a former Party official at the Gilas Bakery who had been enabled by Oppok-Lovely to change his name from Marlen to Marleon[83] and who now had his eye on the post of Third Party Secretary – succeeded in arranging for Gogolushko to be registered as an in-patient at the clinic set up by Janna-Nurse in connection with a new Party initiative to test the resilience of the human organism with regard to certain toxic liquids.

The evening after being told this at the Committee Meeting following his thirteenth encounter with the heeby-jeebies, as he lay on his hospital bed after downing a bottle of ethanol and despairingly nibbling a chunk of plaster off someone's leg, Gogolushko heard the same voice as before say, 'Nikolay, the Word!' This sounded like a command to read, but the only reading material Gogolushko could find was some indecipherable text whose letters blurred together with those of the Instructions in Case of Fire on the non-flammable metal cupboard.

Gogolushko got up early, while it was still dark, and tried to respond to this call, but he had no idea what he should read. There had been such power, however, in the call's unadorned simplicity that he decided he must read whatever he could get his hands on: from the slogans of Kara-Musayev to the chants of blind Hoomer and from Osman-Anon's *Soviet Sport* to the gibberish of Mefody-Jurisprudence. And he began to buy, or rather requisition, everything from *Fundamentals of Explosive Making* to Shabistari's *Rosary of the Mysteries*.[84] But it was, in the end, mysticism that got the upper hand. Gogolushko not only gave up drinking but also began exchanging worldly goods for words of wisdom: four volumes of Simenon from the Party Committee Bookstall for *Gems of Masonic Philosophy*, or three still serviceable Party Committee leather chairs for Yusuf-Cobbler's family heirloom – a book in Aramaic about the Kaballah. Basit-OrgCom brought him Olloyar the Sufi[85] in place of the Party dues that his friend Faiz-Ulla-FAS had so far failed to pay; Huvron-Barber brought him the poetry of Rumi in exchange for ensuring that his wife-murdering son ended up in a labour camp not far from Gilas, to work there as a barber.

Alas, alas, alas, Gogolushko proved unable to read anything of what he had struggled so doggedly to obtain. The books merely accumulated on his shelves like so many dead souls, his sense of mission grew only stronger for being so entirely unfulfilled – and then, one night, overwhelmed by a profound gloom not befitting a member of the Party, Nikolay Gogolushko began to write.

He read the first ten books of his Writings into the Unknown to Basit-OrgCom, who, in his devotion to the Party, not only listened to every word of this balderdash during an official inspection tour of Party cells in the villages but even remarked, 'Yes, very interesting!' Basit's praise may have been sincere, but Gogolushko's writings soon ceased to hold the interest of Gogolushko himself – new and deeper mysteries were already knocking at the door of his mind. Once, after extending an invitation via Kara-Musayev the Younger to Zangi-Bobo the great collector of words, he rashly showed the latter some of his manuscripts, including some unbound pages about the soul's journey through the world in search of the Spring of Life. In the halting Russian that was at that time spoken by over a hundred million people, Zangi-Bobo read these pages out loud. And that night Gogolushko at last understood the true nature of his calling.

Read, Reader! Read about how Nikolay Gogolushko traced the Triangle of the Universe on the Party Committee globe and removed from the secret safe of Osman-Anon – after the latter's mysterious disappearance – the holy Almagest stone that controlled the world. 'Look,' Gogolushko would say to Basit, 'this stone is the centre of the world's gravitational field. Turn the stone round and you will feel it become ten times lighter than it is now!' Basit would obediently rotate this stone that Osman-Anon had once used to knock nails back into his boots or to wedge the door shut on a draughty evening, but he felt nothing – although he always responded to unfamiliar instructions with a nod of agreement. The excited Gogolushko would suggest he take the stone in the other hand. Basit would do as he was told and again feel nothing, although he would agree once again that the gravitation exerted by the asymmetrical cobblestone was now nonlinear and multidimensional.

Alas, although Gogolushko exhausted the simple-souled Basit, who imagined everything in the world to be a manifestation of the cunning subtlety of the Party line, and although Gogolushko made Basit shave off all his hair and accompany him at the Party Committee's expense on a mission if not to Tibet then at least to the Pamirs, to the Yagnobi people on the Roof of the World, he failed to find the Spring of Life – if only because the Party turned against him and ceased to subsidise the now unbridled aspirations of his soul. Yes, Oppok-Lovely expelled him from the Party after he attempted – exploiting his authority as Second Secretary rather than the powers of the Almagest or of the talisman presented to him in the Pamirs – to appropriate for himself the wide-ranging manuscripts of Hoomer on the grounds that they were ideologically dangerous; in fact, of course, he saw Hoomer's words as anti-Gogolushkinist heresy.

This was the time of the correspondence, still famous in Gilas, between Gogolushko and the Party. The closely argued replies of the latter were written by Mefody-Jurisprudence, whom Oppok-Lovely had bribed with an offer of full board and lodging. As for Gogolushko, he penned repentant letters renouncing all he had done during his hours as Secretary of the Party Committee and all he had accumulated as a result of these hours – and calling upon his comrades to follow his example. This apostasy was more than the Gilas Party Committee could pardon; not content with Mefody-Jurisprudence's crushing philippics about Gogolushko's betrayal of the Party's noble ideals, the Committee requested that a meeting of the Party Committee of an important junction station up the line should also be devoted to the case of this turncoat from Communism. And so the expropriator was expropriated and Hoomer's manuscripts ended up safe in the hands of Oppok-Lovely.

Oppok-Lovely showed no mercy. It was decreed at the same meeting that, in view of his failure to supervise his subordinate, Buri-Bigwolf should be dismissed from his post and transferred to the medical clinic to assume responsibility for lice and fleas – since this was the only work that such a 'parasite', as Oppok-Lovely put it, might understand. Buri was replaced as First Secretary by Basit-OrgCom – the same Basit who had for so long played the role of Gogolushko's loyal proselyte and disciple.

'Every Christ has his Judas!' Gogolushko muttered to himself on his way back from the Junction Station Party Committee to the Junction Station itself. Life was no more than excrement – excrement smeared over the body of life. That was how everything had begun, and that was how it was all ending. Gogolushko was not, however, remembering the call he had long ago heard in his sleep – no, it was just that all the space between the rails was smeared with excrement from passing trains. As was his life. At this point something elusive flashed through his consciousness – as if an electrical contact had sparked and at once been broken. He looked in his briefcase for his pen and notepad. But then his thoughts were thrown into confusion by the 16.48 local, which suddenly appeared from behind him. Gogolushko rushed towards the platform, clutching his half-open briefcase in both hands. Just as he reached the rear of the train, there was a whistle, and he had barely managed to thrust his briefcase into the diminishing space between the automatic doors of the Riga-manufactured coach when the train began to move. Gogolushko skipped after it, trying to squeeze through the door or – failing that – to recover his half-open briefcase. The accursed Latvians, however, had done a good job, and the door was unyielding. Gogolushko reached the end of the platform; he could shout and run no further. There was another whistle – and his briefcase was gone.

'That's All!' said the same voice as before, and he felt overcome by the extraordinary fullness of this 'All' – an All in which the whole of Nikolay Gogolushko, so tiny in comparison, was subsumed. For a long time he stood at the end of the platform, staring blankly at the receding local train and the rails left trailing behind it . . .

No, he didn't lose his mind – he had done that long ago – nor did he throw himself under the next train. Far more prosaically, he boarded the next train and travelled on it to the next station. And from there he went by the following train to the following station. And so to Gilas, which he reached only long after midnight. His briefcase had not been handed in anywhere.

After sleeping on the station bench to the sound of Akmolin's hoots and Tadji-Murad's squeals until the arrival of the dawn express from Moscow, he set off back up the line on foot, like one of the *illuminati*. On Gogolushko went, from sleeper to sleeper, gazing glumly at every bit of garbage, every bit of soaked and wind-dried paper; every now and then, or maybe less often still – every half-kilometre, or maybe only every kilometre – he would pick something up and, standing there on the bed of the iron road, read slowly through it. Where was he going, Nikolay Gogolushko the dervish? In search of his briefcase, in search of his bag, of his beggar's pouch.

22

Granny Hadjiya's house had two rooms; it had a tiled roof, and the walls were made from unbaked bricks. The house had been built soon after the War, along with all the other buildings to the right-hand side of the railway; until then the area had been scrubland, stretching as far as the Salty Canal, the Zakh Canal and a nameless black river.

Granny's house was thirty yards from the railway line, twenty yards from the chaikhana and ten yards from Gilas's only tailor's: the 'Papanin Tailoring Co-operative' or, as it was called later – after Izaly-Jew had replaced Moisey-Master as director – the 'Individual Cut Co-operative'.

One room had two windows with gratings and an earth floor covered by a single piece of plain felt; this was where they received guests. A trunk stood in one corner, and on top of the trunk was a stack of flowery cotton blankets. The trunk was the most mysterious place in Granny's house: it was where Granny stored her best china, which was only taken out when Great-Grandad Mahmud-Hodja from Balasagun was visiting; and it was where she kept the special sweets they ate only on Mavlyud (the Prophet's Birthday), Kurban-Khait (the Feast of the Sacrifice)[86] and the First of May (International Workers' Day). There were also three photographs, showing Granny with each of her first three husbands – all of whom had died – and a newspaper that her present husband (the boy's grandad, or rather step-grandad) used to take out if it was an important occasion and he had run out of things to boast about. It was like in the fairy-tales that the boy used to read to Granny as she lay there groaning because of her rheumatism: just as the water of life would bubble up to heal a wound, just as a magic tablecloth would conjure up instantaneous meals, just as a magic club would appear at the darkest moment of a battle and flatten the panic-stricken enemy, so Grandad would take out this newspaper if he was at a loss for words and could think of no other way to salvage his self-respect – if, for example, Nuruddin and Imraan, the Chechens from the Zyryanovsk gold mine, had been throwing their weight about. Nuruddin and Imraan were so rich that they carried whole ingots of gold around with them, and they had once bought ten thousand roubles' worth of goatskin coats and astrakhan hats in a day – enough money to buy two Volga cars or for Granny to live on for the rest of her life and still leave something behind.

And so Grandad would take from the trunk a copy of the 6 March 1953 issue of Pravda *with the TASS[87] report of the death of comrade Stalin. To the boy, Stalin's was a mysterious name. The adults whom the boy obeyed seemed themselves to look up to only two figures: God, who was invisible, and Stalin, who was dead. Confronted with this copy of* Pravda, *the Chechens would fall silent – from fear, from hate, or simply not knowing what to say.*

Granny was not a practising Muslim, although she was of true Muslim lineage. Each time one of her husbands had died, she had married again – so that her children wouldn't have to grow up without fathers. But she seemed to have decided – like a true Muslim! – that four marriages were enough, and she had been determined not to allow the boy's last grandad to die or disappear. Although Grandad did sometimes leave the house after one of their quarrels – and then Granny would leave her room with its trunk and its iron bed and the little hanging rug with a picture of three deer at a watering hole and would sleep with the boy and her three sons.

When Granny moved into this other little room, with its brick stove and its wooden sleeping boards, about two feet off the ground, that took up nearly half the room (once a year, when the boy was told to clean out all the rubbish from the space beneath the boards, he would crawl through the half-dark, wrapping himself in cobwebs, and discover not only the corpses of flies and scorpions but also everything that anyone in the family had lost that year, from Granny's thimble to Grandad's whetstone or Rafim-Jaan's violin bow [the story of Rafim-Jaan's violin is almost a book on its own. Rafim-Jaan, like all children who eat their own excrement when they are little, had once found a large sum of money – 1,962 roubles, in fact – that had fallen, along with the belt of someone who must have been very important, out of some celebrating passing train. Granny had taken the 1,962 roubles to Temir-Iul-Longline, who had kept the money for two days and then given a quarter of it back to Rafim-Jaan, saying that this was what he was entitled to by law as a finder of treasure. What Temir-Iul did with the other three quarters – whether he returned it to some grateful collective-farm chairman or whether he donated it to the State – I do not know. What I do know, however, is that a large part of Rafim-Jaan's 490 roubles and 50 kopeks were immediately spent on a 'Record' television which put the Saimulins – with their microscopic 'KVN' television – to shame, at least until, a year or two later, they acquired the first fridge in the mahallya. *After the purchase of the television, and after he had gone to Lobar-Beauty's Culture and Recreation shop and bought a bicycle (also the first in the* mahallya) *Rafim-Jaan managed to hang on for a long time to his last nineteen roubles and sixty-two kopeks – a hundredth part of the treasure he had found and that had so quickly run through his hands, diverted to Temir-Iul's safe, Granny's trunk and the family's various purchases. But in the end Rafim-Jaan went back to Lobar-Beauty's and bought something unheard of, something no one had ever thought of buying before him; yes, people had bought ties that cost eight roubles each, they had bought exercise books for two kopeks each, they had bought two pens for one rouble, and once someone had even bought a drum for the October School, on the school account – but never had anyone thought of buying the violin that had been on display ever since the shop first opened. But Rafim-Jaan did precisely that – he bought this violin, along with its bow.*

During the first day he didn't allow anyone to touch it except Natka, the daughter of Vera-Virgo – and that was only because Natka let him kiss her under the willow tree in between their yards; all the rest of the day he struggled with the violin on his own but failed to coax so much as a note out of it. He slept with the violin that night, took it out onto the street in the morning and was at once surrounded by the other boys from the mahallya, *all of them offering advice. One boy told him to 'press harder with the hairy bit of wood'. 'There's only one hairy bit of wood round here,' interjected Yurka, 'and that's you!' What Rafim-Jaan was holding, Yurka asserted, was not a 'hairy bit of wood' but a violin bow – and he knew this from a book he had read. Rafim-Jaan handed the violin and bow to Yurka. Disorientated by this display of trust, Yurka moved the bow up and down the strings, but to no effect – the only sound he could elicit from them was a quiet rustle. Ismet the Crimean Tatar told him to press the strings down with his fingers, and Rafim-Jaan passed the violin to Ismet; once again it just rustled and wheezed a little. And then, later on in the day, towards evening, it began to split.*

A week went by and the violin was put away in the loft, without its bow, which had disappeared. Nearly a year later the boy came across the bow under the sleeping boards; by then he had learned that you need to smear it with rosin, but Lobar-Beauty had no rosin anywhere in her shop. Nevertheless, they brought the violin back down from the loft. For a long time – its split body held together only by its strong, silent strings – it just lay around and got under everyone's feet. Sometimes someone would trip on it, pick it up in fury and try to throw it away – but the violin had a mind of its own. Whichever bit you picked up would fly through the air as far as the tension of the strings allowed, then snap back under your feet to the accompaniment of a kind of cross murmur or grumbling hum as the strings shook off their coating of brown dust. In the end, the violin disappeared for good; either the mice had taken it apart and dragged it off bit by bit, or an envious neighbour had slipped in at night, or heaven knows what . . .] and so, in a word, there under the sleeping boards the boy would find everything from Rafim-Jaan's violin bow to his own punctured football and even the seventh volume of the Thousand and One Nights. *Granny especially loved listening to the* Thousand and One Nights *on days when the boy had cleaned out the stove, his shovel ringing like a bell against the stove wall as he removed ashes as* light as air, and then gone out into the yard to fetch some logs and a bucket of coal, which was in fact not coal but coal dust and the only way you could get it to burn was to sprinkle water onto it, mix it into a thick paste and then smear it with the shovel onto logs that were already flaming, smoking and crackling), yes, when Granny moved into this little room, she would lie down in her traditional place on top of the stove and the boy would set to work on her rheumatic legs, first trying to send any sluggish blood back to the heart and then looking for the little nodules that used to appear in one place or another and massaging them away to the accompaniment of Granny's satisfied and suffering-filled groans. And then the boy would begin reading from the Thousand and One Nights – that book that was as endless as life itself, as endless as those endless winter days that began and ended here, in this little room where there was a stove, and Granny, and three uncles young enough to be the boy's brothers, and a step-grandad who used to disappear when Granny upset him. And, in between all of this: long hours at the No. 11 'October' School.

Every year, at the end of winter, they repainted these two little dark rooms. First they prepared the whitewash, to which they added a few drops of a green iodine-like substance, and then – using a brush that left the odd thin streak of green – they painted the walls an uneven white, stopping only at the ceiling, which had long ago been coated once and for all with a varnish grown brown from time and soot. A cable for electrical light, put there by Bolta-Lightning the Gilas electrician, coiled across the ceiling like a snake. Before the installation of electrical light Grandad had conjured every night over his paraffin lamp – blowing on the glass, rubbing it with a special fluffy cloth till it shone, trimming the overgrown wick with a pair of little scissors just as he used to trim his own moustache . . .

And then light would appear, first shrouding the lamp with steam and then – as Grandad lengthened the wick – slowly driving the steam away. Grandad would stand the lamp in the middle of the low rectangular table that was the same height as their cat – she used to rub *against the table so often that her back was going bald – and they would all sit down round the lamp, and round the food laid out on the table, and eat an evening meal which always ended with the words, 'Adam boy busin, pullari kup busin, uiimiz yorug busin, amin!'[88]*

23

There were gypsies in Gilas. Some were the kind you see everywhere, the kind that are said to have wandered across from Europe, in the season when mating camels run wild in the Kazakh steppe and the apricot and the lilac come into blossom in the gardens of Uzbekistan. But Gilas also had gypsies of its own, who were already blending in with the darkest of the Uzbeks – the ones known in Gilas as black cow-pats – and these unforgettable *lyuli* had come not from some far-away Europe but from Achaobod, their very own quarter of the Old City.

The first kind of gypsies taught Gilas how to make the most of the railway line. Once a year the freight train would make an unauthorised stop beside the level crossing (something unthinkable in the days of Kaganovich)[89] and the night would fill with the sounds of impatient prancing and freedom-loving whinnying. And by early morning the Orlov trotters, Turkmen Akhal-Tekes and Vladimir carthorses would have been taken to the Kok-Terek Bazaar and exchanged for Astrakhan wool or ingots of Uzbek gold.

The life of the second kind of gypsies – the *lyuli* – was simpler and richer.

Every Sunday Gilas woke to the whistle of the 7.12 and the sound of Lyuli-Ibodullo-Mahsum shouting '*Sharra-Barra! Sharra-Barra!* Rubbish and scrap!' In spring his donkey-cart would squeal in protest as it struggled, ever more heavily laden with old rags, rare bottles and ancient paraffin lamps, through the deep mud of the sidestreets. Sleepy children would come running after it, clutching bits and pieces they had put aside during the week and were hoping to exchange for something precious from the trunk on top of the driving-box: a bouncy rubber ball, a lollipop, a clay whistle that would start to dissolve in the saliva of a child's mouth long before Lyuli-Ibodullo-Mahsum's next squealing visit.

Towards noon – when the last lollipop had been crunched up, when the balls had bounced into scorpion-infested attics, when whistles whose sound filled the *mahallya* had dropped into filthy ditches and pushed up their levels of fertile silt – another *lyuli*, Adkham-Kukruz-Popcorn, would appear. His panniers slung across the back of his donkey, he would shout out to the whole of Gilas: 'Hot Fresh Kukruz! Hot Fresh Popcorn!'

And the children would again come running, exchanging whatever they had been too sleepy to snatch up in the morning for balls of hot popcorn that looked just like the apricot blossom now coming out all over the town.

Around three in the afternoon Gilas would be deafened by the metallic cries of Asom-Paraff, a half-Uzbek and half-Tadjik as black as any gypsy. After the fripperies of the *lyuli*, his 'Paraffeen! Par-a-ff-e-e-en!' was an irruption of reality that would bring the whole adult population of Gilas out onto the street to queue for another week's supply for their stoves and lamps.

Around sunset, a few hours after the cart with the pitch-black container of paraffin, old Bahri-Granny-Fortunes would appear and call out in a voice as cracked as her divining mirror, 'Fortunes told! Fortunes told to the bold! Let my words bring you gold!' Then she would quietly enter the yard where Khairi-Puchuk sat waiting for her husband, who was languishing in jail or in a distant camp – or she would slip into some other yard, where some other patient wife would then start worrying about whether or not she was obliged to prepare a meal for this Artist of Fortunes who had honoured her with a visit.

No matter where she settled, Bahri-Granny-Fortunes would remain there for several hours – until, it was sometimes said, she had secured her hostess's last kopek. Whether or not this is true, around the same time as the whistle of the 21.13, Gilas would hear the call of her son Lyuli-Ibodullo-Mahsum, now returned from his wanderings and searching for his mother. 'Acha! Hey, Acha-Gar! Hey, Whore of a Mother!' he would call out – and then settle his contented mother on the day's pile of old clothes. The silver coin of the moon, or perhaps bits of broken bottles collected by her son, shone in her eyes like splinters as he carried her away into a night as black as their life and their faces.

Since there was no muezzin in Gilas, some of the devout old men and women, including Garang-Deafmullah himself, looked on these five Sunday cries as calls to prayer and remembered the precise time they had heard them throughout the following week.

Gilas had no quarrel with the first – European – breed of gypsy, especially after it emerged that, in spite of their centuries of wandering, these gypsies had the same words as Uzbeks to designate the fundamentals of life: *dushman* and *nomus*: 'enemy' and 'conscience'. These gypsies certainly brought no harm to Gilas and if they ever fooled anyone with those skinny old nags they sometimes pumped up with air through their arseholes and tried to pass off as young stallions, it was only the odd dumb Kazakh from the steppe. It's true that they left a lot of garbage behind them, but the children soon put this to good use; they took the waste paper to school, and they took everything else, the very next Sunday, to Lyuli-Ibodullo-Mahsum. The latter wrinkled his nose a bit at the smell of his nomadic kinsmen, but that didn't stop him from paying for it with a shiny rubber ball or a faulty whistle that made a sound like a baby with diarrhoea and was a source of endless amusement to the young boys of Gilas.

Leaving behind them horses, garbage and the foulest of curses, the male gypsies went straight from the Kok-Terek Bazaar to the City, where they exchanged their money for hashish and gold, while their wives – forever with babies in their arms and dark bruises under their eyes – begged or told fortunes in the station or beside the Komsomol Lake, evidently led by some tribal etiquette to leave the fortunes of Gilas itself to be told by their settled kinswoman, Bahri-Granny-Fortunes.

Attending to the needs even of the atheistic Russians, Bahri-Granny-Fortunes had established herself – at least until Uchmah-Prophecies started to gain a reputation – as Gilas's one and only soothsayer. The old woman's successful monopolisation of the trade in fate, futures and fortunes was, first and foremost, a consequence of a story involving Janna-Nurse – the daughter, by his first marriage, of the first Russian bigamist in Gilas.

Janna-Nurse worked in the medical commission of the Gilas War Commissariat and therefore had access – to put it baldly – to all the young male members of Gilas. Every girl in Gilas consulted her with regard to the masculine virtues of her chosen one – and she, with honourable impartiality, without exaggeration or belittlement, passed on to her girlfriends and to the friends of her girlfriends and even to the friends of the friends of her girlfriends her knowledge of the physical attributes of the future defenders of the Motherland. At one point Janna-Nurse began to think of herself as Janna-Spy, dropped by the maidens of Gilas into enemy territory, and she often dreamed of herself as Zoya Kosmodemyanskaya gritting her teeth under torture or Alexander Morozov throwing himself against enemy mortars.[90] One night, after flinging herself in self-sacrificial ardour on top of enemy bunkers and pillboxes, she woke to find her heroic dream flowing between her young thighs in the form of a warm stream of moisture.

Another night she saw herself as Janna d'Arc, being burnt on a pyre for reasons best left unsaid. In a word, Janna was a faithful and self-effacing servant to her contemporaries for many years.

But when the grandson of Tolib-Butcher was called up for military service; when this Nasim, who for some reason had been nicknamed Nasim-Shlagbaum,[91] had to stand in the War Commissariat amid a row of other swarthy and scrawny youths; when Ishankul Ilyichevich the surgeon told them all to pull their blue cotton pants down to their knees and bend over with their feet apart to be checked for haemorrhoids; when Janna-Nurse went down the row in her usual way, inspecting the hairy anuses with their little lumps of dried excrement; when she got to the middle of the row ... At first Janna couldn't understand what it was and thought she was being offered a bribe. Yes, just as a long red strip of fillet usually hung from a hook in the shop of Tolib-Butcher, so something unspeakably long was now hanging down, swaying gently and almost touching the floor, between the wide-open legs of Nasim-Shlagbaum. But however dumbstruck this left her, Janna-Nurse's medical knowledge was enough to tell her that this was no fillet; no, it was what she needed to fill her. Two balls as black as bull's liver, in a giant scrotum, framed an unbelievable ...

Janna-Nurse quite forgot about haemorrhoids – as she honourably admitted a few minutes later to Ishankul Ilyichevich. He for his part, as he was examining Nasim-Shlagbaum, had suddenly burst out, 'You bastard, you must have swum to the other side of the Zakh Canal and got yourself infected there by the donkeys. What a tool! How could you grow a tool like that all by yourself? You'll need to wrap it up carefully in Russia or it'll be whipped off you by the winter winds and frosts!'

Yes, after listening to these words, Janna had come back to herself, taken a deep breath and said, 'I'm sorry – I forgot to check him for haemorrhoids.'

The surgeon went off to wash his hands; seeing this monstrosity had utterly destroyed his sense of himself as a man.

Then Janna laid poor Nasim on his side and, barely able to hold back her tears of joy, plunged a shining speculum into the youth's behind, clutching simultaneously with a trembling and icy hand at his unbelievable ...

After that Janna-Nurse knew no peace. For two years, while Nasim-Shlagbaum was freezing his extremities in the Red Army, she dreamed of a shiny steel speculum and the soft, lowered barrier of her chosen one; sensing that nothing else could penetrate her dreams any longer, she slowly grasped the full import of his name. She found out the address of his military unit from his grandfather, Tolib-Butcher – who had at one time been secretly in love with her stepmother, although it has to be said that his professional interest in flesh meant that he had at one time or another been in love with every woman in Gilas – and began writing to dear Nasim. At first she wrote in the name of the trade union committee of soldiers' mothers and sisters; then she sent advice with regard to the care and strengthening of the body's extremities in extreme climatic conditions; and in the end their correspondence took on a friendly, or even more than friendly tone. In a word, when Nasim-Shlagbaum's military service drew to an end, it was clear that he had a girl of his own waiting for him in his hometown.

Tolib-Butcher, however, was now honourably approaching the age of retirement and – just in case any other passport data ever needed changing – he had sent a matchmaker on Nasim's behalf to ask for the hand of the eldest granddaughter of Oppok-Lovely. And so, when dear Nasim returned to everyday life after the obligatory week of alcoholic oblivion following his release from the army, he found he was on the threshold of bigamy. Tormented in her dreams by a secret she had not yet revealed to anyone, Janna was waiting for him with patient determination – while Tolib-Butcher made it clear to his grandson that he was in no hurry to die, that he wanted no more difficulties with documents and that if Nasim didn't marry the right woman he'd get out his butcher's cleaver and start sharpening it there and then on Nasim's tool.

And so, in the daytime Nasim walked quietly around the town – the future grandson of the all-powerful Oppok-Lovely. But in the evenings, when everyone was flocking to see the Indian films put on by Ortik-Picture-Reels in his outdoor theatre, Nasim-Shlagbaum would meet Janna-Nurse – who now called him by the more decorous name of Nasim-Shokolad – among the rushes beside the Salty Canal. In the duck-filled darkness they repeated to one another the contents of their letters while the moon, shining down at them from the clear sky and up at them from the cloudy water, gleamed in Janna's eyes like that same shameful speculum.

Towards the end of the summer film season, when they had got through all their letters and the evenings were turning chilly, they began to kiss – and Janna-Nurse, for the first time in all her years of tormenting dreams, divulged her secret. Yes, thinking she might need to take prophylactic measures, she confessed everything to Natka-Pothecary, the daughter of Vera-Virgo the prostitute and Bolta-Lightning the electrician. After that, Janna-Nurse took to visiting the chemist's every morning; she would say that she needed to go and collect prescriptions, new surgical gloves or purgatives for the recruits, but what she really wanted was to talk to Natka about her evenings by the canal.

There were problems. Ortik-Picture-Reels had already moved to his winter quarters in the 'Sputnik' building, but something was wrong with Nasim. In the words of Janna-Nurse to Natka: 'His . . . er . . . you know . . . his . . . it won't stand up.' Natka had been well informed about such matters since childhood, having kept her eyes and ears open when her father was clambering up poles in order to electrify the town's darkness and strangers used to take advantage of this to come and visit her mother. Her advice to Janna was to touch him as if without meaning to, to lean on him as if inadvertently, to reach out a hand unexpectedly . . .

Nothing, alas, made any difference. It might have been the terrible Russian frosts, the same frosts that had at one time or another destroyed the military might of Genghis-Khan, Napoleon and Hitler; it might have been his grandfather's impassioned threats or it might have been a memory of a speculum being stuck up a rectum – but in any case, whatever the reason, Nasim was himself as bewildered and tormented as Janna-Nurse, who kept touching him without meaning to, leaning on him inadvertently, reaching out a hand unexpectedly . . .

It was then that Natka-Pothecary suggested taking Nasim-Shokolad to Bahri-Granny-Fortunes – Gilas's healer, diviner and sorceress. Since it was unacceptable for someone with Janna-Nurse's medical education to visit a mere quack, it was decided that Natka-Pothecary should take Nasim to the old woman; and since Bahri-Granny-Fortunes only told fortunes to women and the girls didn't want to make Nasim suspicious, it was Natka's fortune they would ask her to tell.

That very evening, in the goose-fleshed darkness beside the Salty Canal, where the rushes were now yellowing and withering, Janna-Nurse introduced Nasim to Natka. And on the following Saturday, Natka and Nasim set off in search of the home of Bahri-Granny-Fortunes.

This was in the *lyuli* quarter, where a hundred hidden gates and low passages led from one yard to another, where the houses abutted the neighbours' barns, and the barns rubbed up against every kind of animal-shed, hut and privy. No one could find their way through this labyrinth except the *lyuli* children or *lyulchata* – black dirty little brats who bombarded the young couple with questions: where had they come from and who were they looking for and couldn't they spare a kopek or a rouble as a keepsake? Fortunately, Natka-Pothecary had brought some dried haematogen with her;[92] she broke off little cubes with her teeth and handed them out as if they were squares of chocolate.

Nasim and Natka lost all sense of direction, but the children led them through one narrow passage after another until they emerged into the yard of Bahri-Granny-Fortunes; there the children entrusted them to the care of some woman from Siberia, either a Chuvash or a Mari,[93] who had fetched up there twenty or thirty years before and who had remained ever since, unable to remember the way back to her home. This poor Chuvash or Mari, who over the years had lost her name, her address, the use of her tongue and everything else that goes to make up an individual, spent her days cooking soup and her nights sorting and washing the bottles collected during the day by Ibodullo-Mahsum. Not once during these twenty, or perhaps thirty, years had anyone asked her why she was there; suddenly seeing people from 'the mainland', she had no idea what they might want from her. The children tugged at her long plaits – which fell right down to her ankles, hanging between the knotty varicose veins of her legs just like the thing Janna-Nurse talked about every morning to Natka – and ran off to find the old fortune-teller.

Bahri-Granny-Fortunes was selling sunflower seeds and lollipops at the bus station. The children lured her back with the promise of dried haematogen, and she popped a piece into her mouth the moment Nasim and Natka offered it to her. She found it too soft and sticky; in return, she offered Nasim and Natka some of her own *kurt* or dried yoghurt balls, and they each almost broke a tooth on it.

'Shall I spell you your fortune, child? Shall I tell you your enemy, child? Show me a coin, child, show me a coin that shines – and my mirror will speak its mind,' she said again and again, until the meaning of the words became as much of a mystery as what it was that Bahri-Granny-Fortunes intended to do when these waves of words had receded. The words rolled from her tongue onto her cracked little mirror and, finding no resting place on its empty surface, were at once succeeded by others. The old woman didn't even ask Natka why she had come, and the questions Natka and Janna had prepared in advance were swept away by a torrent that seemed unstoppable – except that now and again there would be an ominous pause after such words as: 'You have an enemy, child, and he is not kind. Show me a coin, child, show me a coin that shines – and my mirror will speak its mind.'

Natka had only a half-understanding – from her electrician father – of the Uzbek tongue, but she sensed at such moments that she was expected to go back into her handbag, which was now filling up with empty words as quickly as it was being emptied of coins.

When the mirror had done all that was required of it, Bahri-Granny-Fortunes moved on to grains of Khrushchev's Queen of the Fields.[94] She scattered the grains on the floor, sketching out the five-year plans of Natka's destiny according to the system approved at the last Plenum of the Central Committee.

After the maize it was the turn of the cotton thread, and by then it was Nasim who was paying.

'Give me your hand, child. Your little finger, circled with thread, is the willy of a man your heart should dread. May my spinning thread bring you balm, may my circling thread chase away all harm!' And Bahri-Granny-Fortunes tied her thread round Natka's plump little finger, which was adorned only by a cheap ring that a neighbour had given her in return for some ichthyol ointment for a boil on his bottom; Natka had not only managed to obtain this vile-smelling paste for her childhood friend but had even smeared it onto his dark arse. As the old woman did away with the willy of Natka's enemy, she also charmed away the ring that encircled it. Then she moved on to Natka's body, looking for spiritual anxiety and weariness of heart somewhere in the area of her necklace.

Overwhelming Natka with yet more words, she swept away her jumper; the girl was wearing nothing beneath it except her mother's bra, already splitting from the pressure of her young breasts. In the swirl of words, Natka forgot both shame and Nasim. She was already pulling her flared skirt over her head when something happened that took away Bahri-Granny-Fortune's power of speech for years to come, leaving her unable to do anything except sell seeds or tell mute fortunes to the Russians, simply by nodding or shaking her head. A crack of thunder from a pair of dacron trousers – made with a double lining by Izaly-Jew, who had been brought to the tailoring co-operative by Moisey-Master – revealed a male member that at once made Khaira the Chuvash remember that she had been born in Sterlitamak on the Street of the Just Sabre of Salavat Yulayev[95] on the fourth Wednesday of the Month of Nisan of the Year of the Bull (old-style calendar).[96]

When Ibodullo-Mahsum came home in the evening on a clanking cart full of empty bottles; when he found his mother lying there half-conscious; when the *lyulchata* told him how three people, two of them naked and the third veiled by her long hair, had torn through the neighbourhood, sweeping away gates, awnings, shutters and walls with some kind of battering ram (clearing the path for what would later become the branch line to Toitepa) and finally disappearing into the rushes beside the Salty Canal – when Ibodullo-Mahsum came home, all he could do was to pick up the dacron trousers – made with a double lining by Izaly-Jew, who had been brought to the tailoring co-operative by Moisey-Master – and add them to his heap of rags. They had, in any case, come his way for free.

Khaira Gavrilovna Huzangay – born in the Year of the Bull (old-style calendar), a native of the town of Sterlitamak, whose domicile was the first building on the right after the well, on the Street of the Just Sabre of Salavat Yulayev – was invited by Natka-Pothecary and Nasim-the-Handsome, known to some as Shlagbaum-Shokolad, to witness their wedding; they had fled with her to her birthplace in order to escape from the unjust axe of Tolib-Butcher, whose embitterment with life was now absolute, from the inadvertent and fruitless touches of Janna-Nurse and from the now wrecked and unrecognisable labyrinths of the Gilas *lyuli*.

And every night since then Natka-Pothecary has cursed and yelled in far-off Sterlitamak – on her own behalf and on Janna's – as loudly as if she were giving birth to a child head last or feet first.

24

Some years after Fate took him to Brighton Beach and left him with no alternative but to study the Jewish-Odessan dialect of the mighty Russian language, Mullah-Ulmas-Greeneyes was sitting in a dirty bar beside the ocean, listening to the shouts and curses of the other drinkers as they argued about who had informed on whom for the KGB, when he saw an aristocratic-looking young Moroccan in the company of a young woman who might have been from Thailand or the Philippines. When the Moroccan disappeared for a moment – no doubt to perform his ablutions – Mullah addressed the girl, taking a long shot, in Laotian. When the girl muttered under her breath, in the purest Uzbek, 'Bloody green-eyes, one foot in the grave but he still thinks he's a charmer!', he fell off his high stool and quite forgot the words of Thai that had been on the tip of his tongue. But when Mullah picked himself up off the floor and groaned in an equally pure Uzbek – 'Ay, ay, my poor bones! Ay, ay, my poor back!' – it was the girl's turn to fall off her stool. The noble Moroccan, however, had by then completed his ablutions, and he returned just in time to catch her.

In the course of the next few hours Mullah-Ulmas-Greeneyes learned that the young man, Vamek ben Hasan, was from the Moroccan royal family and that his betrothed was the daughter of an electrician by the name of Said Alihon-Tura, who had been born in the Fergana Valley, in the village of Mookat, and who had escaped from the heathen Bolsheviks by crossing the mountains.

Mullah-Ulmas-Greeneyes had heard of this family. In exile in Chita he had met a son of some Mullah Obid-Kori who came from this same Mookat and who must have been related to Said Alihon-Tura, and in a transit prison in Solikamsk he had spoken to Said Alihon-Tura's brother, who had briefly been a Soviet millionaire.

Learning from Mullah-Ulmas about her numerous relatives, the poor girl – who had always thought she had no family at all except for an electrician father and a cleaner mother – was filled with a burning desire to go to Mookat. For his part, Mullah-Ulmas-Greeneyes (whose eminent friend and colleague Pete Shelley May – yes, our old friend Pinkhas Shalomay – was a big fish in some human rights organisation or other) offered to obtain them free tourist visas as long as they promised to travel to a small town called Gilas and visit his wife Oppok-Oyim – whom the reader knows as Oppok-Lovely – and take her some important papers he had acquired during his wanderings. And the young couple also, of course, agreed to take letters and invitations to the countless relatives of Pete Shelley May.

Mullah-Ulmas-Greeneyes managed to obtain for the young couple not only a tourist visa for the region (something almost unheard-of at that time) but also a map showing how to get by train from Gilas to Gorchakov – the nearest station to Mookat. And so the young couple set off on their trans-oceanic – and trans-oxianic – travels.

They were met at the airport by Oppok-Lovely and the Gilas KGB. KGB Sub-Lieutenant Osman-Anon, however, was so dependent on Oppok-Lovely (who, among other things, changed his passport for him once a month to preserve his anonymity) that everyone took him for her bodyguard, while she just introduced him with a wave of the hand and the words, 'And this is, er, what's his name . . .' Once, of course, Osman-Anon had had a surname all of his own, but he had never had much of a family – only an officer father who went missing during the War and a singer mother who was always on tour and who died young, leaving him to be brought up by some second-cousin-once-removed who insisted he call her by the unfamiliar name of 'Mummy'. So it will not be surprising – certainly not to anyone who has given any thought to the psychological consequences of orphanhood – that Osman-Anon ended up fighting on the invisible battlefields of the secret Front.

Osman-Anon felt nervous before his meeting with these capitalist-imperialist agents who had come to spy on his Motherland. The night before their arrival he single-handedly drew up, approved and countersigned a forty-seven-page operational plan, codenamed 'The rooks have arrived'.[97] This included every conceivable measure – ambushes, listening devices, incriminating encounters with the alcoholic Kun-Okhun and Vera-Virgo the prostitute – and it ended with the enemy agents being caught red-handed and then exchanged, on the Kok-Terek Bridge, for the Soviet spy Mullah-Ulmas – and with early promotion for Sub-Lieutenant Osman-Anon.

But let us, at least for the time being, leave Osman-Anon listening, watching and taking notes as he stands at his eternal post on the front line of a secret war – and let us enter the home of Oppok-Lovely, who has laid on a splendid feast to celebrate the arrival of these foreigners bearing news of her errant husband: Mullah-Ulmas-Greeneyes, Gilas's First Dissident and Betrayer of the Motherland. Young Pioneers, who have removed their red ties so as not to inflame ideological passions, are serving cups of tea to the guests as they arrive; Nabi-Onearm and Tadji-Murad, on the other hand, have put on ties for the first time in their lives – at Oppok-Lovely's request – and are ushering the guests to their seats. The number of these guests is growing by the minute.

Oppok-Lovely, like a true Uzbek hostess, is directing proceedings from behind a screen. Cognac is to be taken to Temir-Iul-Longline; vodka (in a teapot) to Tolib-Butcher (even though the swine doesn't deserve so much as a cupful); cheap 'Chashma' Portwein to Kun-Okhun (who'll soon be under the table anyway); tea with sugar to Akmolin (it would be all the same to him if she gave him diesel fuel but he is, after all, her guest).

And in all the hustle and bustle the honoured guests from over the waves got somehow forgotten. After they had sat for some time in a special room set aside for them, Muzayana suggested to Vamek ben Hasan that they go out into the courtyard to see what was going on out there. As they watched Olma the dancer from Khorezm languidly circling her hips and convulsively shaking her shoulders, Tadji-Murad – or it might have been Nabi-Onearm – barged drunkenly into them and began swearing at Vamek ben Hasan, 'Don't just stand there like some great dick! Take some cups of tea round to the other fucking guests!' The noble Moroccan did not understand a single word, but Muzayana took her fiancé by the hand and led him into the shadows beneath a tree.

And as Kabir Mavsumov, the finest public reciter in the whole republic, was reading out the letter Mullah-Ulmas-Greeneyes had composed for his wife ('The sun of my devotion shines as brightly as ever in the sky of my love . . .') – although it has to be said that Kabir Mavsumov was illiterate and so was able to declaim each ringing phrase only after Garang-Deafmullah had first muttered it to him under his breath; yes, as Kabir Mavsumov was declaiming this letter and as Muzayana and her fiancé were moving into the shadows beneath the tree, Kun-Okhun wandered out into these same shadows to have a piss. Having been lying under the table, he had been unable to admire Olma the languid dancer; glimpsing Muzayana and mistaking her for Olma, he staggered up to her and thrust some money – a ten-rouble note he had only with difficulty managed to hide from his wife Djibladjibon-Bonu-Wagtail – into the sleeve of her dress. Vamek ben Hasan's response to this was a punch on the jaw that knocked his fellow-Muslim to the ground, where he went straight to sleep. Osman-Anon, however, was not sleeping; a

KGB agent – as everyone knows – never sleeps. 'Quick! Enemy attack!' he yelled. And Muzayana, who must have inherited something of her parents' instinct for evading trouble, seized her Moroccan by the hand and made off with him into the night. Osman-Anon followed.

All roads in Gilas lead to the railway station, and that was where the young couple ended up. Osman-Anon did everything as he had been taught at KGB school, sprinting past the wool factory (where the nightwatchmen, resentful at being excluded from the feast, fired salt bullets at him)[98] and reaching the ticket window just before the young couple. Wanting to avoid recognition, he had put on the spectacles he had once confiscated from Master-Railwayman Belkov for fraternising with foreigners, but Tanya-Tickets was not easily fooled. 'Not foreign spies again!' she called out.

Osman-Anon scowled ferociously, his scowl somehow gathering together all his incompatible feelings: from irritation with Tanya to Love for the Socialist Motherland and his desperate need for a piss (though not, of course, until he had unmasked these spying foreigners). Auntie Tanya understood all this and asked simply, 'Where do we want tickets to?'

'Stations unlimited,' the KGB agent answered impassively, as if repeating a password. Grasping that he needed a ticket for all possible destinations and time zones within the USSR, Auntie Tanya took a blank ticket, carefully wrote on it, 'Believe the Bearer!' and pressed her stamp down on top of it.

'To be returned on return!' she ordered, not wanting to appear slapdash, and turned to the next of her midnight travellers.

'Where to?' she asked.

A nice young woman tried to explain something in very strange Uzbek, then pushed a map through the window and indicated that they wished to travel to Gorchakov. Tanya asked how many tickets she wanted. The nice young woman mumbled something still more incomprehensible and pushed some pieces of paper through the window.

'What's that?' asked Tanya.

'Dallars, dallars!' said the young woman.

'We don't want any of your dallars here,' said Tanya sternly. 'Payment must be proffered in roubles.'

The Moroccan prince removed a royal ring from his little finger and pushed it through the window. The cramped little office became twice as bright. Two sharp rays of light pierced Tanya's narrow eyes. 'I'm sorry, I haven't quite got enough change,' she said. 'Just wait a moment while I nip across to the buffet and get some off Froska.' And she hurried off on her stumpy legs, the royal ring lighting her path through the darkness.

At four in the morning, accompanied by KGB agent Osman-Anon, the young couple left Gilas station on the Frunze-Djalalabad train; they were carrying two plastic bags full of Soviet roubles, and all the women who worked at the station, from Minigyul the Tatar cleaner to Chinigyul the Tatar cook, were there on the platform to wave them goodbye. And for several years all kinds of heirlooms from the family of the Moroccan prince – gold rings, silver rings, copper and bronze rings, even one ivory ring – were accepted in Gilas as a means of exchange, until the rings grew weary of circulating and, one by one, came to rest where they belonged: in the home of Oppok-Lovely, in a small casket underneath the lid of a white piano that bore the elegiac, if enigmatic, inscription: 'Roenisch 1911 Hatsunay 1964'.

But let us return to the young couple. It was with complex feelings that Muzayana made the journey to Mookat. Imagine a young woman who had travelled the world with her parents and then settled in Brooklyn, where everyone would always think of her as a stranger. Why, anyway, should anyone think of her at all – with a father who attended to light bulbs and a mother whose job was to remove people's garbage? And Muzayana was not without pride; any number of market-traders and shopkeepers, all of them raking in money just as they had done in the Buz Bazaar in Tashkent, had asked for her hand – and she had turned down all her suitors until the day this prince had flown to New York after seeing a family tree in Saudi Arabia which showed that he and she sprang from the same root.

And now Muzayana was on her way to where the leaves of this tree still rustled – just like the silver leaves of the great poplars guarding the entrance to the little side valley that sheltered her village, the Mookat she was about to see for the first time. But how can a mere road take you into your dreams, into your visions, into your longings? Can you enter something that does not exist? Her father had called this his home, because he had been born here, but why did her own heart stir as these mountains drew steadily nearer? Why were their blue stones, red sand and white snow not simply a landscape like any other? Why did all this enter deep inside her, making her ache with *toskà*?

Crooked clay walls, with yellow-eyed apricot trees looking over them; flowers covered in dust; dust covered in oblivion; now and again a veiled woman, or a man on a donkey-cart. What was all this after Manhattan, Brooklyn or Queens? Where had it all come from and why? There was a lump in Muzayana's throat, and Vamek's questions seemed silly, trivial, out of place.

Why, why, why had her father left this village? Why had he not let her be born here, where no iron road had penetrated, warping the earth and its people, twisting lives out of shape?

Muzayana and Vamek were put up by her father's brother, Nurmat-Tura – who turned out to have led a modest yet dignified life, making boots and bringing up his many children, all of whom had already married. As soon as news of Muzayana's arrival got around, visitors began to appear: her uncle's uncle, the nephew of her uncle's brother-in-law, the sister-in-law of her father's nephew, the wife of the sister of the father-in-law of her uncle's niece . . .

Muzayana soon ran out of presents, but the visitors kept on coming. Whole queues of relatives would be waiting for Muzayana and Vamek ben Hasan when they got back from a walk through land that had once belonged to her great-grandfather, Said-Kasum-Kadi, or from the high ravine where Obid-Kori had said farewell to her father and entrusted him to Kirghiz tribesmen who even now remembered that day of exodus. Muzayana began giving presents of ordinary Soviet roubles – the contents of the two bags they had brought from Gilas. Glad to discover that American money was no different from their own, the visitors were overwhelmed with curiosity: what can one buy in America for these three roubles? And what if they add the rouble Muzayana has just given to Abdusamat, or the five roubles she has given to Ruzvan-Bibi, who isn't a relative at all but who has cured Muzayana of the nausea induced either by the change of climate or the number of visitors?

In reply Muzayana would point wearily at Vamek's shoes (if she was speaking to a man) or at her own gown (if she was speaking to a woman), and the visitors would beg to be allowed to exchange their three, one or five roubles for shoes that had trodden far-away paths, for garments that had circled the world on shoulders they loved and revered. Soon not a single item of foreign clothing remained on either the Moroccan prince or the young descendant of the Prophet. Vamek was now wearing a Kirghiz felt cap from the Selpo[99] and traditional (though factory-made) Kirghiz trousers with legs of different colours; Muzayana, for her part, was dressed a little better, having gone to the village bazaar and bought clothes that local widows had made in their homes. But when the young couple had nothing left at all, when they had spent their last kopeks on a lollipop for a newborn baby (named Muzmek in their honour) – then, I am sad to say, the gossip and backbiting began.

In defence of my people, I must say that this gossip and backbiting did not begin entirely spontaneously. Osman-Anon may appear to have been sleeping, but he had in fact conducted no fewer than thirty-seven secret meetings with shepherds, postmen and bank clerks; he had even met one-armed Uncle Seryozha, who had a small newspaper kiosk and whose only secret was a single copy of the weekly *Football* that he had hidden away for some boy or other. Yes, zealous as ever, Osman-Anon had organised an entire secret network of agents that would have stayed secret for ever had not old Symyrbay-Moonshine got drunk every evening by the old mill where cockfights were held and, with a sob of shame in his voice, divulged the names of those who had signed up that day to collaborate with this anonymous spy of a stranger.

The campaign of gossip had been instigated by Osman-Anon. His profession barred him from receiving gifts from Muzayana and Vamek, and there was, in any case, no other course of action open to him. Even if he had expropriated the foreigners – as he had dreamed of doing night and day– he would have secured only a Selpo gown and some socks from the Djalalabad factory.

And so, as I have said, the gifts ran out and tongues began to wag. But Osman had underestimated Muzayana; she excused her lack of gifts by giving brief talks about unemployment, the ruthless exploitation of labour and the general difficulty of life in America. After she had explained such matters not only to the adults but also to whole classes of children – brought to her by Mustafa Djemalovich, a Kurd who taught the history of the Communist Party of the Soviet Union – she went on to demonstrate to the devout Muslim women of Mookat how sexual intercourse is practised in America. 'No, no, come on now!' she would begin. 'How many kids have you got? Twelve? Fourteen? And do you know why? Because you don't use condoms! What? C-o-n-d-o-m-s! Yes, like this one! No, it's not a May Day balloon. It fits over a male member. What's a male member? It's what makes a child. No, I don't mean a husband, I mean the member of a husband – how do you say it in Uzbek? In English it's called a . . .' At this point the women would hide behind their veils, but they would go on listening. And watching. And reporting all they had heard and seen to Osman-Anon.

'And then she wriggled about like this!' they would say, awkwardly imitating the movements of the godless young American. 'Like this!'

And Osman's feelings of fraternal and patriotic respect were only just enough to prevent him from exploiting these honest agricultural labourers then and there, in his room in the collective-farm guest house.

'Like this!' the women repeated. 'Like this!'

'Don't worry!' Osman attempted to calm them. 'We won't let her wriggle out of this one!'

'Yes, that's just what she did – she wriggled about like this! Like this!'

So carried away were these wives of shepherds and horseherds that they left their precious veils behind and hurried back to their homes to search for their foolish and ignorant husbands.

In the meantime, the Moroccan prince took to drinking spirits distilled from millet with Symyrbay-Moonshine – the only man in Mookat who appeared to have any time for him. As for Muzayana, she had not only given up all her clothes but had also worn out the last of her threadbare dreams. She sat there mutely, as if carved from stone, while visitors came and went, and came and went, kissing her feet, kissing the hem of her dress, kissing her numb palms. Childless women ran their hands over her breasts.

It was not long before pilgrims on their way to Mount Suleiman were, as a matter of course, making a small detour to visit the holy girl whose silent touch had cured fifteen men and women of hair-loss – not to mention seven cases of Parkinson's, six alcoholics, four cases of eczema and even one case of haemorrhoids. Muzayana for her part gazed at them blankly, seeing not faces but bright blurs and no longer even trying to find out who her visitors were or why they had come.

In the end it was not the young couple who were arrested, but Osman-Anon. After her guests went missing, Oppok-Lovely had alerted the Ministry of Internal Affairs and the various other security services. Sub-Lieutenant Osman-Anon was duly tracked down; not only had he deserted his post but he had also failed to equip himself with his customary new passport. It is said that three Chekists, seven plain-clothes policemen and a platoon of soldiers from some special unit stormed the collective-farm guest house and found Osman-Anon in his room, reading the copy of *Football* that one-eyed Uncle Seryozha had hidden under the table for some boy. We, of course, know the truth, but Osman-Anon's explanations were in vain; his colleagues punched him in the belly, gagged him and dragged him away.

As for Muzayana, exhausted by her relatives, she waited out the term of her visa, thanked God that her father had chosen to slip over the mountains to China – and made her own getaway by air to America, together with her princely husband. And that is all I know.

25

Gogolushko, however, knew everything. The only thing he did not know about was the Apostolic Cathedral of Saint Thomas. But then no one in Gilas knew about it except Father Ioann, whom everyone called Ivan – or even just plain Vanka – and thought of simply as the crazy caretaker of the Russian cemetery. In the middle of this cemetery there had once stood a rather monstrous edifice popularly thought of as a collective-farm hydroelectric station[100] from before the Revolution. And this building had been quietly covered by a mound of graves, until nothing was left of it except a somehow still rather monstrous bump. Nothing more.

The young boys of the town, admittedly, sometimes said that it was not a hydroelectric station at all, that it went deep down into the earth and that the interior was faced throughout with red-brown granite – of which there was only one other slab in the whole of Gilas: on the top step, just below the pedestal that supported their limestone Lenin.

The Cathedral of the Apostle Thomas, founded according to legend by the doubting apostle himself, did indeed descend deep into the earth – or rather the earth had for centuries climbed up around the Cathedral – and its interior, which had been cleaned by Father Ioann during long years of devout service, was indeed magnificent. Dense, resonant granite – similar to that of Saint Isaac's Cathedral in Petersburg, where Father Ioann had first served as a dean – rose up in columns towards a simple cupola with an opening into the dusty Asiatic sky. What made the interior so magnificent, however, was not the circle of columns – most of them polished to a slippery brilliance – but the spiralling steps, the curve after curve of tapering granite steps. Some of these steps and columns, however, were covered by petrified moss, and it was hard to remove this marvellous moss and its green patterns without damaging the stone itself.

Here were no icons, images, crosses or icon-lamps, nothing to distract the spirit from its aspiration heavenwards. And after making for himself a kind of cradle that hung from the opening in the cupola, Father Ioann had removed nearly everything that had obscured the sumptuous granite; he used to work at dawn, when none of the Orthodox would think of dying – and if they did, then the wake and its attendant downing of vodka would come to an end only on the third day and only that evening would some Anti-Christ like Mefody come to inform Father Ioann of yet another man who had passed on from the kingdom of Satan. Father Ioann was, fortunately, able to make use of these deceased, raising up from this progeny of the devil a kind of impregnable mound around his immaculate Cathedral.

Where there had been windows, there were now niches which opened only into the earth itself and that gave off a putrefactive damp. Father Ioann put black tarred roofing paper over them and sometimes, when the noon sun fell slantwise through the opening in the cupola, the niches would shine with a blue light, and a marvellous sensation of eternal twilight amid the noonday world would fill Father Ioann's heart with the cool of tranquillity.

Only one passion consumed Father Ioann during these long years of service in the desert – he hungered to restore the Cathedral to its former magnificence. This passion enabled him to survive on the offerings brought by a few old Baptist women – in particular by poor Marfyona Mosha, whose heart was torn between hope and fear: hope that Father Ioann, the only man in holy orders for many miles, would administer the last rites to her, and fear that he might pronounce a final curse on her for being of the seed of heretics. During his many years of zeal Father Ioann had grown unused to eating regularly; Easter cakes gave him wind, while eggs made his skin, accustomed as it was to a cold darkness, feel as if it were on fire. His favourite foods were nuts, which he gathered on the border of his dominion, and raisins; he picked the grapes from forbidden collective-farm vines and then dried them in honour of the congealed blood of our Lord.

One passion, as I have said, consumed Father Ioann – and this passion somehow led him to keep a record of the acts of the inhabitants of Gilas: that lost and ill-assorted tribe of the debauched and depraved. True, his annals were incomplete; there was no mention of any event from the many years when Father Ioann was in exile first in Solovky[101] (it was in fact, after being released from Solovky that Father Ioann had first come to Gilas), then in Kolyma,[102] and lastly, not far away at all, in Uchkuduk. No especially subtle reasons had been advanced for his various sentences: Father Ioann had been exiled in order to comply with quotas imposed from above – as a class enemy of the people, as a stateless Nationalist-Cosmopolitan, and then as a recidivist parasite. Father Ioann had never been submissive in spirit and his only fear during his last two sentences – in Kolyma and Uchkuduk – was that the authorities might undertake to improve the Russian cemetery and thus discover the Cathedral he had left buried beneath a burial mound. Before being sent to Kolyma, he had protected it with a slogan picked out in white pebbles, 'Let Village Life be our Focus!' (which he hoped would prevent the impious from focusing their attention on the Cathedral) and with a portrait of the Anti-Christ with a moustache (which he hoped would frighten off any other potential busybodies). He had found it harder, however, to decide what to do before leaving for Uchkuduk: if he were to write some new slogan over the burial mound, then Musayev-Slogans – the very same Kara-Musayev who had sent him into exile but who had now been deprived of his official position and even of his first name – would come to the cemetery in search of enlightenment; if he were to sow the burial ground with the maize so dear to Khrushchev's heart, then Vera-Virgo would bring her clients there. Yes, this question tormented Father Ioann all through the last night before his departure for Uchkuduk until finally – may the Lord forgive him! – he moved his toilet to the top of the mound. His judgment proved correct – no adult ever thought of answering a call of nature in the middle of a cemetery, while the children, for their part, never thought of entering the cabin at all, fouling it instead from every side.

During the absences of Father Ioann, the Orthodox were buried by Mefody; some gave him a three-rouble note, others, more straightforwardly, presented him with a bottle of vodka. But neither his periods of exile, nor the burial services he conducted in between them, were what really mattered to Father Ioann, even though they took up most of his life. What mattered to him was the Cathedral. His entire life was devoted to its restoration; and yet, as less and less of it remained to be cleaned and polished, so Father Ioann grew increasingly uneasy. This was no idle unease about being sent off again in order to fulfil some quota, perhaps this time in the capacity of a Gilas dissident; both his body and soul had grown accustomed to such things, and anyway the Lord always punished his persecutors afterwards. No, what troubled Father Ioann was the question of the destiny of the Cathedral. For many years the work of cleaning it had occupied him entirely, and his only thought had been to restore it to its primordial glory. But now, as the moment of the final scraping and polishing drew ever nearer, Father Ioann's heart tightened and shrank like the decreasing areas of encrustation on the granite columns: what was he to do next? What indeed? Should he display this magnificence to the depraved rabble? 'To what avail is this glory,' he asked the Lord, 'if thick-snouted swine are to come running into it as if into a field of acorns? Why have you tested me all my life,' he asked, 'why have you called upon me to perform such a labour, if now you mean to cast this pearl before the swine that make up the human race? To whom will you entrust your Cathedral? To those who will turn it on the first day into an ethnological museum, on the second day into a goods shed, and on the third to a depot for that capitalistic Belyalov to fill with rotten bast and stinking potatoes?' No, Father Ioann could not reconcile himself to this.

He tried to admonish his pride, understanding that a Cathedral with no people was no Cathedral at all, but who – O Lord! – were these people? Why was the Lord's faith so perfect that the world now wallowed in faithlessness? And if people should trample on this faith, and on a life devoted to the restoration of this Cathedral, would that truly represent a humbling of his pride? Father Ioann was troubled in spirit, and he kept putting off the hour when the Cathedral would once again shine forth in its power and perfection, as it had in the days of the Apostle Thomas.

Yes, it was hard for Father Ioann to believe that the completion of the Cathedral under the earth would complete the restoration of the heavenly Cathedral; it was hard indeed. It was as if the spirit of Doubting Thomas himself hovered over Father Ioann, deepening his doubts.

Even during his days as a dean at Saint Isaac's, when Father Ioann was a young man and Russian philosophy and theology were blossoming, he had begun to realise with chilling horror, as he meditated on the nature of faith, that another's experience of faith counts for nothing, that faith is a sensation, something experienced deep in the heart and impossible to communicate – and that this is why a faith can be built only from words, this is why Christ had needed apostles – imperfect, tormented betrayers as they were – in order to establish his teachings. Yes, Socrates had needed Plato, Christ had needed apostles and evangelists, and Muhammad had needed caliphs. And then, as Father Ioann became more interested in the history of the apostles than in that of Christ himself, the apostle he chose to study was not Judas, that open traitor and Anti-Christ, nor Peter, the beloved disciple who came to deny Christ just as Christ had predicted, nor even the eloquent and exalted John, whose name was the same as

Ioann's – no, the acts of these three were all entirely predictable, dictated as they were by Christ's life and death. The apostle whom Father Ioann chose for his most searching study was Doubting Thomas, whom people call the Twin; this doubter of all that was obvious, this believer whose belief never ran ahead of his experience, did indeed seem to Father Ioann like a twin.

In the journal *Theological Notebooks* Father Ioann published two articles, based on the apocrypha and life of Saint Thomas, who had set out after the Resurrection to Georgia and India. The unusual cast of mind revealed by these articles did not escape notice; it was in fact Father Ioann's unorthodox scepticism that led him to be exiled to Solovky, even if the official pretext for his exile was his Orthodoxy.[103] In Solovky he shared a cell with a certain Mahmud-Hodja – not a theologian but simply an educated Muslim – and discovered, to his astonishment, that Islam too has its versions of the lives of the Prophets. There he listened to stories about Noah's Ark, about how the dog intended to couple with the bitch and multiply – and how Noah, warned by the cat, prevented them from sending the Ark to the bottom of the waters with the weight of their progeny. 'And that is the reason both for the never-ceasing enmity between cats and dogs, and for the look of shame in the latters' eyes,' Mahmud-Hodja concluded gravely. All these stories were so remarkable that Father Ioann went on to question Mahmud-Hodja about the Christian apostles. It was then that Mahmud-Hodja, citing some ancient Uighur literature he had once read,[104] told him the story of the Apostle Thamus, who had travelled as far as the Oxus and the Jaxartes[105] and had even built a Cathedral of his own faith there.

It was this that decided Ioann's fate. At night, by the light of a creaking camp lantern – kept, like everything and everyone there, inside an iron cage – Father Ioann mastered the flourishes of the ancient Arabic and Uighur scripts, as described to him by Mahmud-Hodja. Both the harpoon-like needle of the letter 'T', and the letter 'Ash' – a spring with a backwards-bent tail – would remain for ever in Father Ioann's memory. Mahmud-Hodja had introduced him to the world of an extraordinary people, a people who believed devoutly in all religions from Shamanism to Buddhism and who had translated into Uighur the *Diamond Sutra*, Manichean penitential prayers and the Christian Gospels.

When they were both released from Solovky, Mahmud-Hodja had taken Father Ioann to Gilas; soon after this, Mahmud-Hodja had given up the ghost in his hometown of Balasagun. The orphaned Father Ioann had taken to buying up all the ancient manuscripts in the region, especially those with letters that resembled harpoons and springs. It is said that it was he who first introduced to Gilas the contagion of searching for manuscripts, a disease that would go on to afflict blind old Hoomer, Gogolushko the Party Secretary, Oppok-Lovely the passport officer and the drunken Mefody.

But we have digressed from the agonies of Father Ioann. The day of the very last scraping, the very last polishing, was drawing nearer. What then? Father Ioann was like a mountaineer approaching the very summit of the world, where earth comes to an end and heaven begins; he understood the intoxication that awaited him in that blue, faceted air, with snowy peaks arrayed on all sides; yes, he could sense that dizzying minute, or two minutes, or five minutes. But what then? What then – if his heart did not burst in that never-ending moment? Mountains were simpler, Father Ioann decided; you simply climbed back down again. But how could Father Ioann climb back down again? From the peak of a spiritual feat that had taken up his whole life. And where was he to climb down to? And to what? Was he once again to bury his Cathedral in dirt?

The Lord himself once went up into a mountain and spoke the words: 'It hath been said, "Thou shalt love thy neighbour and hate thine enemy." But I say unto you, "Love your enemies."' But who would place the follower of a different creed above a true believer? Father Ioann questioned the Lord – and searched for an answer inside himself. Deacons, bishops and metropolitans, a Patriarch or a Pope – would even the pillars of Christianity go to this extreme? He searched for an answer inside himself – and felt that he was being tempted to do neither more nor less than to renounce his faith.

One day, or rather night, not long after Easter, Father Ioann came across a boy curled up under a bush on the edge of the cemetery; he stank of vodka, of what people called the green snake. *What could inspire greater disgust? The serpent beneath the Tree of Knowledge . . . Father Ioann wanted to fetch Satan a blow with a cudgel, but – O Lord! – there was nothing to hand except a cross sticking up from a grave. Father Ioann seized this cross, raised it in the air, then stopped short; the boy, a native of these parts, was whispering in Russian: 'Mummy.'*

But the boy did not awake – neither when Father Ioann carried him to the burial mound, nor when he climbed down to continue his work in the Cathedral, leaving the boy to lie under the stars with no covering except Father Ioann's torn sheepskin. Long after midnight, with an excitement that bordered on lust, Father Ioann carried the boy into the Cathedral. Never had Father Ioann known anything like this; it was as if his every movement were being followed by thousands of eyes of thousand-winged yet incorporeal angels, as if his every moan or groan were being heard, as if his every thought were being examined for purity, and he was eager to show that his own lust was not like other people's lust; so it is that a man seeks to commune with eternity, in some sense to master it, but in the end, because of our imperfections, nothing remains but these stirrings of lust . . . Stammering and confused, the Father read the fifty-fifth of the Psalms of David and then made the sign of the cross over the boy. Just for a moment the boy half-opened his eyes, cast them round the Cathedral, the steps and columns, the cupola, the opening into the wide-open dawn sky, and then closed them again.

What the priest wanted now was for the boy to die, and then – it was with horror, with shame, but with an irrepressible longing that he caught himself thinking this base thought – he would administer the last rites to this innocently sinful child and thus fill the Cathedral with meaning; but the boy did not die, and Father Ioann did not kill him for the sake of the fulfilment of his own Cathedral.

What happened was more prosaic. In a state of trembling intoxication, leaving the boy lying before the altar on a stone that represented the Coffin of our Lord, Father Ioann climbed into his cradle in order to remove the last piece of petrified moss; this broke off at the first blow, tore off a piece of Father Ioann's ungainly cope, crashed onto one of the granite steps, chipped a small piece off the step and hurtled downwards again. The old man climbed down after it in agony, as if it were his own heart that had been chipped, but the damage to the step was only slight and Father Ioann turned his face to the heavens in joy, whereupon he heard the slender sound of an underground stream, a slowly mounting, snake-like current . . . Appalled at the remorseless movement of fate, losing his footing on the polished steps, the old man hurried down until, in darkness where the light of day never penetrates, he heard the rustling wings of angels now flying away. Water from the fires of Gehenna was rising unstoppably, along with a stinking steam. Father Ioann would have rushed down to meet this water but a sudden burning pain dragged him back up to the boy, whose eyes were now clear and open. The old man snatched him up in his arms and then, his cope flapping against the polished steps, rushed up to the cupola, to the opening into the sky.

That was the day of calamities, the day of the earthquake that brought about the collapse of the water tower opposite the house of blind Hoomer. Hot mineral water gushed from the Russian cemetery and the resulting flood swept away the graves that had been dug by Father Ioann – or Old Vanka, as most people called him. Coffins and pages from the Father's annals were carried off higgledy-piggledy by the healing waters. Later, however, Oppok-

Lovely got hold of some bulldozers from the local Motor Tractor Station and from three other centres run by the sons of Chinali and had a tower built over the former Cathedral. This tower, known as the Collective Farm Hydroelectric Station and separated by a path from the Russian cemetery where Vanka-Prophet is buried, is now used by the District Health Committee for sulphuric baths.

26

Indian films? Indian films, Indian films!

If anything educated the social conscience of Gilas and its
inhabitants, it was not of course the dismal Socialist Saturdays
during which Gogolushko and Satiboldi-Buildings supervised
the planting of tubercular trees – which grew neither taller nor
broader yet never quite died, and which would be transplanted
again in the course of the next Socialist Saturday. Nor was it the
slogans daubed all over Gilas – including the public toilets – by
Ortik-Picture-Reels. (As you may remember, none of these
slogans were ever read by anyone except Musayev – although it is
true that he was allowed free access, in his search for hidden
meanings in Party decrees, even to the women's toilets. As for
Ortik-Picture-Reels, he nearly drank himself to death on the
royalties he received for his work from the Party.)

No, if anything truly educated, quietened and comforted
Gilas, it was, of course, Indian films.[106] First, their titles provided
the boys with a word game that was popular, even if not always
quite fair. Yes, thanks to the bribes that his stepfather, Shop
Inspector Ryksy, received from local shopkeepers, Kobil-
Melonhead was able to make regular trips to the City and
therefore had a considerable advantage over the other boys.
Making the most of this, he would look at Kutr, the son of Bolta-
Lightning and Vera-Virgo, and ask a succinct question, for
example: 'L.I.S.?' After scratching his head for a bit, Kutr would
repeat some words he'd picked up at home from one of his
mother's visitors and admit defeat, having already bet Gilas's first
condom, which had been left behind by one of those same
visitors. '*Love in Simla!*' Kobil cried out triumphantly as he took
possession of the condom. 'It's never been shown here,' Kutr

whined – but it was too late. Kutr then suggested playing *nuts*;[107] very soon he had not only won back his condom but also won rights to the titles of eight films that no one in Gilas apart from Kobil-Melonhead had ever seen: S. for *Sangam*, F. I. T. D. for *Flower in the Dust*, E. A. M. F. for *Elephants are my Friends*, and so on.

So much for the children. As for the old men, they went to these films so they could weep freely for all their relatives who had died one way or another before, during or after the War – as well as for their own displaced, dislocated lives; the Koreans also wanted the chance to weep freely, to drown the grief of separation from their beloved Sakhalin Island with a still greater *Indian* grief; the pregnant wanted to be sure their babies would be born safely and happily; alcoholics wanted to spend a few hours without drinking – and then, of course, there were the Crimean Tatars[108] and the travelling gypsies, who had Indian blood themselves and goodness knows what going on in their obscure souls.

Once, on the day of Yom Kippur, after writing the film title *Shri 420* (*Mister 420*) with his own urine on the wall of Huvron-Barber's little shop, Yusuf-Cobbler went to see the film itself. Why he went is unclear – he may have wanted to laugh at those who were weeping, or he may have hoped to see a size 420 shoe – but the film affected him more deeply than he expected. Stealthily weeping thousands of years' worth of Jewish tears onto the floor, he saw his tears join streams of other tears flowing across the dank carpets Ortik-Picture-Reels had acquired after they had been 'written off' by the Party; these rivulets rose to the level of his clients' ankles, to the level of their calves, to the level of their bottoms – and soon Yusuf-Cobbler was thinking not only of the Great Flood and Noah's Ark but also of the Mount Ararat of salt-corroded soles and heels that he would soon be required to repair. Be that as it may, he was so shaken that he decided never again to piss against the wall of Huvron-Barber's little shop. Such is the power of Indian films.

But the story I want to tell happened long before *Mister 420*. I want to tell you the story of what happened after *The Railway to Pradesh* (T.R.T.P. – as Kobil-Melonhead would have put it). Or rather not *after* the film was shown, but *while* it was being shown, since Ortik-Picture-Reels showed every Indian film eight times: four times one day and four times the next day. The takings from the first two screenings went to pay the rental, the takings from the next four went to the local Party officials, and the takings from the last two constituted his profit. And Temir-Iul-Longline published a regular supplement listing changes made to the railway schedule in order to co-ordinate it with the film programme and the times workers finished their shifts.

Temir-Iul-Longline was, of course, an important figure. It was often said that his long-lived grandfather Umur-Longline had not only built the local railway but had also been buried somewhere beneath it; this, at least, was how Temir-Iul's father had understood the sentence, 'The iron road was built on the blood of the Russian and local proletariat'. Old Hoomer, the local sage, never contradicted this interpretation – and Temir-Iul gratefully arranged for him to be paid a considerable personal pension. He also, in case Hoomer should ever blurt out anything best left unsaid, ordered an entire Timur team[109] to keep an eye on him.

But it's hard to be sure of anything in this world. There were also certain sharp-tongued old women – like Nakhshon Shtonner, especially if her husband's pension was late – who sometimes tried to make out that Umur-Longline had been killed by Russian navvies: he had, so these women said, been profiteering from their labour – selling off railway sleepers, already coated with tar, to be used for building work in the town. Yes, mouths are different from saucepans – you can't keep a lid on them. And half of the buildings of Gilas did indeed have foundations made from these sleepers. There was no doubt that something had been built on the blood and bones of Temir-Iul's grandfather – it was just a little uncertain exactly what!

But enough of that – let's get back to the film. This particular film – like all Indian films, of course – was simple enough as regards content. Beside the railway line lives the family of the local Teacher, who has taken in the orphaned Gopal and brought him up together with his own daughter; yes, Gopal and the beautiful Radkha are like brother and sister to one another. The Teacher has taught Gopal to read and write; after betrothing him to Radkha, the Teacher even pays with the last of his money for him to go to Bombay and study in the Railway Academy. But after Gopal's departure, the Teacher's family sinks into poverty. The Teacher is growing old and can only teach the occasional lesson, and Radkha is now the breadwinner. She has no choice but to work as a dancer in the station restaurant. There she is seen by the Station Supervisor, who at once begins to think Evil Thoughts.

Meanwhile, Gopal, still in Bombay, is in trouble as the result of an encounter, during the Festival of the Sacred Cow, with Dimna – a student in the year below him and the daughter of the very same Station Supervisor. Dimna is in love with him; in the womb of the monument to the sacred cow, with festivities and fireworks going on outside, she tries to seduce him – but in vain.

Gopal finishes his studies and returns to his birthplace. In the evening he goes straight to the station buffet to drink a cup of Indian tea and – O Vishnu, O Shiva! – whom does he see but Radkha, dancing before a crowd of drunkards? A terrible storm sweeps through his heart. Radkha tries to explain herself – but in vain.

Gopal finds himself a room in a local boarding house. Soon, however, the Station Supervisor receives a letter from his daughter and not only allocates him official housing but even appoints him director of the maintenance section.

A year passes. On one and the same day Dimna returns from

her studies and the Teacher dies of consumption. Since he has no money, he is buried in a part of the cemetery beside the railway line. Not knowing any of this, Gopal arranges to meet Dimna. Radkha hears of this and much else from the station drunkards; forty days after her father's death, she accepts the Station Supervisor's long-standing proposal that she marry his half-wit nephew. This will make her the Station Supervisor's concubine and perhaps, in due course, her rival's stepmother.

News of the Teacher's death and Radkha's fateful decision reach Gopal as he lies in the peachy embrace of the shameless Dimna. Suddenly his eyes open. Abandoning everything, he runs down the railway line to the cemetery. Led by Fate, Radkha is already there, weeping over the tragedy of her life. Gopal and Radkha sing a sequence of songs to one another, explaining everything – both past and present. But there is no way out: they are in the grip of inexorable forces. Nevertheless, love is invincible; there on the grave, beside the Teacher's portrait, they love one another.

Meanwhile, the Station Supervisor and his dishevelled and devilish daughter, hell-bent on revenge, are coming down the line in a handcar – or do I mean handcart? A crowd of fire-breathing locals, armed with sticks and staves, accompanies them.

Gopal and Radkha are standing on the track, embracing. Their clothes and hair flutter in the wind. The handcar, accompanied by wild screams, draws closer. Something terrible is about to happen. But the whistle of a steam engine, coming from behind, overwhelms everything. Nothing can be heard above the grinding and crashing except Radkha's and Gopal's love song. The train sings this too, beating out the rhythm of their eternal song against the rails.

My darling, have no regret for the blood that's been spilt –
These rivers of blood will soon form a boundless sea.

Falsehood and lies will be swept from the face of the earth –
And the earth will be covered by wonderful flowers.
O pyari, pyari tumsa . . .

Temir-Iul-Longline had a son, as pock-marked as he was himself; afraid that this son would soon be disfigured irredeemably, he decided he must find him a wife. He had, however, left this too late. Democritis Chuvalchidi, the son of Auntie Lina (who worked as a cleaner at the Party Committee building) and the late Aristotilis Chuvalchidi (a Greek Communist refugee who had died of consumption far from his beloved Hellas) had already singled the boy out. Democritis had, in fact – if the reader will forgive me for saying this – already buggered the boy.

In spite of the fact that the pock-marked son of the pock-marked father bore the name of the heroic Sohrab,[110] he had turned out to be a gentle and tender-hearted young boy. He used to while away hour after hour in Rukiya's Selpo shop. Or he would go to the Kok-Terek Bazaar and his eyes would fill with tears as he ran dreamy fingers over a newly arrived bolt of woollen suiting or a piece of the very same *fil-de-perse* from which, before the War, Oppok-Lovely had made socks for her husband Mullah-Ulmas-Greeneyes. There was no one in Gilas whose knowledge of these materials and their provenance could compare with Sohrab's.

While everyone in Gilas – even the intellectual Mefody-Jurisprudence – was still wearing cream-coloured single-breasted Chinese jackets behind which could be glimpsed a Ukrainian shirt with an embroidered collar, Sohrab was wearing drainpipes and a tweed jacket he had bought straight off the shoulders of a bewildered old Kazakh who had just arrived, surrounded by rams, at the Kok-Terek Bazaar.

Barely had he acquired the nickname of Sohrab-Sharpie before he had shifted to a broad-checked stitched shirt and flared dacron trousers. And Guloyim-Pedlar, who had started up a cottage industry producing drainpipes and tweed jackets for up-to-the-minute Gilas Koreans, had barely had time to christen him Sohrab-Bell-Bottom before he was sauntering around in jeans made in India.

And so – back to the Indian film.

At the very moment that Sohrab, who was pock-marked but as tender and sensitive as a crêpe-de-Chine mallow, was being corrupted in the wool-washing shed by Democritis son of Aristotilis Chuvalchidi, who never even thought of washing his one and only smelly grey tunic – at that very moment Sohrab's father, Temir-Iul-Longline, was trying to arrange for his son to marry the only daughter of Faiz-Ulla-FAS, the younger son of Umarali-Moneybags and the director of the station FAS, or Factory Apprentice School.

Meanwhile, as in *The Railway to Pradesh*, Faiz-Ulla-FAS was bringing up his nephew Amon, whom he had inherited after the death of his sister; she had died soon after her father, of a heart attack brought about by her inability to remember where it was that the two of them had buried a large bag of both pre-war and wartime gold loan bonds. After educating Amon in his very own FAS, Faiz-Ulla had entrusted him to the care of Master-Railwayman Belkov. And on Amon's return from military service, Faiz-Ulla had decided, in the light of the shameful story of the betrothal of Amon's fellow-conscript Nasim, the grandson of Tolib-Butcher, that it would be best to avoid unnecessary expense and simply marry Amon to his own daughter. He would hardly, after all, need to pay bride-money to himself!

After the first screening of *The Railway to Pradesh* but before the beginning of the second screening, Faiz-Ulla was visited by matchmakers. And who do you imagine had sent them? The Station Supervisor, of course! Learning of this visit, the whole of Gilas held its breath. After all, Zainab and Amon truly loved one another. How could they not love one another when an epic poem had already been written about their love?[111]

Faiz-Ulla-FAS, who had himself betrothed the young couple, had no idea what to do. Were he to refuse the Station Supervisor, he would have to say goodbye to his FAS, to his pension and to the station itself. What else was there in life?

'The Station Supervisor has asked us to visit you. He is honouring you with his attention,' Tadji-Murad began obliquely.

'Not everyone is honoured with the good will of our supervisor,' said Ashir-Beanpole, as if through the crackly, tar-impregnated loudspeaker he used for his hourly announcements about train departures. And then, making Faiz-Ulla blink with surprise, he added, 'You know his son, don't you? A real warrior of a man!'

'Sohrab-Sharpie?' Faiz-Ulla blurted out.

Tadji-Murad tutted in gentle reproach. Then he went onto the offensive, shifting into the Russian he had learned as a con-script in a construction battalion. 'He's a fine fellow, an excellent fellow, a true Komsomol!'

'And his father will be sending him to university!' said the third matchmaker, Dolim-Dealer, sensing Faiz-Ulla's confusion.

Faiz-Ulla was indeed confused. After all, it was clear from the film, which he had seen only yesterday, that when a Station Supervisor tries to arrange a marriage there may be more to it than first meets the eye. And what about Amon and Zainab? Faiz-Ulla had promised to allow them to marry, to lie under a single blanket not as brother and sister but as man and wife. What would happen to Zainab? What would happen to poor Amon, whose friend, Nasim-Shlagbaum, had just run off with Natka-Pothecary, leaving his former comrade-in-arms all alone?

'A thousand thank-yous to our Supervisor, who has been granted wisdom by our wise Party! The most splendid of men, the kindest of men! A man whose speech is as straight and as strong as the iron road he supervises! Only . . . how can we possibly be worthy of his good will and attention? It's four months now since I last paid my Party dues.'

'Heavens!' said Dolim-Dealer, who was an experienced negotiator. 'You don't need to worry about a trifle like that. You can leave *that* to the Station Supervisor!'

'What do you mean?' said Faiz-Ulla, who was at a loss for words.

Continuing to draw on his many years of experience as a seller of bullocks and calves, Dolim-Dealer moved from words to deeds. 'Come on, give us your hand now! Good sense is the road to riches! Say yes! Come on now – say yes! Very well then – let the Station Supervisor pay not just four months of Party dues, but five months! Say yes! Really, come on now – don't shame us in public! Don't worry – he can pay your dues for six months! Look – there's a crowd gathering! Seven months then! All right? Yes?' At this point he shook poor Faiz-Ulla's hand so energetically that the latter's head couldn't possibly move horizontally, in negation, but only up and down, in agreement. 'Ah – he's said yes! He's agreed!' He released Faiz-Ulla's hand and said, 'Praise be to Allah!' letting the world know that the bargaining was over and a deal had been struck. After that it made no difference how many times Faiz-Ulla, who still had no idea what to say, invited them to sit down for a cup of tea – they were already leaving, to the accompaniment of Dolim-Dealer's mind-numbing babble: 'A man's word is his word is his word. Our supervisor will let you know the date of the wedding. But you can start making your preparations already! By the way, are you going to the cinema today?'

In reply to these last words, Faiz-Ulla gave a nod of the head – even more publicly than before.

By one o'clock the whole of Gilas knew what had happened. Akmolin, who at that time of day was usually asleep, was zipping about the station in his diesel shunter, deafening the town with his hooting and tooting as he darted from track to track.

During the afternoon screening Zainab and Amon learned what had happened. At six o'clock Democritis Chuvalchidi learned. The evening's programme was starting at seven. Gilas held its breath.

The trouble was that Gilas had not yet had time to digest the terrible events that had followed the screening of *Djaga*. The public trial was still continuing and it was unclear how the murder investigation would end. But this is a story you do not yet know.

Ezrael, a son of Huvron-Barber and grandson of Djebral-Semavi – the Persian who had ended up in Gilas because of his love for Maike the incomparable poet – had left school after failing, several years running, to pass his fourth-year exams. He was, however, as handsome as Yusuf – not the Gilas cobbler of that name, but the Yusuf or Joseph of the Koran and the Bible and the Torah – and he was married to Shah-Sanem, an Azerbaidjani from the Kazakh village of Kyzyl-Tau.

Somehow the young couple quarrelled, and Shah-Sanem, wanting the world to know how disgracefully she had been treated, went away for a few days to her mother's. It was the month of Ashura, when Shiites remember their great martyrs – and this was too solemn a time for Ezrael, whose faith was the faith of a true Persian, to get the better of his high principles, apologise to his wife in the usual way and bring her back home. After a week, seeing that her husband hadn't come to collect her, Shah-Sanem decided to go back home anyway. Ezrael saw her from the window of his father's barber's shop but pretended he hadn't. The Month of Sorrow was still only young. Wanting to provoke her seemingly haughty and indifferent husband, Shah-Sanem began collecting more of her belongings, as if to prolong her absence until the Month of Sorrow was over. After gathering up a bundle of clothes she didn't need, she emerged from inside the high wall Djebral had built as a shield against revolutions –

but Ezrael's teenage sister Aishe, who had all of a sudden begun to think of herself as a worldly-wise woman, left the house first and went rushing off to Huvron's shop. Learning what Shah-Sanem was doing, Ezrael abandoned Nabi-Onearm even though he had shaved only one side of his face; still holding his cut-throat razor and wearing his white gown, he rushed off after his wife, who was at that moment crossing the railway line. The sun was beating fiercely down, bleaching all sense from everything, and so Ezrael's sorrow all too easily modulated into fury – and it was just then that Akmolin chose to wake up and toot on his hooter. Tadji-Murad answered on his whistle, and this somehow made the heat haze spin more crazily than ever as it streamed up from the embankment. Ezrael looked at Akmolin and Tadji-Murad in sorrowful fury and told his wife to go back home and wait; once the month of Ashura was over, they would be able to sort everything out more easily. His wife seemed unable to understand and continued across the railway line with her bundle. Ezrael then began cursing his wife, shouting out that she was a brainless chicken and that this most sacred of months meant no more to her than a heap of manure. She walked on, through a gathering crowd; the half-shaven Nabi-Onearm, one side of whose face was contracting as the lather from Huvron's Bulgarian soap began to dry, watched especially intently. Had Ezrael taken her by the hand so everyone could see, had he finally taken that stupid bundle off her, Shah-Sanem would probably have turned back – but just then the Kyzyl-Tau bus drew up, and Ezrael still didn't understand. *Ezrael still didn't understand her.* He followed her into the bus, in his white gown and with a soapy razor in one hand. She took a seat by the window, and they remained silent until they got to the whirlpool near the level crossing, close to where the director of the Gilas music school had been run over by a train. There, however, they had to wait for Akmolin's mincing little diesel shunter to pass by, with Tadji-Murad standing on the footplate and whistling – and that was enough to make Ezrael swear out loud, which led Shah-Sanem to turn to the window and weep silent tears. Near the Kok-Terek Bazaar, Ezrael tried clumsily to wipe away these tears, but by then Shah-Sanem was in some kind of stupor – as blank and unfeeling as a bald patch on the head of one of his customers.

'So you just fucking want to be fucking fucked, do you? Well, fuck you!' hissed Ezrael, not entirely without hope. They were now drawing near the river where his grandfather had washed the body of the incomparable Maike. Shah-Sanem said nothing. With everyone watching, Ezrael slashed her throat with his razor.

Blood spurted onto his white gown, onto the tangled hair of the screaming Kazakh girl in front of them and onto a sack with maize spilling out of it beside their feet. Ezrael walked down the bus, which had come to a stop in the middle of the road, and made his way out into the steppe, to the very place where his grandfather had buried the incomparable Maike after hearing from him the terrible words that they had all heard again during the film *Djaga*:

> Blood is never washed away by blood,
> Only tears can wash away blood.

And so, still not having digested the story of Ezrael and Shah-Sanem, Gilas waited breathlessly for the second screening of *The Railway to Pradesh*. In the usual way, an hour before the film was due to begin, music blared out through Ortik-Picture-Reels' loudspeaker, which the railway authorities had 'written off' in exchange for Ortik's adorning a banner with their latest slogan: 'Gain a minute – and lose your life! Take care!' The Beatles sang 'Girl'; Raj Kapoor sang *'Mera djula he djopani'* or 'I'm wearing a Japanese hat' . . . Three quarters of an hour before the beginning, Ortik's Auntie Koshoy-Hola began selling her sunflower seeds – a commodity on which she had a local monopoly; at the same time Ortik's wife began reselling some of the tickets she had already sold. After another fifteen minutes a long queue of people had formed, all of them dressed in their smartest white; Ortik's son Omil was supplying tickets to the tail of the queue at three times the official price. Nearly the whole of the able-bodied population of Gilas was present.

Zainab and Amon sat down on either side of Faiz-Ulla-FAS. Temir-Iul-Longline the Station Supervisor was greeted with loud applause as he strode in together with Tadji-Murad, Ashir-Beanpole, Dolim-Dealer and the for some reason still only half-shaven Nabi-Onearm, who raised his one hand as if to calm the public. Ortik, however, understood this gesture – which Nabi repeated after a whisper from the Station Supervisor – as a signal that the film should begin; he turned out the lights.

Had I the power, I would move the film from the evening to a mindless midday, a midday full of sunlight and languid songs on the radio – but it was inescapably seven o'clock in the evening. Young daughters-in-law were sprinkling their yards with water; patches of shadow had appeared; the newly swept earth was breathing a sigh of relief. And the fervent song of young Gopal and Radkha could be heard from the summer cinema.

Everything happened as scripted. After a day of honest labour, and after pissing against the wall of Huvron-Barber's little shop, Yusuf-Cobbler was still chuckling at the thought of the imminent torrents of tears when the old Teacher handed the departing Gopal his last rupees together with a school certificate for good study and conduct and Akmolin suddenly got up and left: was he *really* just starting his night shift? Ten minutes later, and without waiting for Radkha to do her first belly dance before the drunken railway workers, Zainab got to her feet and walked out to the left, past her mother. A moment later Amon got to his feet and walked out to the right. The audience held its breath, watching the Station Supervisor saying goodbye to his daughter as she set off just as Gopal had set off a year before her. At that moment

Dolim-Dealer touched the Gilas Station Supervisor on the arm and followed Zainab out.

Yusuf-Cobbler had already forgotten what he had been laughing about only minutes before, the Indian Station Supervisor was already thinking evil thoughts and leading the audience to suspect him of still greater evil when the Gilas Station Supervisor – whose suspicions were getting too much for him – also walked out of the cinema, through rivers of tears and Radkha's impassioned singing. Amon and Zainab were already far away, kissing with no less passion.

Some time later, as Gopal entered the station canteen, Democritis Chuvalchidi entered the station buffet run by Froska, the ex-wife of ex-Master-Railwayman Belkov. He ordered a glass of vodka on tick, silently downed it without even the tiniest morsel of food, made his way to the cinema – and found the Indian Station Supervisor furthering his evil designs; there he was up in his office, with the railway line stretching out beneath him as far as the eye could see to both east and west. Democritis glanced lazily at the screen, then surveyed the rapidly diminishing audience till he caught sight of *him*. Dimna threw herself at Gopal and, after singing a song of faithless love, began kissing him in front of everyone. Why didn't he speak? Why didn't he declare his love once and for all? Democritis made up his mind when only six people were left: old Koshoy-Hola, stepping across puddles of tears as she went on selling sunflower seeds; Ortik's son Omil, who was still chewing the last of the seeds he had bought with the money he had made from selling tickets; Musayev-Slogans, who couldn't understand why there were no posters and slogans in India; Nabi-Onearm, who was scratching the still unshaven half of his face with his one hand; and *him, him, him*!

As the handcar, with the whole of the town on board, careered noisily along, the lovers stood on the railway line, just beyond the level crossing, in the last rays of the summer sun. Their hair and their clothes were fluttering in the breeze. Seeing them, the Station Supervisor screamed. The handcar gathered speed, hurtling towards a catastrophe. Tadji-Murad closed his eyes in alarm, but the whistle he had forgotten in his mouth suddenly whistled. There was a hellish wail from the oncoming loco-motive, Gopal and Radkha burst into an '*O pyari, pyari tumsa*' that could be heard all over the town – and Akmolin slammed on his brakes. The handcar, spilling out half its passengers, also stopped dead. And there were the lovers – standing halfway between the handcar and the locomotive and aware only of each other.

Everyone went still. The Station Supervisor's head – everyone slowly realised – was sticking through a hole in the shatterproof glass of the handcar's windscreen. While Tadji-Murad super-vised the extraction of his Supervisor's head, whistling and waving his hands in the air, Zainab and Amon leaped onto the running board of the local train just announced by Ashir-Beanpole – and that was the last that anyone in Gilas ever heard of them.

And as the frustrated audience dispersed towards their homes, after failing to watch the film to its climax and then being robbed of fulfilment a second time, a scene took place beside the level crossing – just beyond the whirlpool that the Salty Canal forms after emerging from the pipe that takes it beneath the road, close to where Ezrael had cursed Akmolin and Tadji-Murad and where the director of the Gilas music school had been run over by a train – a scene such as could never have been seen in any of the films shown by Ortik-Picture-Reels. Two men were walking along the railway line, and one was saying, 'So you don't love me any more? Well, why don't you say anything? Say something, damn you! You bastard! You fucking bastard! Finished with me, are you? Finished? So I'm no use to you any longer, am I? Remember how happy we used to be! We could still go away together. Yes, we could get tickets for the express and just go. Who the fuck's going to find us? Did you hear what I said? Say something then! Why are you crying? Look, nothing's happened. Look, we're together. Just the two of us. And we don't need anyone else, do we? Do we? Why the fuck don't you say anything? Why are you looking at me like that? Because of my clothes? They're just clothes. My mother washes them every other day. Seen better clothes on other people, have you? And I suppose other people's cocks feel bigger, do they? Or . . . Have you . . . Stop a moment . . .' Standing quite still, he hissed into the other man's face, 'So you just fucking want to be fucking fucked, do you? Well fuck you!'

Democritis leaped on Sohrab, threw him to the ground, rolled him over a rail and onto the stones of the embankment and harshly, brutally, raped him.

No, the portrait of the old Greek Communist did not – like the portrait of the old Indian Teacher in the cemetery – look down on this scene from the embankment; the only onlooker was Nabi-Onearm, who was on his way to the bathhouse to wash away the tears from the film – or so he said later. In actual fact, he was making the most of everyone being out of the way and was about to start stealing his quota of cotton seeds. Fired with eloquence by what he witnessed that evening, he chose to testify at the subsequent trial, which ended with Democritis the son of the late Greek Communist being exiled to the land of the Fascist Colonels, without right of return, and Sohrab-Sharpie the son of the Station Supervisor being exiled to the All-Union State Cinema Institute in Moscow and leaving the courtroom singing, in his touchingly girlish voice, that immortal Indian song: '*O pyari, pyari, tumsa . . .*'.

27

None of the children gave much thought to the question of where the Koreans had come from and when they had first appeared in Gilas.[112] Some of the brighter boys – Fazi the grandson of old Boikush, for example – thought of them as Uzbeks who happened to speak a different language. Another boy, who had seen not only Koreans but also Dungans,[113] doubted the truth of this but decided to keep silent – probably because Boikush was selling *kurt* at the time and so Fazi's pockets were always full of incontrovertible arguments.

At school it was thought for a long time – both in the classes for Russian-speakers and, still more, in the classes for Uzbek-speakers – that the Koreans were a particular breed of Russians. Instead of names like Sasha, Yura or Katya, they bore names that the boys considered still more Russian: Vitold, Izolda, Artaxerxes or Klim. Although it has to be said that the parents of these boys all had names like Sasha, Yura or Katya.

But no one saw much of these parents, although the grannies and grandads appeared on the street more often. The grand-parents' names, however, were a mystery – except that there was one old man the children all called Alyaapsindu. Alyaapsindu did not have a son called Petya or even a granddaughter called Lyutsia, and he used to wander about all day between the station and the end house on the street by the Salty Canal. In his straw hat, and with a bamboo staff in his hand, he would go out even in the most scorching heat, stooping a little, as if he were trying to tread on his compact shadow, and repeating his 'Alyaapsindu!' (the Korean for 'Greetings!') to every adult, child or dog that he met.

Then he would return – and somehow it looked as if he were trying to get away from a shadow that had lengthened during the hours he had been walking. He might have been smiling into his thin, whitish moustache as the children followed behind him and called out 'Alyaapsindu!', uncertain if they were pleasing or irritating an old man who seemed as indifferent to them as a pendulum.

The children's parents would appear late in the autumn, after they had finished work in the rice and onion fields. All Gilas would suddenly be filled with their strange and festive-sounding speech and with crowds of men sauntering to and from the cinema, turning their feet out as they walked, jackets flung casually over their bony, protruding shoulders.

The men would take over the Gilas chaikhanas; they now seemed like a particular breed of Uzbeks – more Uzbek than the Uzbeks themselves, who seemed somehow lost amid the sea of light blue Korean shirts and their ever-changing fans of cards. Their wives, meanwhile, remained at home, hulling rice or hanging up onions to dry beneath awnings; those who had already completed these tasks passed the time in little huts by the bank of the Salty Canal, looking after their two or three pigs, and anyone playing football near the canal would smell a mixture of fresh sawdust, salted and peppered cabbage, stagnant water and bitter onion which reminded them that Koreans could never really be anything but Koreans.

The Koreans never worked the fields near Gilas. They travelled to regions known only to elder brothers and sisters who had done geography at school and that sounded strangely exotic to everyone else: Kuban and Kuilok, Samarasi and PolitDept, Shavat and Sverdlov. No one in Gilas ever saw them working; the town knew them only as conquerors.

The Koreans didn't even trade in the Gilas bazaar. During the winter, while Korean men with names like Boris, Vasily and Gennady were walking around the streets or enjoying the chaikhanas, old Uzbek women would take the opportunity to dart down Papanin Street and clinch deals with Korean women with names like Vera – or Faith, Nadya – or Hope, and Lyuba – or Love. The Uzbek women would then spend the rest of the winter at the bazaar, selling back to the Koreans the rice, onions and peppers they had bought from them only a few months before.

But not *chimchi*. *Chimchi*! This explosion that turned an Uzbek boy's tongue inside out, this fusion of every Korean smell, this peppery fire that warmed the breath of the Korean women calling out their wares in the winter bazaar, this bitter Korean cabbage with veins as tight and white as violin strings, circled by a girdle of blazing-hot peppers just where the white of the stalk changes to the green of the leaves – how could this *chimchi* that was the symbol, emblem and nickname of every Korean be sold by a mere Russian or Uzbek, by a Tatar or a Bukhara Jew? Each knows his own: Akmolin has his shunter, Kuchkar-Cheka keeps a seat warm in a chaikhana, Zakiya-Nogaika washes and combs wool, Yusuf-Cobbler resoles shoes, and even Ozoda, with the encouragement of her aunt Oppok-Lovely, keeps an eye on the traders in the small Gilas bazaar – while *chimchi* is sold by Koreans: by Vera – or Faith, Nadya – or Hope, and Lyuba – or Love.

They did this, however, only when their husbands had stopped going out onto the street. January and early February – a bleak time of year in Gilas – was a kind of dead season for the men. It was a time when they sat in their homes; the previous year's debts had been paid back, and the money left over had been spent in the chaikhanas and on some new item of consumer goods; one year this would be televisions, another year mopeds, and a third year refrigerators. It was a time when they sat and watched television, or else cleaned their mopeds, or slammed the doors of their new fridges – although the now-orphaned old Uzbeks in the chaikhanas sometimes made out that this dead time was when the Koreans did their wildest gambling, that they met every night at Gennady's, or Vladimir's, or Mikhail's and that the lights always burnt until dawn.

And this was the season when the Koreans killed their pigs. The flames of their blowtorches glimmered against the frozen yellow grass by the Salty Canal and vied with the frozen yellow sunset over the fields.

It was said that the Koreans ate dogs, that this helped to prevent them catching TB – an illness to which they would otherwise be especially vulnerable because they spent their working lives up to their knees in water; it was said that in February, before leaving for the fields of Kuban or Kuilok, of Shavat or Samarasi, they borrowed money from Tolib-Butcher, from Satiboldi-Buildings or, more often, from Oppok-Lovely – to be repaid the following autumn; yes, all kinds of things were said of them, but every spring, all of a sudden, they would disappear, leaving as hostages their strangely named children – their Lavrentys and Emmas, their Violas and Ruslans, their Artyomchiks and Ophelias.

28

The director of the Gilas music school was called Sevinch; the conductor of the Gilas Pioneer-and-Trade-Union Wind Orchestra – or brass band – was called Soginch. By a whim of nature one of the two was deaf in his right ear, while the other was deaf in his left ear. Both, however, had been brought up in the same orphanage – in Samarasi – where they had been taken as small children during the years when fathers were being unmasked as kulaks and mothers were being liberated from their veils,[114] leaving no one to take care of small children except the State that was already taking such absolute care of their parents. The State gave Sevinch and Soginch their brassy names – which meant, respectively, 'Joy' and 'Desire' – and imbued them for the rest of their lives with a love of martial music. So strong was this love that, many years later, when the chamber orchestra of the Gilas music school took nine minutes to get through a Beethoven quartet, Sevinch frowned. 'Languid,' he said crossly, 'and far too drawn-out. I want the same again – but this time in three minutes!'

But that was towards the end of Sevinch's life, which we shall come to in due course. And it is not very important anyway. What was important, what really mattered, was that Sevinch's and Soginch's lives, ever since the orphanage in Samarasi, had been like the two rails of a single track, tied inseparably together and running in close parallel. And this orphanage had also instilled in each of them the need to come first in whatever he did; there was, after all, only one of anything – one pot of food in the dining room, one textbook in the library, one hole in the squat-toilet – and so the children had to learn to be quick off the mark. Either by 'tramping along stony paths', as Marx had written on the wall of the corridor, or by 'trampling one's comrades underfoot', as someone had written in the toilet.[115]

And so it was Sevinch who collected the most red paper stars in an envelope – one for each time his work was marked 'Excellent' – and who ended up with more of these red stars than there are stars in the sky; but it was Soginch who won the gold medal in their last year at school – for a version of Lermontov's 'The Novice' in which the hero was Stalin himself. Soginch adapted the poem so skilfully that the leopard Stalin wrestled in the night brought to mind not only Hitler, but also, in turn, Bukharin, Radek, Trotsky[116] and even that only recently unmasked enemy of the people Akmal-Ikrom.[117] There was no counting the tears shed by plump Auntie Tonya the Cook, whom the trade union had invited to join the examination board, when she read how Stalin confessed to Lenin, and through Lenin to the immortal Karl Marx himself:

> I would have died, I've often thought,
> Had you not lived, had you not taught.

But when they were both sent to the Higher School of Music and Arts in the City, as part of the post-war Komsomol intake of the era of rebirth and reconstruction, it was Sevinch who was appointed the conductors' course-leader; he had donated to the State all the red paper stars he had been awarded during his ten years at the orphanage.

Soginch then wrote a denunciation, stating that Sevinch and countless others were rootless cosmopolitans[118] – snakes who had sloughed off their surnames and so camouflaged their true nationality. And so Sevinch and half of the course were deported across the Kazakh steppe and into deepest Siberia, to some Fuisk or Kuisk or Fukuisk or other.

And Sevinch became known as Moses, and he and Soginch were separated.

In this Fuisk or Kuisk or Fukuisk, like a cat taken far from its home, Sevinch discovered that he possessed a phenomenal memory: he needed only to glance at a score by Stravinsky – who was banned – or Bach – who was permitted – or at an account in *Pravda* of Beria's trial[119] or Khrushchev's Secret Speech – and the whole of it would be superimposed, phrase by phrase, on the rhythmic pattern beaten out by the names of the stations through which he had passed along the iron road to Siberia. Inexorable *toskà* had etched these names deep into Sevinch's soul: Salar, Gidra, RadioStation, Shumilov, Gilas, Kirpichny, Sanitornaya, Sari-Agach, Djilga, Darbaza, Chengeldy, Arys, and so on, up till the final chord or sentence, now linked inseparably to his present Fuisk or Kuisk or Fukuisk.

A few years later, however, Khrushchev's Thaw set in, and Sevinch's People's Symphony Orchestra went on an extended tour not only of the Soviet Union but even of Western Europe, demonstrating to the world that our provincial musicians were at home with Mahler, Hindemith, Berg and even – to the surprise of many – Karlheinz Stockhausen. The day they arrived in Paris, after the Orchestra had been awarded a First Prize in Milan for their performance of an anonymous masterpiece that had been languishing in the Italian National Archive before being embraced by Sevinch's capacious memory, Sevinch was invited by one of his violinists, Joseph Levi-Sprauss, to accompany him to the house of a distant relative – a certain Claude Lévi-Strauss who turned out to be studying the myths of some Irokoiz or Karakez or other. When Sevinch, who was engaged in his usual mental activity – this time he was fitting one of the symphonies of his beloved Beethoven (the one with the famous knocking of Fate – *Ta-ta-ta ta-a! Ta-ta-ta ta-a!*) to the names of his Siberian railway stations, starting from Salar; when Sevinch suddenly remarked *à propos* of nothing that only between Chelkar and Emba did myth part company from music, the startled Lévi-

Strauss carefully noted down his words – and published them three years later as if they represented a world-shaking discovery. And even Levi-Sprauss's unsophisticated tastes – the way he eschewed raw oysters in order to chew on cooked meat and potatoes – were exploited by this relative of his and used in the title of another of his controversial books.[120]

Lévi-Strauss, alas, had tapped only the most superficial layer of Sevinch's phenomenal memory. Had he been more attentive during that evening in Paris, or had he gone once or twice to visit his relative in that Siberian Fuisk or Kuisk, he would have been able to classify the entire world into isomorphic structures. After all, the Sermon on the Mount was connected to the Ya-Sin Sura or 'Heart of the Koran'; Pushkin's and Alisher Navoi's analyses of the tangled net of human passions were part of the same intricate web; and even within the confines of Gilas one could hear the development both of a famous theme of Shostakovich and the endless whirling of Solzhenitsyn *Red Wheel* . . . But I must not allow myself to be carried away.

While Sevinch was in Siberia, preparing to enrich world scholarship, Soginch had been making tea for the Head of what was by then called the Department of Reconstructed Popular Instruments. Then the Head of Department had died and Soginch had conducted the orchestra in a performance of Chopin's 'Funeral March' ornamented with a few delightfully Uzbek grace notes. There was a shortage of qualified cadres during those years, and so Soginch, in spite of his youth, became the new Head of Department.

Soginch would have gone on serving tea, first to the Deputy Head of the Higher School of Music and Arts, then to the Head and then to someone still higher, conducting requiems as long as his age allowed – had it not been for the onset of Khrushchev's Thaw and the return from exile (they travelled, as we have seen via Vienna, Milan and Paris) of Sevinch's People's Symphony Orchestra. These two events happened to coincide with the sudden death of the Deputy Head, and so Sevinch was appointed Deputy Head in his place. His appointment was announced at a general Party meeting, with eight representatives of the City Party Committee – from the General Secretary to the woman whose role was to offer the speaker a glass of kefir[121] – sitting on the presidium, as well as a now grim-looking Soginch and a now jovial-looking Sevinch. While the Head held forth about mistaken and repressive policies in regard to culture and art (policies he had zealously enforced during the preceding five years) the colour of Soginch's face changed from white to green, while Sevinch's face glowed ever more vividly.

Soginch then did as he had done for many years, and began making tea for the new Deputy Head of the School. Serving the tea, however, proved harder than making it. Sevinch's secretary made Soginch wait while her boss spoke to the financial director and the accountant, and it was several hours before the Head of Department was allowed to go in and congratulate the new Deputy Head; he did not, of course, proffer the pot of now cold tea. This humiliating tea ceremony was repeated day in day out. After wasting four packets of top-grade tea, which he had been given by a student who managed a food shop, the Head of the Department of Reconstructed Popular Instruments resolved to visit the Deputy Head of the Higher School of Music and Arts only when summoned.

Khrushchev crowned maize 'Queen of the Fields', Sputnik flew off into Space and Khrushchev's 'Cosmic' Seven-Year Plan came and went. The Department of Reconstructed Popular Instruments was reconstructed to include a national choir – and the post of Deputy Head of the School was abolished. Once again Soginch was Tsar.

And so now it was merely as an ordinary lecturer and the

conductor of an orchestra from some Fuisk or Kuisk or Fukuisk that Sevinch would sit in Soginch's lobby, waiting while Soginch ran a finger over a lady student's eyebrow or brushed up a few lines of his dissertation about the reconstruction of the traditional plectrum.

From time to time – so people said – the two of them would curse one another for all they were worth, each trying to channel his curses into the other's good ear while advancing his own deaf ear . . . And so their closely bound lives would have gone on – but for the scandal that for many years deprived the distraught Oppok-Lovely of her beloved singer, Bahriddin. It was discovered – alas! – that the reconstructed department had been supplying Bahriddin with female trainees outside working hours.

Once again they saw eight representatives of the City Party Committee – from the General Secretary to the woman whose job was to offer a glass of kefir to the speaker, although this was now someone new, her predecessor having been promoted to the office of supplying kefir to the Provincial Committee. Once again the General Secretary, adorned with all his medals, raged and fumed – this time about a terrible epidemic, a morass of amorality blighting socialist-realist art. And so the department was closed and all the members of staff, including Soginch and Sevinch, were deported to Gilas.

This new place of exile was not far away, and the brief train journey through an area of wasteland, with nothing to remember but two long curves and one level crossing with a horizontal *shlagbaum*, had an effect that no one could have predicted: Sevinch's photographic memory, charged up in readiness for new and astonishing feats, went as blank as a film exposed to bright light; it burst, faded, dissolved, was carried away, reduced to nothing, leaving only a monotonous yellowy-brown and the black and white flickering of the solitary *shlagbaum*.

It was at this time that Soginch first became known as Aaron and that Sevinch met a writer by the name of Chingiz Aitmatov, who was composing something to do with a railway line across the steppe. It would be truer, however, to say that this was when Aitmatov met Sevinch, who had been recommended to him by Lévi-Strauss, Roman Jacobson, Chomsky, Derrida and another seven or eight luminaries of world culture. Moved to the depths of his heart, Aitmatov immortalised this meeting through his terrible story about a man named Mankurt whose memory has melted away.[122] Mankurt's name, however, derives from a misunderstanding; Aitmatov had failed to grasp that Sevinch, lamenting his lost memory, had somehow managed to come up with the French word *manquer*. Yes, writers get things wrong and make things up. The sad but simple truth is that Moses Sevinch had forgotten the names of the stations he had passed through during his journey to Siberia and – as an inevitable consequence – everything that he had linked to these names during his years as a conductor in his Siberian Fuisk or Kuisk or Fukuisk. And the years before his exile contained nothing memorable at all: only an anonymous orphanage childhood and its brass band. But since he kept singing Dunayevsky's marches[123] under his breath, he was appointed head of the music school.

And so Soginch would have to hang about in the corridor, waiting for Sevinch to remember, at last, that his secretary had summoned Soginch in order for them to fix up a meeting – a meeting that, like so many previous appointments they had arranged, Sevinch would at once completely forget about.

Around this time half of the orchestra followed Mullah-Ulmas-Greeneyes into emigration, some going to Brighton Beach and others to Israel, while those who were refused visas went to the Old City to join the new Shash-Maqam ensemble that had been set up to play the music of the Bukhara court.[124] Putting on an embroidered skullcap, exchanging one's violin for a *gidjak* and well-tempered polyphony for wailing monody was simpler, after all, than changing one's country.

The Patriarch who was setting up this ensemble loved vodka and flattery. So said the poet Habib-Ulla – who, after drinking till dawn, would often find himself sitting in some doorway or other. In his loneliness he would take out two kopeks and a list of telephone numbers from a hidden trouser-pocket, go to a public telephone and begin ringing the numbers in alphabetical order. The Patriarch of traditional music was, as a rule, the only man who picked up the phone; more often than not he turned out to be meditating on the theme of wine in Classical Persian poetry. Habib-Ulla would tell him that a new interpretation of this mystery had come to him in a dream, and, half an hour later, he would be sitting beside the Patriarch, reciting something oddly familiar along the lines of:

> The Shash Maqam resembles ruby wine,
> But what is wine if not the Shash-Maqam?[125]

Overwhelmed by such beauty of feeling, the Patriarch would moan, put a hand to his heart and take down a *doutar*[126] hanging from a nail on the wall. He would start to play; the music he played was as thick and dense as a hangover, and now it was Habib-Ulla who would moan, 'Look, look – here comes Tamburlaine's magnificent cavalry! Their gowns and their horse-cloths are gold brocade. And here comes the cupbearer, the pourer of wine, the raiser of spirits! O cupbearer, pour wine for us!' Habib-Ulla would start to rave and hallucinate. His spirit, stinking of the night's vodka, would spread its wings until it took up the entire room. 'Cupbearer, bring wine!' he would repeat, almost sobbing. The obedient old Patriarch would put down his *doutar* and bring in a bottle he had put aside in case Tamburlaine and his horsemen should appear – and, with their eyes half closed in the dawn light, the two friends would silently do justice to this bottle, in order for the Patriarch to pick up the *doutar* a second time, while Habib-Ulla, like a whirling dervish, let himself be carried away into a slow, dizzyingly blissful dance.

'No one but you, no one but you can understand this music,' the Patriarch would say afterwards, weeping over Habib-Ulla while the latter snored in ecstasy.

Before long the half-Jewish orchestra had drunk their All-Uzbek Patriarch into the grave, leaving the orphaned Habib-Ulla to knock back plain vodka without musical accompaniment. But we have again allowed ourselves to be carried away.

What I wanted to say was that Sevinch felt more deeply orphaned than even Habib-Ulla, the orphaned poet of the Old City. Sevinch had lost not only his music, not only his career, not only what was left of his orchestra – he had lost his memory. And he did not drink; he did not know the saving grace of vodka. He forgot everything. He forgot when he was meant to be at the music school and he forgot how to find his way there alone; every day either some student, in exchange for Sevinch's signature in his course book, would have to accompany him to the outer fence of the school grounds and hand him over there to the care of his secretary – or else Musayev-Slogans, who had lost not his memory but his mind (not to mention the first part of his name), would lead him through dusty and sloganless sidestreets until Sevinch's secretary tracked them down at a crossroads.

It was at this time that Sevinch – who no longer even knew his own name and whom others knew simply as Moses or Musa – became an artist. No longer burdened by memory, he saw everything as if for the first time. And since the language he had mastered in his orphanage, the mother-tongue he had acquired with no mother to help him, was already drifting into oblivion (the curses he had got his tongue round only later in life – those monstrous, magnificent, multi-layered and multi-storied variations on pricks and cunts and mother-fucking curs that he had learned in Fuisk or Kuisk or Fukuisk – had long ago vanished into thin air) Musa was left with only a mute longing, a sense of grey *toskà* that he tried to brighten with cheap watercolours. Little by little he painted over all the writing paper and all the music paper in the music school; after that he began practising murals in the teachers' toilet. Next it was frescoes on the ceiling of the small room he had been allocated for the period of his exile by the good-hearted Oppok-Lovely – who, as a result of her failure to get any passport data out of the music school's nameless director, was able to issue a brand-new passport to yet another would-be émigré. Everyone was following in her husband's footsteps and leaving Gilas for foreign parts. Everything in Gilas was diminishing – everything, that is, except Musa's *toskà*; like water in a fairy-tale well, this grew only deeper and deeper.

Musa's devoted secretary, after shedding silent tears in the teachers' cloakroom, proposed a motion at a meeting of the music school trade union calling for the children to be educated in the spirit of syncretism and a holistic and integral approach to art – and, since no one understood a word of this gobbledegook except that it meant something very serious indeed, the director was allowed to spend his sleepless nights painting over every wall, door, cupboard, desk and pane of glass, and even the solitary, tinkling grand piano – which, in any case was really an upright with a plywood extension tacked onto it by Kozikvay the school carpenter.

Next the secretary made representations to the summer and winter cinemas and – in return for a bottle of Ambassador Vodka and a jar of home-pickled cucumbers – Ortik-Picture-Reels not only gave Musa the free run of his walls but even allowed him to use the brushes and paint he was issued with as an official slogan-painter. This, unfortunately, led to problems: the depth of Musa's *toskà* impelled him to submerge Ortik-Picture-Reels's snow-white screens beneath wave upon wave of indelible patterns, as a result of which film after film, even a comedy like *Operation Y*, evoked from the frustrated inhabitants of Gilas only floods of tears – floods that washed away the last rotting remnants of the strips of carpet that the Party Committee had long ago 'written off' in exchange for a few slogans no one except poor old Musayev-Slogans ever bothered to read.

Wanting to avoid a scandal, the music school secretary hurriedly got hold of a couple of pairs of not-quite-matching, not-quite-white sheets. Swallowing down his indignation with pieces of lightly pickled cucumbers, Ortik hung the sheets over the rainbow colours with which the music-school director had tried to paint away his *toskà*.

To his secretary's relief Musa soon came to understand the vanity of his attempts to conquer the flat world of planes – the world of walls, ceilings and asphalt surfaces – and he transferred his attention to his own body. The secretary found this easier – Musa didn't try to paint his face, since he couldn't see it, and what he painted on his wrists and hands could be taken for tattoos from the harsh years of his orphanage childhood.[127] It was harder, however, in the heat of summer. Musa would stare languidly out of the window and sweat; the office would fill with different-coloured vapours; and his occasional visitors, allowed through only in cases of extreme necessity – the accountant on pay day, the supplies manager on delivery day, Soginch on days of school orchestra concerts (the secretary was hoping he might revive her boss's memory) – would emerge from this office in shock, their voices shaking as they tried to describe what they had seen there.

Soginch, however, was in shock not because of the vapours but because Sevinch had forgotten him. Sevinch remembered him neither as a friend nor as an enemy and greeted him at each concert as if they were meeting for the first time. For a while Soginch took out his irritation and bewilderment on the orchestra, threatening the lead violin with his stool or hurling his music stand at the percussionist, but after the occasion when he threw his baton at one of the flutes and his musicians responded by mounting a surprise attack on him in the dark, repeating as a diversionary tactic the words, 'This'll teach you to paint on the walls, this'll teach you to make a mess of the fizzy-water stall!' – after that evening his behaviour changed. He organised orchestra trips to nearby collective farms; he arranged for those who had suffered at his hand to be awarded Lenin Certificates and for everyone else to be given Lenin Badges. He was, however, obsessed by a thought that allowed him no respite.

It was around this time that Musa came to the end of his Self-Painting Period and entered his Colour-on-Colour Period. With the salary he still received as School Director he began buying entire boxes of watercolours and using colours from one box to paint on colours from another box: blue on red, red on yellow, then purple or orange on green. This so amazed him that he not only stopped going out to work but even gave up leaving his room. And Soginch, sitting in the director's armchair when the secretary was out during her lunch break, finally grasped the utter hopelessness of his orphaned fate: were Sevinch sitting in this chair, his own existence would be endowed with at least an illusion of meaning. But as things stood . . . And so Soginch decided to act, to put into effect a plan he had been thinking about for a long time.

What you are about to read is a story of complex treachery – and Gilas heard about it only after Soginch had died from a wasting illness the aetiology of which Janna-Nurse had been unable to determine from any available reference book and which she suspected was a sickness of the soul. But you need to know a little more about Musa and his habits if you are to understand this story and the plot that Soginch devised.

Once a week Musa used to walk across the level crossing in order to wash himself in the bathhouse – a habit instilled in him at the orphanage and which remained with him until his dying day. There, during his Self-Painting Period, he had washed the paint off his body in a private cubicle for which he paid fifty kopeks. Since entering his Colour-on-Colour Period he had found it painfully dull to look at the colourless water and his own pale body, but even oil paints would have been easier to wash away than habits instilled in a Soviet orphanage.

Soginch was also fated by his years in the orphanage to go once a week to the bathhouse – although he went to the main room rather than to a private cubicle, since he had never been one for self-painting and no soap in the world could ever wash off his two orphanage tattoos: 'I'll Never Forget Dear Mother' and a portrait of Stalin with his moustache brushing against Lenin's beard.

Relying on Musa's orphanage ways, Soginch decided to act. Having bribed his percussionist by promising to make him not only a Shock Worker of Communist Labour but also his personal assistant, he threatened the lead violin, grabbed his bow, hit the viola player on one ear with it and stuffed the viola player's handkerchief up the trombone. After Soginch had left, the percussionist did as instructed and persuaded the orchestra – composed by then, after numerous departures to Israel, of the purest riffraff from Gilas – to mount another revenge attack. It was decided that this should take place as Soginch (Soginch had intended his place to be taken by Sevinch, but the percussionist, alas, turned out to have ideas of his own) returned from the bathhouse and was crossing the deserted railway line, at a time when even Akmolin would have left his shunter on one of the sidings and be making his way, together with his current apprentice, to enjoy some home-grown tobacco and home-distilled vodka in Fyokla-Whispertongue's shop.

All that day Musa had felt a certain malaise. It was as if a bell were about to ring in his head and something special were about to happen – something along the lines of the Last Day at the orphanage, the First Day of that vast and terrible thing called Real Life. In the early afternoon, when he took up his brush and the usual two boxes of paint, he felt a deadly boredom; after dipping his brush in carmine red, he held it suspended for a moment, then put it back into the same carmine red. He cleaned his brush, dipped it in methyl-orange, then put it back into the methyl-orange. A drop fell from the brush, kept its form for a moment, then dissolved back into what it had come from. Musa washed his brush again and did the same with the ultramarine, with the cinnabar red and with a pale yellowy-brown. Now he was sweating with excitement. His penis began to swell with blood just as it had done in his small orphanage bed. Frenziedly opening box after box, he repeated the same process with one colour after another. The glass he used for washing his brush became a turbid brown. After the forty-eighth box he threw down his brush and gulped down this brown liquid that by then smelt of every one of earth's smells.

In the bathhouse he vomited, but the brown liquid he had poured down his throat had for some reason turned a poisonous green. His need to study this surprising change, and the feeling of burning in his now spent and shrunken penis, led to his leaving the bathhouse ten minutes later than usual.

It was during those ten minutes that everything happened. After arranging for the attack on Musa, Soginch was unable to resist the temptation to go and watch. Leaving the bathhouse just before the appointed time, he walked along the Salty Canal and past the little whirlpool it forms after running beneath the road close to the level crossing; he intended to continue, hidden behind a truck full of cabbages due to be unloaded the following day, to the place of execution. But the bribed percussionist proved to be the basest of traitors; after shadowing not Sevinch but Soginch, he led the orchestra in a savage assault on its own con-ductor – an assault spiced by such pre-rehearsed divertimentos as

'This'll teach you to threaten the violin!' and 'And that's for gagging the trombone!'

Ten minutes later, there on the railway embankment, Moisey or Musa Sevinch tripped over Soginch, who was lying there half dead. He recovered his balance, then bent down over Soginch and passed a clean hand over his bloody face. Soginch opened his eyes and, seeing Sevinch's face above him, sank his teeth into Sevinch's hands. Sevinch let out a howl, which blended with the howl of a diesel engine coming towards them out of the darkness. In the light of its headlamps, Sevinch saw how the blood spurting from the stump of his bitten-off finger was blending with Soginch's blood both on Soginch's face and on his own hands – and he understood the meaning of everything. The sight of blood dissolving into blood made him stagger backwards as he let out a cry that was swallowed up by the howl of the advancing locomotive.

The first Gilas knew of all this was the following morning. A clot of blood was found on the level crossing; a crow was trying with its sharp crooked claws to bury this blood.[128]

29

Before the War, during the years of mass executions and Cultural Revolution, it was thought progressive when Aisha, a Nogai[129] widow who had been brought to Gilas as a young orphan, gave birth to a fatherless girl by the name of Saniya. But when, during the year after the death of Stalin, Saniya gave birth to yet another fatherless girl, Zumurad-Barrenwomb blurted out, 'She'll end up a witch!' Uchmah, the Karaite[130] granddaughter, by Saniya the Kumyk,[131] of Aisha the Nogai, did indeed grow up to be a witch.

It began harmlessly enough with her predicting who would get what mark for calligraphy from the otherwise unpredictable – given his nocturnal drinking bouts – Golovchenka; when, however, Hemmler the German geography teacher failed all the Korean girls for referring to themselves as White and these Korean girls then used their knowledge of martial arts to punish Uchmah for accurately predicting their collective failure, she stopped going to school. And from then on she foresaw only bad fortune.

The first terrible news she brought to Gilas was the news of the true end of little Hussein, the younger son of Huvron-Barber and grandson of the Persian Djebral. When Hussein disappeared, everyone thought he had died at the hands of the Djukhuds – Bukhara Jews who tempted little boys with sweets and then kidnapped them. It was said that a group of Djukhuds would take a boy to one of their homes, spread out one of the large oilcloths they called *supras*, sprinkle this *supra* with flour and then stand there in a circle round the boy, whom by then they would have stripped naked. One after another they would hold out a sweet, beckon the boy and stick an awl into his flesh. The boy's blood would drip onto the flour, and the Djukhuds would use this flour to bake their Passover matzos.

This web of lies so frightened Yusuf-Cobbler that he not only stopped peeing every evening against the wall of Huvron-Barber's little shop but even went so far as to hang the magic word 'STOCKTAKING' on the door of his own shop and disappear for the best part of a week. His disappearance only fanned the flames. Everyone started remembering how Yusuf, now they came to think about it, had always been excessively friendly to children; even the very oldest of the old women began to mumble, 'Yesh, he wash alwaysh inviting ush.'

But then Uchmah, playing beneath Djebral's high wall, blurted out, 'Water, he's in water – washed by water.' And then, jerking her head and repeating the word as if it had no more meaning than the call of a bird: 'Zakh! Zakh! Zakh!'

Representatives of the *mahallya* took her to Sergeant-Major Kara-Musayev the Younger. That very day Kara-Musayev the Younger arrested the two dark sons of Lyuli-Ibodullo-Mahsum, and on the fourth day the boys confessed that they had drowned Hussein in the Zakh canal. A month later, after Hussein's swollen corpse had been dragged out of the water thirty kilometres from Gilas, near the Kerbel dam, Yusuf-Cobbler came back to Gilas and, without opening his shop or even pissing against the wall of Huvron-Barber's little shop, went straight to the home of Aisha, Saniya and Uchmah. There he not only repaired free of charge all the footwear he could find but also presented the women with a real *supra* made from oxhide, a set of cobbler's awls and ration coupons for flour and sweets.

Bahri-Granny-Fortunes, however, did not forgive Uchmah for depriving her of her two grandsons. For three days and nights she conjured over the scorched head of a ram; in the middle of the third night, the night of the full moon, she tore the ram's tongue out by the roots, ate it and fell asleep.

But she must have miscast or misspelled her spells; it was not Uchmah who died but Bahri-Granny-Fortunes herself, and her death was preceded by hours of continuous vomiting. Ibodullo-Mahsum tried to go as quickly as possible to Huzur, the male nurse who was the son of Dolim-Dealer, but every last backstreet and alley in the *lyuli* quarter had been swamped – so Dolim-Dealer was always telling people during the years that followed – by the vomit of the dying old woman. The children shut themselves up in clay hovels whose walls began to collapse, as if undermined by an avalanche, and Ibodullo's squeaking cart couldn't get through. And the yellowy-blue torrent carried the old woman's body out of her home and through the gap that had once been cleared by the powerful battering ram of the grandson of Tolib-Butcher.

Bahri-Granny-Fortunes' curses may, nevertheless, have occasioned Uchmah at least slight inconvenience. Sergeant-Major Kara-Musayev the Younger charged Uchmah with being an accessory after the fact, for failing to pass on information she possessed about the terrible murder of little Hussein. Kara-Musayev, however, only opened the case after being bribed by Ibodullo-Mahsum, and he never brought it to a conclusion; nor indeed did he ever have the opportunity to press another criminal charge. He was already about to lose everything, about to become mere Musayev-Slogans.

Many years later, as Musayev-Slogans sat in Huvron's chair, visibly suffering as he struggled to reconcile the meanings of two slogans up above the mirror, one in Uzbek and the other in Russian, about how citizens must keep their eyes and ploughs well peeled and work to purge weeds from every field, Huvron-Barber suggested he call on Uchmah and perhaps even ask her forgiveness. If Musayev liked, they could go together; it was, in any case, time for Huvron's lunch break.

And so Musayev, half-shaven and still struggling with the riddle of the slogans, and Huvron, still wearing his white gown, set out together to call on Uchmah. They found her sitting outside casting pebbles on the ground. When Musayev began to look around, as he always did, for a slogan to divert his mind, Huvron quickly asked her to forgive the ex-sergeant for the criminal charge he had long ago brought against her and never formally dropped. In reply, Uchmah deftly removed Huvron's razor from his pocket, made a small cut in her ring finger and let two drops of blood fall on the pebbles. The first made a rustling sound; the second rang out like a bell and bounced back up. 'Zangi-Bobo, Zangi-Bobo,' she said without hesitation.

Just then Aisha rushed in; she had retired from her job as a wool-washer and now worked part-time as a postwoman. She had learned about the uninvited guests from Ibodullo-Mahsum, to whom she had just delivered two dirty envelopes from the Gulag, and had rushed back to protect her granddaughter; uninvited guests had never brought her anything but suffering.

Still holding her undelivered newspapers, in which Musayev-Slogans had quickly found solace for a mind worn out by inactivity, Aisha saw the razor in Huvron's hands and took fright, imagining he was either going to follow the example of his elder son and murder someone or else – in return for some service of Uchmah's – was about to shave the whole family free of charge, just as Yusuf-Cobbler had once repaired all their shoes to repay them for some other small service. '*Kit-shi! Kit!* Away! Go away!' she hissed at him.

The following day it was Huvron-Barber's turn to hang up his STOCKTAKING sign. He then set off with Musayev-Slogans to call on Zangi-Bobo, an old man who had spent his entire life sitting by the entrance to the Kok-Terek Bazaar and selling *nasvoy* – snuff spiced with chicken droppings and a little mint. It was Huvron-Barber's hope that Zangi-Bobo would free Musayev from the affliction of slogans. Zangi-Bobo had, after all, devoted his life not so much to trading *nasvoy* as to gathering words. Every word he had heard or seen, every word directed at him or let drop in his presence, every imported, impossible, indecent or indecipherable word – in a word, every word Zangi-Bobo had ever encountered, even if only once in his life, was immediately noted down on a piece of paper and then transferred in the evening to one of thirty-two large books each of which corresponded to a letter of the Russian alphabet. In actual fact, there were thirty-five books; he had had to begin supplementary volumes for three of the letters. Zangi-Bobo's one remaining uncertainty was the question of what to do with various enigmatic Russian words he had encountered over the years. Mefody-Jurisprudence, the town intellectual, was unable to explain these words except when alcohol loosened his tongue – and even then he could explain them only by a string of other words that sounded colourful but were, if such a thing is possible, yet more incomprehensible. And so the number of enigmatic words in the dictionary seemed destined to go on multiplying for ever, and Zangi-Bobo was torn between a wish to purge his dictionary of this suspect vocabulary and a sense of scholarly duty that kept sending him back to Mefody's barrack.

Zangi-Bobo was fond of Huvron-Barber, and he welcomed him with open arms. He led his guests into the courtyard, where they found a large rug covered with dog-eared pages from ancient books, in the shade of a vine. Bringing out a tablecloth, the old man explained, 'I've stopped hiding the books in the toilet. I don't think anyone's going to arrest me because of them now.'

'Certainly not when I've brought you the man who did the arresting,' said Huvron, nodding towards Musayev-Slogans.

The old man fell silent for a moment, recognising the former sergeant-major. Musayev's father, the scourge of Gilas, had once been in the habit of trampling Zangi-Bobo's *nasvoy* into the ground beside the gates of the Kok-Terek Bazaar, at least until the day – O merciful Allah! – that he went blind.

Musayev understood little of the subsequent conversation, devoid as it was of the clear good sense embodied in slogans, and so he was just looking around in his usual way when he gave a start of delight; he had spotted an upside-down tin railwayman's badge on the crooked wall of the toilet. Bending his head so he could see better, he read out syllable by syllable, 'A min-ute of play can des-troy your life'.

'A min-ute of play can des-troy your life,' he repeated out loud, then began to think about what this might mean. While he was thinking, Huvron managed to explain to Zangi-Bobo why he had brought Musayev along; Huvron did not know how Zangi-Bobo could help, but he trusted Uchmah's intuitions. Zangi-Bobo, however, had no idea how to respond. And so the three men sat over their cooling tea – the slogan-reader and the word-gatherer wrestling with insoluble riddles, while the barber sat in silence between them. Suddenly Musayev said, '"A min-ute of play can des-troy your life." Literally, this means, "If you play for a minute, you will annihilate your life", or more clearly, "You will expend your life in vain", or "Your life will be wasted". What does this mean? Sheikh Muslihiddin Sa'adi[132] says, "If you're drowning in the ocean, what difference does the rain make?"'

Huvron-Barber was himself a descendant of Sa'adi and he froze, astonished to be hearing such wisdom from the lips of a former policeman whom the whole town considered an idiot.

While the barber listened, Musayev drew on at-Tabari[133] to expound the meaning of the first half of Sa'adi's sentence before making a subtle philosophical leap which allowed him to relate the meaning of the second half of the sentence to the slogan on a banner by the entrance to Mukum-Hunchback's chaikhana: 'A Chatterbox is a Gift to Spies'. It was said that Mukum received this banner in exchange for a dirty tablecloth which had served as the standard of a Red Army unit during the long years of basmach rebellion and which the Museum of Military Glory had therefore required as an exhibit. How this old tablecloth had first come into the possession of Mukum-Hunchback was a mystery – although it was suspected that his father, who had died as a true Communist, had at one time been an important basmach leader and had captured it himself. Mukum-Hunchback, in any case, kept his counsel, in accordance with the advice on the banner whose meaning Musayev-Slogans was at that moment trying to interpret.

Meanwhile Zangi-Bobo remained pointedly silent, since the words pouring from Musayev's mouth had all long ago been entered in his thirty-five books. But when Musayev, growing ever more excited, like water nearing the centre of a vortex, began to behave as if he were addressing thousands of people in a stadium, and when his voice began to gurgle in his throat, like Uchmah's during her prophetic frenzies – then Zangi-Bobo pricked up his ears, while Huvron-Barber couldn't help but feel a professional anxiety occasioned by the sudden leaps of Musayev's Adam's apple. Musayev rolled his eyes; his brain gave a dry rattle like that of the last two coins left in a money box; then he flung out his arms triumphantly and, his mouth foaming, pronounced the words, '*No pasaran!*'[134]

Huvron-Barber went back home in the evening, but Musayev-Slogans stayed behind in order to absorb the truth of words straight from the pages of the thirty-five books; as for Zangi-Bobo himself, he just lay down as usual on his mattress beside the window. On the windowsill, as always, was his Arrow wireless, with its two knobs and a needle that enabled him to drift across the world, encountering first a Chinaman who seemed to be casting raindrops on water, then an Indian whose sharp voice cut into Zangi-Bobo's soul, and then the thundering prayers of an Arab. What he listened to longest, however, was Persian, with its chains of trailing adjectives that twirled into infinity like the motifs on a carpet; a familiar word would make Zangi-Bobo tremble with joy, but then he would drift away again on the short waves of his Arrow, carried by the tide of languages streaming across the night sky of summer. His hearing grew sharper and sharper until, after a wheeze and a rattle from the wireless, a Uighur began a simple little song:

> *Bu sozni eshitken zaman chetki akh,*
> *Bolup chekhrasi ul zaman misli kakh,*
> *Ketip khoshidin erga khamvar olup,*
> *Bu sozler kongul ichra azar olup . . .*

As always when he recognised every word, Zangi-Bobo slipped into blissful sleep . . .

Musayev-Slogans, however, was unable to sleep at all. He was lying close by, beneath the spreading vine; at first he simply felt bored gazing up at the meaningless stars in the spaces between the vine's dusty foliage and the bunches of ripe grapes – and no less bored listening to the strange squeals, howls and crackling that filled the night-time ether. The ex-policeman felt heavy and wasted at heart, as if some slow-acting force had deprived him even of the slogans that were his last refuge. The Uighur came to the end of the slogan-free song that had lulled Zangi-Bobo into sleep. Zangi-Bobo's snores were followed by silence, then by signals in which Musayev discovered a strange property: their pipping and peeping was precisely synchronised with the twinkling of the stars in the vine's dusty spaces. One by one, however, the stars would drop down, clustering into yellow, mouth-watering bunches only just above his head.

Something achingly sweet filled the breast of the ex-sergeant, as if he at last understood the meaning of everything. Rising soundlessly and without putting on his down-at-heel boots, he began to walk slowly towards the barn.

On his way there, he stirred up the sheep, which were sleepily chewing the cud; leaning against their fence, he began to piss. Hearing the stream of his urine, the sheep too began to make some kind of rustling sound. Musayev smiled and continued on his way. There was no light in the barn. As he groped for a switch, Musayev found some matches beside a five-branched candlestick. Half closing the squeaking door, he struck one and used it to light three of the candles. In their flickering light he saw the thirty-five books, standing in a long row on the shelves for drying apricots. He moved quickly towards them, but the candles started falling out of their holders, and, after picking up two that had gone out, he burnt himself on a third and threw the candlestick onto the straw floor so he could clean off the wax that had stuck to his burnt skin.

A moment later he went up to the books. After standing there for a while, Musayev struck another match and opened the first book that caught his eye. The flame lit up the top left-hand corner of the page, and he caught sight of the word: *samar*. This blood-red word was followed by five explanations. He greedily read three of them (1 – fruit; 2 – result; 3 – harvest), but by then the match had burnt down to his fingers. He tossed it into the darkness and struck another match. This lit up another word, either *semiz* (fat) or *semorg* (a mythical bird rather like a phoenix), but he moved the match straight back to the first corner; once again, however, as he was searching for the last two meanings of *samar*, the match burnt his fingers.

The third time he was holding the match in the right place and so he quickly grasped the word's last two meanings, but they were followed by a sentence where all he could make out was the word *yerga*. Musayev lit yet another match, but his fingers were trembling so much that it just flared and went out immediately. His heart had almost stopped beating. He felt he knew this sentence already; his fingers – and time itself – were moving more slowly than his heart and his thoughts. At last he lit another match and feverishly read the words: '*samari yerga urdi*' – 'his fruit fell on the earth'.

Something inside him really did seem to break off and fall – fulfilled or perhaps full of failure – to the ground. In the smoke-bitter darkness of the barn he struck match after match; one new word after another floated up to him, but he was unable to take them in.

That same signal from the stars or the ether was knocking at his heart and beating against his bare, burning feet. '*Samari yerga urdi . . . samari yerga urdi . . .*' What all this meant he could not have explained, although there was a moment when something lit up inside him – not a slogan, but the plywood arch over the entrance to the collective farm, whose name, 'The Fruits of Lenin's Path', had somehow never been entered into the dictionary – but this was only a momentary illumination, a flash of lightning, a last fragile ark of memories, and then there was another tear, or drop of wax, or match head, falling onto the earth, beneath his burning feet . . . '*Samari yerga urdi . . . samari yerga urdi . . .*' He himself was now burning on the straw, along with these half-open books whose pages were now being turned not by hands but by fire, and he could see words rising from these books in the shape of flames and their ashy shadow was falling back down beneath his burning bare feet. '*Samari yerga urdi,*' he whispered for the last time – and these words were the last words to burn in him, their dazzling sweep was the last thing he sensed.

Musayev died three days later in the Kok-Terek hospital; Zangi-Bobo had come to the end of his life a day before him, having outlived his own mind. The two men were buried for some reason by Huvron-Barber, although he was not related to either of them. Zangi-Bobo's relatives did not dare to attend the funeral, since the fire that began that night in his barn had spread to the house of Soli-Stores, the eldest son of Chinali and chief heir to his vast wealth.

That night, banknotes accumulated by Chinali and his son burnt in great sackfuls. Thrown up into the air by the flames, the notes and their ashes fell into neighbours' yards, onto patches of wasteland, into the Salty Canal and into the hands of onlookers. Stinking water from the canal was poured over Khiva carpets while arms of flame stretched along lengths of gold-embroidered cloth from Bukhara; slates – enough slates to cover the whole of Gilas – were continually cracking and exploding, scaring away the volunteers with their buckets of water; the volunteers themselves were struck not so much by the extent of the fire as by the extent of the wealth left untouched. Soli-Stores was able, just with the money he happened to have in his pyjama pocket, to buy a Pobeda car from the Korean Filip Ligay and send him off to the City in it to bribe the fire service to come.

A caravan of fire engines arrived towards six in the morning, after which they remained registered in Gilas for ever. They arrived just as the porcelain was catching fire, after the timber had finished burning and molten glass had poured like water into the Salty Canal. Soli's wife had just sold 700 rolls of satin at knock-down prices; needing somewhere to store what was still undamaged, she used the money to buy half of a house on the opposite side of the road.

The firemen worked fast, and water pumped from the Salty Canal soon formed a pond bounded by Soli's robust outer walls; sticking up out of the pond were burnt rafters and a metal TV aerial pointing towards Moscow. The firemen also dragged two badly burnt men from the adjacent buildings. As the reader knows, these were the former Sergeant-Major Kara-Musayev the Younger and Zangi-Bobo, who had clung on dementedly to a two-button wireless, tearing the plug out of the wall along with the socket and surrounding plaster.

Soli-Stores abandoned the gutted house and built himself a vast new house, inadvertently sending the price of building materials sky-high and then feeling he had no choice but to keep the prices of the materials he sold retail to others at the same high level. The fire thus continued to afflict Gilas for many years and the swimming pool created in the grounds of the old house was only a partial compensation. Most of the children would just flounder about in it for a few minutes before washing themselves clean in the now glassy-clear Salty Canal. Only the very bravest would take a deep breath and dive down beneath the remains of girders and beams, bobbing back up to the surface with silver Russian teaspoons, translucent Chinese porcelain cups or even a wad of sodden counterfeit banknotes . . . But not everyone was brave enough – and anyway, what the children found most often were one-inch nails and splinters of slate.

'What about Uchmah?' you will probably ask. Uchmah became pregnant. And only she knew by whom. No one else had any idea who had thrust this child on her: whether it was Huvron-Barber – in revenge for the deaths of Kara-Musayev and Zangi-Bobo; Yusuf-Cobbler – out of gratitude; the spirit of that inveterate womaniser Kara-Musayev; or just some passer-by. All she ever said, when the subject of her baby came up, was 'Shafik! Shafik!' – which was how she pronounced the name 'Shapik', the name of the first boy in her matrilinear clan.

Shapik grew, as people say, not by the day but by the hour, but somehow he grew into a thin and gangling idiot who used to scratch his bottom and then suck his dirty index finger. On his seventh birthday, when he looked seventeen yet had the mind of a baby of seven months, Oppok-Lovely gave him both the uniform and the civilian clothes of Sub-Lieutenant Osman-Anon, who had mysteriously disappeared. What Shapik liked most were the khaki breeches and the black *kitel* with blue shoulder-straps, and he used to wander along the railway line in them, resembling a giant crow and never failing to terrify both Akmolin, who had spent time in the camps in the days of Kaganovich, and Nabi-Onearm, who seldom let a day pass without stealing cotton seeds.

Soon after his eighth birthday deep wrinkles appeared on his face and he began to speak – if what Shapik did with words can be called speech. Once a word had formed on his tongue, it was as if it were glued there, unable to slip, or slide, or leap off it again.

And so, as if he had the hiccups, he would go around whispering, shouting or just plain speaking this poor importunate word, until after anything between four and ten days it would disappear of itself and for ever, sometimes yielding to a long and tense silence, sometimes giving birth to another word that would prove equally stubborn and hard to evict.

At the age of ten he looked like a withered-up old man, even though at night he still slept in a communal bed between his grandmother and his great-grandmother, whom he cuddled up against like a baby barely weaned from the breast. And they accepted him as a baby – until the night when, lying between Aisha and Saniya with his left hand on Aisha's right breast and his right hand on Saniya's left breast, he drenched them with a copious fountain of semen. The howls of the two elder widows woke the youngest widow, who promptly took her son away to sleep in her own bed. But there is no need for the reader to feel anxiety – nothing happened to the grandmother or the great-grandmother, neither of them gave birth to any strange beast, and everything returned to normal except that they each kept secretly looking at Uchmah, wondering in silence if she would soon bear the fruits of incest. But they waited in vain. Shapik did not become his own son and his own father in one person any more than he became his own grandfather, great-grandfather, grandson or great-grandson.

By the age of eleven, however, Shapik had come to look exactly like the late Hoomer, the patriarch of Gilas. And Oppok-Lovely, who had just set up a commission for the preservation of Hoomer's heritage, decided to take Shapik away from his family, saying she needed him as a model for the writer's portrait – although what she really wanted was to intimidate the now excessive number of chroniclers in Gilas: the alcoholic Mefody-Jurisprudence, whom she had already appointed to her commission, Nakhshon the town's human rights activist, who had quite lost her head after the death of her husband, and all those wretched folk storytellers trying to earn twenty-five roubles a page. If any of these chroniclers overstepped the mark, she would release her poor, witless boy from confinement and ensure that they caught sight of 'the spirit of the late Hoomer' roaming about the garden. Shapik would, inevitably, be making the most of the few pleasures he had been granted by life. He would scratch his behind and suck his index finger; he would keep stammering one and the same word (usually a fragment of some obscenity – the only protest his feeble soul could manage); or he would spray his seed over the roses and dahlias. All this, linked to the image of the already mythical Hoomer, made Oppok-Lovely's visitors feel as if doomsday had dawned.

And only Oppok-Lovely's scribe, the little boy supplied to her by the No. 11 October School, knew the truth; being the same age as Shapik, and having already been entrusted with the task of recording Hoomer's heritage, he had also been allocated the daily tasks of reading to the young cretin from the writings of the old seer and playing the odd game of nuts with him.

Uchmah, meanwhile, wanted to revenge herself on the woman who had taken her child. For days on end she sat in her empty yard beneath a naked and no less orphaned sun, baking her brains as if to cook up some act of vengeance. Finally she realised what she should do. During the night of the next full moon she transferred all her powers of prophecy to the son of Mukum-Hunchback, a boy known as Bakay-Croc who only a year before had lost both his legs; he had been about to steal a wheelchair from a goods wagon in the middle of the night when the train began to move . . . The morning after this full moon Bakay-Croc uttered his first prophecies; Uchmah, for her part, ceased to be a witch and never menstruated again in her life.

Bakay-Croc declared that he had seen in a vision that the future belonged to the legless and crippled; whoever lost a leg, he affirmed, would stride into eternity. He was like a motionless monument, like a speaking statue, and he soon acquired a multitude of followers. They gathered at night in the scrubland beside the Salty Canal, wrapped themselves in white cotton sheets and began rolling about until one of them let out a howl as he or she smashed a limb or dislocated a joint and so broke through to enlightenment. Next came a wave of fanatics who, also wrapped in sheets, chose to lie down like their prophet in the paths of oncoming trains. It was this that led to Akmolin's retirement, after forty-five years in charge of his diesel shunter with no interruption apart from his five years in the camps as a young man. Rif the Tatar, meanwhile, made large sums of money helping Father Ioann at the Russian cemetery, burying unattached legs, irrespective of faith or size, in return for appropriate bribes.

It was the Jewish Yusuf-Cobbler, as it happened, who was fiercest of all in his denunciation of this new faith, but his rage sprang less from religious than from economic considerations; he thought that the decreasing number of feet would wear out less footwear. Soon, however, he realised that one foot wears out a single shoe in half the time that two feet take to wear out two shoes and so he began to calm down, though he still took the precaution of economising on nails and elastic.

Little by little the adepts of the new faith began to use not only the power of the word but also physical force to recruit to their order those who still lived without meaning or belief. They began by smashing the legs of Raphael the younger brother of the late Timurkhan – who in the end really had been run over by a train. Then a car with no number plate ran over the legs of Lobar-Beauty, who was in charge of the Culture and Recreation shop, and Gennady Ivanovich Mashin, a local football star and trumpet player, was 'swept off his feet' during a friendly game.

It was at this time that Yusuf-Cobbler composed his bleak yet well-known prayer: 'O Lord, cut them down to size from both ends. Top them and tail them. May there be no end, O Lord, to your eternal justice . . .'

Oppok-Lovely, irritated as she always was by any rival concentration of power, let alone one whose effects were so damaging, acted straightforwardly and wisely; she undermined the material base of the new faith by going from town to town and buying up all the cotton sheets – which neophytes and proselytes were required to wrap round their bodies – and then stacking them in the tuberculosis hospital. Bakay responded by calling down curses on her during one of his Monday sermons and declaring a Holy War. The reward for the head of this female Satan and the destruction of her empire would, he promised, be eternal bliss – a blessing that could otherwise be won only through castration and the loss of both legs. And so, on the night of the second Monday after this sermon – the night of a total lunar eclipse – a party of volunteers was dispatched to the house of Oppok-Lovely. Oppok-Lovely, however, was not at home; after going to the City to arrange for pensions to be granted both to Uchmah ('loss of the family breadwinner') and to Shapik ('incapacity for labour'), she had decided to spend the night there with her younger daughter Shanob.

The vengeful Uchmah had long ago foreseen the storming of Oppok-Lovely's house but she was now – alas! – unable to interfere in the course of events either by speeding up bureaucratic procedures or by making Oppok-Lovely think better of her sudden act of kindness. Alas! And out in Oppok-Lovely's garden the moon began to burn up; along with the moon, the shadows of trees and people began to turn to ashes, twisting up like scorched sheets of paper and curling into nothing; the two-legged turned one-legged, the one-legged became legless and the legless lost their heads as well as their shadows.

And suddenly, as the first of the volunteers were carried by their own momentum against the house door, the light disappeared completely – and every last shadow along with it.

Everything became one ghastly darkness. Earth had covered both Sun and Moon with darkness.

'Bloody . . . Bloody . . .' Shapik repeated in his lonely bed, and the storming party entered the house.

After turning the house upside down and finding only the naked Shapik, they dragged him out into the yard just as the moon was squeezing her way out through the crooked slit between darkness and darkness. Shadows slipped down onto the earth and thickened; only this naked young ancient seemed unchanged. He scratched his behind, sucked his finger, inconsolably repeated his 'Bloody fuck . . . bloody fuck . . .' – and suddenly drenched Bakay, who was sitting on his low-wheeled trolley with his back to Shapik, with semen as dense as the light of the moon.

Bakay did not wear trousers, since he had nothing to wear them on, and his tunic had ridden up – and so Shapik's semen trickled slowly and stickily down Bakay's buttocks . . .

When the moon had reappeared in all her fullness, the crowd wrapped Shapik – who was once again shooting semen into the night garden – in some huge pages from books made of leather and other skins. They glued these pages to him to make up for the absence of cotton sheets and, so bewitched by the moon that they forgot to set fire to the house, set off with this scroll to their sacred mound beside the Salty Canal, intending to carry out a ritual sacrifice.

In the light of the full moon, they rolled him over once, twice, a third time – but not once did Shapik cry out; all they heard was the crackling of dry grass and rushes. Then one of Bakay's two-legged followers, wanting to earn eternal bliss without having to sacrifice his legs, suggested setting fire to the scroll. They tried to do this. But the leather burnt poorly – probably because it was damp from the idiot's secretions or from the ink of countless words.

Another new recruit suggested dousing the scroll with petrol. Yet another ran to the garage beside the level crossing as fast as the legs he didn't want to sacrifice could carry him; he came back with two cans of petrol. The crowd was going crazy. The excitement infected Shapik inside his womb of paper; he moved on from his usual one or two syllables and began abusing the listeners with the nearest he ever got to an entire sentence: 'Bloody fuck . . . bloody fucking . . . bloody fucking hell . . .'

Two full moons shone from Bakay's eyes with a dead light as he indicated with a nod of the head that his comrades-in-arms should pour petrol over the scroll. They grew as excited as children preparing to make calcium carbide explode in a puddle.[135] Two of the two-legged splashed the petrol over the leather envelope and withdrew, having earned the spiritual credit they needed. And just as a third man was about to toss a match at the scroll, Midat-Clubfoot, a Bashkir who had been lame from birth and who had waited for Bakay all his life with the passion of St John the Baptist waiting for Jesus, used his one good leg to aim a kick at this scroll wrapped round a human being – and it began to roll slowly and heavily down the hill. And at that moment the third man threw his match.

The explosion shook all Gilas. The earth quaked. Dogs hid in their kennels, howling and scratching their stomachs; bees left their hives and flew up towards the moon; the town's nuclear war alarm blasted away like the trumpet of Jericho, not ceasing until the following morning.

Only then did Gilas understand what had happened. Fatkhulla-Frontline – the mind, conscience and honour of Gilas – whose one eye needed only half as much sleep as the two eyes of others, went out as usual at five o'clock to take his seven sheep to graze beside the canal. There he found Hoomer; Hoomer had long been thought dead, but that dawn he had come back to earth to walk naked among scorched bodies and crutches, in scrubland that had been burnt to a cinder, and repeat words that Fatkhulla had heard before only as a young soldier on the Second Ukrainian Front: 'Fucking . . . Bloody fucking . . . Bloody fucking hell . . .'

This meeting and this Sabbath of the Dead were too much for Fatkhulla-Frontline; he drove his trembling sheep back to Gilas. There he roused Tordybay-Medals, Satiboldi-Buildings and the whole *mahallya*, so they could decide together how to drive away these evil spirits.

When the menfolk of Gilas, armed with hoes, spades and pitchforks, reached the canal, there was no sign of either Hoomer or Shapik, only the relics of this new faith of the one-legged and the legless, a faith that had been consumed within only days of its birth. They buried everyone and everything straight away, in the scorched scrubland; and a few months later it was decided to cover the area with asphalt, so that a new 'October' summer cinema could be built there.

In her old age Uchmah worked there as a ticket-seller; she was also the fortunate recipient of both the pensions that the benevolent Oppok-Lovely had gone to such pains to arrange for her.

30

However much I have put this off, however much I have attempted to conceal, I have no choice in the end but to tell you. Otherwise, none of this makes any sense at all. Or hardly any sense.

In Gilas, just beside the railway line, behind the water tower, there lived a blind old man, half-Tatar and half-Uzbek, by the name of Hoomer. His wife was half-Armenian and half-Jewish; her first name was Nakhshon, and her surname was either Donner or Shtonner. I can't remember. Or I've got confused. Never mind. And so, Hoomer no longer left the house, but Nakhshon – a once beautiful seventy-year-old with eyebrows now thick as a moustache and a large wart just above her upper lip that had once been seen as a beauty spot – used to participate as a volunteer in electoral commissions. On election days she would go round Gilas with a voting urn and call either on Kun-Okhun, who would be too drunk after loading coal all night to walk to the polling station, or on Mefody-Jurisprudence, who was always as good as de-voted by his devotion to principle; last, she would call on her blind husband and spend half an hour with him, perhaps drinking tea and nibbling the sweet cakes she had obtained from the voting commission. And on Sundays in summer she would visit the Kok-Terek Bazaar and sell a first edition of Ozhegov's Russian Dictionary, a pre-Revolutionary Herbert Spencer or perhaps the psychological writings of William James. She was, in short, someone who spread culture and enlightenment wherever she went.

Nakhshon and Hoomer had no children. Occasionally, after a Young Pioneers' parade, the Timur Team from the October School[136] would bring them three kilos of potatoes and a piece of the household soap allocated to the team by the administration of the wool factory. This is all that anyone knew about them. And that Nakhshon was a fine cook. So thought Oppok-Lovely, who knew everything about everyone and who, alone of the adult inhabitants of Gilas, used to visit their little room just beside the railway line, behind the water tower.

But now let me tell you what no one at all knew.

Hoomer was, of course, the patriarch of Gilas. No one could say how old he was because even the most ancient old men of Gilas remembered him as having always been old. As a young man, this son of an interpreter for the occupying Tsarist forces had worked as an interpreter for the Russians building the first railway line to Turkestan; he had had to gallop about the steppe on post horses, getting stuck in sandstorms and snowstorms while freedom-loving Kazakhs mutinied or more mercantile Sarts sold sleepers for the foundations of houses – as a result of which both Kazakhs and Sarts had to be tried in court. Hoomer interpreted not only the judges' verdicts but also the instructions of the officers in charge of dispatching the prisoners to Siberia, where there also happened to be a railway under construction, although that one was being built by Buryats and Khakas.

The task of the Sarts was to lay down the rail running north from Tashkent, while the task of the Kirghiz and Kazakhs was to lay down the rail running south from Akmecheti. After the brigade from Tashkent and the brigade from Akmecheti had met and the first rail had been officially joined, each brigade would go on to lay the second rail on the territory of the other. So if the Sarts had laid their first rail as far as Shiili before they met the Kirghiz and the Kazakhs, they would have to lay their second rail only between Shiili and Akmecheti, whereas the Kirghiz and the Kazakhs would have to lay their second rail all the way from Shiili to Tashkent. Is that clear? Crystal clear? To the Kirghiz, the Kazakhs and even the Sarts, it was clear as mud.

*

At the end of the fourth winter, covered in scabs and filled with a fierce mutual hatred, the two half-frozen hordes of short-lived Asiatics – the original workers had all died long ago, as had their replacements – met beneath a lurid sunset close to a Kazakh camel drivers' shelter outside the town of Turkestan – just as the Russian geographers and engineers had intended. It is probable, however, that this success would not have been achieved but for the mental and physical agility of Hoomer; as he shuttled between courts and executions, he had felt as if he were drawing together two ends of a length of thread, holding one in his right hand and the other in his left.

There, in the light of the steppe sunset, instead of going for one another's throats, the two bands of workers threw down their hammers and pickaxes, leaving their twelve Russian armed guards to hammer in the last 'Turkestan Railway Regiment' link of rail while they themselves set off in two separate groups to the town, to offer prayers to Hazrat Hodja Ahmed at his ruined shrine.[137] Hoomer-Interpreter did not know what to do: should he remain for the ceremony of the tying together of the two ends of the iron thread that now led from Akmecheti to Tashkent or should he follow those whom he had come to see as tongueless without him?

In the end he plodded off after the workers, his box-calf boots crunching through snowdrifts as he followed a line of his own between the two trodden-down paths, keeping in view these two hordes that seemed like two black eyes against the white snow – like two frozen pupils that had thawed out and fallen onto the ground far ahead of him. Hoomer was not without feeling and, as an educated scion of these same wild tribes, he wept as he followed them, longing in the depth of his heart to be reconciled with them and to regain the innocent and unclouded eyes of his youth; but all of a sudden some troublemaker would turn round and, encouraging the others to join in, would shout and holler and throw things in his direction – pellets of clay from under the snow, balls of snow already black with dirt. Then this trouble-maker would fall in again with the purposeful stride of his comrades and they would walk on in silence until someone from the other crowd turned round and caught sight of Hoomer plodding along in his unbuttoned greatcoat. And the same thing would happen again.

As they approached the shrine, the two crowds merged into one; Hoomer lost sight of them as they entered the mausoleum, and he was left on his own in the steppe. By the time he got there himself, the men were already at prayer, having taken their places before and behind and on each side of the shrine. Hoomer found himself a place at the back and, never having prayed in his life, resolved to copy the movements of the men standing in front of him. They bowed to the ground; Hoomer bowed to the ground too. They straightened up; and before Hoomer had fully straightened up himself, they were back down on their knees again. Hoomer struggled to keep up. Kneeling down and putting his forehead to the ground, he suddenly felt the ineffable absurdity of what he was doing. But this absurdity was so full and complete, so remarkable, that when, after straightening up for a moment, the believers bowed down again before the Almighty, Hoomer lowered his head to the ground with the sensuality of a man who is discovering sensations he has never felt before. It would have been difficult, so Hoomer thought, to conceive of anything more absurd than this pose – your bottom in the air and your nose down by someone else's feet – but in its humiliating absurdity, in this humiliation that had nothing to do with either another man's bottom sticking up in front of you, nor with your own bottom sticking up behind you, nor even with having your face covered in snow that someone else has been standing on, in this shared humiliation before something higher Hoomer found a sensuality both sweet and astringent and as he stood there with dirty snow and snowy dirt flowing slowly down his face and as he silently moved his lips in a prayer he had been taught by his Tatar grandmother from Orenburg, he found himself waiting impatiently for the man standing on the platform with his back to them all to shout out '*Allahu Akbar!*'[138] and bow down so they could all bow down and become part of the earth once more.

That night, lying with his fellow-believers beside the saint's grave, Hoomer tossed and turned beneath his Russian army greatcoat. He dreamed of a man coming to do his ablutions and carefully washing his legs, his feet, each of his toes and the gaps between them, then winding calico foot-cloths round his feet and ankles – all in order that, after a little while, a second man should lift him up, all clean and prepared, and carry him about the world just as one might carry some carcass. But the man Hoomer found himself thinking about was the man compelled to carry the washed man through the world, the man sentenced to carry another man on his shoulders, just as one carries the clothes on one's body, just as one wears a beard or a pair of spectacles or one's own name . . .

Disturbed by this dream, he woke up. Night was staring down into the ruined buildings and its bright stars seemed sharp and protruding. Falling back into sleep, he dreamed of two dogs snarling at one another as they approached him – only they weren't dogs but tame wolves, a pair that had lost a cub, and the she-wolf went on howling for her cub all night long.[139] The wolves began walking all over him and suddenly he felt that, instead of biting his hand, the male was touching his soft forearm with its naked member – like a dog about to wet him with its seed. He stayed flat on the ground. The mating season was beginning and it was time for the male to run wild; the she-wolf would just go back to her kennel and howl.

Still flat on the ground, Hoomer woke up, looked at the stars – now linked with one another into a single thread – and slipped back into his dreams. The iron road had become an iron thread, but he couldn't make it out clearly; he couldn't tell if it was black or white.

Then he heard the voice of the muezzin calling the faithful and obedient to their early morning prayers, at the hour when you cannot tell a white thread from a black thread; and later that day, in a covered wagon, Hoomer took an official notebook with a lace tie and began to write the first page of unofficial text he had ever written – a page that marked the beginning of his career as a writer.

Now that you know about this day and this night, it is easier to explain and understand many things in his subsequent life. I saw those first pages of his awkward – and therefore over-literary, excessively stylised – text[140] only once, and at a time when they were covered with water, but they were bright, probably as bright as Hoomer's face that day he prayed in the snow . . . This text, I remember, was called:

The Railway
(a traveller's notes)

I.

He did not know his father. Neither his given name, nor his surname, nor his profession. Nor even whether he really was his father. And so a word that for everyone means something near and clearly defined, as perceptible as the sound of someone panting or the hairs coming out of a man's nostrils, was for him only a word. A primordial word: 'Father'.

'Mother' was simpler. His mother had died as she gave birth to him and they had wrapped her in a cloth she had been weaving.

Her other pieces of cloth had been given to the ritual washers and mourners; a little ladder had been stuck, according to custom, into the sand by her grave;[141] and she had been forgotten.

He was brought up by Gulsum-Khalfa,[142] a homeless old woman who chanted prayers over the dead. She was lame and half-blind. This had made her late for the funeral, but she had sat out the remaining forty days of mourning and had been the only adult to remain in the empty yurt. For all this she had received not even a handkerchief and so she had appropriated the newborn child, hoping he would come in useful as she grew older still. And she knew that if the worst came to the worst she would be expected to weep for him too – and so have somewhere to live free of charge for another forty days.

But the little boy clung to life. The following spring he was crawling about beneath a wilful goat that Gulsum-Khalfa had earned with her funeral tears, and at the age of five, when Aspandiar's horsemen raided the village,[143] he escaped with the goat into the wilderness. He walked with the goat to the end of the world, to the place where water begins, talking to her and drinking her milk. And there he buried her after she had choked to death on too much salt; and there, on her sandy grave, weeping tears perhaps still saltier than the water his goat had drunk, he was found by Russian salt-diggers.

He dug salt with them for seven years, until they all died. When the last of their corpses had been loaded onto a boat, he slipped on board with them, leaving this deserted world and sailing over the sea towards a place whose name he did not know, although he secretly guessed that it would be the same other world that lame, blind old Gulsum-Khalfa had invoked at funerals in order to frighten people.

One night, as he lay among the corpses, which were too salty to decay, there was a crash that split the hold in two. Water rushed in; the corpses were carried in all directions, almost crushing the boy beneath them. But the boy was carried to the surface by a powerful stream of something viscous from far below, and he saw with horror that the sea, split in half by the upended boat, was on fire. 'This is hell!' he thought, and a wave of fire swept over him. But it was only the surface of the sea that was burning – down below there were just flashes of lightning, through which corpses, letting out bubbles, were floating up to the surface. Keeping the corpses above his head and taking in through his scorched mouth the air that had collected beneath them, he kicked out with his legs, heading deep into the abyss . . .

Clinging to the scorched corpse of the man he called Old Ivan, he was washed ashore. The sea went on burning; the flames in the sky vanished, turning into stars. The boy lay in the other world and tried with his young mind to remember what his stepmother had said would happen to him because of all the sins he had committed. But nothing happened at all. The sea went on burning just the same, except that the waves were carrying its waters further and further away. And in the morning, when the soot-blackened moon melted away in a black corner of sky, the hot sea was no longer hell but a mere bonfire, attached to a fragment of some tower that had been overturned in the middle of the sea and that stuck up into the sky like an absurd little ladder, with fragments of the boat hanging down from it.

The boy did not know whether or not people buried their corpses in this other world, but he dug a pit in the black and oily sand just in case. He dragged Old Ivan, whose skin had exuded a white shroud of salt, into this dark pit, then made a crooked ladder out of bits and pieces of the boat, stuck it into this Russian's grave of black sand and recited a short prayer about the One and Only who neither begetteth nor is begotten and there is none like unto Him.

This other world was strangely empty. The boy waited a long time for someone to come for him but, since no one came, he set off along the deserted shore to where he could see dark trees in the distance. That, he thought, was probably paradise. And indeed it was.

In an empty garden, growing close together, were apricots like yellow suns, cherries like red lamps, and peaches whose cheeks were covered in tender down – as well as figs, which the boy had never eaten before. But what astonished him were the pomegranates. The boy had neither heard of them nor seen anything like them; they looked more like how Gulsum-Khalfa had once described her withered heart – but when, after turning one over in his hands, the boy ventured to take a bite, what spurted out were forty crimson bees that stung his tongue with their sweet-sour poison. 'Now I really am dying!' the boy said to himself as he fell asleep. 'Now I will see the souls of the dead, a sight never granted to those still living.'

The first man to come to the boy in the other world was a gardener with a moustache and with eyebrows that met in the middle; he spoke a strange and unintelligible language. He took the boy to a house where people washed him for seven days before sending him to a huge kitchen where saucepans hissed like the sea. There the boy ate and ate until his cheeks were red, after which he was taken to the chancellery, where he was taught a few words of their strange language. Then the musicians taught him how to wiggle his belly and bottom in a strange dance. Last of all, they tied his hair into a little pigtail and took him to the palace chambers. 'Here I will see God!' the boy thought excitedly, and he looked round the empty bedchamber. But no one entered except a sweet-voiced man in a gown, probably an angel of God; he stroked the boy's pigtail and began questioning him in his unintelligible language.

The boy was astonished at the way half-blind Gulsum-Khalfa had deceived those who lived in the previous world, frightening them with stories of Munkar and Nakir interrogating people after death,[144] one holding a hammer, and the other an anvil: 'A lie –

you'll lie flat as a pancake! Another lie – you'll be beaten to dust!'
No, this angel of God spoke in the sweetest of voices, stroking
the boy and accompanying each stroke with a tender 'M-m-m-
m!' Then he languidly took off the boy's clothes. As if feeling for
any sins that might still remain in the boy's body, putting one
moist hand against the boy's buttocks and another, rougher hand
against his willy, he murmured, 'A nightingale of the bedchamber!' From the other room came slow sweet music, the
music God's servants had played when they taught the boy how
to dance. The angel of God threw off his gown and pressed not
wings but a hairy chest against the boy's shoulder blades, whirling
him away in an ever quickening dance. The boy's head was
whirling too; he did not know what to do. The angel of God
untied the last of the cloths round his waist and the boy, seeing
what was being thrust towards him, began to whisper in terror his
one and only prayer about the One and Only who neither
begetteth nor is begotten and there is none like unto Him.

The music had become a one and only drum, pounding into
his heart, when the door was suddenly flung open and, in a white
dress, in flew – a woman. In naked shame the boy rushed to the
window and, cutting his burning skin against splinters of glass,
vanished into the garden . . .

Lying down in the deepest depths of this garden, covering
his nakedness with a fig leaf that swelled with the blood from
his cuts, he tossed about in delirium and wondered where
people go after death in *this* world. Back to his stepmother
Gulsum-Khalfa?

2.

The crowd was turning nasty, and under this mind-numbing sun
the men's tall Astrakhan hats looked like huge black flies. He

quickly adjourned the meeting – saying it was time for the Muslims' midday prayers – and hurried to the white tent to speak to the commander of the Cossack railway penal detachment, to warn him of possible trouble.

All through the afternoon and until late in the evening he stood there like the hoopoe and gave flat and monotonous answers to this motley rabble, but there were now thirty mounted Cossacks on guard, half-asleep astride Akhal-Teke horses that continued to prance about even beneath the merciless sun. During the night, with bloodshed seeming as inevitable as that blood-red head in the daytime sky, he was woken by the slightest rustle or movement of sand in the wind, but then everything would go quiet again and only just before dawn was the alarm raised and the Cossack detachment roused: the native railway-workers had all escaped into the desert. On the outskirts of the camp they had stuck two rails into the sand and tied three sleepers between them, to make a small ladder climbing up into the sky.

The Cossacks were sent out in pursuit in parties of twelve, to the four points of the compass and each of the four points in between – and towards noon two of the parties returned, together with thirty half-dead Yomuds.[145] The rest of the Cossacks had been slaughtered in the sands; two nights later, God knows how, their sun-and-sand-blackened heads were quietly slipped into the camp. It was decided that the thirty captured fugitives should be given similar treatment, that their thirty heads should be exhibited just as heads are exhibited in the main bazaar of the city of Merv.

But his Tarot cards told him that these thirty fugitives, these thirty condemned men, must themselves lay down the track that leads to their death and that their brothers, fathers and sons would all come and work beside them – whereas their immediate execution would lead only to another cycle of deaths ... Anyway, a severed head in Bairam-Ali is as good as a severed head in Merv

. . . What mattered was that the State should grow greater and mightier.

This last argument convinced the Cossack commander. He was afraid, however, that these damned Asiatics might take it into their heads that they were building a ladder to help them run away into the distance and so he gave orders that, until they reached Bairam-Ali, they should lay down only a single rail; he knew in any case that his opposite number in Chardzhou had already taken the same decision.

For three months, under a mindless sun, the thirty condemned men dug through sands; when they reached solid ground they covered it with gravel as white as the rays of the desert sun in order to build an embankment five feet high.[146] During the night the shifting sands would slip down into the half-filled trench, mix with the gravel and so reinforce the embankment's foundations. Sun, sand and wind raged together, as if in alliance, but the embankment was eventually made ready, the first link of rail was laid by the Cossacks, the first curve was laid by the Yomuds – and then, in the middle of the night, as he was thinking about his non-existent father, he heard some kind of rustling, some kind of stirring.

'Sand in the trench again,' he thought bitterly. Waking up before anyone else, he left his tent at dawn. O God! Where the rail came to an end, a second ladder was sticking up into the sky. It too was made of bits of rail with three sleepers tied between them; and a dead man, an old Yomud, had been thrown against it, feet on the bottom rung and head hanging back over the top rung. Pulling on his jacket, he walked up to the dead man. Thick blood was oozing from his throat, dripping onto his beard, down onto the sleepers and onto the sand. In a trench below the iron ladder, he saw – half-buried in bloody sand – the green-eyed youth who appeared to have sent his father up into the heavens. A hand with a knife smeared with congealed blood was sticking out, as were his legs, which seemed to be still trembling . . .

There was no understanding these crazed Yomuds; it looked as if they had freely chosen to die. The whole scene was like a giant playing card, as he said later to the Cossack commander: the top half a King, the bottom half a Knave. The commander ordered both father and son to be buried in the trench and the last three links of track to be taken up and re-laid so that the line would pass at a distance from these two madmen in their trench and their ladder sticking up into the desert sky.

But there is no bad without good. A dozen relatives of the dead father and son appeared out of the desert, as if they had heard the news from the wind or the sand or the blind desert sun. They were allowed to weep over the graves – and were then sentenced to continue building the railway. The three women in chadors were to cook their scanty rations as they all headed further and deeper into the desert.

Using the rail that had already been laid, one third of the prisoners used railway wheelbarrows to fetch fresh gravel and new lengths of rail while the others dug a trench in the burning sand, leaning to one side as they dug so as to make the most of shade no wider than a man's hand.

One day, after he had galloped the length of this rail – riding the Akhal-Teke colt that had been given to him, along with a revolver, on the day the new recruits had arrived; after he had quickly overtaken the wheelbarrow-pushers, who seemed to be moving as slowly across the earth as the sun through the sky; after the week's rations (a freshly killed sheep and a sack of Russian potatoes) had been taken to the quartermaster's yurt – he felt the touch of a hot hand on his sweaty elbow. As if burnt, as if stung by a carpet viper, he trembled and spun round on his heels. In front of him, half-opening her chador and whispering impassionedly, stood a seventeen-year-old beauty – one of the cooks.

'What do you want?' he asked her.

She repeated her whisper, but either because the air in the yurt was on fire or because he himself was on fire and drops of sweat had run into his ears, he heard nothing and saw only the beckoning movement of her hand as it disappeared into the flowery folds of her chador. She turned and went outside. He knew that the Cossack guards might catch sight of them any moment, but curiosity and a force stronger than caution or fear led him after her.

'*Eger guich bilen alaymasalar, ozum-a bermerin!*' (If I'm not taken by force, I shan't yield!), she kept repeating. He didn't understand what she meant by this, but her ardent tone inflamed his young blood. He took her hand. She did not resist.

'What do you want?' he asked again. But this time it was as if he were demanding payment for the risk he was already taking – holding her hand within shouting distance of both the Cossack guards and the horde of her fellow Yomuds. She understood him and pointed into the distance, to where he had just come from on his colt.

'It's forty days today.[147] And you're a Muslim. Tonight we can ride *there*!' Speaking the words as if she had learned them by heart, she disappeared beneath the awning of the kitchen yurt.

Like the sun, he was on fire until evening, remembering and trying to interpret her every word and gesture. It seemed as if the sun would never set, as if it were a head that had been severed and wouldn't let itself be buried in the earth, but finally a first white star came out in the green sky, as white as her hand coming out of her green sleeve. A little later he let his colt drink the remaining water and walked off on his own to wait for night beside the slowly cooling rail that had just been laid.

He sat down beside the lame track. He tried to think about the railway: they were going to lay the second rail after all, though without fully nailing it down, so that the new recruits could use a handcar instead of a wheelbarrow to transport the rails and gravel – but his thoughts quickly slipped away to the seventeen-year-old beauty. Her words were a torment to him: 'If I'm not taken by force, I shan't yield!'

'*Eger guich bilen alaymasalar, ozum-a bermerin!*' he said over and over, wondering if she was referring to Cossack abuse of her maidenly purity or whether this was her way of asking him to act passionately and decisively. Whatever the truth, all he could see was her lips whispering these words; they blotted out everything in front of him.

Night came. There was a breath of what passed in those parts for cool air, and the moon rose obediently to light up the whispering dunes that seemed to be counting their pale grains of sand. Snakes slid out of their holes. A desert owl gave a solitary hoot. He went up to the quartermaster's yurt and, more excited than ever, began to wait. It was as if everything had been a delirium of the sun, a fruit of the heat haze of his consciousness. If she hadn't come yet, she would never come – and perhaps it was all just a trick she had been put up to by the Cossack commander, who was now watching from his white tent. A hundred such thoughts went through his head, and he didn't hear her creep up from behind to touch his elbow. As if stung, he spun round and seized her hands.

'Over there!' she said. Understanding that everything would happen *over there*, he led her out of the camp and into the patch of camel-thorn where his colt was languidly sniffing out scarce blades of grass. They jumped up onto the colt's still warm back; the girl put her arms round his waist and they rode off. His eyes were scanning the ground ahead but his heart was beating behind him – below his shoulder blades, against her springy breasts. The moon galloped after them, her mane of stars flowing in the wind. And when the moon had climbed up into the sky and was hanging over the little ladder of rails and sleepers, as if meaning to slip down onto the mound of sand where the trench had been, the girl gently slipped down from the colt's back and walked towards the grave, letting the bright moon of her face shine out freely. He slipped down after her. The colt neighed and, when he started to pull it in, asked to be set free. He released the colt and followed the girl with uncertain steps. Her scarf, which had remained in place during their wild gallop, was blown off by the light of the moon; the girl had thrown it off along with her cloak, releasing the shining, sinuous curls of her hair. He walked after her, not knowing what would happen next but trusting to the mystery of this night. Just by the ladder, she flung open her arms, which shone in the moonlight, and threw herself down onto the mound. He rushed towards her and was almost on top of her when he heard her resonant sobs; they were like claps of thunder from a clear, starry sky. She was weeping, repeating her incomprehensible '*Eger guich bilen alaymasalar, ozum-a bermerin!*'

He stopped, like a reined-back colt, but only for a second. Then he was kissing her hair, which was full of tears and sand, kissing her back, which was trembling from her sobs, kissing her arms which lay stretched out to either side by the base of the two iron rails pointing towards the shameless moon. His body was an unbroken colt and it longed to drown in this desert night. He went on kissing her, greedily, until he suddenly recognised that she was somewhere a long way away. It was as if she didn't see him, didn't sense him, didn't remember him or even know that he was there; she was writhing on top of this grave of sand in a kind of numb oblivion, as if she wanted to scatter the sand into the starry sky above her or else bring the stars down over her grief like grains of sand.

He moved away from her, still lying on his side on the grave. His revolver in its holster was sticking into him and he realised soberly how useless and irrelevant he was in the presence of her deathly-bitter love. He squatted down awkwardly and, feeling sudden pity for this unfortunate creature of God, began to stroke her head, her hot temples and her tangled hair.

Slowly she turned her tear-stained face away from the dark sand and laid her head on his knee. He cautiously kissed her on the temple and then, lifting aside her heavy hair, on the neck. She did not resist. He felt awkward and ashamed and she seemed aloof, but his desire overcame everything. Once again he lay down beside her, and once again his revolver was in the way and he took off his belt and holster and threw them down by the base of the absurd little ladder and just as it seemed that nothing could stop him he saw the girl slowly point the revolver's gleaming barrel straight at him. Instead of seizing hold of it or striking it out of her hands, he jumped up in surprise; and while he stood there in the middle of the desert, paralysed with shame at the thought of being shot with his trousers half-down, Barchinoy shot herself through the heart. Birds that had settled for the short night on tamarisk bushes or stumps of *saksaul*[148] flapped their sleepy wings; a carpet viper that had sensed their love and crept up towards them rustled back into the night, and a little stream of blood coiled down the trail it left in the sand.

Before dawn he buried her in that same trench, under that same ladder that tore open the sky. Taking his colt by the bridle, he set off along the railway line back to the camp.

On his return he was arrested, and the Cossack commander opened an inquiry. In the lock-up, from which the Yomuds had been sent out to work but which still harboured their dense and heavy smell, Lieutenant Lemekh interrogated him about the events of the night. His replies were by no means the whole truth, but then how could he be understood by a man who only wanted to know one thing: had he or hadn't he fucked the bitch after she'd snuffed it? How could a man like Lemekh understand his simultaneously confused and enlightened heart? Getting no clear answer to his impatient questions, Lemekh lost interest and passed the case on to a sub-lieutenant. The sub-lieutenant turned out to be army intelligentsia, full of questions about what had motivated both him and the girl, but, since the sub-lieutenant had no clear idea of the motives underlying the interrogation itself, he too lost interest and found some excuse to pass the case on to a sergeant. The sergeant simply gave the young man a good beating for 'trampling on the honour of the Empire with your uncontrolled cock'. The beating was painful but uncomplicated. Deep inside him, however, nothing shifted, nothing changed. In the afternoon they poured a little newly delivered water over his bloodstained face; he was then passed on to the quartermaster, to help bring in the supplies. The quartermaster's only complaint was that the young man hadn't kept him better informed: together they could have given it to her good and proper – mane and tail.

The quartermaster was followed by several more Cossacks of lower and lower rank, but the only one he remembered was the one-eyed Bulba, a filicide, who suddenly bared his member and climbed on top of him. As the thirty-stone Cossack hung over him the young man felt that once this was over he would have no choice but to take his own life, but he somehow managed to free himself. Without understanding why, he found himself hissing, *'Eger guich bilen alaymasalar, ozum-a bermerin!'*

He grabbed hold of the water bucket and swung it with all his might at Bulba's one eye, but the bucket just buckled against his forehead. Bulba knocked him angrily to the ground, spat at him as he pulled up his trousers and then left him for dead, meaning to come back later and remove the body.

But he did not die. With his dim and confused consciousness he could still see the same interminable light that had wedged itself between the previous night and everything that had happened since; this light was like a gap, an abyss, a breach that nothing from the everyday world could bridge.

'Eger guich bilen . . . eger guich bilen,' he kept whispering, as if Barchinoy's love for another were an illness, a plague, a pestilence that had infected him.

In the evening, when the Yomuds returned, he was transferred from the lock-up to the quartermaster's yurt. To stop him running away, they gave him another thrashing. And this was a good thing, since it quietened, at least for a while, the ache in his abandoned heart, a heart that no one in the world needed. But towards midnight his sense of *toskà* grew unbearable; like a shadow, he left the tent, dragging his bloodstained body behind him.

It had not occurred to the Cossacks to beat up his young accomplice; already corrupted by a taste of nocturnal freedom, the colt offered him its back. He clambered on and guided the colt towards Barchinoy's grave.

They found him early the next morning, half-buried in sand. As a warning to everyone else, he was left lashed to the ladder for the entire day. His lips cracked; dry salt came out of his eyes; but not even the desert sun could burn away his *toskà*. Towards evening a passing fox sniffed at him and licked the blood off his feet; and a vulture that had been baked red-brown circled above him, then flew away to invite his family to a nocturnal feast.

'They can lick and drink my blood – but what do *I* have to lick and drink?' he repeated to himself as he drifted in and out of consciousness. The sun turned into a red-brown fox – or perhaps it had been a red-brown fox all along – and disappeared beneath the edge of the desert.

Because of the ache in his heart he begged God for a quick death, but God rejected him as an unbeliever, abandoning him as black night overtook the desert. With the last of his strength the crucified man called on Satan for help, but towards midnight, when he sensed something troubling the still air, when he heard a creak from the topmost rung of the ladder, he realised that this was not Satan but Azrael, black as a night raven, blinding his tired eyes with the flapping of black wings. And no sooner had Azrael, without asking a single question, pierced his heart and his liver in order to suck out his soul, than a crescent-feathered arrow passed with a whistle in between his head and his shoulder and plunged into the wooden sleeper. And Azrael, changed into a night vulture, was flapping his wounded wings up in the sky, while his hangers-on flew after him.

3.

An old man was chanting over him the words: 'And in this valley a name is untied from its bearer – as if the letters of the alphabet should abandon a book or a path should lose its direction. But what are you without a name, without books and without a path?' asked the blinded one. 'Speak if you can!

'Time in this valley is released from its traces, sand does not make up deserts, stars do not indicate darkness. But what are you without day, without reckoning and without light? Speak if you can!

'There you will be deprived of questions, there you will be deprived of deprivation, there and not there you will be not you. And what will then be left? Speak, if you can!'

Here the first dozen pages of Hoomer's notes break off. There is a gap, and then the manuscript continues. But while you have been reading it, I have realised that there is something else you need to know. I will begin, I think, from the very end.

On the day of calamities, when the earth quaked and a goods train going through Gilas was derailed, when the shock of the train hitting a pillar beside the station caused five cans of petrol to explode and the explosion brought down the water tower – on this day of calamities a torrent of water and flaming petrol swept away the white clay hut where Hoomer was then living alone, since his wife was taking part in some trial of Crimean Tatars,[149] and carried reams of burning and half-burnt and singed and occasionally unsinged sheets of paper through the town. After

240

the seven days of the flood, the old women began drying the pages in the innocent sun; then they screwed them up and used them to light fires in their hearths. Zangi-Bobo used them, along with pages from Peryoshkin's Fifth-Year Physics Course, to make cornets for sunflower seeds and *kurt*; Mefody-Jurisprudence used them to make cigarette papers.

But it was the ever alert and erudite Mefody who first discovered what had been written on these pages – what blind Hoomer had dictated and Nakhshon had written down in her fine hand. Mefody discovered this in the presence of Kun-Okhun, as they were smoking home-grown tobacco along with a little hashish that Kun-Okhun had obtained from Dolim-Dealer in exchange for a sack of stolen coal. Realising that the smoke was curling into the shapes of letters, they read, letter by letter, the words: 'Yusuf and his brother . . .' Frightened almost to death, Mefody stared at Kun-Okhun; Kun-Okhun, lumpen and uneducated as he was, swallowed the wisps of letters that were still hanging in the air yet somehow failed to take in anything at all. Mefody, however, having been trained long ago to deduce cause from effect, was appalled to discover that there was indeed still part of a slobbered-over letter 's' on the end of the roll-up. What they had seen in the air was a title; what followed was a compactly written text about how the illegitimate son of a great Russian explorer and a local washerwoman was sent by the Turkestan Geographical Society to study in Petersburg.

The hashish they were smoking was the kind known as 'Death'. Suspecting that it might be inducing hallucinations – Kun-Okhun had taken it into his head that he was a Party member and was now somehow managing to sing the Internationale with neither words nor melody – Mefody rushed to his briefcase, where the stack of dried pages of Hoomer, ready to be used for cigarette papers, lay beside Thomas Mann's novel and his 6 March 1953 copy of *Pravda*. He began reading at random: about the death of Umarali-Moneybags, about some old fellow called

Obid-Kori and . . . about the insane future of Sergeant Kara-Musayev the Younger (at that time still the Gilas head of police), who was doing his best to have Mefody sentenced for parasitism in accord with article 108 of the Criminal Code because then there would be no one left in Gilas who knew anything about the Law . . .

Mefody read many strange things in these pages but, when he got to the end of them and came to his 6 March 1953 copy of *Pravda*, he started rambling on in his usual way about Yusufs, exiles and betrayals, and this, as always, ended with Kun-Okhun peeing on the bald head of the unfortunate lawyer, although this time Timurkhan, having died beneath the wheels of a train, was unable to be present as a witness.

But somehow these precious pages, like the original tobacco smoke, vanished into thin air. Mefody blamed Kun-Okhun: after peeing on Mefody's bald patch, he had disappeared for what he referred to as 'a big job'. Kun-Okhun, however, could remember nothing; he just kept repeating that he was a freight handler and that he was not a member of the Party. Mefody then began prophesying to small groups of friends – in return, of course, for bottles of Portwein no. 53 – about what lay in store for Oppok-Lovely and, above all, for the soon-to-go-insane Kara-Musayev the Younger. When everything happened just as he had said it would, when Kara-Musayev's mind was taken over by slogans and Oppok-Lovely began renaming half the inhabitants of Gilas, everyone who had heard Mefody's prophecies began to suspect that Kara-Musayev had been framed, that the whole story of him and the young Uighur girls had been a fabrication of Oppok-Lovely's.

Wishing to gain control not only of Gilas's past and present but also of its future, Oppok-Lovely announced a public investigation into the matter of these manuscripts. We cannot be sure who first told her about Hoomer's chronicles – it might have been Osman-Anon, although at that time he still had an ordinary surname and was not yet a full-time employee of the KGB – but we can be sure of one thing: that Oppok-Lovely offered to pay twenty-five new roubles for every page that was brought to her, even if the page had been soiled.

Oppok-Lovely's next decision was to buy Mefody-Jurisprudence – lock, stock and barrel, with all his eccentricities. Mefody was allowed to keep his beloved briefcase; Kun-Okhun was allowed to pee – in the apple orchard behind Oppok-Lovely's house instead of outside the station – on Mefody's head of hair, which was now flourishing from an abundance of phosphorus; Oppok-Lovely guaranteed Mefody full board and lodging – including supplies of vodka and pickled cucumber; and in return Mefody had only to remember and retell everything he had read on that ill-starred and smoke-filled day.

Mefody's words were written down by a young boy who had lost his parents; Imomaliev, the director of the October School, had recommended the boy to Oppok-Lovely, saying he was intelligent and had good handwriting, at a time when he needed Oppok-Lovely's patronage to arrange for some repairs to the school building. Oppok-Lovely had not only enabled him to get the roof mended but had even sent Imomaliev, with trade union authorisation, to the Artek pioneer camp[150] – so that he could educate Artek riffraff in Uzbek ways.

At first the boy wrote on oxhide parchment, but when Oppok-Lovely discovered that Tolib-Butcher was palming her off with the hide of Korean dogs she spat in his face and began using A4 paper from Finland. The next problem was that Mefody, wanting to prolong his sinecure, began making things up, fabricating absurd stories of his own which later researchers, recommended to Oppok-Lovely by the eminent Pinkhas Shalomay, soon recognised as forgeries. The story of Hoomer and the railway line, for example, turned out to be the purest invention, and researchers also cast doubt on the story of Kun-Okhun and the Party recruitment drive after Stalin's death and heaven knows what else. Not every forgery, however, was the work of Mefody.

On hearing that you could earn twenty-five roubles a page, everyone in Gilas had begun scribbling down stories, but after a while people became more cunning. 'Yes,' they would say, 'we used to light our stove with pages of Hoomer. Our boy seems to have read a few pages – and the little rascal never forgets a thing. Listen now . . .'

At first Mefody simply ground people down with his cross-examinations and then dictated his summary of their stories to the boy from the October School, but then Oppok-Lovely appointed Nakhshon to the heritage commission – even though she had aged with grief and lost her memory, which had been kept alive only by her husband. Nakhshon, however, had lost none of her intransigence; many people, in fact, thought that her eyes protruded not because of Grave's disease but because of the peculiar corrosiveness of her soul.

After the appointment of Nakhshon the flood of stories began to dry up – but only as far as Oppok-Lovely's heritage com-mission was concerned. People did not stop talking to one another. Ortik-Picture-Reels told the story of Gopal and Radkha to the secretary of the music school over a bottle of vodka and some pickled cucumber she was treating him to in exchange for more brushes and paint; Nabi-Onearm, caught red-handed plundering socialist property, managed to get Kuzi-Gundog to put down his shotgun by telling him the story of how Garang-Deafmullah had shot away the end of his cock; Garang-Deafmullah, no longer alive, appeared to Tolib-Butcher in a dream and frightened him by foretelling the story of his grandson Nasim-Shlagbaum.

Self-taught chroniclers even appeared at the Kok-Terek Bazaar, attempting at least twice to sell little *samizdat* booklets they had compiled, but Oppok-Lovely got to hear about this and promptly removed Kun-Okhun from his duties as a freight handler and provider of hair-fertiliser and entrusted him with a new responsibility – that of beating up revisionists and pretenders. After two or three exemplary beatings, these pseudo-chroniclers disappeared from the town, although one of the railway guards who traded in tea said he had come across similar manuscripts somewhere or other in the Kazakh steppes.

This, however, does not concern us, just as it did not concern Oppok-Lovely. And so, when Pinkhas Shalomay's experts had finished separating the wheat from the chaff – although it was not always easy to tell which was which – Oppok-Lovely had the final manuscripts carefully bound: one in deerskin, one in sealskin, one in crocodile, and another – which had clearly never belonged to Hoomer and which might equally well have been an early forgery of Nakhshon's, a late invention of Mefody's or simply a faithfully recorded popular legend – in the kind of leatherette used for upholstering doors. She then put the volumes away in her most distant and hidden room, where she kept her one letter from her errant husband, locked the door and sewed the key into an amulet she had worn round her neck ever since she was a young girl in the Komsomol.

We can now return to our pages, which begin as abruptly, after a passage that has been devoured by fire, as they break off.

. . . near him. Nogira had been run over two years before by the very first train to come down the line; she had lost part of her mind and all the fingers of her right hand except the ring finger, on which she wore a little glass ring. And he developed a passion for taking this lanky twelve-year-old back to his home. On scorching summer days, as the whole district slept and Nogira sat by her gate, drawing lines in the dust with her ring finger, he would pass by as if on his way to the well; as if on the spur of the moment, in a voice that disgusted him, he would say, 'Nogira, I've got some lollipops. Would you like one?'

'Yes,' she would reply, jumping up eagerly.

'Run along then. And you can bring some stale bread for the animals. I won't be a moment.'

There was no need at all for deception. That was what was so disgusting – the way he always began with this absurd deceit, as if someone were listening.

She knew, as if by instinct, how to dart through his gate unnoticed. Then he would enter the yard himself, glancing from side to side. He would put the lid on the water-bucket and prepare the bread – as if he were about to feed the animals. Then he would walk towards the bread-oven shed – knowing that the idiot girl would be waiting for him there, quiet as a mouse.

He would go inside, close the crooked door behind him, walk through the sharp strips of dusty light, lay the girl down on the cotton hulls, pull off her trousers and begin pushing his huge red cock against her fleshy, still hairless crotch. 'Do you know what this is?' he would whisper, swallowing down his saliva.

'Cock.'

'And what am I doing with it?'

'Fucking.'

These words would further inflame him, and he would begin to push a little harder than he should. She would groan, as if the cyclops pushing against her flesh really had penetrated deep inside her. Then he would place it between her legs and let himself go – and she would groan because of the weight of his body. The cotton hulls under her legs tickled and rubbed his cock and he would shoot his load. Then she would lie there with him, only after a long time asking, 'Where's my lollipop?'

He would wipe himself clean with cotton hulls and sit on a rung of the little ladder that stood pointing towards the chimney. She would stand up to pull her trousers on, and the sight of her reddened crotch would excite him again. He would beckon her closer and say, 'The lollipop's in my pocket. Take it yourself.'

She would slip her left hand into one pocket – and find only a thick and swelling emptiness. Then she would put her damaged hand into the other pocket; pushing the stumps of her missing fingers against a stump with no fingers at all, she would use her one whole finger to pluck out a lollipop that had stuck to the damp cotton.

Then he would pull out his shame, which was aching with tension, and she, sucking the lollipop she had earned, would move her ring finger up and down it in shameless gratitude, tracing the same incomprehensible letters that she would be tracing tomorrow, and every day, in the burning noon dust of the vill . . .

This is followed by some burnt passages that I can make neither head nor tail of, and then by some complete and coherent pages, evidently not in the handwriting of Nakhshon.

. . . did not want to recall how he had to run away from the village. When he next saw the iron road, beside which the Cossack detachment had eventually shot the thirty Yomuds and Tekes, and along which they had been unable to run a train for an entire year because, every time they checked the line with a handcar, they came upon a section of dismantled track with ladders sticking up into the sky over the trenches where the dead had been buried and they would have to repair the track again during the day only for it to be dismantled again in the night until in the end they decided to abandon this section of track that kept climbing up into the sky and lay down a parallel section seven miles clear of this ill-starred place of either justice or vengeance – but I have lost track of my thought. Let me start again, let me return to where this fraught and fractured sentence began . . . When he next saw the iron road (that is, the original section of track, which climbed steeply up into the sky at both ends – above where the father and son and Barchinoy were buried, and above where the thirty Yomuds and Tekes were buried) he understood that the four hills at the corners of the desert horizon were his childhood's four points of the compass, his own four corners of the world which he had been carrying inside him all these years, always subordinating the daily path of the sun to this line from the 'double-humped hill' through the 'bald hill' above which the sun stood at noon and on to the 'grave hill'. Yes, this was the site of his childhood home, now buried beneath the sands and traversed by this absurd railway line that kept climbing up into the sky; it was here that he had pastured the goat that had fed him and Gulsum-Khalfa, and it was through the gap between the 'sandy hill' and the 'grave hill' that he and the goat had escaped from the horsemen of the cut-throat Aspandiyar.

Sitting on the bottom rung of the ladder, he unwound the rag, stiff with dried blood and sweat, from around the bullet-wound on his shin, and thought about how he had returned to these parts in search of his father but in the end had just had to run away. A spider was spinning its eternal thread over his head, and the thirty warriors he had destroyed, thirty young men beloved of women, thirty young men who had never become husbands or fathers, lay beneath his feet, while the sun cast its light down upon them.

Thus wrote Hoomer in the Turkestan sunset, in a winter-cold officers' coach, hiding in his compartment from the crowds of triumphantly drunken Russians.

31

Once again, I don't know whether I told the truth about that night. No, no, I don't mean the truth about the events themselves – everything happened as described in these pages; what I mean is – the truth about who was responsible. The easiest thing is to blame it all on Uchmah; but it has also been suggested that the ageing Oppok-Lovely was driven to extreme measures by her longing for her errant husband; there have been attempts to implicate Nakhshon; and there have been mentions of Musayev and God knows who else. Mefody-Jurisprudence – who had by then been deprived of his sinecure, so that Kun-Okhun had had to go back to peeing on his head outside the station instead of in the apple-orchard behind Oppok-Lovely's house – came out with all kinds of nonsense about the triune nature of Hoomer, Shapik and I forget who else; but people with more sense were quick to relate this to Mefody's deep-rooted and profoundly Russian belief that a bottle of vodka should always be shared between three, a belief which, since the death of Timurkhan, had been elevated, in the lawyer's alcohol-pickled mind, to the status of an article of faith. But no one, no one in Gilas thought about the role of the eldest son of Fatkhulla-Frontline – the war veteran who was the mind, conscience and honour of the *mahallya*; no one considered a drawing teacher and retired engineer by the name of Rizo-Zero.

Rizo had been born during the War, after the shell-shocked and half-blinded Fatkhulla had been sent back to Gilas in order to mobilise the women to shock labour on behalf of the war effort. This had led to the three-eyed Rizo, later to be known as Rizo-Zero, being born to the beautiful though small-eyed Zebi. I say three-eyed because above the bridge of his nose lay a small pit the size of an almond that looked like a miraculous third eye.

Making the most of his rights as a war veteran, Fatkhulla sent his son off to the railway institute at the age of seventeen, expecting him to return to his native Gilas as one of Kaganovich's esteemed engineers – but Rizo concerned himself at the institute with matters very different indeed. No, no, not the ones you're thinking of – he didn't drink, he didn't smoke, he didn't seduce women; what he devoted himself to, God knows why, was not the theory of railway construction on loess soil or on sand, but the theory of shadow.

Not only did he read, and write summaries of, everything he could find on this subject in any of the libraries – he also used to sit in the sun for whole Sundays on end, studying the slightest variations in his own shadow on the roof, by the lake, in the student hostel or in the stadium. Any student whose coursework or diploma dissertation touched however tangentially on this problem would find their way to him through an improbable number of intermediaries, and he would gladly compose an essay on 'Shadow in Dostoevsky's Petersburg Novels' for an evening-class student of printing or 'The Shadow of Gogol in the Work of Bulgakov' for a girl who had undertaken a correspondence course in the Humanities. His generosity, however, bore fruit that for the main part proved bitter: the printer's essay was rewarded with a diploma he did not wish to receive, and the correspondence-course student was all but forced to embark on a doctorate. She was courted by three different supervisors, each trying to win her for their department and thus wrest her away from the regular festive rations to which she was entitled by virtue of her position as technical secretary to some Party committee or other.

But Rizo-Zero did not rest on his laurels. He progressed ever further. When he returned to Gilas with a rather mediocre diploma, the best his father could do for him was to find him a job as assistant to Master-Railwayman Belkov. But by then Rizo-Zero had already learned to annihilate his own shadow. Just before sunset on a summer's day, while old Alyaapsindu was dragging behind him a shadow as long as his long years, Rizo-Zero was able – by means of some system of mirrors, or through the properties of mysterious objects, or because he had acquired the ability to emit an invisible light through his third eye – to walk behind him down the very same sidestreets with only the tiniest spots of shadow beneath the soles of his feet, as if it were high noon.

After an argument with Ilyusha the Korean (usually known as Ilyusha-Oneandahalf because Rizo's donkey had long ago bitten off half of one of his ears) Rizo annihilated Alyaapsindu's shadow as well. The old Korean never again went out of his house; instead he went out of his mind, was overwhelmed by *toskà* and died.

It was around then that Rizo-Zero was fired by Master-Railwayman Belkov. He found himself a job as a drawing teacher and appeared to lose all interest in shadows.

It was not long, however, before people began seeing Rizo-Zero up on the roof at night with a telescope; and then, during a drinking bout, Ilyusha-Oneandahalf informed the whole of Gilas that Rizo had taken up the study of stars and was especially interested in solar and lunar eclipses. Ilyusha even tried to intimidate Zukhur, who was refusing to sell him vodka, by threatening that Rizo would bring down a terrible eclipse on the town.

Zukhur went straight to the *mahallya* committee to report this to Fatkhulla-Frontline. Fatkhulla tried to calm Zukhur, as if his power extended not only over his son but also over any eclipses his son might call down. Nevertheless, Fatkhulla thought it better to be safe than sorry; on returning from the chaikhana that evening, he took Rizo aside and approached the subject obliquely: 'Your mother and I are ageing, my son. Yes, the old folk of Gilas are quietly dying out. Hoomer, Umarali-Moneybags and now Alyaaps . . .'

'But that's not because of *me*,' Rizo-Zero interrupted anxiously. '*I'm* not to blame.'

'Of course not. But there's something else. I've heard you've taken it into your head to call down an eclipse. Please don't – why upset people? Especially when Zukhur's just received a consignment of Russian potatoes. He's promised us a whole sack.'

'Father, what on earth are you saying? Have you no fear of Allah? Are such things in the power of a mere mortal? Not a hair will fall from your head unless He so decrees.'

'That's what I'm saying: don't do bad things. If you've got to do something, do something good.'

And Fatkhulla explained what he and his Ukrainian comrade Petro had done in the War to get German prisoners to talk. Rizo-Zero heard him out, holding in his hand a potato that Zukhur had given his father. Only when his father had finished did Rizo, wanting to show at least some loyalty to science, start to demonstrate what brings about an eclipse; the lamp stood for the sun, his father's face was the earth, and Zukhur's potato – the moon. Rizo-Zero circled the moon round his father's face and, at the very moment when its shadow fell on Fatkhulla's one eye, they heard loud shouts from outside, from somewhere around Oppok-Lovely's house. Other shadows leaped and coiled their way into the house and began creeping across the wall. Fatkhulla grabbed his soldier's belt, from which there always hung a crooked Chust knife, and dashed outside. Rizo-Zero dashed after him. Through the dusty vine they saw the moon shrivelling up before their very eyes, like a scrap of paper caught by a flame . . .

'I told you not to!' the father shouted, and clipped his son on the ear. The son, still holding the potato-moon, said not a word.

The whole of Gilas was pouring out onto the street. Poor Fatkhulla was so ashamed he didn't know where to look with his single eye.

The following morning, after finding out about the terrible explosion by the canal, Fatkhulla – the mind, conscience and honour of the *mahallya* – cursed every part of his son Rizo from head to toe and threw him out of the house.

Rizo-Zero wandered off down the railway line, examining his thoughts. Thoughts structure themselves according to the path one follows; yes, during his years as assistant to Master-Railwayman Belkov, Rizo had learned to resolve even the most stubborn of contradictions between the two rails beneath him. On this occasion, he was thinking: 'I'm walking one step at a time, from sleeper to sleeper. My foot rises, then comes down on the sleeper in front. It settles there. My other foot does the same, with the same movement. What then remains on the sleeper behind? Stop! Let's go through that again. There – my foot is still on the sleeper behind. On the sleeper in front lies only emptiness. And then my foot goes and fills that emptiness, occupying that empty space. But if only a moment ago it was occupying the same form of space on the sleeper behind, doesn't that mean that this emptiness has moved from the sleeper in front to the sleeper behind? It seems then that I move forward, while my empty shadow does precisely the opposite. And if we consider my movement from the level crossing to the wool-washing shed as a whole, then has this emptiness I occupy not carried out the same movement in reverse, from the wool-washing shed to the level crossing? Let me draw a little diagram.' And Rizo-Zero bent down over the sleeper and began, with a sharp stone from the embankment as his stylus, to draw a diagram on the creosoted sleeper:

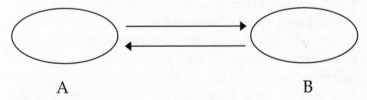

A   B

'Here we have the presence, the existence of ellipse A, which is to be transposed, as indicated by the arrow pointing to the right, to its present absence: ellipse B. When it reaches ellipse B, its absence, displaced by its presence, will be transposed to ellipse A; that is A and B will exchange places, but their forms, since nothing in nature can be either destroyed or created, will remain identical during this exchange, that is . . .' – but before Rizo had pursued his thought to a clear conclusion, there was a piercing whistling, a waving of multicoloured flags and Tadji-Murad, calling Rizo-Zero every name in the book and turning the air blue with his curses, was rushing towards him, closely followed by a wagon he had just uncoupled. Rizo-Zero's thought rushed forward to meet him but, instead of a pure and empty form, it encountered Tadji-Murad's choicest curses: 'What the fuck are you doing with your arse stuck up in the air waiting for some fucker to fuck it? Fuck your fucking arse – these wagons will make one great cunt of you! Rizofucking Zerofucker!'

Flabbergasted at the discrepancy between the pure transcendence of thought and the crude language being flung at him, Rizo barely managed to straighten his stiff back before Tadji-Murad, hurtling through space almost as fast as his whistles and curses, slammed into him like one wagon into another and knocked him out of the path of the wagon that had been sent rolling along the gradient.

As they lay there getting their breath back – one from physical exertion, the other from the sudden disarray of his thoughts – Nabi-Onearm, using the freewheeling wagon as cover, jumped across the track with a sack of stolen cotton seeds, tripped over Rizo's large thought-bearing shoe and crashed to the ground, scattering seeds over the railway bed.

'You fuckers!' shouted Nabi-Onearm, seizing the high ground, as he always did, by being first to leap to his feet. His index finger was drilling into the sky, but this time he did not get the chance to speak. Kazakbay-Happytrigger, a guard at the wool-washing shed and the owner of the cows Nabi's seeds were meant to be feeding, suddenly lost his nerve. Afraid that he too might suffer public exposure, he took a potshot at Nabi with his double-barrelled shotgun, cleanly removing the finger with which the one-armed man was pointing at the heavens. Nabi let out a howl and fell to the ground as if dead. Tadji-Murad jumped to his feet to get back to his waving and whistling and inadvertently kicked poor Rizo's forehead with his heavy railwayman's shoe. In the blinding light of this blow, Rizo-Zero saw two rails rushing from one horizon to the other in a vain attempt to meet, suddenly noticed the sleepers that locked them so inseparably apart, and, understanding the meaning of everything in an instant, was thrown into a total eclipse of consciousness.

32

*That summer, cosmonaut Kitov flew into space; when the loudspeaker
in the bazaar announced this, the boy's aunts were all in the yard,
ironing shirts and trousers for his circumcision. The boy was standing
beside them, and he was the only one to hear the voice of all the radio
stations of the Soviet Union. He was the first to hear the cosmonaut's
surname, Kitov, although the bazaar loudspeaker was interrupted just
then by the wheeze of the station loudspeaker, that is, by Ashir-
Beanpole wheezing out his eternal, 'Attintion, attintion, citizin
passingers, thi Sir-Darinsky–Darbaza–Chingildi locil train will bi
arrivin' it plitform three. It will bi stoppin' fer one minit!'*

*The boy began to jump about in unaccustomed joy, perhaps because
he was proud of understanding what 'to fly into space' really meant –
unlike the time before, when it had been his aunt Nafisa, throwing her
briefcase up into the sky, who had called out, 'Lyaganov has flown into
space, Lyaganov has flown into space!'*[151] *That time the boy had felt
scared: someone had gone and flown into the sky, with no wings, with
no equipment, with nothing at all. Either he'd quarrelled with his
wife or else he was wanting to spite someone: he'd just gone and flown
up into the sky like Nafisa's briefcase – out of which exercise books,
text-books and fountain pens had come raining down.*

*No, this time it was the boy who had been first to hear the news:
'Kitov has flown into space, Kitov has flown into space!' Only the boy
had nothing to hurl into the sky; it was the school holidays, and
tomorrow would be his circumcision and the yard had been carefully
tidied and sprinkled with water.*

*He felt as happy as if the colt he had been promised a month ago had
already been brought into the yard. Tomorrow he would have to sit on
the colt and ride round and round the fire till he felt drunk, so that it
wouldn't hurt afterwards. He leapt over the patches of sunlight that
fell through the thick dusty curtain of the vine and onto the damp,*

shadowy earth, just as the colt would prance and gallop if it understood what it meant to fly into space. 'Kitov has flown into space! Kitov has flown into space!'

Nobody reined the boy back – neither the various 'aunties' who lived nearby, nor his granny coming out of the dark house. He knew that tomorrow would be his special day, and so he leapt about until he felt exhausted, until his grandad – or rather step-grandad, since the boy did not have a grandfather of his own, or, for that matter, a father – came in through the gate. Grandad went straight into the dark house, followed by Granny, by Aunt Nafisa and Great-Aunt Asolat and even by Robiya, who was helping them. She was the aunt of Kobil-Melonhead, who was now outside Huvron-Barber's window, playing nuts underneath the cherry trees with Kutr, Hussein, and Sabir and Sabit, the two lyuli boys. Kobil-Melonhead, of course, didn't know a thing either about Kitov or about outer space.

The boy longed to go and tell them the news he had been first to hear, but he didn't want to lose his name-day specialness[152] by leaving the house, and so, not quite knowing what to do with himself, he wandered inside after the women, into the dark house, so that he could at least show off about Kitov to Grandad.

But he had barely crossed the threshold before he heard Grandad say in a hopeless tone, 'It was a lot of money. I didn't have enough.'

Granny gave a long sigh; one of his aunts began to cry.

Grandad had clearly been talking about the colt. The boy's eyes filled with tears and he stood rooted to the spot. The aunts wandered out of the inner room and stumbled into the boy in the half-dark. They were crying quite openly – goodness knows why – until Granny came and sent them into the yard, saying it was a sin to cry on the eve of a holiday. She didn't see the boy.

All this made the boy angry. He wiped away his tears and went out onto the street, having quite forgotten about Kitov and even about his own specialness.

No, he did not find Kobil outside Huvron–Barber's window – the only boys playing nuts were Kutr and the two lyuli boys, Sabir and

Sabit. Hussein was sitting on the ground, leaning back against the wall of his house. It was clear that he had already lost and was looking not at the nuts but at the tall figure of Shapik, who was picking his nose beneath the cherry trees.

Old Alyaapsindu was walking down the noon alley, dragging his short shadow behind him. Just as the boy reached the players, Kobil-Melonhead came running up behind the old man, shouting, 'Bitov's in space! Bitov's flown into space!' Neither the boy, nor old Alyaapsindu, who went on dragging his shadow along without a backward glance, bothered to point out to Kobil-Melonhead that it was not Bitov but Kitov who had flown into space;[153] nor did the boy feel like saying that it was he who had been first to know, that it was he who had told Kobil's Aunt Robiya. No, the boy no longer wanted anything under the sun.

'And they didn't buy him a horse,' Kobil concluded. Blankly, the boy went up to him and boxed him on the ear. Kobil said nothing, and only Shapik, like a motor gradually gathering speed, began stuttering his 'Bloody . . . Bloody fuck . . . !'

The players were distracted for a moment, even though the game was nearly over. And then, instead of either winning the last nut or losing everything he had already won, little Sabir just grabbed the nut and ran off with it, shouting out, 'Quick, Sabit, scarper!'

Sabit had longer legs than Sabir and he dashed after his younger brother, but Kutr managed to trip him up. Sabit crashed down on top of Shapik. They started fighting; little Kutr was going for Sabit's balls, but Sabit for some reason went for Shapik, who was completely innocent. And only a shout from Fatkhulla-Frontline put an end to all this. Kutr and Sabit rushed off in different directions, and Kobil and the boy were left on their own in the shade. Musayev walked by in the sun, muttering slogans. Then Kobil-Melonhead suggested they play films . . .

And so the afternoon drew to an end, empty and useless. In the evening Satiboldi-Buildings and everyone from the mahallya *began to gather in their house to cut carrots for the* plov *and get everything* ready for the following day. Nabi-Onearm was one of the first arrivals and, being unable to do anything very useful with only one hand, he naturally began to organise those who came after him. He sat Tadji-Murad, Rizo-Zero and Faiz-Ulla-FAS down to cut carrots, and he sent Kun-Okhun and Timurkhan off to chop wood and break up coal. Tolib-Butcher began cutting up the sheep; Temir-Iul was put in charge of setting out the tables and benches; Fatkhulla-Frontline sent messengers round the mahallya so he could get an idea of how many guests would be coming; Garang-Deafmullah checked that everything was in place for the ritual; Tordybay-Medals brought his son Sherzod, who was going to take the place of the boy's colt; and even Ortik-Picture-Reels, after showing one of his Indian films, turned up at midnight for a cup of tea.

The women of the mahallya were working away in the inner rooms; only Oppok-Lovely had yet to return from the City, having gone there to invite her idolised but elusive Bahriddin to the feast. A little further down the street, in Aisha's house, Saniya and Uchmah had sewed countless kerchiefs and napkins from calico they had requisitioned from the house of Soli-Stores. 'Stolen goods are the strongest!' Aisha declared, finding that Soli's calico was so sturdy that her scissors were growing blunter more quickly than she could dash to and from the little shop of Huvron-Barber, who was himself hard at work sharpening not only her scissors, but also the knives being used to cut carrot and onion, lean meat and fat, potato and pumpkin, melon and watermelon.

In a word, the entire mahallya was at work. Even Uncle Monya, the hunchbacked Jew about whom no one knew anything at all, was applying a fresh coat of paint to his gate.

By midnight, Rif the Tatar gravedigger, had dug a splendid fireplace. Over it hung a vast cauldron, big enough to cook the thirty-five kilos of rice that Murzin-Mordovets, accompanied by Zangi-Bobo and Mefody-Jurisprudence, had brought in his car from the Kok-Terek Bazaar. Murzin gave the bottle he had earned to Mefody, since he himself, as he put it, 'would soon be back on the road chasing *roubles'. Mefody united his immemorial trinity, and soon he, Kun-Okhun and Timurkhan were on their way to the station to perform their eternal ritual.*

That night the boy did not sleep. This, for once, was not because of a lack of supervision on the part of the adults, but at their insistence. It was essential to be tired for tomorrow's circumcision, in order to get through it more easily – and there may have been other reasons as well. Many things, after all, were happening that night for the first time: it was the first time that Rokhbar was baking naan bread in Granny's oven; it was the first time that Grandad wasn't making fun of his friends Djebral the Persian from Shiraz and Fatkhulla the Tadjik from Chust, each of whom had only one eye, but on opposite sides of their faces. Instead of knocking their foreheads together, he was observing everything from the shadows with the dignity expected of a master of the house and whispering to his child-messengers, who transmitted his instructions to Nabi-Onearm, who then jabbered away for all he was worth . . .

But however the boy tried to stay awake and keep an eye on everything – since that was what Granny had told him to do – all the same, towards morning, after eating piping hot naan bread straight from Rokhbar's oven, he sat down where Grandad used to store huge black watermelons during the winter and curled up for a moment on the cotton hulls. He could hardly have slept long – probably it was no more than the tiniest scrap of sleep – but while he was asleep he saw many things: he was deep in a palm forest, with no sky to be seen at all, and he happened upon a tree stump swarming with wasps – and then from behind this stump appears Rokhbar, who turns out to be Nabi-Onearm, who is sucking his one hand, which has been dipped in either pain or honey. 'I'm the beekeeper,' Granny says to Oppok-Lovely, who for some reason has lost not her hand but her leg. 'Let's dip your willy in this.' The boy feels frightened, sees Shapik weeping and Sabir and Sabit laughing, then hears the words, 'Come on, try these on . . .' When his amputated willy turns in his hands to a pen, he thinks sadly about the colt that was meant to save him, but all he can see by the tethering post is a ladder . . . and then he sees the very same ladder in Rokhbar's oven shed and he hears Granny's very real voice: 'Come on, try these boots on . . .'

The boy sat on the bottom step of the ladder and, only then remembering his dream, began to try on the new boots.

'They're not too small, are they?'

'What good is it to me that the world is so big if my boots are too small?'[154] the boy said in a voice hoarse from lack of sleep. The women burst into laughter, and Rokhbar slapped her baker's glove against her thigh as she said, 'A real little young warrior!'

He walked off in his new boots, which really were a little tight for feet that had spread out during a barefoot summer, but they were gently and snugly tight, as if long barefootedness had made his feet grow a protective sheath. As he walked out of the gate, they made a knocking sound against the five-kopek piece cemented into the ground for good fortune; it was as if his feet were pure bone.

It was already dawn, a quick summer's dawn. Izaly-Jew's cocks woke Lyuli-Ibodullo-Mahsum's donkey, and Lyuli-Ibodullo-Mahsum's donkey woke the cows on the Samarasi Collective Farm. The old war veteran Fatkhulla-Frontline excused himself for half an hour and drove his veteran sheep to the scrubland by the Salty Canal. Last of all, the Koreans' pigs started grunting; their smell, which had ripened during the night, was carried by the dawn breeze towards the station, where Akmolin was hooting and a sleepy Tadji-Murad was frightening equally sleepy crows with his whistle. And along with the dawn, though the sun was still below the horizon, the guests began to arrive for their plov.

The first, on his own, still all wrinkled and curled up from the night cold, was Rakhmon-Kul, one of the sons of Chinali; Garang-Deafmullah welcomed him with a prayer, and the two of them shared a bowl of plov. Then came the two drivers – Murzin the Mordovian and Saimulin the Chuvash; they had decided to fill up a little before setting out on their journeys. After that Dolim-Dealer, Oppok-

Lovely's heir, brought four men who worked as weighers at the Kok-Terek Bazaar. Next Tadji-Murad, whistle in hand, brought Akmolin, who had left his shunter in the siding opposite the little shop of Yusuf-Cobbler; then Yusuf-Cobbler himself wandered in, wearing his green embroidered Margilan skullcap in honour of the plov *he was about to eat and bowing to all sides to be sure not to miss anyone. Then came: Huvron-Barber; everyone from the cotton factory; the Tatars from the wool factory; eleven Korean footballers about to set out for a friendly match against their fellow-countrymen at the 'Political Section' collective farm; and Lyuli-Ibadullo-Mahsum. Next, holding his hand just below his heart in Uzbek fashion, came Master-Railwayman Belkov. Garang-Deafmullah was no longer able to keep up with saying a prayer to welcome each guest, and so Fatkhulla-Frontline – who had returned from taking his sheep to pasture – and Nabi-Onearm – waving his one hand Shiite-style[155] as he greeted Ezrael, the son of the Persian Huvron-Barber – had to help him out, saying prayers of welcome in separate corners of the room. After being welcomed, each guest was served* plov; *they ate decorously, drank a lazy cup of green tea, listened to another prayer from either Tolib-Butcher or Kun-Okhun – who had sobered up after performing his nocturnal duty towards Mefody-Jurisprudence – and then got to their feet and set off to work.*

Party First Secretary Buri-Bigwolf brought Gilas's First Veteran, who had only recently been released from the Gulag; this, of course, was Mullah-Ulmas-Greeneyes – the husband of Oppok-Lovely and brother-in-law of the late Oktam-Humble-Russky, the town's First Bolshevik. Vying with Buri-Bigwolf, Tordybay-Medals brought Gilas's Senior Inhabitant, blind old Hoomer. Hoomer fussed about for a while and asked confusedly to be introduced to the culprit. When the boy went up to him, the frail and transparent old man put his calico bag to one side, whispered something in the boy's ear and, patting him on the head, gave him some kind of amulet – earth from under Gilas's first railway sleeper, or a sliver of the first brick from the cotton factory, or maybe a bit of paper sewn into a black velvet triangle – and pronounced a blessing. Hoomer, however, gave off a smell of chloroform and valerian; the boy was quick to move away from him, and the old man – thank God – was taken off to eat plov with Mullah-Ulmas-Greeneyes, who was smiling the stupid smile of a man who is never quite sure what language he will be addressed in.

At eleven o'clock it was the turn of the women to eat; they were served the remains of the plov and a freshly cooked pea soup. But by then the boy no longer knew who was coming and who was going. He had to go next door to Aisha-Nogaika, to wash in a tub before the ritual. It was bad enough to have to bathe in a tub under the supervision of Auntie Aisha and of Janna-Nurse, who poured water over him and rubbed him down with a loofah – but what he hated still more was the way all three widows kept darting about, one bringing him a little jug, another a little towel, another some more warm water, each of them considering it their duty to wash his willy – which had wrinkled up out of embarrassment – and to crack some joke at its expense. And then, after he had been washed and dried all over, Auntie Uchmah turned away to blow her nose and then touched his willy again with snotty fingers – as if his willy were a handkerchief! Ugh! And then her snot dried over his foreskin and even after he had been dressed up in his holiday finery the boy kept trying to wipe away this crust with the help of his satin trousers, but they just slid over it, making his willy swell and somehow expanding Uchmah's revolting trail.

As he came out of Aisha's house, he saw that the other boys were all playing nuts under Huvron-Barber's cherry trees: Kutr, Shapik and Hussein, Sabir and Sabit, Kobil-Melonhead, Kara and Borat . . . Just before one o'clock, when he was feeling hungry and sleepy, someone gave him a small cup of vile, bitter cognac, saying it was medicine. Then he was given a handful of raisins and placed on the back of Uncle Sherzod, who was going to take the place of the colt and whirl him around the bonfire.

The memory of his brief dream stung the boy's heart and he put his arms round Sherzod's strong neck. They went out into the yard. The *fire was not yet burning properly. Someone hurried off to fetch a stack of papers they remembered seeing in a bag on the floor; but the papers wouldn't burn. Bakay said they should throw paraffin on the fire, but there wasn't any; children were sent to get some petrol off Murzin or Saimulin, but the two drivers had already left; in the end someone ran to the garage by the level crossing and came back with not a can of petrol but a whole drum. They threw some on and there was a burst of flame, giving off the same sickening heat that the boy could already feel building up inside him; then he and Sherzod began circling the bonfire.*

The fire burnt. The flames seized sheets of paper and carried them up into the air. All the children except Hussein and the two lyuli came running to watch Kakhramon Dadayev – whom Oppok-Lovely had hired in the City – playing five tambourines at once.

The fire burnt. As he passed by, old Alyaapsindu saw that his shadow was dancing even though his body was barely moving; but for the help of Rizo-Zero, he would have fallen to the ground in shock.

The fire burnt. Sabir and Sabit led Hussein towards the Zakh Canal, while Hussein's father, Huvron-Barber, sharpened Garang-Deafmullah's razor for the circumcision.

The fire burnt. Blind Hoomer returned to his musty home and felt a sharp pain in his chest as he discovered that he had left behind the calico bag of papers that he never allowed himself to be parted from. But there was no one to help: Nakhshon had gone away to take part in some trial of Crimean Tatars, and the Young Pioneers were all on holiday.

The fire burnt. The staring, whirling faces made the boy feel more and more sick: Uchmah, who had covered his willy with snot; Janna-Nurse, who hadn't wiped off this snot; Tolib-Butcher, who was pressing up, in the dense crowd, against the plump bottom of the half-

blind Boikush; Tadji-Murad, Boikush's son, who still had his whistle round his neck and who chose not to notice what was going on because Tolib-Butcher set aside two kilos of boneless meat for him every week (the boy's granny got the bones from this portion).

The fire burnt. Sabir and Sabit led Hussein to the deserted bank of the Zakh canal, dived into the water and called to Hussein to come in after them. Hussein, forbidden to swim by the strict beliefs of his Shiite family, stripped naked and stepped cautiously into the water. First out of mischievousness, then out of intoxication with their own power, Sabit and Sabir began pushing Hussein under. Hussein cried out. 'Shut up or I'll fuck you!' shouted little Sabir; his elder brother, already tormented by wet dreams at night and a constant need to masturbate during the day, shuddered from the rush of blood to his head and his cock and said, 'Now we can bugger him!' Hussein was crying; they pushed him back under.

Exhausted, Hussein said he didn't mind what they did – as long as they took him out of this icy water that was already filling his innards and making him want to vomit. On the bare bank, pushing his face into the thick hot dust and spreading him out 'like a crayfish', Sabit burnt Hussein's aching and pulsating arse with his quick ejaculate, after which Sabir wriggled about on top of him while Sabit knelt on the ground, gripping Hussein's head between his knees and pinning his arms as he howled and vomited; Hussein's face was covered with saliva, tears and snotty semen.

When the still semen-less Sabir finally got off him, Hussein's battered arse let out a stream of diarrhoea and pressurised gas. Enraged by this, the two brothers tied the boy's hands behind his back with his T-shirt and tied his trousers round his ankles.

'I'll kill you! I'm still going to kill you!' Hussein howled. Sabir and Sabit caught sight of old Zangi-Bobo in the distance, gathering mint to enrich the nasvoy he made from tobacco and chicken droppings; they took fright and tried to stuff Hussein's shirt into his mouth. Hussein bit Sabir's hand till it bled, but Sabit kicked him hard in the eye and, *while Hussein was recovering, succeeded in gagging him. Hussein could hardly breathe for snot and blood, and his whole body was in convulsions.*

'Careful, he's dying,' said Sabir in fright, 'Let's throw him into the water!' shouted his elder brother.

They tried to lift Hussein but only managed to remove the tie from his legs. In the end they just rolled him along the bank and pushed him, covered in dust and blood, into the water.

Hussein struggled still more convulsively and the gag came out of his mouth. He gasped in air and let out a wild cry.

'Throw a stone at him!' squeaked Sabir, seeing Zangi-Bobo jumping about in the distance. Sabit began looking for stones to throw at Hussein's choking head. The first stone turned out to be earth; on hitting the head, it spread into a dirty stain on the slowly moving water. The second stone missed, but the third was well aimed; there were no more shouts or gurgles, and the head disappeared beneath the water. And it was not long before the bloody puddle on the surface of the Zakh canal had faded away.

Sabit was still holding a stone in his hand. Sabir was trembling. 'Are you going to dive in too?' Sabit asked him. Sabir trembled still more and shouted, 'Dive in yourself, you bastard!' Then he began to run along the bank, afraid that Sabit had decided to kill him too. Sabit, afraid that Sabir would tell everyone what had happened, ran off after his brother. And only Zangi-Bobo saw the two boys, who were letting out blood-curdling cries as they tore along the steeply gullied bank.

The boy vomited onto Sherzod's back. There were shouts and squeals all round, competing with Kakhramon Dadayev's five tambourines. Someone screamed; someone rushed up to the boy; someone hurried to put the fire out. There was general mayhem. The boy was carried out of the circle, but he went on vomiting. Even when he seemed to have vomited up every drop of cognac and every last raisin, he went on vomiting yellow, bitter bile.

266

'Now! Now!' someone shouted – and he was carried under the trees and into the house. On the way, his hands were tied tight – as were his ankles, now released from their boots. Then he was thrown half-unconscious onto a soggy bed and someone huge and merciless pulled down his trousers. With his last gasp of vision the boy saw faces pressed against the window – Janna-Nurse and her niece Natashka, and Shapik's mother Uchmah, and Kobil-Melonhead and Kutr and . . . a sharp pain, like the crest of a wave of shame, lifted him high, high, high above the ceiling, high above the blue sky and the dazzling yellow sun, right into the darkness into which Kitov had flown.

'So I'm dead,' the boy thought with a calm sense of doom. And no sooner had he grown used to this thought than the window was flung open and howls and screams came flooding in, and, when he opened his eyes in the other world, he saw Uchmah and Janna and all the same excited faces as before. Someone's huge hand quickly showed him a tiny ring of skin, which was oozing blood and through which he could see a red lamp, and then Garang-Deafmullah hobbled to the window and threw this useless piece of flesh through the iron grating, and the women all screamed as they fought for this magic ring that would help them bear children . . .

And the boy closed his eyes.

There seemed to be no end to the screaming of the women outside.

In her youth Zebi-Beauty lived up to her name and never harboured a breath of evil inside her. Once, at a reception to mark the return from the War and the Gulag of Mullah-Ulmas-Greeneyes – Gilas's Traitor-to-the-Motherland and First Veteran – she bent down to pick up a naan bread and let out a loud fart. The subsequent silence hung in the air. Fortunately, her seven-year-old son Barot was there at hand, and she cursed him, clipped him across the ear, and sent him packing. And the poor mite's indignant 'But what have *I* done?' hung in the tainted silence.

But the reception continued . . .

How people loved Bahriddin!

There was probably no one people loved like Bahriddin-Singer. In Mukum-Hunchback's chaikhana there was a poster that showed this 'Sea of Faith' (which is what his Persian name means) emerging from a music box made to look like the Ka'aba – or from a Ka'aba made to look like a black music box filled to the brim with the treasures of the Uzbek nation. All of Gilas kept coming back to gaze at this poster, pretending they needed more of the limp naan bread sold in the chaikhana.

Oppok-Lovely quite lost her once white but now greying head over Bahriddin. In between stamping documents – each of which earned her twice the monthly pension of her brother Oktam-Humble-Russky, who was now living out his last years in an old people's home – she tried to think up an excuse, any excuse, perhaps even a splendid Bolshevik funeral for her own brother, for arranging a banquet, so that she could extend an invitation to Bahriddin-Singer and publicly, in front of the whole of Gilas, present him with a gold-embroidered gown, slip his arms into its sleeves and tie the gold-embroidered belt round his waist; for a moment at least, in front of everyone she knew, she would throw her arms round him, hold him in her embrace – and then, then she would die happy. Yes, she would forget her errant husband and die happy.

But Oktam-Humble-Russky, alas, was too principled a Bolshevik to die before the final victory of Communism; and Oppok-Lovely's own daughters had quiet 'Komsomol-style' weddings in the City, in student dining rooms, without ceremony and without singers; and her son Kuvandyk the garage mechanic even went so far as to marry a Russian girl, having first developed a taste for Russian vodka; and Bahriddin himself proved more than a little elusive.

And no sooner had Oppok-Lovely found an excuse for a banquet – the elevation of her returnee husband to the position of 'Bearer of Dying Languages' in an institute in the City – than she heard terrible news: Bahriddin, her beloved Bahriddin, the 'sea of her faith', had set up a brothel staffed by the female music students of some damned Soginch or Sevinch . . . The girls had wandered about stark naked, angelically singing the finest songs in their repertory as they went about – or lay about – their business. And then some minister of some kind of internal affairs had turned up just at the wrong moment; the naked angels had been singing at the tops of their voices as he passed by. Anyway, whatever the reason, news came from the City that Bahriddin-Singer had been stripped of everything: titles, laurels, medals, regalia. And he had been sent into cultural exile on the naked shores of the Aral Sea, which was already drying up and shrinking.

A few years later, Oppok-Lovely, who had remained loyal to her idol amid the sea of other mature and maturing voices, heard from Pinkhas Shalomay's nephew, who was a student of Bahriddin's and who often sang at weddings instead of him, that Bahriddin was returning from exile. Oppok-Lovely at once sent off a messenger to tell him that she would be glad to arrange the same 'most angelical singing and other rites' for him in her hometown of Gilas. With the help of her protégé Ali-Shapak – formerly the public weigher and now the Head of the Kok-Terek Bazaar – she took over the weighing hall, furnishing and decorating it so that the director of the medical institute could send an entire course of female students there to extend and deepen their knowledge of anatomy and physiology. Alas, Bahriddin turned out to have abandoned angelic young women and turned his attention to dogs.

After disappearing for a week, Oppok-Lovely's special messenger spent the next two weeks telling the inhabitants of Gilas about how Bahriddin, that sea of faith that would never dry up or disappear, had bought some land from some Kazakhs. Yes, he had bought four hills and a valley between Chernyaevka and Sharabkhona. Bahriddin and his dog would sit on one hill; the opposing dog would be placed on the opposite hill; judges, seconds and fans would occupy the other two hills – and then the dogs would battle it out in the valley below.

Within a few years Bahriddin's Labon was the undisputed champion of fighting dogs from the Urals to the Aral Sea, from the Pamirs to the Pacific. Bahriddin then sacrificed his invincible Labon, burying him in the valley between the four hills, and the First Secretary of those parts – who had been enabled by the influx of fans not only to balance his budget but even to build factories and a whole new regional infrastructure – cordoned off the whole area and put up signs saying: 'Stop! Danger! Danger Zone!'

After listening to her idol on the radio as he sang, in a voice crimson with *toskà*, a line of Babur, 'I'm your dog – tie me tight to the chain of your hair,'[156] Oppok-Lovely took it into her head to summon the best dog-breeders among the local Koreans, so as to pay tribute at least through the most refined canine cuisine to the King of Dogs sacrificed by her King of Song. Once again she sent a messenger to the City – only to discover that Bahriddin had withdrawn from the world. He received no one at all; all day and all night he read the classical texts he had once sung at weddings for roubles: for roubles promised him by the master of the wedding feast; for roubles thrust into his pockets, under his belt, under his embroidered skullcap and even – as if into the slit of a postbox – into the resonating chamber of his one-stringed *tar*,[157] for roubles hurled at him by his countless devotees of every sex.

This rock of faith was now reading ancient texts and trying to lay bare their most secret meaning – a meaning that was opening his eyes to his own true nature . . . For three years and three months he read the volumes he had slowly gathered from villages of both plain and mountain. And when he knew these volumes better than all the musical academies and institutes of philology in the country, when the depth of his knowledge had turned his hair grey, he resolved to communicate this knowledge to the people.

A new institute, it is said, was founded to house the manuscripts he had gathered, while he himself dressed their meaning in the simple clothing of his wisdom-filled voice. His decision to return to his public coincided with the departure of Mullah-Ulmas-Greeneyes to the United States, thanks to Pinkhas Shalomay (and with the help of a reference from his former mathematics teacher, Alexander Solzhenitsyn). Enraged and distressed by the scheming of that vile Pinkhas, who had taken away her husband just as she was being given back her beloved Bahriddin (who had now, apparently, dyed his hair black again) – yes, enraged and distressed as she was, the ageing but still determined Oppok-Lovely, who was about to retire from her position as Gilas passport officer, decided to kill two birds with one stone; in order to lament the loss of both her youth and her husband, she dispatched a messenger once again to Bahriddin-Teacher, offering him gold jewellery that the wife of the last Emir of Bukhara had sold as she lived out her last poverty-stricken days in the small town of Kermina and that Oppok-Lovely had obtained in exchange for issuing Pinkhas Shalomay – or rather Pyotr Sholokh-Mayev – with his very last Soviet passport.

Quick as lightning, urgent as the whistle of one of Kaganovich's steam-engines, the news flashed through Gilas: Bahriddin, that ocean of Oppok-Lovely's faith, was coming to Gilas! Large-denomination banknotes were quickly exchanged for smaller denominations, so that their possessor could make more frequent approaches to the idol with tokens of grateful appreciation.

Oppok-Lovely brought a brigade of young Tatar women from

the wool factory to spread paint and whitewash over buildings, fences and trees. The brigade leader, Zakiya-Nogaika (her father had been an eminent member of the Jadid movement[158] in the Crimea, and she herself had first come to these parts to instruct the local women in reading, writing and the new life but had ended up as a wool-washer in a shed by the Zakh canal) happened to mention an occasion when Domla Halim, the most famous singer at the court of the Emir of Bukhara, had come to visit her father in the Crimea: her father had bought a piano in his honour and Domla Halim had liked the instrument, putting his stick between the pedals, placing his spectacles and his prayer beads on the music stand and laying his turban and gown on the flat lid. Inspired by this story, Oppok-Lovely released a brigade of Georgians and Ossetians from their duties at the cotton factory and got the Korean Chen-Duk – whom she had once transformed with a stroke of her pen into the Kazakh Chendukbayev and who was now the director of a pig farm up in the mountains – to sell her the 'Roenisch 1911' grand piano that he had inherited, along with the directorship of the pig farm, from a local Volga German who had been deported after the War to the homeland of his distant ancestors.[159]

While the Georgians and Ossetians were transporting the piano – and bringing a large billiard table from the Gilas library to fill the space left behind in Chendukbayev's office – a new inscription appeared beside the words 'Roenisch 1911': 'Hatsunay 1964', scratched by a crooked Ossetian knife. Zakiya-Nogaika, however, painted out both these inscriptions, covering the entire piano, including all sixty-four keys, with snow-white paint intended for the bodies of cars. She was especially diligent in her treatment of the little protruding black keys, on which it was so strangely easy to pick out the simple Tatar songs of her far-distant and enlightened youth.

At last, after everyone had changed their money and those who were not very well off had had their trouser pockets made so deep that they could dig about in them all evening, pretending that they were searching for a wad of notes as they muttered, 'No, Bahriddin's not quite himself today. Pity we can't lock him up with a tape recorder first thing tomorrow morning!' – yes, after the paint on the fences, benches and ceilings of the 2,375 adult inhabitants of Gilas had dried, after even the snow-white paint on the Roenisch-Hatsunay piano had finished drying, there appeared for the first time in the history of Gilas a messenger from Bahriddin. He came in a brand-new car, drew up outside Mukum-Hunchback's chaikhana and asked the way to the house of Oppok-Lovely, a building familiar to every adult, child and animal in Gilas. And within a couple of hours the whole of Gilas knew that Oppok-Lovely had suffered a stroke.

What happened to Oppok-Lovely during the following years belongs to another story. All I can say now is that this stroke left her half-paralysed and, when she was a very old woman – an old woman who had neither been reunited with her husband Mullah-Ulmas-Greeneyes nor been granted a chance to embrace her elusive Bahriddin – she was often to be seen in a small pram, being wheeled around Gilas by the devoted Zakiya-Nogaika, who had succeeded with the help of Oppok-Lovely in posthumously rehabilitating the name of her Jadid father and who therefore received a special pension along with a monthly delivery of macaroni, canned meat and black pepper. Zakiya-Nogaika used to wheel Oppok-Lovely up and down the town; on Sundays they would go as far as the Kok-Terek Bazaar, where Oppok-Lovely, who was festooned with little cloths, ribbons and hand-kerchiefs, would untie these home-made purses and give money to plump Froska, the fizzy-water seller who had once been pined after by the entire male population of Gilas – or to Tolib-Butcher, who had never forgiven Oppok-Lovely for enabling his younger brother to retire before him and had revenged himself by slipping large bones into her parcels of top-quality meat – or to Yusuf-Cobbler, who had gone on pissing against the wall of

Huvron-Barber's little shop until he watched the film *Shri 420*, by which time the wall was blanketed with moss and ivy; and so Zakiya-Nogaika and Oppok-Lovely would pass through the bazaar, with Oppok-Lovely untying one cloth purse after another, settling her accounts with the world and growing ever lighter like the holy tree the boys had once found in the cemetery, and then returning in the same pram, letting herself be pushed by Zakiya-Nogaika across the railway line and down crooked sidestreets, and then, back at home, still sitting in her pram, taking into her hands first the one and only letter and photograph she had ever received from her errant husband, who had been condemned to eternal study of the mighty Greater-Russian language in Brighton Beach, and then her own one and only passport, with its photograph of a woman whose hair was snow-white from birth rather than from old age; and her dry eyes would shed tears as Zakiya-Nogaika – who suffered from Parkinson's disease – sat by the piano, her trembling yet rigid fingers picking out the simple Tatar songs of her far-distant, enlightened youth on stumpy keys that time had once again made black.

Notes

1.   A Sufi spiritual community.
2.   Koran 112:1–4
3.   The Cheka, or 'Special Commission', was the original name for what was later successively renamed the OGPU, the NKVD, the KGB and the FSB.
4.   Similar to pilaf.
5   The conventional Soviet name for the Second World War.
6.   The Tsarist authorities often exiled both soldiers and sailors to Central Asia for infringements of discipline. Such titles as this were not uncommon.
7.   The bazaar most frequented by Russians, as the name perhaps implies.
8.   A bourgeois stove was the normal term for a stove that was small, round and made of cast iron. It was thought to be greedy for fuel yet to give out little heat – hence the name.
9.   The Communist Youth Organisation.
10. Every Uzbek town is traditionally divided into a number of *mahallyas* or communities. Gilas contained at least five *mahallyas*.
11. Recruited from Central Asian prisoners, this Legion probably numbered around 200,000. And the Germans did indeed often mistake Uzbeks for Jews.
12. Until 1928 the Arabic script was used for both Tadjik and Uzbek; in 1928 the Latin script was officially substituted. The official pretext for this 'reform' was the assertion that the Arabic script was unable to accommodate the technological demands of the twentieth century; the real reason was the desire of the Soviet government to distance the people of Central Asia from Islam. In 1940, the Soviet authorities decreed another change of script: from Latin to Cyrillic – so as to make it easier for everyone to learn Russian.

13. In 1924, when the Bolsheviks created the republic of Uzbekistan, the Sarts and the Uzbeks were officially declared to be a single ethnic group. Historically, however, they are distinct: the Sarts mainly urban and mercantile, the Uzbeks nomadic and tribal. In the early twentieth century the Sarts outnumbered the Uzbeks; Uzbekistan could equally well have been named Sartistan.

14. Maurice Thorez was the leader of the French Communist Party.

15. Palmiro Togliatti was the leader of the Italian Communist Party.

16. Demosthenes, the famous Athenian orator, is said to have overcome a speech impediment by practising declamation with a mouth full of pebbles.

17. The Inuit people live mainly in Alaska, Canada, Greenland and in the far east of Russia. The Khakass, Buryat, Evenk and Nivkhi are all indigenous peoples of Siberia.

18. Stalin died in 1953. In 1956 Khrushchev denounced his crimes in his famous 'Secret Speech' to the Twentieth Party Congress. This marked the start of a relatively liberal period known as 'The Thaw'.

19. Solzhenitsyn studied mathematics as a young man, and he worked as a schoolteacher for several months before the outbreak of the Second World War. After his release from the Gulag, he spent several years in exile in Kazakhstan.

20. The Communist Party's children's movement.

21. A famous Uzbek film from the 1960s, about Uzbek spies in Germany.

22. In the Arctic Ocean.

23. The Koryaks, of whom there are around 4,000, live in the Far East, on the Kamchatka peninsula.

24. Odessa was an important Jewish centre for many years. In 1941, for example, Jews numbered 30 per cent of the population.

25. Every Komsomol member was required to pay a monthly contribution to the organisation.

26. Soviet citizens needed passports in order to travel around the country. Internal passports were introduced in some parts of the Soviet Union in 1933; in Gilas, however, they were evidently introduced only in the late 1960s.

27. It is customary at a Muslim funeral for every direct male descendant to wear a belt.

28. Islam encourages burial as soon as possible, preferably before sunset on the day of death.

29. Kokand is a city in the Fergana Valley, and the territory of the Kokand Khanate included much of present-day Uzbekistan. Khudoyar was Khan from 1845 until Russia annexed the khanate in 1876.

30. According to the Koran, Gabriel came to Mohammed when he was resting in Mecca and brought him the winged steed Buraq, who carried him first to the Temple Mount in Jerusalem and then up into the heavens, where he spoke both with the earlier prophets and with Allah. Allah told him to order the Muslims to pray fifty times a day. Moses, however, told Mohammed that this was too much to ask; at his instigation, Mohammed went back to Allah several times to beg for a reduction. In the end it was agreed that Muslims should be required to pray five times a day.

31. Nazar, the hero of this poem by Muhammadniyoz Nishoti (born in Khorezm in 1701), is a faithful servant to a king. The king sends him on a long journey to find the water of life needed to save his sick son and heir.

32. The suffix 'Kori', attached to a man's name, indicates that he has memorised the entire Koran.

33. An important, mainly Russian city in eastern Uzbekistan, named after the commanding officer of the Russian armies that conquered Turkestan in the late nineteenth century. In 1924 it was renamed Fergana. Oyimcha's father had evidently built himself a stone house in an attempt to

emulate the Europeanised lifestyle of the city's élite; houses in the small towns and villages were usually built of clay.

34. i.e. modern European carriages rather than traditional Central Asian ones.

35. A delicacy: horsemeat sausage.

36. A town not far from Moscow that was famous for its textile factories.

37. Uzbeks look on bread as sacred. Even treading on it accidentally is sinful.

38. The word is correctly used to denote a single-breasted (often military or naval) jacket with a high collar.

39. This notoriously untranslatable Russian word can mean anything from spiritual anguish to a vague yearning or restlessness. One can feel *toskà* for a loved one, for the motherland, for God; one can feel *toskà* with or without a specific cause.

40. The suffix 'hodja', attached to a man's name, indicates that he is a direct descendant of the Prophet or one of the first four caliphs.

41. A town, and province, in the Fergana Valley.

42. The pilgrimage to Mecca.

43. 'Jadid' was the name of a modernising tendency within Islam in the early twentieth century; the word's basic meaning is simply 'new'.

44. Pishpek is now known as Bishkek and is the capital of Kirghizstan. In Soviet days it was called Frunze.

45. A once important Silk Road city, located near Tokmak in Kirghizstan.

46. One of the Muslim nationalities of western China.

47. There are references to 'dishevelled mountains' in the Koran.

48. Said to be the longest epic poem in the world.

49. A stringed instrument, related to the lute.

50. Alisher Navoi (1441-1501) was a statesman, a scientist and – above all – an important poet. He was the first major poet

in the area corresponding to present-day Uzbekistan to write not only in Persian – the language of the court – but also in Chagatay, the ancestor of contemporary Uzbek.

51. The 'muallaka' was a genre of pre-Islamic Arabic poetry. Imr-ul-Kais was the greatest poet to compose in this genre.

52. The bridge – thin as a hair – that a Muslim has to cross, on the back of 'the sheep of his righteous actions', in order to reach Paradise from the Place of Judgment.

53. A religious/political party that flourished in the years before the 1917 Revolution.

54. i.e. the Grand Duke Mikhail Aleksandrovich – General Governor of Turkestan and the younger brother of Tsar Nicholas II.

55. i.e. the building where the Gilas Party Committee had its offices.

56. Cf. Lenin's famous slogan: 'Communism is Soviet Power plus the Electrification of the Entire Country!'

57. Lazar Moiseevich Kaganovich (1893–1991), himself a Jew, was a loyal henchman of Stalin's and commissar for transport from 1935 to 1937.

58. The names of two of the cheapest Soviet red wines were 'Vermooth' and 'Portwein'.

59. An Armenian revolutionary federation.

60. See note 6.

61. England, still the world's greatest colonial power, was a frequent object of random criticism by Soviet journalists and politicians during the 1920s and 1930s.

62. On 2 September 1920 an insurrection in Bukhara, supported by the Red Army, ended with the declaration of a People's Republic of Bukharia.

63. Mikhail Kalinin was the formal head of the Soviet state from 1919 until 1946. Unlike most of the early Bolshevik leaders, he was neither Jewish nor part Jewish.

64. During the 1920s the Communist authorities set great store by their (largely successful) campaign to 'liquidate illiteracy'.

65. There were terrible famines in the Volga region in 1891 and 1921. Worse still was the man-made famine of 1932–3 induced by Stalin's collectivisation campaign. The K-M troika may also have enjoyed playing at offering help to the Russians; usually, after all, it was Russians who patronised Central Asians.

66. The basmach were Muslim anti-Soviet fighters in Central Asia between 1918 and the mid-1930s. The movement's importance peaked in the early 1920s.

67. In 1934 the Soviet government established the Jewish Autonomous Region, popularly known as Birobidzhan, in a sparsely populated area some five thousand miles east of Moscow. This was intended to be the national homeland of Soviet Jewry.

68. 1937 marked the peak of the purges directed by Stalin against the intelligentsia.

69. Burkhanutdin al-Marginoni, born in 1090, compiled four volumes of Sharia Law under the title *Hidoya* or *The True Path*.

70. '1924 saw the dissolution of all the preceding administrative entities and a complete rewriting of the map of Central Asia, on the basis of "one ethnic group, one territory"' (Oliver Roy, *The New Central Asia*, London: I.B.Tauris, 2000, p. 61). But the various ethnic groups were inextricably mixed, and so their separation by the Soviet authorities was artificial. Thus the mainly Uzbek inhabitants of Mookat were arbitrarily reclassified as Kirghiz.

71. Many people sent to the Gulag were charged with treason, under article 58 of the Criminal Code.

72. The Taklamakan Desert is in western China, in what is now called the Xinjiang Uighur Autonomous Region.

73. There was a popular belief that the moustached Iosif Stalin was an illegitimate son of the moustached Przhevalsky.

74. Mefody was evidently one of the many lawyers arrested that year.

75. The Solovetsky Islands (often known simply as Solovky) were the location of the first Soviet labour camp; this operated from 1922 to 1939.

76. An industrial city near the Chinese border. Mefody had evidently worked there as a 'free worker' after being released from one of the many labour camps in the region.

77. A Code was typically 100 pages; a Commentary typically six times the length of a Code.

78. Mefody is, of course, referring primarily to the brother of Joseph, the Biblical Patriarch. His words, however, also conjure up the ghost of another 'Benjamin': Venyamin Yerofeev, the author of what is perhaps the most celebrated evocation of alcoholism in Russian literature: the short novel *Moscow Circles (Moskva Petushki)*.

79. The fortieth day after someone's death is an important day of remembrance. A year after death marks the end of the period of mourning.

80. First Secretary of the Uzbek Communist Party; he was expelled, and shot, in 1938.

81. Cf. Koran, Sura 36, verse 77, translated by Yusuf Ali as 'Doth not man see that it is We Who created him from sperm? yet behold! he stands forth as an open adversary!'

82. To protect the south-eastern border of Finland, a line of defence was built across the Karelian Isthmus in the 1920s and 1930s; this later became known as the Mannerheim Line. The Soviet attack in 1939 was halted at this line for over two months.

83. 'Marlen' is an amalgamation of 'Marx' and 'Lenin'; 'Marleon' is an amalgamation of 'Marx' and 'Leonid' – the first name of General Secretary Brezhnev, the Soviet leader from 1964 to 1982.

84. A sixteenth-century Sufi treatise.

85. A seventeenth-century Uzbek Sufi poet.

86. Kurban-Khait or Kurban-Bayram is a commemoration of Abraham's sacrifice of a ram instead of his son Isaac.

Families who can afford to sacrifice an animal will do so, and there is a complex code stipulating how the carcass should be distributed among friends, family and charitable concerns.

87. The main Soviet news agency.

88. 'May your father be rich, may he have lots of money, may our house always be full of light, Amen!'

89. See note 57.

90. Two of the most famous Komsomol heroes from World War Two.

91. A *shlagbaum* (the word is borrowed from German) is the vertical barrier by a level crossing that descends to stop vehicles crossing a railway line when a train is expected.

92. Haematogen is a yellow powder obtained from egg yolk and considered a blood tonic. A somewhat chocolate-like substance prepared from haematogen was commonly prescribed by Soviet doctors as a cure for anaemia; people often ate it just as a sweet.

93. Both the Chuvash and the Mari are indigenous Siberian peoples.

94. A reference to a campaign of Khrushchev's. After taking it into his head that maize was an especially valuable crop, he insisted on its being sown throughout vast areas many of which were unsuited to its cultivation. The plants were sown according to a special system – in fours, each plant forming a corner of a square – the purpose of which was to allow tractors to move freely up and down the fields. The often repeated slogan 'Maize is the Queen of the Fields!' is splendidly alliterative in Russian: '*Kukuruza koroleva polei!*'.

95. Officially promoted, under the Soviet regime, as a Chuvash national hero.

96. Khaira's mind is still disordered: she remembers her birthday according to a wild mixture of calendars. Nisan is the first month of the Persian – and Jewish – year; the 'Year of the Bull' is Chinese; the terms 'Old Style' and 'New Style'

are normally used with reference to the switch in 1918 in Russia from the Julian to the Gregorian calendar.

97. The title of a famous painting by the Russian landscape painter Aleksey Savrasov (1830-97).

98. Guards and nightwatchmen at institutions of minor importance were issued with air rifles and salt bullets. These were intended to wound but not kill.

99. i.e. Village Consumer Society. Every village or small town in the Soviet Union had a similarly titled shop for the sale of clothes and household items.

100. There were, of course, no collective farms before the Revolution – let alone collective farms with hydroelectric stations.

101. See note 75.

102. A vast area of north-eastern Siberia; in effect, one huge labour camp. The Kolyma camps operated from 1932 to 1956 and enjoyed a particularly grim reputation.

103. It was not long after the Revolution that the Church Authorities began to collude with the Bolsheviks.

104. The Uighurs, who live in Xinjiang (the west of China), are now Muslims but were once mainly Syrian Christians.

105. Now known as the Amu-Darya and the Syr-Darya, these two great rivers used to flow across Uzbekistan and into the Aral Sea. Since the 1960s, however, so much water has been taken from them in order to irrigate the cotton fields that they now barely reach the Aral Sea. Once the fourth biggest inland sea in the world, this has decreased in volume by 75 per cent.

106. Compare Monika Whitlock: 'For millions of Tadjiks and Uzbeks, the 1970s are captured by the mingled sensations of ice-cream, sunflower seeds, and Raj Kapoor, super-star of the Bombay screen, belting out numbers from *Samgan* and *Shri 420* on a hot, black night. The ability to sing showstoppers all the way through in Hindi without understanding the words became and remained a

characteristic of the Central Asian Brezhnev generation' (op. cit., 102).

107. One nut is placed on the ground. The players, standing some distance away, try to throw their own nuts as close to it as possible.

108. Almost the entire population of Crimean Tatars was deported to Central Asia in the summer of 1944. A quarter of them died during the journey and the following months.

109. Many Soviet schools had a 'Timur Team', who were supposed to help the weak and the elderly in much the same way as British Boy Scouts. The title is derived from *Timur and His Team* (1940), a story by the children's writer A. P. Gaidar (1904–41) about a gang of village children who secretly do good deeds, fighting hooligans and protecting families whose menfolk are in the Red Army. The book was made into a film in 1941 and remained part of the school curriculum up into the 1990s.

110. Sohrab is one of the heroes of the greatest Persian epic, Ferdowsi's *Shahnameh* or *Book of Kings*. Matthew Arnold's 'Sohrab and Rustum' is based on the most famous part of this epic.

111. A reference to *Zainab and Amon*, a poem about the love between two collective-farm workers and their fight against restrictive traditions by Hamid Olimjan (1909–44), a leading Uzbek poet and First Secretary of the Uzbek Union of Writers.

112. Monika Whitlock writes that the first wave of Koreans 'stumbled across the Kamchatka peninsula into the Russian Far East to escape famine in the early twentieth century. Stalin moved 172,000 of them from Vladivostok to Soviet Central Asia, presumably for fear they would collaborate with the Japanese. There they were joined by many more through the 1940s and 1950s, until half a million lived in Uzbekistan alone' (op. cit., p. 100).

113. See note 46.

114. 'For Soviet reformers and Uzbek nationals the (veil) drew a boundary line; it was either the nadir of backwardness and oppression, or the hallmark of age-old Uzbek self-respect, dignity and honour. Women deveiled at gunpoint. Women reveiled at the point of a knife' (Kate Brown, 'Behind the veil of freedom', *TLS*, 8 April 2005).

115. This parodies a sentence from Marx's preface to the French edition of *Das Kapital*: 'In science there is no broad high road, and only he can attain its shining peaks who, not fearing exhaustion, is ready to tramp along its stony paths.'

116. Bukharin, Radek and Trotsky were all important Old Bolsheviks. Seeing them as potential rivals, Stalin had them eliminated.

117. See note 80.

118. From 1948 until his death in 1953 Stalin promoted an increasingly vicious anti-Semitism; this culminated in the 'exposure' of the alleged 'Doctors' Plot' against the lives of Soviet leaders. During this period Jews were commonly referred to as 'rootless cosmopolitans'.

119. During the months after Stalin's death, Lavrenty Beria, Nikita Khrushchev and Georgy Malenkov ruled as a triumvirate, but Khrushchev soon outmanoeuvred his rivals. Though Beria was never, in fact, publicly tried, he was shot later in 1953; Malenkov resigned as chairman of the Council of Ministers in February 1955. For Khrushchev's Secret Speech see note 18.

120. Claude Lévi-Strauss (born 1908), the founder of structural anthropology, is famous, among other things, for his books about the musical structure of myth. Another book is titled *The Raw and the Cooked.*

121. Similar to yoghurt.

122. In his novel *The Day Lasts Longer than a Century* (initially titled *Small Station in the Tall Grass*), Chingiz Aitmatov refers to a Kirghiz legend about a tribe that left their prisoners lying in the sun with raw camel hide stretched

over their heads. As it dried, the camel hide would compress the prisoners' skulls and so destroy their minds. The prisoners were then known as *mankurts*. In Aitmatov's words: 'A *mankurt* did not know where he was from. He did not know his name, did not remember his childhood, his father and his mother – to put it more simply, a *mankurt* did not realise that he was a human being.'

123. Isaak Osipovich Dunayevsky (1900–55), the most successful Soviet composer of the Stalinist era, wrote mainly songs and marches.

124. Literally, *Shash-Maqam* means six modes. Theodore Levin and Razia Sultanova write that 'the Central Asian *maqam* represents a vast yet integrated artistic conception that encompasses music, metaphysics, ethics and aesthetics' ('The Classical Music of Uzbeks and Tadjiks' in *The Garland Encyclopedia of World Music*, vol. 6, New York & London: Routledge, 2002, p. 909.)

125. Habib-Ulla appears to be half-remembering lines from Pushkin's *Mozart and Salieri*: 'Of all life's pleasures, love is second only to music – but what is love if not music?'

126. A two-stringed, fretted lute with a low pitch, common in most of Central Asia.

127. Most orphanages contained at least some children who had been criminalised while living on the street. These children would pass on their criminal ways – including a taste for tattoos – to the other children.

128. In the Koranic version of the Cain and Abel story a raven shows Cain how to bury his brother.

129. The Nogai Tatars, of whom there are now around 75,000, live mostly in the north-western part of the Russian republic of Dagestan.

130. Karaism is a form of Judaism that accepts no scriptures except the Tanach – the Jewish Bible, rejecting later accretions such as Rabbinic Oral Law.

131. The Kumyks, of whom there are around 300,000, are an

indigenous people of the North Caucasus. They live mainly in the lowlands of north-eastern Dagestan.

132. Sa'adi (1207–91) is one of the three most famous Persian poets.

133. Abu Ja'far Muhammad ibn Jarir at-Tabari (839–923) was a Muslim scholar and theologian.

134. 'This famous Spanish Civil War slogan ('They shall not pass') was first spoken in July 1936 by the Spanish Communist leader Dolores Ibárruri Gómez, also known as La Pasionaria.

135. Children in Gilas used to throw calcium carbide in a puddle, place an upside-down can on top of the puddle to collect the acetylene gas released in the ensuing reaction, then drop a match through a small hole in the tin. The gas would explode and the can would shoot up into the air.

136. See note 109.

137. Hodja Ahmed Yasawi was a Sufi poet and philosopher. He died in 1166 or 1167 (or possibly 1146), and was buried in a small shrine that attracted many pilgrims. In the fourteenth century Timur the Great erected an immense mausoleum complex over the shrine; on his death in 1405, the buildings were left unfinished.

138. Allah is great!

139. The wolf is a symbol of Turkish identity; there are many myths of Turkic tribes or their leaders being descended from wolves.

140. Hoomer does indeed allude to numerous works of literature. These include: *The Conference of the Birds* by the Persian poet Farid-Ud-Din Attar; the Turkish oral tales collected in *The Book of Dede Korkut*; Nikolay Gogol's *Taras Bulba*; and Andrey Platonov's *Soul*.

141. It was a Turkmen custom to place a small ladder beside a grave – so the souls of the deceased can climb up to heaven.

143. The word 'Khalfa' indicates that she was well educated and that she was allowed to preach to women.

143. Aspandiar is an ancient Persian name. And in the 1920s a number of Turkmen tribes chose a leader named Aspandiar as their 'king', in order to put up a unified resistance to the Bolsheviks.

144. Two angels (not mentioned in the Koran) who interview the dead in their graves and provide a glimpse of heavenly reward or infernal punishment in the life to come.

145. The Yomuds are a Turkmen people, originally nomadic.

146. Cf. 'The route (. . .) included a 150-km stretch over shifting sands. No other railway had been built in these conditions and after the tracks had been buried, swept away, or left hanging in the air each time it was laid, doubts grew about the railway's feasibility (. . .) only the laborious process of elevating the railway on a continuous embankment finally solved the problem (J. N. Westwood, *A History of Russian Railways*, London: George Allen and Unwin, 1964, p. 126).

147. See note 79.

148. A thorny shrub, the main source of firewood in the Central Asian deserts.

149. I.e. of activists who were demanding the right to return to the Crimea. And see note 108.

150. A prestigious holiday camp for Young Pioneers, in the Crimea. The children sent there were, almost without exception, from the families of the Soviet élite.

151. It seems that Nafisa was confused, or that the loudspeaker in the bazaar was indeed unclear. The first man in space – in April 1961 – was Yuri Gagarin. Nafisa may have misheard 'Gagarin' as 'Lyaganov'; in her confusion, she appears to have added the Russian suffix 'ov' to the Uzbek 'lyagan', which means 'dish' or 'flying saucer'.

152. Circumcisions, though widely practised, were officially disapproved of, and people went through the motions of pretending they didn't happen. The boy may have heard his grandparents inviting guests to his 'name-day'.

153. The loudspeaker in the bazaar, which relayed the main

Soviet radio stations, does not appear to have improved during the years since Gagarin/Lyaganov first flew into space. The cosmonaut's name was in reality neither Kitov nor Bitov, but Titov.

154. An Uzbek saying.

155. It is a traditional Sunni Muslim custom to hold your cupped hands before your mouth as you pray, reciting the prayer as if into your hands and then drawing your hands across your cheeks, as if spreading the prayer into your face. Shiites often perform a similar gesture with just one hand. Central Asian Muslims are mainly Sunni, whereas Persians are mainly Shiite.

156. Zahir-Ud-Din Mohammad Babur (1483–1530), born in Andijan in the Fergana Valley, was the founder of the Mughal Empire in Northern India.

157. A single-stringed instrument related to the two-stringed *doutar*.

158. See note 43.

159. Between 1763 and 1772 around 30,000 Germans were encouraged by Catherine the Great to settle in the Volga steppe. By 1897 the Volga Germans numbered nearly 1,800,000. Around a third of the population died in the famine of 1921, and in 1941 they were nearly all either drafted into the army or deported to Siberia or Central Asia.